Praise for JoAn

"The connection betwe
coming to terms with lo
him adds strength and i
more than the average fi
detailed descriptions, real-life issues that resonate... Verdict: An excellent start to a promising community series with a stunning Olympic Coast setting."

—*Library Journal*

"Perennial favorite Ross delivers the emotionally intense first book in her small town contemporary romance series, Honeymoon Harbor... Ross has always been known for her ability to create truly memorable characters whose stories resonate sharply. This amazing book is touched by pain and grief, but also love and hope. A wonderful novel!"

—*RT Book Reviews*

"A widower gets a second chance at love with his wife's best friend in this...sweet first book in Ross's Honeymoon Harbor series... Fans of cozy small-town romances will be willing to read further in the series."

—*Publishers Weekly*

More select praise for JoAnn Ross

"Ross's Shelter Bay series spotlights her talent for blending vibrant characters, congenial small-town settings, and pressing social issues in a heartwarming contemporary romance."

—*Booklist*

"Beautifully descriptive and gently paced, this heartwarmer captures coastal small town flavor perfectly."

—*Library Journal* on *Seaglass Winter*

"It isn't often readers find characters they're willing to spend a weekend with. However, that's exactly what Ross accomplishes...enveloping the reader in the lives of two endearing, albeit flawed, characters."

—*RT Book Reviews* on *The Homecoming*

Also available from JoAnn Ross

Honeymoon Harbor

ONCE UPON A WEDDING (novella)
HERONS LANDING
HOME TO HONEYMOON HARBOR (novella)

JoAnn Ross

Snowfall on Lighthouse Lane

Recycling programs for this product may not exist in your area.

ISBN-13: 978-1-335-55678-3

Snowfall on Lighthouse Lane

This edition published by arrangement with Harlequin Books S.A.

For questions and comments about the quality of this book, please contact us at CustomerService@Harlequin.com.

www.HQNBooks.com

Printed in U.S.A.

As always, to Jay, who never stopped believing.

CHAPTER ONE

October
Washington State coast

LIFE, AS AIDEN MANNION knew firsthand, could be dangerous. Anything could happen. You could be hit by a taxi while sightseeing in Times Square. Run headfirst into a tree while skiing down a diamond run pretending you were Bode Miller. Or you could be a cop who got up one morning, headed off to work on the joint police/Department of Homeland Security detail you'd been assigned to and, out of the blue, end up in the ER getting a slug dug out of your thigh while your partner was being wheeled off to the morgue.

He watched the fishing boats chug along beneath a gray quilted sky from the deck of his family's vacation house. Out on the horizon a storm was brewing, bringing to mind all the ships that had sunk into the sea off this wild, rugged Washington coast. Including ancestors from the Harper side of his family.

He took a long drink of coffee. It was black and thick and sweet. It was his thirtieth day waking up without a hangover. "Which has to be an improvement, right?"

"Too bad no one's around to give you your one-month chip." The dry response had him realizing he'd spoken out loud. It also made him laugh for the first time in a very long while.

"You always were a smart-ass."

"Takes one to know one, dude," his former partner shot back with that flash of grin that was the last thing Aiden remembered seeing before all hell broke loose. When Bodhi Warfield's ghost had first appeared on the ferry headed to Honeymoon Harbor, Aiden had thought he was a hallucination. That was weird because, after attending Bodhi's funeral—with all the pomp and ceremony that occurred when a police department lost one of their own—he'd purposefully waited until he'd gotten here to the coast house to start drinking. Having witnessed too many drunk driving deaths during his LAPD patrol days, no way was he going to risk causing another.

But after drinking himself to oblivion for the first several weeks and, waking up with a hangover the size of Mount Olympus, he'd come to the conclusion that being a drunk was getting boring. So, he'd just stopped. Cold turkey. The same way he'd quit the cops. But Bodhi had continued to hang around.

"Don't ghosts get cold?" Aiden asked.

Bodhi glanced down his California beach-tanned chest at the Hawaiian-print board shorts he was wearing instead of the leather biker dude duds he'd been wearing when killed. "Surfers are too chill to get cold," he said.

They'd been an odd couple. The laid-back surfer—who'd changed his name from Broderick to that of Patrick's Swayze's surfer bank robber character from *Point Break*, then had joined the cops mostly to piss off his liberal psychologist professor parents—and the Marine turned vice cop who still carried an edge from his bad boy days. But that difference had made them a great team. Like Starsky and Hutch. *Men in Black*'s Agents J and K. *Lethal Weapon*'s Murtaugh and Riggs, and *Miami Vice*'s Crocket and Tubbs, who even Bodhi had reluctantly admitted would win on the chill factor.

"But hey," his partner would say, whenever the topic would come up, "they were just actors playing roles. We're the real deal, Mannion."

And they had been. Until they weren't.

"Someone's coming," Bodhi said.

Apparently death gave you preternatural senses, because it was another few seconds before Aiden heard the car rumbling across the bridge over the creek fed by glacier waters that would soon be icing up for the winter.

The house had been built on the cliff where the mighty Pacific—ill named, Aiden always thought, since there was nothing peaceful about it—constantly warred with the land. The towering sea stacks offshore, many with trees still growing atop from when they'd been part of the mainland, were proof that wind and water would always eventually win.

Built for a whaling captain nearly a hundred years ago, the house was two stories with a widow's walk around the top. Seth Harper, who'd taken over his family's construction company (which had originally built the house) and was engaged to Aiden's sister, Brianna, was the only person, other than his immediate family, who knew what had gone down the night Bodhi had lost his life. The night Aiden had lost his way.

The driveway was long and lined with towering, shaggy Douglas fir trees. He walked around to the front of the wraparound deck and watched the familiar SUV come into view.

"It's your dad," his partner said, without even bothering to look up.

"Seems to be." He knew his parents worried, but he'd

reminded them that he was no longer that wild-ass boy who'd gone off to war. All he needed was a little time to adjust. Something he could do better on his own. During their twice-a-week check-in phone calls, he hadn't shared the fact that he wasn't exactly alone.

"He's bringing change."

"And you know that how? What, is my life written down on some big *Life and Times of Aiden Mannion* board somewhere?"

Aiden had been raised Catholic, but life had turned him a hard-core agnostic. Had it not been for his former partner's ghost showing up, he would've gone full-out atheist, but maybe there was something to the life after death thing, after all.

Unfortunately, every time he tried to pry some details about the afterlife from Bodhi, he'd get only a shrug and the response that it wasn't his place to tell, but not to worry, it wasn't boringly pastoral and the music was a helluva lot cooler than just harp players.

That was encouraging. Not that Aiden was in any hurry to find out for himself. He'd assured his mom that yeah, he might have issues, but she didn't have to worry about him being suicidal. Part of him wondered if his imagination had recreated his partner to help him overcome the gut-wrenching guilt that in the beginning had hung over him like a cold, wet shroud. If that was the case, it seemed to be working, so he wasn't going to dig too deeply into the question.

He watched his father park the SUV and climb out with a cooler that Aiden knew was filled with meals his mom had cooked. She'd sent John Mannion out with a similar cooler last week. And every week since Aiden had arrived back in Washington.

"You don't have to keep coming all the way out

here," he greeted his dad. "The freezer has enough food for any army."

"You know your mother. She believes in the food pyramid. Which is why she sneaks green stuff into her dishes. I also picked up a pizza at Luca's."

"Loaded?"

"Is there any other kind?" John carried the cooler past Aiden and Bodhi and into the kitchen. "If you moved back to town, you could have all the pizza you wanted. And Luca won't make you put vegetables on it."

"I'm happy where I am."

Sure, he was drifting, okay, maybe stalled, but what was wrong with that? Wasn't a guy entitled? He had, after all, been shot. Maybe not that badly, but it should give him a pass.

"I went to Mom's birthday party. And that wedding," he pointed out.

"Four months ago. And you only went to the wedding because your sister guilted you into it because her fiancé's, who used to be your best friend, mother had come back from Yellowstone Park to officiate."

It had been hard enough to sober up enough to drag himself out to the family Christmas tree farm just out of Honeymoon Harbor for his mother's birthday celebration, but at least that had been just family who—except for his grandfather, who seemed to have lost his conversational filter—had treated him with kid gloves.

Then Brianna had taken him out to the barn, supposedly to show him all that had been done to fix it up for summer theater companies while he'd been away, and to tell him how she and Seth Harper were trying to decide whether to have their next year's summer wedding here in the barn or in the garden of her bed-and-breakfast, Herons Landing.

"And speaking of weddings," she'd mentioned offhandedly, "Seth's mom is going to officiate Kylee and Mai's ceremony tomorrow."

"You mentioned that, too."

"You should come."

"Why? Kylee was yours and Zoe's friend. I barely knew her. And I've never even met Mai."

"In the first place, you can't hide away like a hermit forever. In the second place, you should go because you've been ignoring my fiancé, who used to be your best friend, and it's not like an hour or so of socializing with a few old friends is going to kill you. And third—" she ticked the reasons off on fingers tipped in a turquoise polish that reminded him of the Caribbean "—we're all worried about you, Aiden. Including Seth. And me."

"You're playing the Catholic guilt card," he'd grumbled.

She grinned, looking not the least bit guilty. "It's my superpower."

And so, unable to say no, he'd caved. And while it had admittedly been good to talk with Seth, it still weirded him out thinking about his best friend and his sister having sex. Unfortunately, Brianna hadn't warned him that Jolene Wells would also be there. That was probably because his sister had no way of knowing about his and Jolene's past.

"You sure have a lot of secrets for a guy who always came off so uncomplicated," Bodhi said. Aiden glanced over at his father, who, after putting the pizza in the center of the table, had begun loading up the refrigerator. Fortunately, he didn't appear to hear a thing. That meant Aiden's ghost, hallucination, or imagination, was a private one.

Aiden followed his dad to the kitchen and got out

some paper plates and napkins. "It hasn't been that long," he belatedly responded to his dad's comment.

"Four months."

Four months, one week and five days, he thought. There had admittedly been those lost weeks when he'd first arrived.

"I need your help," his dad said as he popped the top on two bottles of beer.

"I'm not drinking."

"Good for you. This is a nonalcoholic winter ale your brother made."

"Because nothing says I'm an alcoholic like drinking a nonalcoholic beer."

"Or it could say, I'm a smart guy who wants to keep my wits about me while the morons around me are getting plastered," John Mannion suggested in that deceptively mild tone that somehow possessed as much power as Aiden's former drill instructor's shouts. "Why don't you withhold judgment until you taste it?"

Shrugging, Aiden took the bottle, tipped it to his lips and swallowed. But not before rolling it around in his mouth. He may not be an expert, but he'd drunk enough beer over his lifetime to recognize good stuff when he tasted it.

"This is really great." Good enough if you gave it to a guy without a label, he might not realize it was alcohol free.

"Can you imagine Quinn doing anything that wasn't?"

No. Quinn Mannion always been the quintessential perfect eldest child. A real-life Eagle Scout with the badges to prove it, along with being head altar boy at St. Peter the Fisherman's Church, had made him a hard act to follow. Which was why Aiden hadn't even tried, instead going for a gold medal in rebellion.

Quinn had been making big bucks as a corporate lawyer in Seattle when he'd up and quit, come home to Honeymoon Harbor and started a brewery and pub, following in the footsteps of their ancestor Finn Mannion, who'd been forced to shutter the Mannion family pub during Prohibition. The beer was as perfect as everything else Quinn did. It was dark, with an honest-to-God beer flavor that carried a hint of seasonal spices.

"He makes a summer version, too," John said. "It's got a citrusy taste that's great for cookouts. It got a lot of buzz locally, so he's going regional with it next summer. This is the first season, but I suspect it's going to do as well as his Captain Jack Sparrow."

That beer had won a bunch of awards, Aiden knew. It had also made it down to LA, where it was strictly a draft beer, because, according to Quinn, most distributors and bars kept kegs cold all the time, allowing for a consistent flavor advantage. The kegs also protected the beer from light. And proving that Quinn hadn't exactly given up capitalism when he'd walked away from his big bucks lawyer gig, he'd told Aiden that kegs had bars buying and selling a lot more than in bottles.

"Damn, I miss beer." Bodhi heaved a huge sigh and shook his sun-bleached hair "And pizza. It's a bummer having to live vicariously through you, since you've never exactly been Mr. Party Guy, but the past few months have been brutal."

"You could leave," Aiden shot back. Then cringed, when his dad, who'd been dishing up slices of pizza glanced up. *Damn.*

"I didn't mean that the way it sounded," he backtracked. "I meant you didn't have to hang around to keep me company just because Mom's worried about me."

"Parents worry. It comes with the job. But this is a

busy time, getting ready for the Christmas tree-selling season, so I'm only staying long enough to eat a slice of pizza and offer you a proposition."

"Okay."

While his mother could be a velvet steamroller you could see coming from a mile away, his dad had stealth ninja skills that had you agreeing to something before you knew what had hit you. Like that judge who'd been tempted to throw up his hands and send Aiden to juvie. But without attempting to use the power of his office, which John Mannion had far too much integrity to ever try, he'd deftly worked out a deal where, so long as Aiden stayed out of trouble for the last two months of high school, he could enlist in the Marines when he turned eighteen and have his juvenile crime spree record expunged.

Because his father had gone to bat for him, risking his own reputation, Aiden had started growing up on the spot by keeping to his part of the deal. Later the Marines, as tough as his Afghanistan deployment had been, had proved to be the best thing that had ever happened to him.

They sat at the table where he and all his brothers had carved their initials, to the feigned consternation of his mother. The fire in the kitchen fireplace, which before electricity had made its way to this upper part of the Olympic Peninsula Coast had served as both heater and oven, added a wood-scented comfort. Bodhi was sitting on the edge of the counter, tanned legs swinging.

"Axel Swenson had a stroke." John Mannion broke the comfortable silence.

"That's too bad." Aiden and the chief of police had had an adversarial relationship, which he had to admit, had all been on him. "How is he?"

"Okay. There are some memory issues that may or may not clear up. And lingering weakness in his right arm, but he's going to undergo therapy for that."

"That's good to hear." Brianna had called and told him that their grandfather Harper had had a TIA, commonly referred to as a ministroke because it supposedly doesn't leave behind the damage of a "real" stroke. While Jerome Harper continued to insist all was fine, Aiden knew his mother worried about her father more than she let on. Although he knew enough not to talk about this with his grandpop, Aiden hated the idea of losing the gruff old family patriarch.

"Yeah. Axel might have a chance of coming back to work, but his wife put her foot down. She wants him to focus on getting better, then she's booked that cruise to Alaska he's been promising her for the entire forty-five years of their marriage."

"Sounds about right." And a lot like Seth's parents taking off to see the country in a motor home. Apparently boomers aged into nomads. But not his parents. He couldn't imagine them ever leaving the farm they'd gotten married on. Built a house and raised four sons and a daughter on.

"Here it comes," Bodhi warned.

"I'd like to see those glaciers before they're all gone, myself," his dad said. "Maybe your mom and I can book one of those cruises next year. After the new trees are planted."

"I'll bet Mom would like that." Aiden couldn't remember the last time his parents had taken a real vacation, other than a few days here at the coast house.

His dad took another pull on the brown bottle with the snow-flaked fir tree on the label. "The thing is, it's going to be hard to find someone to fill Axel's shoes."

Bang! The damn ninja star hit its mark.

"No."

John lifted a brow, but didn't bother to pretend not to know that Aiden had jumped a step ahead. "Why don't you just hear me out?" he suggested. "I did bring pizza. And beer."

"What would Mom say if she knew you'd stooped to bribery?"

"As it happens, we're on the same page about this. Well, except for maybe the triple meat on the pizza. Which she needn't know about."

His mother had always been into healthy eating before farm-to-table became a concept. Her one exception was her award-winning fried chicken that had been passed down through generations of Harpers before her becoming a Mannion by marriage.

"My lips are sealed."

"Mine, too, unfortunately," Bodhi moaned. "That Italian sausage would be making my stomach growl." He put a hand on his buffed-up abdomen. "If I had one."

It was all Aiden could do not to roll his eyes. While he liked pizza and burgers as much as the next guy, Bodhi had always worshipped in the church of carnivores. With fries and onion rings on the side. Their woman captain, a fortysomething vegan who was into yoga, had always sworn Bodhi's arteries must look like the Pacific Coast Highway at rush hour and claimed he was a walking heart attack waiting to happen.

Unfortunately, Bodhi hadn't lived long enough to test the validity of her accusation.

"I'm not talking about a long-term commitment," his father said. "Unfortunately Axel had his stroke on the night we were at Mannion's, celebrating his twenty-fifth anniversary in the job."

"He could've taken that as a sign it was time to get out of law enforcement," Aiden said.

"There is that. My point is the position is open and we need someone. Now."

"You're the mayor. Appoint someone. Anyone but me."

"You're the only viable candidate. Don't get me wrong, we've got some good young deputies, but they're green. We're also a small town with a small budget, so the others who have more experience under their belt are either volunteers or retired from other cities and don't want to get back into full-time police work."

"I fully appreciate their thinking."

"This isn't the same as what you were doing in California," his father said. "Instead of working the rough streets chasing down bad guys, you'd mostly be helping out Honeymoon Harbor citizens."

Previous generations of Mannions had been doing exactly that since their arrival on the Olympic Peninsula, though he was the only police officer in the family that he knew of. The tallest building in town, discounting the clock tower, was the three-story gray town hall built in 1876 by one of Seth Harper's ancestors. The bronze plaque on the side of the building named Finn Mannion as mayor. The same position his dad had held for years. Partly, he'd say, because no one ever wanted the unpaid job, and that kept anyone from running against him.

"Take it from me, any streets can be rough these days," Aiden said.

"Your dad obviously doesn't watch *Dateline*," Bodhi said. "Hell, if you watch that show enough, you'd never leave your house."

Aiden bit back the smile, not wanting his dad to think he was smiling at the idea of Honeymoon Harbor's former bad boy playing Andy Griffith for the Pacific Northwest's version of Mayberry. His mother used to claim that just because his name meant he'd been born from fire, didn't mean he needed to be constantly setting them at every opportunity. He'd admittedly been the family black sheep, a wildling who'd constantly rebelled at what he'd viewed as the constraints put on him growing up with the town's mayor as his father and a high school principal mom.

He routinely got into fights, could have papered the wall of the bedroom he'd shared with his brother Burke with parking tickets, and had once gotten caught TP-ing the house of a guy who'd stood up his teenage sister, Brianna, for the Spring Fling.

Luckily, he seemed to have inherited whatever family gene had made his uncle Mike the Mannion family charmer, and Aiden would have been the first to admit that he'd talked his way out of more trouble than a lot of guys would have gotten away with. But even his family name and charm came screeching to an end when he swiped a twelve-pack of Coors from the back of a delivery truck outside Marshall's Market. That had caused the judge to issue his ultimatum and give seventeen-year-old Aiden a choice: the military after graduation or he could leave the courtroom and go straight to juvie.

"The city council approved me hiring you this afternoon."

Given his former reputation, that showed how desperate they were. "Good for them. Now you can go back and tell them to come up with another candidate because I'm not interested."

"We're not meeting again until next month. Are you suggesting the town go without a police chief while we're doing a hiring search?"

"You could always contract with the county sheriff's department."

"They're good people," John allowed. "But although Honeymoon Harbor has always been the county seat, we value our independence and prefer to run our own town."

Which, as mayor, his dad had always done well, while managing to handle expanding growth with environmental concerns. "Even if I were to consider it, which I'm not," he said quickly, holding up a hand, "the operations I worked in LA weren't play-by-the-book deals. I spent a lot of time undercover that definitely didn't involve playing with others."

Other than his partner, who'd always had his back. "How do you know I even have leadership skills?"

"You know, I watched a documentary on the History Channel last week," his dad said mildly, as he appeared to sidetrack the conversation. But Aiden knew that he was just buying time to set up another ninja attack. "How, since 1775, Marines have embodied our country's standards of courage, esprit and military prowess. You may have taken off the uniform, son. But you'll always be a United States Marine. There isn't anyone who'd be better."

"He's got you there, dude," Bodhi chimed in again. "Besides, now that you're not drinking yourself into a stupor trying to get over misplaced survivor's guilt, you're going to need something else to do. I gotta tell you, dude, I'm getting cabin fever hanging around here."

Aiden hated to admit it, but they both had a point. Now that he was sober, he was beginning to get bored. And restless. And there was also the fact that he owed his dad. Without this isolated coast house to crash in when he'd gotten out of LA, he wasn't sure how far off the rails he might've gone.

"How long are you talking about?"

"Well, ideally, you'd settle in and like the job—"

Aiden crossed his arms. "How. Long?"

"If you find you don't feel like the job's a good fit for you, only until we find a replacement. Say, sometime mid-February?"

"That's six months."

"He can do math, too," Bodhi said.

"Why don't you sleep on it?" his dad suggested. Then, savvy politician that he was, he turned the conversation to the Seahawks's chances of making the Super Bowl while they finished off the pizza.

"Having been a detective in a previous life, I happened to have noticed that you failed to mention a salient fact," Bodhi said as they stood in the doorway, watching Honeymoon Harbor's ninja disguised as mild-mannered mayor drive back down the tree-lined road toward the coast highway that would take him along the Strait of Juan de Fuca to Honeymoon Harbor.

"Which would be?" But Aiden knew exactly what he was referring to.

"That the guns-for-drugs deal we were on was going to be your last bust. You were getting out and transferring to the youth gang suppression unit."

The unit had been established to try to keep kids from turning to gangs in the first place, so cops like him and Bodhi wouldn't have to be rearresting them. And it would hopefully save the lives of the kids, innocent bystanders and police officers.

"That was the plan."

"After the clusterfuck, you were also offered a police shrink and paid leave to get your head back together."

"I didn't want either one."

He'd already been on the brink of burnout. That night had continued to play through his mind and pushed him over the edge into the deep dark pit he'd finally begun to crawl his way out of. But he hadn't done it alone. Because damn if somehow Bodhi hadn't shown up as backup.

"Would you rather have ended up being the dead guy?" his partner asked.

"What the hell kind of question is that?" But Aiden knew. And yeah, given a choice, he would've willingly changed places and been the one having "Amazing Grace" played by a kilt-wearing, bagpipe-playing homicide detective at his gravesite.

"You always talked about how your father's spent years serving your hometown. And how that big brother of yours is such a Boy Scout. But guess what, dude? You've got the same blood running in your veins. You may have joined the Marines because your only other choice at the time was juvie, but we've dealt with enough kids back in the 'hood to know when a basically good teenager is acting out. Which you definitely must have been to get the judge to force you off that dangerous path everyone thought you were headed down. But the deal is, deep down inside, you're a stand-up guy. The kind who'd stand up for your fellow jarheads—"

"You weren't there."

"I didn't need to be. I've watched you in action. It was like you had that *protect and serve* motto tattooed over your heart. How many funerals of gangbangers and their victims did you go to?"

Aiden shrugged. "I've no idea."

But he did. Because every damn one of them was embedded in his mind. He went to the funerals of the teen bangers, not just to watch for the killer to show up—that happened more times than you'd think—but also in respect of their friends and families who'd loved them. The same with the victims, but those had been harder, because many had been so damn innocent. Like the toddler shot sleeping in the tub—the one place her mom thought she'd be safe—during a drive-by shooting at the wrong house.

"Getting back to my question, would you rather have had your parents burying their son in that flag-draped casket instead of mine?"

"That's an impossible choice." Struggling out of the quicksand pit of despair those memories triggered, Aiden opened another bottle of the winter ale and wished he hadn't dumped all the real stuff down the drain thirty days ago.

"Aren't you glad it wasn't your choice to make? Or mine either? Life's out of our hands, dude. All you can do is ride the wave you get, and stay upright as long as you can. Then, if you're lucky enough to survive the wipeout, you get back on the board and wade out into the surf again. No one makes it through alive, Mannion. And to quote the great Mark Foo, 'It's not tragic to die doing something you love.'"

"Isn't Foo the guy who died surfing?" Although Bodhi had a degree from UCLA in philosophy, of all things, mostly all he'd ever talked about was someday quitting the cops and joining the pro surfing circuit.

"Yeah. He bought it on his first ever session at the Mavericks Big Wave competition at Half Moon Bay. That made it kind of a sucky omen, but he wouldn't have wanted to go out any other way."

"So you'd rather have drowned than gotten shot?"

Tanned shoulders shrugged. "It's six of one, half a

dozen of another. I got the same rush from chasing bad guys down a dark alley as I did doing barrels in shallow water."

Aiden had learned that surfing move was more dangerous than in high water because—not that he'd ever intended to try it himself—sand apparently was like concrete when you hit it, which left more than a few surfers with broken necks.

"You never really loved being a big-city cop," Bodhi pressed his case. "It was too impersonal. That's why you went to all those damn funerals. To make a connection. But, bro, those were some really effing painful connections."

Aiden didn't answer. There was no need. Sometimes he figured he'd gotten more than a lifetime of violence in Afghanistan, which was why he'd only lasted six months on the SWAT team before asking for a transfer. SWAT had felt too much like war.

The Gang and Narcotics unit working with Homeland Security had been just as bad, triggering nightmares he wouldn't classify as full-blown PTSD, but had made him so edgy he couldn't stop wondering if maybe he *had* slipped up somehow that night Bodhi was killed. Clusterfuck, indeed.

Hell. Maybe his dad was right. Maybe playing police chief for a few months might not be such a bad thing while he figured out what to do with the rest of his life, now that drinking his way through it hadn't turned out to be a viable option.

"Women like men in uniforms."

"So?"

"So, you could try it out on that redhead from the wedding."

"Are you talking about the bride?" Who, if Bodhi

hadn't been able to tell from the two Wonder Woman figures on top of the wedding cake, wouldn't be the least bit interested in him.

"No, the *other* one. With the sexy streaked auburn hair. The one you were pretending not to be scoping out. While Gidget was doing her best to pretend to not notice you."

"I've no idea what you're talking about." But he did. At the time he'd tried to tell himself that long, deep burgundy hair with the sunlit copper streaks was as impossible to miss as a flashing red stoplight. The fact that it was tousled in a way that looked as if she'd just gotten out of bed had caused the numbness inside him begin to stir.

"Dude, there were so many sparks flashing back and forth between the two of you, I'm surprised that flowered arbor over those two brides didn't burst into flames."

"*Gidget's* name is Jolene Wells. She grew up here, too. But I was a year older so we didn't move in the same crowd." That part was true. Especially since Jolene hadn't belonged to any clique.

The mean girl queen bees had called her out for being trailer trash; the nerdy girls hadn't seemed to notice anyone else around them, given that their noses were always stuck in books; and the girl jocks were always out on the field, doing their own energetic, athletic things. Being a guy, Aiden hadn't missed noticing that sweaty, superfit girls could be hot and had dated enough to know that they could be every bit as energetic in the back of his truck as they were running, kicking soccer balls, shooting baskets and slamming each other's shins with field hockey sticks.

"Jolene and I barely knew each other."

It was a flat-out lie.

Aiden had never forgotten those secret nights when they'd lain on the deck of his boat anchored in Serenity Cove, talking and looking up at the stars. There'd also been a lot of making out, that had, on more than one occasion required a cold shower when he'd gotten home, but as the daughter of a former teen mom, Jolene had had no intention of risking pregnancy. Also, he'd been trying to stay on the straight and narrow to avoid going to lockup, where the actual juvenile delinquents would probably love nothing more than pounding on the guy whose mom had kept sending them to detention.

Granted, he'd screwed things up with her, but he'd been about to try to fix that until another fateful night years ago, when time and tide had literally shifted and…

Nope. Not going there.

"Okay. If you're not really into her, which I'm still not entirely buying because there sure as hell was something going on there, the redhead wasn't the only fox there. Like that cute brunette who had the sexy librarian glasses, pinned up ponytail and pencil skirt thing going on."

"Chelsea Prescott *is* a librarian."

"So I overheard when she was talking about cataloging romance novels with your sister. Who'd have thought the Dewey Decimal system could be so sexy?"

"Life isn't all surfing and sex."

Aiden's mind, distracted by an unbidden memory of Jolene Wells stripped down to a thong and a barely there lace bra, had him automatically falling back on that sex and surf line he'd repeated so many times. Just to yank his partner's chain because they both knew that despite his laid-back attitude, Bodhi had been the sharpest and most successful undercover cop in the unit. Aiden had often thought that was because bad guys never bothered to look beneath the stoner surfer act he was able to slide into like a wet suit.

"Maybe life would be better if it *was* all about surfing and sex," Bodhi shot back, on cue. "Seriously, though, Mannion, have you considered that part of your problem is that you need to get laid?"

"Maybe I don't have a problem. And maybe I don't need to get laid." He hadn't even thought about sex until that damn wedding. When a certain bedhead-tousled redhead started invading his dreams. Despite leaving him hot and bothered, they were an improvement over the nightmares that had driven him deep into the bottle.

"Said no guy ever. There's also the fact that you also told me how your dad worked his tail off to save you from landing in corrections."

It had been a long night on a stakeout down the street from a major gun dealer's house, where they'd stunk up the car with takeout from a food truck.

"So?"

"So, maybe you owe him."

"What, did you learn that guilt card from watching my sister while we were out at the farm?"

"It worked, didn't it? She got you to sober up for two days in a row so you could go to that wedding where you and the redhead connected."

"We didn't say a word to each other."

Jolene had seemed as eager as he'd been to avoid any memories of that night. Not that he hadn't thought about her. A lot. Especially when, during those long, lonely nights as a Marine sniper when he'd spent hours lying as still as a stone waiting for a shot and she'd filter through his mind. Memories of her pressed up against his body, even though she'd only ever let him get to second base, had helped keep him determined to get home alive.

On the way home from basic training, he thought back on all those rom-coms his sister made the family watch when it was her turn to pick a film for movie night and had, for a fleeting moment, considered holding up a boom box outside her window, like John Cusack in *Say Anything*.

Or, he could make a fool of himself by serenading his girl from the high school bleachers, like Heath Ledger in *10 Things I Hate About You*. He couldn't overcome his fear of heights to climb up a fire escape like in *Pretty Woman* because one, he didn't have a fear of heights, and two, there was only one fire escape in Honeymoon Harbor, and that was on the courthouse.

With all those things going through his head, before leaving for basic training, after stupidly breaking up with Jolene, he'd been headed to the beach, where he'd heard she was at a party. That wasn't his first choice, because if he was going to make a fool of himself, he'd rather do it in private. But if he could talk her into taking a walk, or even better, a midnight sail with him, he'd do whatever it took to make things right. Be honest about his feelings and, although it was selfish, and looking back, Aiden realized that they'd been way too young to be thinking about forever-afters, to ask her to wait for him.

"I noticed the zone of silence between you both. Which only made it more obvious something was going on."

"Maybe to you. Because you've got this ghostly superpower thing going on."

"That's true. But others noticed, too. Your sister and that red-haired bride were talking about it."

"You eavesdropped on my sister?"

"I was just kind of hanging around and overheard the conversation. And by the way, you never told me your sister was so hot."

"She's marrying my best friend. And besides, a player who goes through women like tequila shots isn't allowed to say anything about Brianna. Not even when you're dead." Aiden dragged a hand through his hair.

"For the record, my playing days are over and I didn't say I wanted to do her. Sorry," he said as a storm moved across Aiden's face. "Wrong choice of words and I apologize if you thought I disrespected your sister."

"I didn't just think it. You damn well did. And if you were real, I'd have knocked you on your ass."

"I was merely pointing out that she's got a cool blonde Hitchcock vibe going for her. The kind that makes a guy want to muss her up a little."

Which, dammit, had Aiden thinking of Seth messing her up on a regular basis. There probably wasn't enough Clorox in the state to wash that image out of his head.

"Correction. You are not allowed to so much as *think* of my sister. Period."

"Fine." Bodhi lifted his hands. "Am I allowed to at least say that I didn't exactly eavesdrop on she-who-must-not-be-named, but the way she and her friend kept looking over at Jolene, then back at you, then her again, like they were watching a match at Wimbledon, was a clue that I wasn't the only one curious about whatever backstory you two were hiding."

"There *is* no story."

Not one he'd ever tell. He suspected Jolene would be even less likely to. It was ironic and crummy that by going to the damn wedding he hadn't wanted to attend in the first place, he'd probably taken away from her enjoyment of it. Because if there was one person on the planet Jolene Wells undoubtedly never wanted to ever see again, it was him.

"What the hell are you doing here, anyway, Bodhi?" It was not the first time he'd ask the question. He'd yet to get a decent answer.

"Hanging with you."

"But why?"

"Why not?"

"Because if you've been sent here to earn your wings by getting my life back on track—"

"*It's a Wonderful Life* was fiction. At least I think it was. But I'm not interested in getting any wings. And no, I wasn't sent here to fix your life, as fucked up as it is right now."

Bodhi frowned and scratched his blond goatee that he'd taken to wearing a few months before he'd gotten blown away by that AR-15. "Even though you might as well have been the guy who died, given how you've been hiding from life out here, I sure wouldn't mind seeing you headed in a new direction that'll make you happy."

They'd been partners long enough that Aiden could tell when Bodhi was holding back. He also knew that for all his beach bum vibe, the guy was as tough as steel and impossible to drag anything out of until he was ready to share. So, he could wait him out. It wasn't as if he had a helluva lot else to do with his days.

"You're not real, either. You're just a hallucination." He'd gotten a concussion when a round of shots against his chest protector had knocked him off his feet onto the pavement. Headfirst. It made sense his brains would've been scrambled.

"Would a hallucination tell you to get laid?"

Not only had Aiden not been thinking about sex, he hadn't missed it. Until that moment he'd spotted the one woman he had no business thinking about walking across a summer garden, her full skirt swinging like a bell, and felt both his gut and groin tighten in a totally inappropriate way.

He'd wondered, at the time, if she'd come back to town for good. Although he'd originally planned to return to the house as soon as the vows were exchanged, instead of cutting out, he'd wandered through the crowd who'd lined up to get plates dished up by Italian chef Luca Salvadori, who'd catered the event, listening to gossip that had been amped up to eleven by news of a hometown girl being nominated for an Emmy.

Not being an awards-show watcher, except for occasionally tuning in to the CMAs, Aiden hadn't even known there was a category for makeup. But he was glad that Jolene had managed to escape Honeymoon Harbor, where she'd been a target for those spray-tanned, bleached mean girls and a subject of what he knew to be bald-faced lies about sexual conquests from guys who would never deserve a girl like her.

Although Bodhi was right about them circling each other on the fringes of the gathering, there'd been a moment when their eyes had met, causing a rosy color to bloom in her cheeks. Undoubtedly from embarrassment at what had happened the last time they'd been together. That was enough to tell him that she didn't want to have anything to do with him. For more than one reason.

Still, as he turned away, Aiden was glad she was doing well. Better than well. He had been surprised to hear from his sister that they'd both been in Los Angeles at the same time. And not only that, she'd been living in Beverly Hills. What would he have done if he'd known? Probably nothing because what would an Emmy-nominated makeup artist from the hills want with a cop living in a downtown studio apartment that had holes in the walls from where previous renters had hung pictures, and was surrounded by city infill construction.

He'd also been relieved to overhear Jolene's mother tell his mom that right after the reception, Jolene was leaving for Ireland, to work on a miniseries. That meant their paths probably wouldn't be crossing again.

Which, Aiden had attempted to convince himself, was a good thing.

CHAPTER TWO

November
Los Angeles

FOR A WOMAN born literally on the wrong side of the tracks in Honeymoon Harbor, Washington, Jolene Wells was living her dream life. Not only did she live in the Beverly Hills Triangle—it might be a rental apartment in the flats, aka "South of the Tracks" from when the old Pacific Electric streetcar traversed Beverly Hills—but her famed 90210 zip code was the same as where Jason Priestly and Luke Perry had hung out.

Maybe their characters were fictional, but still. And, as the leasing agent had pointed out, she was steps from Rodeo Drive. Which, while way too pricey for her budget, offered some wonderful window shopping. It was also pet friendly, not that her lifestyle allowed for as much as a goldfish. But that didn't stop her from watching ABC7's *Eyewitness News* "Pet of the Week" adoption segment and thinking maybe, someday.

She'd also, with a lot of hard work and some Tinseltown luck that could've come right out of an old MGM musical script, almost won an Emmy as part of the makeup team for a six-part miniseries set in 1950s Ireland. Although, as the cliché went, it had been an honor to have been nominated, privately she still thought it sucked losing out to yet another Tudor series. How many versions of Henry VIII did the world need, after all?

Still, the amount of press the series had received wouldn't hurt her fledgling business, which she was getting closer to getting off the ground. She'd been making her own organic skin care and makeup going back to her early days at the salon where she'd been discovered and nearly every actress—and quite a few actors—she'd worked with, had asked to buy it.

Unfortunately, her life had been so busy that she'd kept putting off the actual business part of the idea. But while the indoor scenes at been filmed at the same Wicklow County studio as *Braveheart*, the location shoots had been done in the west. During those long, winding bus drives being shuttled back and forth between the Kerry and Clare coasts, she'd had plenty of time to think. And plan. Now, she just had to figure out a doable way to implement that plan. And if heaven would send down an angel investor, that'd be the icing on the cupcake.

Although the press gained by her nomination had caused a burst of even more lucrative film and TV offers coming in, she'd been seriously considering a change. All those movie stars had shaken Hollywood up when they'd come out with stories of abuse, but the brightness of their movie star status had overwhelmed so many of those working unnoticed in the trenches—makeup artists, hair and food stylists, wardrobe mistresses, grips, animal and child wranglers, fixers, and all the other jobs that films couldn't reach the screen without.

She hadn't minded that making a movie involved hard work and long hours. She'd learned a strong work ethic from her mother. What she hadn't expected was that the moment she walked onto a location, she'd be seen by many as new prey.

That was why, right before leaving Ireland, she'd signed her name to a lengthy online list of women and not a few men, who'd decided to go public about the harassment behind the scenes. Behind Hollywood's bright lights. Even knowing that might hurt her future employment opportunities, she'd decided to leverage whatever little bit of influence she had received from her Emmy nomination to speak out. Besides, who really cared about people who the guys at the top of the food chain considered easily replaceable?

So, needing a break from those long hours an overseas location entailed, she'd decided to spend the rare downtime until the new year looking for an investor and mentor who could help her grow her start-up and get her products out into the cosmetics and day-spa marketplace. So far, the producers of *Shark Tank* had turned her down twice, but she'd sent in a new audition video, mentioning her Emmy nomination, so hey, maybe the third time would be the charm. It could happen, right?

Her flight had been delayed on the tarmac at Kennedy, and now it was dark as her flight glided down its path into LAX. On an average night from the air the city looked like jewels spread out as far as the eyes could see, with the mountains supplying spots of dark contrast. But this was November, and going with the idea that there was no business like snow business, the abundance of holiday lights could undoubtedly dazzle from space.

The moment she turned on her phone after landing, it exploded with emails and texts, but since everyone was eager to get off the plane after the delay, she decided to check them out once she got to the limo. If anything major had occurred, like World War III breaking out while they'd been in the air surely the pilot would've announced it.

Her limo driver, provided by the production company (proof that her nomination *was* worth something), was waiting for her in the baggage area. In some towns where she'd traveled for work, the black-suited woman with a name tag reading Charlene, holding up a sign with Jolene's last name would've drawn some double takes from passengers trying to figure out if she was someone famous. Here, neither one of them earned so much as a glance.

It was only after they'd escaped the LAX traffic and were on the 405 that Jolene decided to check her messages and emails. Most were from various bloggers and entertainment reporters, none of whom she was in any mood to speak to at the moment. Scrolling down, she noticed a text from a reporter at *The Hollywood Reporter* with a subject line asking for a comment on the attached photo. Opening the link, she found herself looking at her actor boyfriend outside a club with an actress he'd been working on in Australia. A reboot of *The Thorn Birds.* A decision she found ridiculous, given that Richard Chamberlain would *always* be Father Ralph.

Still, since Chad Dylan possessed the combination of egoism and insecurity she'd noticed in so many actors, she'd kept her opinion to herself when he'd gotten the callback, then won the role. In the photo the actress who played Meggie, Tiffany Rule, was showing off a diamond as big as the iceberg that had sunk the *Titanic* on the fourth finger of her left hand while her new fiancé, aka Father Ralph, aka Jolene's former boyfriend, was grinning down at her as if he'd just won the Powerball.

"Good luck with that," Jolene murmured. Tiffany,

at twenty-five, had already been divorced twice, most recently from an A-list director who, apparently bewitched by her charms (or, more likely, Jolene thought cattily, her blow jobs), hadn't required her to sign a prenup. After inheriting half of his considerable fortune in a surprisingly quickie divorce a mere six weeks later (which suggested he'd been a very bad boy doing something he'd wanted kept silent), Jolene suspected those very same barracuda divorce lawyers who'd gotten serial bride Tiffany her windfall were already at work crafting a prenup to ensure that she'd keep every penny when marriage number three broke up.

Jolene wasn't surprised Chad had been unfaithful. They'd been a couple for only four months, and for three of those months they'd been working in different parts of the world. While he hadn't ever found time to make it to Ireland, she'd traveled once to Perth for the sheep station scenes and the second time to Kauai, that, as in the original miniseries, served as a stand-in for the remote tropical island where Meggie had her tryst with Father Ralph.

In Perth, Chad had taken her on a romantic tour of a part of the world that was the polar opposite from her native Olympic Peninsula. But in Kauai, he'd claimed work pressures, and most of their time together had been spent with the cast and crew. Including Tiffany.

Had she caught vibes? Well, duh. What man wouldn't notice a hot blonde who looked like Malibu Barbie? Which was so not Meggie from the book, but knowing the casting director, she wasn't surprised Tiffany had gotten the role. Chad had assured Jolene that even during his and Tiff's (yes, that's what he'd called her, which should've been a flashing red warning light) lovemaking scenes, he'd been thinking of her. She hadn't believed that for a moment.

Still, again, it wasn't as if she'd been in love with him. Although she'd overheard the script supervisor tell the cinematographer that you could probably hear the wind blowing between his ears, he'd been cute and convenient. And, she admitted, though it might sound cold, utterly disposable. Which was why she wasn't curled up in a fetal position on the limo floor, her wounded heart shattered.

Only one man had ever possessed that much power over her.

She'd told Chad from the beginning that marriage wasn't in her plans. Neither was love. She'd had both those fantasies sucked out of her growing up. She'd made her own way, happy with casual relationships. To be honest, if they hadn't spent so much time apart, she and the poster boy for narcissism probably wouldn't have lasted two months. The only thing different was that she was usually the one to walk when things started looking as if they were edging toward something serious. Rather than trusting a man with a relationship, she preferred to count on herself.

Having dropped out of school at sixteen after a life-altering event she'd locked away in a far corner of her mind, she'd worked with her hairdresser mom for a year, sweeping up hair, cleaning the salon bathroom, dusting the product shelves and occasionally touching up a client's makeup. It was then she'd discovered that she enjoyed helping women feel happy and good about themselves, women like her and her mom who couldn't afford to go to fancy salons.

Which was why, after earning her GED, she'd followed in her mom's footsteps and attended cosmetology classes at Clearwater Community College. Hearing from one of the instructors that there was a lot of money to be made in Los Angeles, after receiving her degree, she'd bought an old clunker and made her way south down I-5. She'd ended up spending too many nights in that old car, and it had cost her time and money she couldn't afford to transfer her license from Washington to California, but eventually, she'd gotten a job in a quirky West Hollywood salon where both she and her thrift shop vintage clothes fit right in.

She'd been content for the next few years, making friends and enjoying the laid-back SoCal lifestyle, and although that song about it never raining in California hadn't turned out to be totally true, there was a lot more days of sunshine than where she'd grown up.

She'd just turned twenty-one when a producer, scouting the salon for a shooting site for his 1950s film, had signed her to work as an assistant to help with hair and makeup. Because, since she looked as if she'd stepped out of a midcentury time capsule, she obviously had the era's style down pat.

She'd spent every spare minute learning her trade, eventually landing jobs on TV shows and the occasional movie or miniseries, that had, this year, resulted in her Emmy nomination as a key makeup artist in the Outstanding Makeup for a Limited Series or Movie (Non-Prosthetic) category. While the Creative Arts Awards might not be included in the big prime time Emmy extravaganza show, they were held in the very same theater as the one everyone was more familiar with. Win or lose, the highlight of her night, indeed, her life, was being able to fly her mother to Los Angeles to be her date.

Gloria Wells had not led an easy life. Jolene's father

had been—there was no sanitized way to put it—a professional criminal and binge drinker. He'd grown and sold marijuana before it had been legalized, cut and sold timber from federal lands, illegally harvested oysters and clams that he then sold to Seattle restaurants and markets, and finally, while drunk, he'd decided it would be a good idea to take his S&W .38 to Port Angeles and rob the state liquor store. The episode had ended with him being incarcerated in the Clallam Bay Corrections Center. Six months later, he'd been killed when a huge tree limb from an old-growth Douglas fir had crashed down on him while he'd been clearing winter debris from hiking trails on a trustee prison work crew.

Jolene and her mother had always been a team. Despite the bullying from classmates who'd mock her for wearing clothes their wealthier parents had donated to the thrift stop, despite her father's criminal behavior and alcohol-sodden binges, despite never knowing when the police might be back knocking on the door, Jolene had never doubted that her mother, who seemed more like an older sister than mom, had always loved her. Gloria had lost her own parents when she'd been a teenager, which had led her into the arms of Jake Wells. Which, in turn, had resulted in her getting pregnant at sixteen, and becoming the married mother of a newborn at seventeen.

Realizing that she'd never be able to count on her husband for steady support, Gloria graduated from high school and had managed to attend the community college, often taking Jolene to class with her when couldn't find anyone willing to babysit in exchange for highlights or a trim. After getting her degree, she began cutting hair in their trailer outside town.

When men began showing up at all hours, after getting back from fishing, or after their shifts at the old mill, rumors began to swirl around Honeymoon Harbor that Jake Wells's wife was doing tricks out of the trailer. That had never been true, but it hadn't stopped people, mostly former mean girls who'd grown up to be mean women, from talking.

Still, Jolene's mother brushed off the talk and worked long hours barely supporting them by cutting and coloring hair without having paid for the state license that she couldn't afford. And no, she hadn't paid sales tax either, since she'd run a cash-only business.

As soon as Jolene landed her first job in LA, she starting sending money home, despite her mother's objections. While the West Hollywood salon might not charge Rodeo Drive prices, the customer base was loyal and with tips, Jolene was able to make more in a week than her mother made in a month.

Once she'd broken into Hollywood's entertainment echelons and began negotiating pay even above the pay scale set by the Make-Up Artists and Hair Stylists Guild, she was able to help her mom upgrade to a manufactured home, with an extra bedroom where, now duly and legally licensed, Gloria had opened a salon. Because her mother was every bit as talented as many of the hairdressers Jolene had worked with over the years, the salon had thrived, allowing her recently to sell the house, and use the profits, along with a small business loan, to hire Seth Harper, Brianna's fiancé, to remodel the old lighthouse keeper's house into a new salon and day spa.

Although Jolene had never returned to Honeymoon Harbor, instead paying for her mother to fly to Los Angeles once or twice a year, right before leaving for Ireland, Gloria had asked her to return home to help pick out colors for the building. And she'd asked if Jolene would be willing to do the wedding makeup for Kylee Campbell, Mai Munemori and Mai's mom.

Although Jolene and Kylee Campbell had never been all that close, two things they'd shared were their artistic creativity and their outsider status. That was why, as much as she hated going back to Honeymoon Harbor, Jolene had reluctantly agreed. But she'd refused to charge for her work, declaring it her wedding gift to the couple.

While she might not believe in love for herself, it had been impossible not to get swept up into the romantic moment when the two women had exchanged vows in the backyard of their darling restored Folk Victorian home beneath an arbor of white wisteria.

Mai's mother, who'd flown in from Hawaii (Kylee had tragically lost hers in a car accident her first year of college) had carried Kylee and Mai's adopted daughter up the aisle immediately after the vows had been exchanged. At four months, baby Clara looked adorable in a white lace gown. The ceremony was part wedding, part christening and 100 percent perfect.

Except for one thing Jolene hadn't counted on. Aiden Mannion, the last person on the planet she'd expected, or wanted to see, had been there. He'd changed from the last time she'd seen him so many years ago. He'd bulked up, his biceps like boulders beneath his suit jacket, and his shoulders seemed broader, wider, although that could be that he seemed to be standing at attention most of the time. His face was leaner, accenting a stubborn jaw and shadowed with what seemed to be either sadness or exhaustion. Lines he hadn't had before fanned out from eyes that had deep circles beneath them.

But despite all those changes, those vivid blue eyes had, for an instant when they'd met hers, turned intense and dangerous. They'd also sent her hormones spiking in a way she knew had brought heat into her cheeks. Unfortunately, blushing was the bane of a redhead's existence. Then the shields came down and he turned away, walking off in the opposite direction. Apparently he'd been no more eager to see her than she'd been to see him. That had admittedly stung.

She reminded herself that the woman seated in the backseat of this limousine headed to Beverly Hills was no longer that young messed-up teenager she'd been that night Aiden, Honeymoon Harbor's bad boy, had rescued her from her own stupidity. Which was embarrassing enough. It was what had come after…

No. Don't think about that. She was strong, confident and had been an Emmy nominee, dammit. She'd come a long way from the girl who'd provided constant fodder for gossip. The wounded girl who'd humiliated herself that fateful night.

And damn. Here she was, thinking about it again. Thinking about Aiden Mannion. And those hot, dangerous eyes.

Just when she was wishing she could have her memories erased, a new text dinged. From, of all people, Chad.

Sorry. I feel like shit. The news wasn't supposed to get out til I talked with u. Hope ur okay. We agreed, no strings, right?

"Right," she muttered, shaking her head. See, this was why she didn't allow herself to get emotionally involved. Because of guys like Chad Dylan. Who, before he'd taken on those two first acting names, had been—wait for it—Norman Bates. Seriously, what kind of sadistic parents would stick their kid with a name like that? And how could he have possibly survived the inevitable schoolyard taunts and end up with an ego the size of Jupiter?

"My GPS says left," the driver, who must have thought she was talking to her, said.

"Sorry. I was talking to myself."

"I do that a lot." Charlene smiled up at Jolene in the rearview mirror. "Casualty of spending so many hours alone in this car."

"Do you like your job?"

Personally, Jolene had always considered the California freeway system to be one of the lower circles of hell. Which was why she always was so grateful whenever she could score a ride.

"I do, surprisingly enough. I get to choose my hours, that lets me be home with my kids when they get up in the morning and go off to school."

"You have kids?"

That was, she'd always thought, a downside to her nonmarriage vow. She enjoyed her friends' children and would love one or two of her own someday. Her boyfriendless, homeless life might be in flux right now, but the one thing Jolene was certain of was that she wasn't ever going to get married, and single motherhood wasn't anything she wanted to tackle. How could she ever manage being a mother in her line of work? It wasn't as if she could put them in boarding for however long she was working on a movie.

"Three. Two boys and a girl," Charlene answered. "Though I'm speeding too fast toward an empty nest. My twins are in middle school, and my oldest is a junior in high school going on thirty. I'm going to curl up in a wet puddle of tears when she leaves home. I don't even want to think about coming home to an empty house once the twins leave."

"So you're not married?"

"No. In the cliché of all clichés, my investment banker husband took off with his secretary. They're currently enjoying the good life in Bali, that, surprise, surprise, doesn't have an extradition treaty because he also absconded with a lot of money he'd been socking away in offshore accounts."

"Wow. I'm sorry." Didn't that story make her own breakup seem insignificant? Like whining about a head cold to someone with terminal cancer.

Charlene's black-suited shoulders lifted in a shrug as she turned onto Santa Monica Avenue. "Don't be. Best thing that ever happened to me and the kids." She glanced up in the rearview mirror again. "Seems like we both lucked out. You earlier than me. You escaped the mess and expense of a divorce."

One of the things Jolene had always enjoyed about her job was that she was able to work in the movie business, while staying beneath the radar. Which was why she'd never dated any actors, until Chad, who not only thrived on the paparazzi, but would initiate coverage. Early in his career, when he was down in the part of the credits when most people would have left the theater or clicked off the TV, he'd make a call to certain friendly, and hungry paps to let them know where he was going to be.

The first time it had happened, they'd gone to a movie in Westwood, standing in line for their tickets like everyone else. When they'd come out of the theater, they were met by a loud, buzzing swarm of two dozen photographers.

"They're like wasps," he'd told her on the drive back to his rented house, because heaven forbid he ever been seen at her lowly apartment. Even with its 90210 zip code. "If one or two know you're going to be there, the rest show up."

"You called them?" Jolene wasn't naive. She knew such things were done. But she'd never heard anyone admit it.

"Sure. Everyone does it," he assured her. "In fact, my publicist is working to get me a paying yogurt gig. All I have to do is get myself photographed eating a lot of a certain brand of yogurt. Enough Instagram, Snapchat and YouTube hits, and I'll be able to move out of the Valley."

"You can make that much? Just from having your picture taken while living your normal life?"

"You may have been in the business longer than me, sweetcheeks, but if you're on my side of the camera, yeah, it's like what studios used to pay publicists to do for their stars. If you play your cards right, and get enough hits, fans, followers and likes, you can shoot up to the top. Look at the Kardashians."

"They're not actors."

"Of course they are… Don't frown, it'll give you wrinkles." Which was akin to leprosy in Hollywood. He reached over and rubbed a thumb on the lines that had furrowed on her forehead. "It's just part of the celebrity industrial complex."

"But you're not exactly a celebrity." As soon as she'd heard the words come out of her mouth, Jolene had known she'd said the wrong thing. But instead of getting annoyed, he'd flashed his light-up-the-screen boyish grin and returned his hand to the leased Porsche's steering wheel. "But I will be. That's what those paps with the cameras are for. It's how it's done, baby."

Apparently the publicity worked. It wasn't long before he'd gotten the role of Father What-a-Waste, and she'd found herself showing up on the cover of tabloids and carrying pepper spray because having a camera flash in your face in a dark parking garage could be freaking scary.

They were driving past The Regent Beverly Wilshire, that had served as the *Pretty Woman* hotel, and was bejeweled with holiday lights. Rodeo Drive had also rolled out the red carpet for holiday shoppers with red ribbons adorning the trees, poinsettias and a bazillion white lights.

"Uh-oh," her driver murmured.

"What's the problem?"

"We're blocked off."

Jolene could see that for herself. Her heart and stomach sank when she viewed the police roadblock and the flashing lights of the phalanx of police and bright red fire trucks.

CHAPTER THREE

CHARLENE PULLED OVER and they both stared at the three-story building. The flashing red, blue and white lights reminded her of the aluminum Christmas tree and color wheel her mother had bought for two dollars at Goodwill. When she'd been eight years old, Jolene had found the revolving colors wonderfully festive. Tonight they were anything but.

"What floor are you on?"

"The third," Jolene said, staring up at the gaping hole leading into her apartment. Because it was the top floor, she'd laughingly told friends who'd helped her move in that she was now living the Beverly Hills penthouse style.

"Oh, damn. I'm sorry."

"Me, too." Fire hoses were spraying huge streams of water into the windows, but while she was not a firefighting professional (though she had done the makeup for a few episodes of *Rescue Me* that included creating fake burns on a victim's face and arms), she could tell that the entire floor was toast. Burnt toast.

Could this day be any worse?

"I'll be right back," she said, opening the car door.

"I'm not going anywhere," Charlene said.

She made her way toward the crowd of people huddled together, watching the action. Many, she suspected, were looky-loos, drawn by the lights and sirens. Others she recognized as neighbors from the building.

A police officer stopped her at the wooden barricade. "Sorry, ma'am," he said. "But no one's allowed in right now."

"That's my apartment." She pointed to the corner, though smoke was pouring out of all the windows on that floor. "I just wanted to ask a question." Which, now that she was closer, she realized was not the time while everyone on the scene was working hard to save the building.

Just then a firefighter in yellow turnout gear and a helmet who was talking on a radio came walking toward her.

"Hey, Jolene. I thought that was you," the woman who'd moonlighted as an expert on one of those *Rescue Me* episodes Jolene had worked on, greeted her. Her badge revealed she'd worked her way up to captain. "I remembered you telling me you lived here and was wondering on the way to the call if you still did."

"I do. Did," Jolene corrected. "I guess it's bad up there, huh?"

"The good news is that the fire detectors worked, and everyone got out. The bad news is this building still hasn't upgraded to sprinklers, so I'm afraid you're looking at a total loss."

Although there was nothing humorous about this situation, a laugh escaped. "It figures."

"Yeah. I heard about your breakup when we were watching *ET* before the call came in. I'm sorry for your shitty day."

Didn't it just figure that she, Chad and Tiff had already made *Entertainment Tonight*. Jolene laughed again because it was better than crying. "It's just stuff.

I haven't lost anything that can't be replaced." Including her cheating boyfriend. "The important thing is that everyone's safe. Do you have any idea how soon I can get in?"

"The short answer is you can't. The investigators need to go through after cleanup's done. But, honestly, Jolene, there's nothing there. The guys who went in clearing the floor, looking for people and pets, report that it's going to be cinders down to the insulation and charred studs."

"Well." Despite, or perhaps because of the additional time in New York, yet more jet lag hit like a sledgehammer. Her mind was fuzzy, and not from all the smoke lingering over them. "Thanks for saving the rest of the building. At least the other two floors are okay. Being homeless is tough anytime." Having slept in her car when she'd first arrived in the city, she knew that all too well. "But at the holidays, it's even worse."

"You've got that right. Unfortunately, it's one of the most common times for fires, what with all the lights and trees and candles people put up. We've already put a call into the Red Cross in case anyone needs help getting relocated. Oh, and you haven't asked, but you should be able to pick up your car tomorrow. Fortunately, with the garage being subterranean, it should be fine."

That was something, Jolene decided.

The radio on the fire captain's jacket crackled. "Got to go," she said. "Take care."

Jolene looked up at the building one more time, then turned and walked away. The Red Cross van was arriving as Jolene reached the limo. Grateful that she had someplace to go, she called her best friend, a caterer she'd met five years ago on a Western movie shoot in Old Tucson.

"Are you okay?" was the first thing Shelby Carpenter asked her.

"I'm fine. Except for the fact that my apartment is now ashes."

"Tell me you're kidding."

"I wish I could. The fire department's still here."

"Damn."

"Yeah. Trying to find a silver lining, either the sight of the cop cars chased the gossip press away, or they decided not to risk getting arrested for interfering with an emergency response. Whichever, I don't have to answer questions about Chad and Tiffany."

And fortunately, since she wasn't a celebrity, she imagined the story would morph into the newly engaged couple's wedding plans in a day or so and she'd happily disappear back into the crowd of invisible people who keep the industry humming.

"That could be. More likely, in stroke of good luck for you, a certain dick of a director who'll go unnamed, but those of us who've worked on his dystopian teen movies know all too well, just got hit with a flood of sexual harassment accusations. They've all run like lemmings up to Bel Air to stake out his mega-mansion."

"That's something." Jolene knew very well who Shelby was referring to. She'd once threatened to contact her guild rep if he dared pat her butt a second time. She'd also been vocal about warning others against working with him. With varying levels of success.

"Are you sure you're okay?" Shelby asked again.

"I'm fine. Really."

"At least now I can confess I never liked Chad," Shelby said. "The two of them deserve each other."

"You won't get any argument from me about that."

"So you're not in tears over him?"

"Hardly."

"Since we won't have a night together until after Christmas, Ètienne took tonight off and is cooking. But I can send him to the restaurant if you want to have a good cry and girl binge on junk food and ice cream."

Ètienne Gardinier, Shelby's fiancé, was a local chef who had a trendy bistro, Epicure, on Melrose. Every time Jolene ate there with her best friend, she half expected to see Heather Locklear walk in from the Melrose Place apartment complex. Ètienne looked like a god, had a sexy French accent, his food was to die for and, amazingly, he was also a really good guy.

"Big girls don't cry." It had been Gloria's motto, passed down from mother to daughter.

"We're having beef bourguignon, and unlike in the *Julie & Julia* movie, it's not going to be burned to a crisp."

"I swear, if you don't marry that man soon, I may break my no commitment rule and try to steal him for myself."

"Sorry," Shelby said with the easy confidence of a woman who didn't have to worry about her boyfriend getting engaged to another woman behind her back. "But I've got dibs."

"If you weren't my best friend, I'd have to hate you," Jolene said.

Thirty minutes later, she was at Shelby and Etienne's decked-out-in-tasteful-white-fairy-lights Venice contemporary that boasted both ocean and mountain views and greeted with a glass of cabernet and hug from Shelby, along with a continental two-cheek kiss from Ètienne, who heartily assured her that the *caca boudin* wasn't good enough for her.

"Shit sausage," he translated when she lifted a questioning brow.

Ètienne was the complete package. Handsome, talented, wealthy, cooked like a dream, had an accent designed to make any woman with working ovaries want to bear his children and he lacked the temper so many male chefs seemed to possess. And best yet, from the day they'd met at Food Fare, one of the most recognized and popular culinary fund-raisers in Los Angeles—he'd treated Shelby like a queen. And tonight, he knew just what to say to make Jolene laugh.

"Proving yet again that French cuss words are superior to English," she said.

The main floor was open concept, the kitchen boasting a wall of windows to show off the view, sleek black cabinets, a long marble slab for pastry, stainless steel countertops and a French stove like the one Brianna had Seth put in Herons Landing, but this one was even larger, and matched the stainless steel of the countertops.

A twelve-foot-tall white-flocked Christmas tree decorated with porcelain and blown glass food and cooking utensil ornaments added colorful whimsy to a modernist interior that could have easily been stark, but was instead inviting, and cheered Jolene up a bit. Although the tree might be pushing the season because it wasn't yet Thanksgiving, Shelby explained that since Epicure was booked every day and evening of December with Christmas parties, they were determined to celebrate their first Christmas together in their own time.

The beef bourguignon filled the house with a mouthwatering aroma, served with a rich cauliflower soup swirled with browned butter and a crusty bread that Etienne had, natch, made himself, and baked winter pears with a caramel sauce were as delicious as expected and soothed Jolene after her terrible, horrible, no good, very bad day.

An hour later, jet lag had caught up with her and, after they both insisted she would not be allowed to help with the dishes after her horrible day, Jolene stumbled upstairs with her luggage to one of two guest suites, washed her face, brushed her teeth, changed into a tank and pajama pants and collapsed into bed. She was just about to drift off to sleep when her phone rang.

Reaching out for it in the dark, thinking it was more press, she was about to turn it off when she noticed the familiar Honeymoon Harbor area code. But it wasn't her mother's ringtone.

"Hello?"

"Jolene?" the vaguely familiar voice asked.

"It's me." She wondered if it was one of those cases where the spammers had faked the area code to look like one in her contacts list.

"This is Sarah Mannion. I'm sorry to call so late, dear, but I left a message and was afraid you might have missed it."

"Oh. Okay. Sorry, Mrs. Mannion. I just got back to town a while ago and haven't checked them all." Wondering what the wife of Honeymoon Harbor's mayor could possibly be calling her about, Jolene's fogged mind suddenly cleared as a terrible thought occurred to her. "Is it about Mom?"

"In a way."

"Did something happen?" While Honeymoon Harbor wasn't in a snow zone, it did get its share of cold temperatures this time of year that, when combined with the rain, could turn the twisting Olympic Peninsula roads treacherous. Hadn't her mother lost her own parents on Hurricane Ridge one winter? "Is she okay?"

"That's the thing." There was a long pause. Sarah Mannion was principal of Honeymoon High School and the entire time she'd been a student there, Jolene had never heard the woman at a loss for words. Until now. "I'm afraid I'm going to have to break a confidence," she said finally.

"Okay." Could she just get to the damn point?

"There was a suspicious lump on your mother's mammogram."

Now Jolene was fully awake. She was sitting straight up, her heart beating like she'd just finished climbing Mount Olympus back home. "And?"

"That's the problem. I don't know. *She* doesn't know. Because she refuses to go in for the ultrasound the doctor ordered."

"Shit." Realizing she was talking to her former principal, Jolene said, "Sorry."

"Don't be. You're not alone. Caroline Harper and I are, as far as I know, the only ones she told. And that was probably only because we were getting our hair done at the salon when she got the call. Caroline and Ben have been traveling around the country in their motor home, but instead of staying somewhere warm and sunny like any sane Northwesterner would do, they came home for the holidays this week.

"Which was fortunate, because she kept your mother busy showing off the new spa rooms, while I got your number off Gloria's phone. It was on the front counter next to the computer, I suppose so she can more easily book appointments that call in." The fact that the always-composed Mrs. Mannion had uncharacteristically rambled those unimportant pieces of information revealed how upset she was. “But we can’t convince her that this isn’t anything to take lightly.”

“She hates hospitals.” Jolene’s grandparents hadn’t lived long enough for her to have ever met them and her mother never talked about their deaths other than they hadn’t died quickly after their accident. Her aversion to anything medical was so strong that she’d even had a midwife deliver Jolene at home rather than Harbor General’s maternity wing.

“I know. Because of her parents,” Sarah said. “That was a terrible time.” Of course, Mrs. Mannion, who’d grown up with Jolene’s mother, would know more about those days that she would. “But we’ve tried to convince her that she doesn’t even *know* what she’s dealing with. And the longer she puts it off, if there is anything to be concerned about, she’ll have more problems.”

Jolene blew out a long breath. “I’ll be on the first flight I can get out tomorrow.”

“I hate to ask this of you, because I’ve always prided myself on being a stickler for honesty, but if you could not mention my call…”

“Don’t worry. I won’t say a word. I’ve been working eighteen-to-twenty-hour days on a location shoot in Ireland. Going home for a holiday break makes sense.” Not that anything about today made sense, but Mrs. Mannion didn’t need a play-by-play of unfortunate events.

As she ended the call and opened her browser to look for flights, Jolene’s losses suddenly came crashing down on her. Not Chad. He was already nearly forgotten, and wasn’t she lucky to have escaped falling in love with a man who’d so easily and blithely cheat on her?

But the fire scene, that she supposed her fuzzy, jet-lagged mind had tried to lock away, as was her habit with all things bad, suddenly came roaring back in a blaze. She could smell the smoke that her eyes and lungs still burned from. She could hear the roar of the flames, the pumper trucks pouring what had to be gallons of water through the hoses like gigantic water cannons. A loud generator was running portable outdoor lights and in the glow Jolene could see ashes floating in the air like black falling snow. She heard shouts, the crackling of the radios, the explosion and shower of glass as her bedroom window burst out.

There was a game movie crews often played sometime during their first week on the job. They'd sit around together at the end of the day, drinking, sharing stories about previous projects they'd worked on and asking, "If your home was on fire, what three things would you take?"

Apparently it had started years ago when one of the hairdressers had been going through therapy, and had been given that to do as one of her exercises. It had been designed to get the hairdresser to realize what was truly valuable to her. On a new set, it allowed others on the crew to know a bit about you, that helped with bonding, which in turned was intended to create group cohesion. Of course it was taken for granted that people would lie for fear of revealing too much. But it killed time and as each crew member went on to work on other projects, then those people, in turn, moved on, the game had spread like a virus.

And now, here she was, playing it all alone, in the surreal moment running across the movie screen in her mind in full Dolby Vision HDR 3D.

She was inside her apartment, surrounded by flames, but miraculously safe as she walked calmly around, choosing what she would save.

The first thing was her DVDs of *Gilmore Girls*, including the revival. She'd started watching the show every week with her mom when it had first aired the year Jolene turned thirteen. Later, she'd bought two sets of DVDs—one she'd sent to her mother—and sometimes they'd watch them together, Jolene in LA, Gloria in Honeymoon Harbor, synchronizing their DVD players, and pausing them when one or the other had a comment.

It seemed that each time they'd watched an episode, they found something new they hadn't noticed before. Jolene wondered if that was because their relationship, as close as it was, had never been static, and perhaps they focused only on events relevant to where they were in their lives at that time. There was no way she was going to leave those behind.

The second thing she chose was a leather-covered makeup box filled with small bottles of essential oils for making her skin care products. It had taken her months to collect them, and she couldn't launch her new career without them.

The third, which she had to pass through even higher flames into her bedroom to retrieve, was the needlepoint pillow her mother had surprised her with the day she'd gotten into that junker car and headed off to seek her fortune in California. Given the long hours Gloria worked, she knew it had been stitched late into the night while Jolene had been sleeping. The background color was a cheery sky blue usually seen only during the short summer on the Olympic Peninsula, and the words, stitched a contrasting sunshine yellow, read *Home Is Where The Heart Is. Heart* hadn't been stitched as a word, but as a cardinal-red heart.

"Just remember," Gloria had told her, "wherever you

go in your life, you'll always know that you're loved. And have a place to come home to."

In her vision, Jolene's eyes were clear, but in real life she could feel them filling up.

The scene cleared. The smoke blew away, presumably over the ocean. The fire sizzled and went out. The firefighters wrapped up their equipment and drove away, leaving the ground wet and covered with ash. And the building she'd lived in for eighteen months, longer than she'd ever lived anywhere, was still standing with its third floor looking as if it had faded to black.

"It's just stuff," she'd bravely told Shelby and Ètienne, as she had everyone else she'd spoken with that night. "It can be replaced." But as she opened her phone app to search for a flight, she realized she'd been wrong.

She could buy more oils. And she could undoubtedly find more DVDs online. But the pillow that she'd often hold to her breast while watching *Gilmore Girls* on the phone with her mom, or when her outwardly gilded life seemed dark or lonely, that homemade pillow that had epitomized all the sacrifices her mother had made with such unconditional love, had been turned to ciders. And was truly gone forever.

Which was when Jolene's eyes flooded over, and not wanting the couple in the bedroom down the hall to hear, she buried her face in a down pillow and sobbed.

CHAPTER FOUR

AFTER A RESTLESS night's sleep, and checking out flight schedules, Jolene decided that now that she was back to being homeless, it made more sense to drive to Honeymoon Harbor so she'd have a car while she was there. Google Maps put the trip at seventeen hours. If she stopped in Oregon for a night, she'd only have a seven-hour trip left, and that would only add a day to the trip. Also, that way, if her mother's recheck did show anything wrong, she wouldn't have to worry about a car rental or about searching for a new apartment until everything was settled in Washington.

"It's a good plan," Shelby said the next morning. Ètienne had already left to go shopping at the farmer's market and the laundry Jolene had brought home from Ireland was currently tumbling in the dryer to give her a clean start on her trip. "You said you wanted to take time off to concentrate on launching your beauty line.

"Knock on wood, your mom's lump is just a false alarm. But, the cosmetics would be something the two of you could do together during any downtime she might have from any treatment she might end up needing. Also, you need to leverage your name recognition from the Emmy buzz. Just because so many people in the business know how excellent you are, you're not exactly a household name."

"My name may be mud after signing that #TimesUp harassment list."

"If they blacklist everyone who signed it, there'll be no more movies because there won't be anyone to work on them. But since the breakup and engagement is going to be tabloid and blogger fodder, it won't hurt to be out of town."

"True. I'm knocking on wood *and* crossing my fingers that Mom's situation is like you said, a false alarm. But I've been feeling guilty about never going home. She went through a lot to essentially raise me alone. I owe her."

"You went home this past summer for that wedding."

"Just for the weekend." And, if you discounted Aiden Mannion showing up at the wedding, had survived.

"You also fly Gloria down here and show her a great time at least once a year," Shelby reminded her. "She had such fun when you took her shopping for a new glam dress for the Emmys. You also pitched in with the funds for her day spa. It's not as if you've deserted her."

"True, though most of the money for the new salon and spa came from her never treating herself to anything and saving all her money instead. And if there's anything living in this city and working in our industry has taught us, it's that money doesn't guarantee happiness. Family is the most important thing."

"You won't get any argument from me on that. I don't think my sister could've gone back to work if Mom and Dad didn't live ten minutes away to take care of her kids." As darling as the toddler triplets were, the few times Jolene had met them, they'd worn her out with their energy. And she was ten years younger than Shelby's sister.

"My mom's been hinting at being a grandmother," Jolene said.

"And?"

"Not going to happen."

"Never say never," Shelby said. "Ètienne and I had The Talk—" she put air quotes around the words "—last week."

"How did that go?"

"I thought two sounded like a reasonable number, because my sister and I have always gotten along so well. But he pointed out that two allows the kids to team up against us. He grew up with five siblings—"

Jolene held up a hand. "Please don't tell me you agreed to match that?"

"Just because my eggs are aging as we speak doesn't mean I've lost my mind. Or course not. But he thought three might work better."

"But wouldn't three against two put you at even more of a disadvantage?"

"That's what I asked. But he assured me that with multiples, there are always power struggles going on. So, their army, so to speak, is splintered. While we maintain a united front."

"You make it sound as if you'll be planning the D-Day invasion. Or Henry V's battle against the French at Agincourt." Jolene knew that one well, having headed up a three-person makeup team for a performance at the Pasadena Playhouse.

"You're awfully young to be so cynical," Shelby returned.

"Perhaps. But it's served me well. If I'd been crying my eyes out over Chad, I'd have crumbled when I saw the fire. Instead, here I am. A new plan already in the works." Not wanting to even allow a negative thought about her mother's possible condition, she bit into one of the buttery croissants Ètienne had made before she'd even gotten out of the shower and nearly moaned. "I swear, your man is a culinary god."

"I know." Shelby patted her washboard stomach. "Even with all the sex we've been having, I had to add kickboxing to my workout routine to work off the extra calories I've been eating."

"I don't know which to be more jealous about." She took another bite. "I take that back. It's his food. Definitely."

"I'd argue that, but I don't want to rub my good fortune in. And getting back to my point, if you stick around town, you'll probably end up getting sucked back into a project, because if you were an actress in a Christmas romance novel or movie, you'd be cast as the workaholic city girl who gets swept off her feet by a small-town cowboy. Or better yet, a sheriff. With a badge. And a big gun on a leather belt slung low on his hip."

"Big gun being a metaphor."

"Exactly. But my point was this way you'll be off the grid out in the middle of nowheresville."

"Honeymoon Harbor has Wi-Fi. And cell service." Shelby Carpenter was a rare specimen: a native Los Angelean, so to her anything beyond Santa Barbara might as well be on another planet. "But I get the point, and it did occur to me."

"Hopefully, it'll be no big deal." Shelby sobered.

"That's what I'm hoping, too." Jolene couldn't imagine losing her mother. She also knew that she could well have a fight on her hands. One she was determined to win.

AFTER TAKING THE clothes out of the dryer, showering and repacking, having been notified that she wouldn't be able to retrieve her car until late afternoon or early evening, she went shopping to pick up a duffel bag and a few toiletries and other essentials that she hadn't been able to bring back on the plane. Fortunately, she'd bought a jacket and rain boots in Ireland that would be perfect for the Pacific Northwest. Since she'd planned to spend the next few weeks creating new products, and she'd lost everything in the fire, she also dropped into Earthwise Soapmania, where she filled two boxes with basic organic ingredients.

She and Shelby spent the rest of the day at the beach, eating a going-away lunch while admiring—and scoring on a 1-10 scale—tanned and buff surfers and volleyball players.

The sun was already setting into the Pacific when Jolene received the text that the investigators were through with the fire scene and she could retrieve her car. Which she immediately did, then followed Shelby back to the Venice house.

"Since Étienne's working tonight, we're on our own. And, I may or may not have the DVD to the best girlfriend movie ever."

"Let me guess. *Beaches*."

"Well, we could watch runner-up *Romy and Michele's High School Reunion*, that would probably be more suitable, given that you're going back to where you'll run into all those girls from high school—"

"Please. I'm trying not to think about that."

"*Beaches* it is. Why don't you take those shopping bags up and finish packing while I set up the DVD player, change into jammies and get out the ice cream."

"You're on. I think I'll also call Mom before it's too late. Besides, I don't want to talk with her when I'm crying like a baby after watching that tearjerker."

"We'll be strong."

"Says the girl who cries at *Sleepless in Seattle*."

"That's an emotional love story!"

"It's a crazy woman stalker story."

"Cynical," Shelby repeated. "The movie's a classic. Because, unless you have a heart of stone, most of us secretly hope that something crazy and magical can happen and we'll fall in love and live happily ever after."

"I'm honestly glad you've found a man who'll give you that," Jolene said. "And, I'm not so stone-hearted or cynical that I don't believe that you and Ètienne are a rare couple that will make it. But—" she shrugged "—I guess I just don't have the love gene."

"Remind me of this when you invite me to be your matron of honor."

Jolene laughed. "Not going to happen."

Once upstairs, she changed, finished packing, then sat down on the bed to call her mother. "Hey, Mom," she said when Gloria Wells answered. "How are things going?"

"I was just about to call you," Gloria said. "I've been a little preoccupied lately, you know, getting the spa opened and working on my social network presence—Did I tell you I joined the Honeymoon Harbor women's business association?"

"No, but that's great." And hopefully might give her some allies in her battle to get her mother in for that recheck.

"I went to my first meeting yesterday. Brianna hosted this month's luncheon at Herons Landing. And by the way, she probably outdid Martha Stewart in Thanksgiving decorating. It was fun. And informative.

"We voted to all have booths in the barn the Saturday after Thanksgiving at the Mannions' annual Christmas farm holiday festival and give out numbered cards for people to fill with numbered stamps, one from each of our booth. Then, when it's filled, they put it in a big bowl. It doesn't cost anything to enter, then at the end of the day, we're having a big drawing of products or services from each of our businesses. I'm giving away a spa day and hair and nails makeover for my share of the grand prize, and selling sample kits of your skin care line to anyone who stops by my booth for a stamp."

"That's a wonderful idea. And should boost Christmas sales."

"That's the plan. Brianna thought it up. She'd read about it in one of her books on ways a bed-and-breakfast can work with other businesses to create a cooperative environment. The Mannions are donating trees for various social groups to decorate by theme. They'll be finished the night before the festival and will be auctioned off to raise money for various community organizations like the food pantry, the Boys and Girls Club, and the after school program."

Knowing that Brianna Mannion had left a high profile job in Las Vegas as a hotel concierge who catered to high rollers to return to Honeymoon Harbor and open Herons Landing, Jolene figured she probably knew a lot about the hospitality business.

"I'm sure it'll be a smashing success."

"So, like I said, I've been really busy, which is how I didn't even hear about your breakup until gossipy Mildred Marshall came in for a cut and perm today. I think she loved being the first to tell me. I'm so sorry."

"It's no big deal. Seriously. Chad and I had reached our sell-by date anyway."

"Well, I'm glad you don't sound heartbroken. Of course I'd never met him personally, but from how he was always getting himself in magazines and gossip columns, he didn't seem like the best husband material. You need to find a man good enough to spend your life with."

This from the woman who'd married the entirely wrong man for all the wrong reasons, but now, as the women's lunch report proved, seemed to be doing just fine on her own. Except for that damn breast lump that her mother didn't know Jolene knew about.

"I'll try to fit that in," she said mildly, not wanting to get into a discussion that could go so wrong on the phone. "Meanwhile, I called to tell you that I'm coming up for a visit."

"To Honeymoon Harbor? But you were here just here a few months ago." An occasion as rare as snow in LA. "What's wrong?"

Her mother had reason to be suspicious. But she also didn't sound as if she were doing cartwheels. Probably because she realized that she'd never be able to keep her secret safe in a small town whose Facebook page was probably the first thing most people turned to for their morning news. If it turned out she did need treatment, it would be all over town in a heartbeat.

"Nothing." Jolene hoped. "I was just thinking while flying back from Ireland how much fun we had when I was back home this summer."

"Weddings are always fun."

If you discounted everyone coming up to assure you that one of these days, you, too, would find your perfect match, wear a princess gown and toss a bouquet of flowers at a group of women seeming willing to do anything to up their odds of finding their own Prince Charming. As happy as she'd been for Kylee and Mai, that particular wedding turned out to be especially uncomfortable, thanks to Aiden Mannion showing up.

"Anyway, I'm between projects and want to work on my business plan for my skin care line, so I was thinking until after the new year would be a perfect time to get away. And hey, maybe even some of the women in your group would have some marketing ideas."

"I'm sure they would." Yep, her tone suggested she wasn't entirely on board with the program. Jolene had planned to wait until she'd arrived to tell her about the fire, but decided she'd toss in the one thing she knew her mother wouldn't be able to resist. "There's something else."

"Oh?"

"There was a fire in my apartment building yesterday."

"Oh, no! Why didn't you tell me right away instead of letting me babble about my silly businesswomen's lunch?"

"It's not silly and I'm truly happy about your networking."

"Forget the networking. Are you all right?"

"I'm fine. I wasn't even home yet. But it appears to be a total loss. So, essentially, I'm homeless."

"You'll never be homeless," Gloria said. "Not as long as I'm alive." And didn't that cause a frisson of fear to skim up Jolene's spine? She didn't even want to think about losing her mother. "Of course you need to come home right away. It is, after all, your house."

"Mom. It's not my house."

"Well, technically not, since it's not the one you grew up in. Or the manufactured one you paid for, which I was able to get enough money from when it sold the very first day to pay Seth to remodel this place. So, you helped pay for this one, as well."

"With money I earned because you were such a great role model and encouraged me to take those beauty classes. So, let's stop arguing about who owes who what, and just enjoy the holidays."

There was a long enough pause that had Jolene looking down at her phone to ensure they hadn't lost the connection. Although, as she'd told Shelby, Honeymoon Harbor did have cell service, it could be iffy.

"That sounds like fun. I'll fix up your room. And make pot roast."

"Am I dying?"

Her mother laughed at the line from the *Gilmore Girls* episode when Rory had questioned her grandmother about why she'd had her cook a pot roast, which had turned out to because Emily Gilmore had invited the Reverend Boatwright to dinner to give twenty-one-year-old Rory the Sex Talk.

"Aren't I a little old for you to be worrying about my sex life?"

They'd always laughed at the place where the reverend explained to Rory that her virtue was her most precious gift and how, if she gave it away too soon, to the wrong man, when the right man came along, she'd have no gift to give. So she'd have to buy him a sweater instead.

As humorous as it had been, it had opened up a mother-daughter discussion about safe sex that included her mother assuring Jolene that despite having become a mother at seventeen, she was the best thing that had ever happened to her.

"Well, as Rory told the good reverend, my ultimate gift ship has long sailed, Mom."

"I'm shocked... And are you accusing me of using pot roast as a ploy to bring up the topic of you someday getting pregnant?"

"No, but you can't deny that you've been angling for grandchildren."

"I have not," Gloria said, not quite truthfully. "You've made yourself very clear that the best I could hope for, preferably, before I'm in my dotage living at Harbor Hill nursing home is a grandpuppy."

"It's assisted senior living." Jolene knew because while going to school she'd done events there for the women residents. It had been amazing what a little blush, a new lipstick and a haircut could do for morale. "Besides, you know I'd never put you in a nursing home."

Yet while she couldn't imagine her mother growing old, dotage was definitely more appealing than losing her to cancer. Jolene was going to get her to that damn recheck if she had to drag her there kicking and screaming.

"And getting back to the pot roast," Gloria said, "I merely thought it'd be a nice dinner to have on rainy fall night. I can put it in the Crock-Pot before I go to work."

"That sounds good." The roast had always been saved for special occasions, causing a twinge of guilt that a visit home could be considered an event. Her mother had always been there for her, but by leaving Honeymoon Harbor, she'd essentially cut the most important person in her life out of her life.

Now, forced to consider a future without her mother in it at all, Jolene worried that because she'd admittedly wanted a different, more secure life for herself than Gloria had experienced, she hoped her mom didn't think she looked down on her in any way.

Which wasn't the case. But how could she explain that returning to Honeymoon Harbor was like returning to the scene of a near fatal accident?

"What's your itinerary?" Gloria asked, dragging Jolene's mind away from a memory flash of Aiden, bruised fists clenched, a thunderstorm moving across his face.

"I'm leaving early tomorrow morning. I thought I'd spend the night in Oregon. There's an organic floral farm in the Willamette Valley where I get a lot of precious oils."

"Oh, I was so relieved you weren't hurt I didn't think about your oils. I'm so sorry."

"It's just stuff," she repeated. Not like losing her mother. *That* she had no intention of doing anytime soon.

After assuring her mother she'd call after she'd stopped once she settled into a motel room tomorrow night, and yes, she had the numbers for her mother's cell, and the landline she'd kept due to iffy cell service in spots on the peninsula, she went back downstairs, where Shelby was waiting with the DVD player on Pause and two pints of Ben & Jerry's Chocolate Caramel Cheesecake.

Two hours and three minutes later, they'd nearly gone through a box of Kleenex and all the ice cream. Along with a bag of white chocolate-covered pretzels Shelby had stashed away for PMS therapy.

"If you ever got viral cardiomyopathy like Hillary, I'd give you my heart," Jolene said.

"You couldn't. Because then you'd be the one who dies in the end."

"But you're nicer, so you should be the one to live. You said it yourself—I'm cynical. Just like C.C."

"At least we'll always have today's sunset."

"I'm didn't want to say anything, but I'm pretty sure I heard Bette Midler singing 'Wind Beneath my Wings' as the sun sank into the water." Jolene reached into the pocket of her pajama pants and pulled out her phone. "We don't have a photo both like Hillary and C.C., but we do have burst mode."

She lifted the phone, and still weeping, and laughing, shot the series of selfies.

"Hashtag BFFs forever."

CHAPTER FIVE

"WHAT THE HELL did you think you were doing?" Although it took every ounce of patience he possessed, Aiden reminded himself that blowing up at the deputy police chief he'd inherited from his predecessor wouldn't be a wise officer management move.

"I responded to a 911 call. Accessed the situation and handled it."

"You didn't do a damn thing."

Don James shot out his jaw. Which, once upon a time ago, when Aiden had been Honeymoon Harbor's teenage brawler, would've made a perfect target. Although the Marines had taught him discipline, there were times, like now, that professional police adulting sucked. "The wife said she slipped. He backed her up." He shrugged. "End of story."

"It was a 911 domestic abuse call. Washington law states there needs to be an arrest."

"Laws are written by politicians who've never spent a damn day on the street," Don countered.

Like this guy had ever been on the street. Aiden suspected that if he'd spent an hour working in the tough spots in LA, James would fold like a cheap lawn chair and go running home to his mommy.

"They're written to keep order. And we've been tasked with serving and protecting the public."

"Seems to be pretty one-sided these days," James

muttered. "Whatever happened to listening to the guy for a change?"

Donna Ormsbee, who'd taken the call, broke in. "Maybe when guys stop hitting women, we'll do that. Or at least admit it when they do." Donna had been working as both office manager and 911 operator for as long as Aiden could remember. When Honeymoon Harbor had its annual downtown Halloween Trick or Treat night, she'd always hand out home-baked cookies from the McGruff the Crime Dog jar on her desk.

"I don't remember anyone asking you," Don James shot back, to which Donna responded by running a hand through her long slide of silver hair, middle finger extended. The gesture's FU effect was minimized a bit by the sequined dancing turkey on the front of the orange sweater she was wearing as a lead up to Thanksgiving.

Aiden had thought being police chief of Honeymoon Harbor, which was the county seat of Salish County, would be a snap after what he'd been through. Humping his butt across the mountains of Afghanistan in temperatures hot enough to fry an egg on his armor had been no Sunday stroll in the park. Fighting gangs and gunrunners in the second-largest city in the country had come with challenges that had nearly gotten him killed. But he was quickly learning that small-town police work came with its own challenges. Especially when you'd been appointed to the job another guy had expected being promoted to.

"You're not being paid to hang around the office," Aiden said, deciding to lower the conflict level.

Beefy hands moved to James's hips, fingers like Vienna sausages splaying on his brown leather Sam Browne belt. "You want me to go back to the Palmer place?"

"No." That was the last thing Aiden wanted. "I want you to go out and patrol the harbor. And stop by the food bank on the way. We're delivering Thanksgiving dinner boxes."

Steely brows climbed the wide forehead. "Now you've turned me into a damn delivery boy?"

"We have the vehicles. We're already driving around on patrol. The food pantry is slammed with work this time of year and needs all the volunteers they can get. Makes sense for us to do our civic duty and help out. Stop by the pantry office and Margie, who's in charge of the food drive, will give you some boxes and a list of addresses. I figure if all of us do our part, we can reach everyone who needs help this season."

Muttering beneath his breath, James pulled on his gloves, yanked his hood over his brimmed hat and stomped out into the slanting November rain.

"He's pissed off so many people over the years, I'm not at all surprised the city council didn't appoint him chief," Donna observed as they watched him pull out of the parking lot, tires squealing.

"Yet there have to be people claiming nepotism with me having the job. Given that the head of the council and my dad, who just happens to be mayor, have been fishing buddies all their lives."

"Only a fool would think that," she scoffed. "You're obviously the far more qualified candidate."

Aiden decided not to mention that he hadn't wanted to be a candidate in the first place. "I remember the chief being tough, but fair. I'm surprised he never fired James."

"He would've been if he hadn't been Chief Swenson's brother-in-law. Now that the chief and his wife have planned to retire to Costa Rica after their cruise, he's pretty much on his own. You could fire him in a New York minute if you wanted to."

Aiden did want to. But for the time being, he was only serving the remainder of the former chief's term. If he did fire the chief deputy, and he was leaning in that direction, given the politics of the situation, it might cause a fracture in the community. Or worse yet, maybe the guy had friends on the council who'd appoint him chief, that would be a disaster for not only the force, but also the town.

Aiden had been on the job only six weeks, but already he was surprised how much he was enjoying the work, and *that* he never would've expected. He figured a lot of people in Honeymoon Harbor found it ironic that former bad boy Aiden Mannion had ended up the town's police chief. They weren't alone. Most days, Aiden couldn't believe it, either.

He pulled on his jacket and dark blue baseball cap with the Honeymoon Harbor police shield embroidered on the front (because the wide-brimmed brown campaign hat he'd inherited with the job made him feel like Smokey the Bear) and headed over to Wheel and Barrow, figuring he'd find Amanda Barrow, wife of Eric Palmer, at her plant nursery. That would give him a chance to talk with her without her husband.

Like most states these days, Washington took allegations of domestic violence seriously, including having a mandatory arrest provision for police officers investigating incidents of potential violence. The problem was, that law required officers to arrest the "primary aggressor" if they had probable cause to believe that an assault or other serious domestic violence offense has taken place within the last four hours.

And since James had screwed it up, Aiden was working against the clock.

He found her in the shop, making a fall flower arrangement.

"Hey, Ms. Barrow." He greeted her in the same calm, steady tone he'd use to convince an Afghan goat farmer that the armed-to-the-teeth American Marine was a friendly. "How's it going?"

"Fine." She wasn't showing any bruises, but Aiden knew that abusers learned early to hit where it didn't show. He did wonder about the scarf around her neck.

"I don't know how things were where you lived before, but we watch out for one another here in Honeymoon Harbor. If you're worried—"

"I'm fine," she repeated, her eyes, red-rimmed as if she'd recently been crying, met his, then quickly shifted away. As color rose in her cheeks, instinct and experience kicked in, telling Aiden that this wasn't her first rodeo.

He'd run Eric Palmer's record, which showed some speeding tickets and a disturbance call at a sports bar that hadn't ended in an arrest, and three domestic disturbance calls in the last eighteen months that hadn't gone anywhere because both husband and wife denied a problem. There was also a note in the file that said the Palo Alto cop responding to the calls had known something was hinky, but he couldn't do anything without Amanda willing to press charges.

"Do you or your husband own any guns?"

Her eyes widened. "No."

That she knew of. In addition to facing fines and imprisonment, people convicted of domestic violence offenses were prohibited from owning firearms and couldn't qualify for a concealed weapons permit in the state. Violating the law was a felony and could lead to additional criminal penalties. Which didn't mean that bad guys, including wife abusers, couldn't easily work around that deterrence.

"I know Deputy James spoke with both of you—"

"And we both assured him that the call was a mistake," she broke him off again. She'd turned pale when he'd walked into the shop, but now her cheeks were flushed with emotion. Fear? Embarrassment? Probably both. "I'll admit I was angry. I'm sorry if I interfered with police business simply because I tripped over the coffee table while marching out the door to drive away during an argument."

Aiden had been to enough domestic violence calls to know that coffee tables were commonly blamed for injuries. Even more than the clichéd walking into a door, because a fall could explain broken bones and body bruising.

"Did the deputy inform you that a misdemeanor domestic violence conviction is punishable by up to ninety days in jail?"

He decided not to mention the fine, because while Amanda's landscape and floral business seemed to be flourishing, he didn't want to risk money worries keeping her from filing a charge against her husband.

"He did. And, although we didn't discuss the topic at length, I will point out that the relevant word is *conviction*."

And, damn, right there, she'd told him exactly what he needed to know. But, from the upward tilt of her chin and her steady gaze, he knew wasn't going to get anywhere today. It wasn't like he could drag her into the station, handcuff her to a chair and interrogate her under a bright light until she caved and admitted to what they both knew was the truth.

"I hate to be rude, Chief Mannion, but this in my busy season, with Thanksgiving, Christmas and New Year's so close together, so as much as I appreciate you dropping by, I really need to get back to work."

"Right. I know from growing up on our Christmas tree farm how busy this time of year can be." Aiden reached into his pocket and took out a card. "This has the station number, as well as my cell," he said, handing it out toward her.

"Your personal cell?"

"I told you, we care about each other here. I promise, if you ever need anything, anytime, day or night, I'll make things work out okay."

She took the card, glanced down long enough to read it. The regular cards listed only the contact number for the station. Just as he had in LA, Aiden had a special batch printed up with his personal information on it. Because, hey, you never knew.

"Thank you." Her brown eyes seemed to glisten, but it could've just been a trick of the beam of light from the sunbreak slanting through front windows. "Have a good day, Chief Mannion."

He touched his fingers to the brim of his hat. "You, too, Ms. Barrow."

"Amanda," she murmured.

Progress made. Baby steps, Aiden reminded himself. "Amanda," he repeated. "And I'm Aiden."

"The mayor's son. Who was a Marine. And then worked for the police in Los Angeles."

"That would be me." Small towns. She hadn't been in Honeymoon Harbor that long herself, but it seemed she already knew his history. He wondered if she knew how his career in California had ended. Which might not give her a lot of confidence in his ability to live up to his promise to keep her safe if she did ever press charges.

He was nearly to the door when she called after him. "Chief Mannion?"

He turned back. "Aiden," he reminded her.

She turned around and took an arrangement of mums, autumn leaves, acorns, and some other flowers he didn't know the name of from the cooler. "For your mother, Aiden."

It wasn't what he'd come for. But, like the use of first names, it was a start. He'd take it. For now. "Thank you. She'll love it. She was talking about coming by for a Thanksgiving centerpiece."

He didn't know if that was true, but since Sarah Mannion always decorated for any holiday as if she were staging a photo shoot for one of those slick country home magazines he saw in the magazine section of the market, she could have shown up at the nursery any day.

As he pulled away from the nursery, off to deliver his own food boxes, Bodhi appeared in the passenger seat. "When are you going to learn that you can't save the world?" he asked.

"I know that." He'd learned it during his first deployment. "But that doesn't mean I should stop trying."

"So, you going to keep that badge?"

"I'm still weighing options."

"And your others would be? Other than returning to LA?"

"That's not an option."

"You were getting bored hanging around the coast house, cool as it was," Bodhi pointed out. "The same way you got bored being a drunk."

Aiden couldn't argue with either of those things, so he didn't bother trying.

"Of course, on the other hand, you could also get bored playing the sheriff of Mayberry."

"Or not. And I'm chief of police. The sheriff's jurisdiction is outside town." He turned onto Evergreen Way, headed out of town to deliver one of the boxes to the Marlows, a family of five living in a double-wide. Evan Marlow had broken his back when his log skidder had overturned and slid down a muddy bank after a heavy rain. After two operations, he was still in a wheelchair, waiting for his disability to be approved. His wife, Ellen, had gone to work waitressing at the diner, but they'd definitely fallen on hard times with three kids under the age of thirteen. "How many times did we manage to accomplish the *protect* part of protect and serve?"

"Big picture? Or day-to-day?"

"The second."

Aiden knew they'd done good work getting bad guys off the street. But the one-on-one interactions usually involved altercations. Although he'd handed out more of those domestic violence cards that he'd cared to count in LA, the number of cases and calls involved moving on. And even though late at night—when he was staring up at the ceiling, listening to the white noise of the freeway traffic two blocks from his apartment building—unable to sleep, he'd think about those victimized women he'd left cards with, the majority he'd never had time to check back on. At least two he knew of had ended up dead.

Amanda Barrow could be one of his success stories. Change that. She *would* be one. Honeymoon Harbor was small enough that he could keep an eye on her. Watch out for her husband. Maybe, if he made a habit of dropping into the nursery as a customer, buying flowers for his mom, his sister, or even Donna, who'd probably like prettying up her corner of the office, she'd feel more comfortable talking with him. He might be able to make a difference. That wouldn't be such a bad way to spend his life.

Maybe he could even go out once in a while. And not just meeting Seth for wings and beer at his brother's pub, but with a woman. Like a date. Brianna kept trying to fix him up with her friends. Maybe he'd take her up on that one of these days. Maybe he'd meet The One. The one he could imagine building a future with. Like Seth and Brianna. Kylee and Mai. His mom and dad.

The idea of teaching his son to fish off the dock, like his dad had taught him, or having tea parties with his daughter, and grilling burgers in the backyard while his kids climbed on a playset and his wife planted posies in the garden (that deer would eat and their dog would invariably dig up) once would have sent him running for the hills. Strangely, now that he was back in the very town he once couldn't wait to get out of, it was growing increasingly appealing. The only problem was, whenever he imagined it, there was only one woman in the picture. One he'd never have because he'd burned that bridge where Jolene Wells was concerned.

"We were busy being big bad undercover guys," Bodhi pointed out, bringing his wandering mind back to the topic at hand. "Once we made an arrest, our cover was blown with those bad guys, so we had to keep moving on."

"Yeah. That was my point. We were like sharks, always moving forward." And not looking back, because the truth was, if you spent too much time dwelling on what you couldn't fix, it would eat you up. The adrenaline boost that had also contributed to those sleepless nights had been great in the beginning. Like Bodhi said, they'd lived on the edge, just like all those buddy cop movies and TV shows. But it'd lost its appeal. Which was why he was transferring out of the undercover guns for drugs detail the day after the night that had changed everything.

"You know, this isn't such a bad place," Bodhi said, looking out the window at the historic buildings, the jagged, snow-clad mountains and lush green forests, and the quaint harbor, all that could've been a set for a movie set in Victorian times. "Remember *Twin Peaks*?"

"Sure. The exterior scenes were filmed here in the state."

"Remember when Agent Cooper drove into town? And told Diane that he'd never seen so many trees in his life? I didn't really appreciate it on TV. But, man, the guy nailed it. These are frigging big trees. And the mountains are awesome, too. Though I'll bet surfing in these waters would freeze your balls and shrink them to the size of marbles."

"Since I don't surf, I wouldn't know."

"You should've tried it while you were in California. You might not have burned out."

"I didn't burn out." *Exactly.*

"Dude. Don't lie to your partner. I was just saying."

"Don't you have somewhere else to be? Like saving guys from jumping off a bridge, or showing them images from their future life?" Aiden asked through gritted teeth. As soon as he asked the question, a thought occurred to him. "Can you see the future?"

"Nah. That's fictional. Or maybe a higher level." Bodhi swiped a hand through his shaggy surfer hair.

"I'm still new at this stuff. Which may be why I'm here." He turned thoughtful, the way he'd do when they were working out a case. "At first I thought I was here for you. To help you adjust and keep from doing something stupid like eating your gun. But hell, Aiden. What if it's just me? What if I'm not ready to quit you?"

"Like I'm supposed to have an answer for that?"

"Nah. I was mostly wondering out loud. You'd think, if a guy was going to continue to live in some parallel universe, he'd be set up with some kind of mentor," he mused. "Like when you're a rookie cop and you're partnered with a more experienced officer who teaches you the ropes. Or at least you should be given a handbook after you die. *Dead for Dummies*."

Aiden laughed even as this conversation reminded him of the ones he'd have in Afghanistan. His fellow Marines tended to fall into two categories. Those who believed themselves invincible, who tended to lessen exponentially with each succeeding tour, when their thinking turned to more of an odds deal. Like how many tours could a guy do before his ticket was punched?

Then there were those, like Aiden, who every time he went beyond the wire, knew it could be his last day on earth. They were the ones who'd sit around talking about what happened when you died. They'd lost one of their team in a helo crash in the Kush Mountains and it occurred to him that there hadn't been any discussion before or after the boots and helmet ceremony where, if anywhere, that guy might have ended up. Despite his Catholic upbringing Aiden had decided that dead was dead. And death was final, right? But maybe not.

"When you..." *Damn*. There were times when the pain was as raw as it had been that night. This was one of those times.

"Died?" Bodhi prompted.

"Yeah." If Bodhi wasn't a hallucination, this was definitely the most existential conversation Aiden had ever had. "When that happened, was there that tunnel of light, you know, like people who've been through near-death experiences talk about?"

"Nope. Not that I remember, anyway. One of the last things I remember was thinking *holy fucking shit, we've been ambushed* and feeling like a sitting duck in the crosshairs. Then you were shot, and I figured both our asses were grass… Then the next thing I knew I was on the ferry with you, where I ended up in your parents' rad beach house."

"If you went straight from being killed to landing on the ferry, then how would you know the music wherever you'd been between those times was cooler than harps?" Having been a detective, Aiden could not only spot a clue when he heard one, he could also spot when someone's story changed.

"I said that?"

"The first night." True, Aiden had been drunk a lot of the time. Which was why he'd figured Bodhi was a hallucination. But he'd been sober for nearly three months and here his partner was, back sitting shotgun, just like the old days.

"Huh. You've got me there." As Bodhi appeared to be pondering that time gap a please-ticket-me-officer red Miata convertible raced by him, headed in the opposite direction.

"Hey, it's just like old times," Bodhi said as Aiden did a wheel-burning U-turn and sped up to get behind it. "Do we get to use the siren?"

"I doubt that will be necessary." The car had a California plate. Since they were the only vehicles on the road, he turned on his bar lights.

The driver may have been speeding, but at least she was paying attention, because her brake lights flashed. Then her turn signal, as she pulled over to the side and waited.

CHAPTER SIX

AS JOLENE PASSED through scenery that changed from Venice Beach to the verdant miles of California's agricultural flatlands north to the dazzling white peak of the Cascade's Mount Shasta, through the Siskiyou Mountains, to Oregon's Willamette Valley's farms and vineyards, into the lush green of her home state she realized that she'd done exactly the right thing to drive. All those hours of alone in the quiet of the car had given her time to think about her life, which had mostly been centered around work ever since she left home.

Although a very strong part of her wanted to take one of the state's iconic ferries back home, if for no other reason than to stand on the deck, the wind tangling her hair, breathing in the scents of salt and fir, too impatient to risk getting stuck in a long line of cars, she decided to keep driving to Honeymoon Harbor, which involved two bridges. The first was the Tacoma Narrows art-deco-inspired suspension bridge, which many, including her, considered one of the most beautiful bridges in the world. Crossing over the high, gray-green span, she realized how much she'd missed this land of tall green trees and sparkling blue water. The weekend of Kylee and Mai's wedding had been so hectic, she hadn't focused on the scenery.

Her plan to save time was thwarted when the Hood Canal floating bridge opened to allow a Trident submarine pass through, and yes, she did get out of her car to watch, just like most of the occupants of cars stuck on both sides of the bridge. “It never gets old,” a sixty-something man standing with his wife beside her, said.

“No,” Jolene agreed. “It doesn’t.”

Despite her initial annoyance at the delay, she found herself as thrilled as she’d been as a child the first time she’d seen an aircraft carrier cruise by Honeymoon Harbor to the sea. Seemingly everyone in town had come out to wave goodbye to the sailors lined up on deck. When one man showed up with a bugle and played “Anchors Aweigh,” the crowd had sung along.

As memorable as the event was, the sub and support ship ended up costing her nearly an hour. She’d called her mother about the delay, but Gloria had said not to worry, she’d simply turn the Crock-Pot down to low.

As she’d turned on Water Street, heading toward Old Fort Road, which in turn led to her mother’s new home on Lighthouse Lane, Jolene realized she must have been speeding when she glanced up in the rearview mirror and saw the red, blue and white lights flashing atop a Honeymoon Harbor police SUV.

And wasn’t that just what she needed? Flipping the arm on her turn signal, she pulled over to the side of the two-lane road. Then, because she’d seen enough police-sponsored public service videos broadcast in LA, she cut her engine, lowered the window down a quarter of the way, put her hands on the steering wheel and tried to stop her heart from beating out of her chest.

It certainly took him long enough. Deciding he must be running her plates, Jolene took three deep breaths, closed her eyes and practiced a visualization skill she’d learned from a yoga instructor the studio had hired for a TV actress for her daily meditation. The extra perk was that the instructor was more than willing to share guided meditation techniques with other members of the cast and crew.

Jolene imagined herself lying on her stomach on an impossibly empty tropical beach, while benevolent rays of sun overhead warmed her skin. And because it was her fantasy, she'd added a darkly tanned beach boy rubbing coconut oil onto her back. It was working…

She could hear the rush of the waves, the softer sound of the frothy sea foam kissing the white sand. The slight rattling of palm fronds swaying in the wind, the distant music of a ukulele playing "Somewhere Over the Rainbow," and the knocking of…knuckles on the car window?

She opened her eyes with a yelp and covered her heart with her right hand before remembering to put it back on the steering wheel.

"Are you all right, ma'am?" the deep voice asked.

Ma'am? Seriously? She turned her head slowly, carefully, and found herself looking—holy guacamole!—straight into a pair of neon blue eyes set off by an indigo rim that were all too familiar. Impossibly, her already wildly beating heart kicked into overdrive. Not to mention her rebellious hormones that had always refused to behave themselves where this man was concerned. In a week of strange and unfortunate events, bad boy Aiden Mannion wearing the uniform of a Honeymoon Harbor police officer topped the list.

Her mouth went as dry as the Santa Ana winds that roared in from the Mojave Desert, bringing all those wildfires to LA. Hoping she could speak, she managed a not-too-shaky, "Aiden?"

Those lips she was horrified to realize that she could still taste, after all these years, quirked a bit at the corners. "Yeah," he said, as if reading her mind. "It's a surprise to me, too."

"So, you're a police officer now?"

No, idiot. He's just wearing that uniform because he thinks it makes him look hot and dangerous. Which, dammit, it did. Especially with that gun at his hip. Jolene didn't like guns. At all. But she had to admit that Shelby's metaphor was right on the money. It did give him a sexy Western movie gunslinger look. Like Denzel Washington in the remake of *The Magnificent Seven.*

"Police *chief.*" He tapped the badge on his jacket.

"Wow." Realizing her disbelief echoed in her tone, she backtracked. "I didn't mean… Well… That's great. So, I guess you're living here now?"

Although, duh, that was obvious, he gave her a long, silent look, as if considering the question. "It seems so. Do you happen to know how fast you were driving?"

"No. Really," she said, when an ebony brow arched. Of course he'd probably heard that excuse a bazillion times before. "My mind was on my mom. If I was speeding, and I must have been or you wouldn't have stopped me, it's because she may or may not have cancer."

"That's one I've never heard before."

"It's not an excuse. Honest. It's the truth."

Any trace of humor immediately faded from his face. She'd often thought that when God had been handing out good looks, while all the Mannion brothers had received more than their share, Aiden must've gone through the line twice. His black curls, incredible blue eyes framed by long, sooty lashes and arched lips, above a finely chiseled jaw, were unfairly beautiful to have been given to a man. Jolene doubted there'd been a teenage girl in Honeymoon Harbor who hadn't crushed on him. With the exception of Kylee Campbell—who, although she hadn't come out yet, nearly everyone knew she was lesbian—and Zoe Robinson, who'd been inseparable from Seth Harper.

Despite having never been part of the "in crowd," in this one case Jolene had joined the Aiden Mannion fan club majority. And for a brief, shining time, until his arrest for stealing that beer, she'd been his secret girlfriend.

"Your mom has cancer?" he asked, his expression turning serious.

"I don't know. And I truly didn't say that so you'd feel sorry for me and not give me a ticket, which I must deserve, and I probably shouldn't have told you about her because it's supposed to be a secret. Even I didn't know until your mom told me."

One dark brow arched. How did he do that? "My mom told you that your mother may or may not have cancer? And you can take your hands off the wheel now."

"Oh. Thank you." Her hands were so wet and clammy they'd left marks on the black leather. Drawing in a deep breath, she tried to regain her Zen, but this time the image of the beach boy with the wonder hands looked exactly like Aiden Mannion. Which was no help at all.

"And no, your mother didn't tell me that Mom has cancer. She only called to tell me that Mom's mammogram showed a suspicious lump and the doctor wants her to come in for an ultrasound. Which, apparently, she refuses to do."

Now she was squeezing her hands so tightly together, her nails were biting into her skin. "That's why she—your mom—broke a confidence and called me. And why I'm here. To convince her to go in for the test, if I have to drag her there. And to stay with her in case something turns out to be wrong. To help her get through it."

"It's probably a false alarm."

Said a man who, despite having handled more than a few breasts over the years, undoubtedly didn't know anything about breast cancer. But she appreciated his attempt to reassure her. That was the thing about Aiden. Despite his reputation as a troublemaker, he'd always had a warm and caring heart. Like the time he'd come across a great horned owl with a broken wing.

The way his sister had told the story, he'd risked his hand being mangled to wrap the wounded bird in his sleeping bag, then taken it to the Northwest Raptor & Wildlife Sanctuary where he'd visited every day until it had been set free. Most of the fights he'd gotten detention for in high school had been for protecting kids who were being bullied. Aiden Mannion had been the champion of the weak and broken. Including her.

Until the wedding, it had been fourteen years since she'd last seen him. Since the night that had changed her life. And as horrific as it had been, those events had taken her onto a different path, one that had led to LA and the strong, competent woman she was today. And, while she'd prided herself on all that she'd achieved, Jolene had never forgotten that it was Aiden who'd made it all possible. Because if had hadn't been for him, she might not have lived to be here for her mother.

"Thank you," she managed to say through those still bone-dry lips. Without warning, all the events of the past days, along with the fear of losing her mother, came crashing down on her and to her horror, Jolene felt hot tears overflowing her eyes to begin flowing down her cheeks. "I'm sorry." She dashed at the moisture with the back of her hands. "I just can't bear the thought of losing her."

"I understand. Here." He dug into his jacket pocket, pulled out a square of fabric and handed it through the top half of the window.

"Thanks." Uneasy about blowing her nose in front of him *(Like you haven't done a lot worse?)*, she dabbed at her wet cheeks and sniffed. "I've never known a guy who carried a real handkerchief." Let alone one in camo print.

"My dad sent me a bunch when I was deployed in Afghanistan. They came in handy to use as a mask to help from breathing in all the dust."

"Oh. That makes sense." She'd learned from Brianna, whom she'd kept in touch with, that he'd been deployed twice over his enlistment. She'd worried about him the entire time. "I'm sorry. I'm usually not so emotional." Damn. Her eyes were misting up again. "It's just been a rough week."

"Been there," he said mildly. "I hope everything turns out okay with your mom."

"That's it?" she asked as he tucked the citation book back into his inside jacket pocket. "You're not going to give me a ticket?"

"You get a pass on the first one. Especially since the speed limit has dropped five miles an hour since the last time you were here," he added, as if not wanting her to think he was giving her any special favors because he felt sorry for her. Or guilty. Not that he had all that much to feel guilty about.

Yet he had gone out of his way to avoid her at Kylee and Mai's wedding. Was that because of the way she'd humiliated herself the last time they'd been together?

"Well, okay. I appreciate the pass and promise to pay

more attention to the posted limits while I'm here." The temperature was dropping as the streetlights turned on and the sun disappeared into the bay, making the water shine like a gleaming gold wedding band. "I guess I'll be seeing you around, then."

"I suppose so," he said, his deep voice causing butterflies to flutter their wings in her stomach. Instead of hitting the ignition button and driving on, Jolene sat there, looking up at Aiden, his blue eyes locked on hers, holding them prisoner. She couldn't have looked away if snowcapped, volcanic Mount Baker, that loomed from the north over the harbor, suddenly erupted.

The moment must have lasted only seconds, yet to Jolene, it felt as if the world had stopped turning. Finally, the whistle of a train approaching the nearby crossing shattered the suspended silence.

His eyes shuttered, the same way they had at the wedding. "Tell your mom hi for me," he said his tone turning brusque, as if informing her that they were done here.

Whatever she'd thought she'd seen in his gaze was gone. Maybe embers of emotions she'd assured herself had cooled had been stirred, causing her to imagine his hot and hungry look. Because now she was looking up at the assumedly tough alpha male her mother had told her on the drive home from the reception had become an LA police detective after leaving the Marines. Knowing Aiden's propensity for protecting the underdog, he'd probably found his niche in police work.

There'd been a time, back when she was in her teens and too romantic for her own good, she'd often imagined the two of them together. Probably not here in sleepy Honeymoon Harbor, because, as her mom had often said, Jolene had been born leaving, but in some bright and bustling city where their tarnished reputations wouldn't follow them and they could start an exciting new life together.

But she'd since come to realize that a young girl's dreams had as much substance as sea foam, evaporated by life's tides. Despite her mother's attempts to create some normalcy in their family, Jolene had grown accustomed to rough waters. Until a tsunami had swept away the last of her innocence, leaving her not completely cynical, as Shelby so often accused, but definitely a realist.

"I will," she said. "And tell *your* mom thanks for me."

With that she drove away as he walked back to his black-and-white SUV. Although temptation tugged, Jolene did not allow herself to look back.

CHAPTER SEVEN

"WELL, THAT WAS INTERESTING," Bodhi greeted Aiden as he climbed back into the cruiser.

"Just a traffic stop." Aiden started the SUV, turned back in the original direction he'd been headed and continued on to deliver the food basket.

"You didn't give her a ticket."

"She wasn't going much over the limit and everyone's entitled to one break."

"Yet there was that moment."

"I've no idea what you're talking about."

But he did. Looking down into her green eyes, time had spun backward and he'd been back on the boat he'd shared with his brothers, the anchor dropped in Serenity Cove. Looking back, their surreptitious romance had been remarkably innocent, given the chemistry between them. And their bad boy/easy girl reputations.

But, perhaps that had been the point. For some reason whenever they were together, the chip fell off his shoulders and he could be himself. He'd often wondered if she'd felt the same, but since teenage boys weren't known for their verbal skills with girls, especially ones that kept them in a constant state of arousal, he'd never asked.

"You looked as if you'd been knocked off your feet by a sneaker wave when she rolled down that window."

"You're so full of it." Sneaker waves struck without

warning, higher and stronger than typical waves and were infamous for sweeping even the strongest swimmers out to sea. No way was he going to admit that the description was too close for comfort.

And yet they'd somehow managed to have a conversation. Of sorts. Of course, she hadn't exactly had a choice given that he'd been wearing a badge of authority. He wondered if she seemed so nervous because of that badge. Or maybe her mom's cancer scare. Or maybe having to talk to him had brought back that night where everything got so fucked up. As if *she'd* been the one hit by the sneaker wave.

It had been all his fault. If he hadn't broken up with her, she would never have been on that beach on that night, with that douche of a guy. She would have been with him. Safe, except for her heart, which he was bound to have broken eventually.

"She's the one, isn't she? The one you talked about that night we got drunk after the meth bust. The one who got away."

"We're not talking about her." Given her mom's possible health problems, Jolene already had enough on her plate. The last thing she needed was to be reminded of what had to have been the worst night of her life.

Did she blame him? Was that why she'd made a point of staying on the far side of the garden at the reception? Or maybe, although there was no reason for it, could she have been embarrassed by what she'd done? Given the screwed-up state of her mind that night, did she even remember what had happened? He'd certainly fallen through the trapdoor of an alcohol blackout after he'd first gotten home and had been trying to drink Washington State dry.

He wished he could talk with someone, like his sister, who, being a woman, might know better what might be going through Jolene Wells's mind. She and Brianna hadn't been close friends, but he vaguely remembered Brianna inviting Jolene to her birthday party. But if he talked to his sister about it, he'd be breaking a promise to Jolene that he'd made fourteen years ago. So, essentially he was damned if he did. And damned if he didn't.

"And now we're back to you being unable to accept that you're not responsible for everyone on this planet," Bodhi said.

Then why the hell did it feel like he was? And even if that were true, if you wanted to get technical, as police chief, he *was* responsible for everyone in Honeymoon Harbor.

"Don't you have somewhere else to be? Maybe someone else to haunt?"

"Not at the moment." Bodhi leaned back and put his flip-flops up on the dash. He wasn't wearing his seat belt, but Aiden figured it probably didn't matter. "Why don't you stop by the Italian joint for some takeout?" he suggested. "Nothing like a big plate of lasagna and some crusty bread on a cold, rainy night."

"You don't eat."

"No." Bodhi flashed a grin. "But I can vicariously through you." He patted his six-pack stomach that he hadn't lost to death. "Without having to worry about carbs."

As he pulled into the crowded parking lot of Luca's Kitchen, it occurred to Aiden that with Jolene back in town, he'd just added one more name to his list of people and events haunting him.

WITH HER NERVES still jangling as if she'd downed three triple-shot salted caramel lattes, Jolene passed the Harper

Construction offices on the way to her mother's. Seth Harper, who'd taken over the family business that dated back to the nineteenth century, had remodeled the pretty Folk Victorian where the wedding had taken place.

Seth had also remodeled the lighthouse keeper's home into her mother's new salon and spa. The original house, which had only been large enough for a bachelor lighthouse keeper, or the keeper and his wife if they didn't mind being crowded, was now a rental vacation home. Her mother, it appeared, had become an entrepreneur, growing wings in the years since her husband's death. Despite the grief he'd caused them, both Jolene and Gloria had been heartbroken when the accident had taken his life, but, in truth, the odds of him getting his act together had been slim to none.

He'd tried to be a good husband (as far as Jolene knew, he'd never cheated on her mother), but he'd always had a streak of larceny and a seeming inability to connect his actions to any consequence.

Maybe it was because she'd just had that brief, forced conversation with Aiden, but it occurred to Jolene that both she and her mother had fallen for bad boys. The difference was that Aiden was now—and wow, wasn't she still trying to wrap her mind around that idea?—Honeymoon Harbor's chief of police. While her mother's bad boy had ended his life as an imprisoned felon.

The remodel had been completed while Jolene was in Ireland, and her mother had moved into the second-floor apartment Seth had built above the salon. This second home had been built by the earlier lighthouse keeper as his family had started growing, eventually resulting in eight children. It was, as so much of those in Honeymoon Harbor, on the National Register of Historic Places, making remodeling difficult. Still, Seth had kept to the original Victorian style, while adding red shutters to match the retiled red roof and a wide front porch with a decorative white railing.

Her mother, who'd emailed her photos daily during the construction, had explained that before the 1850s, only Southern homes had boasted verandas to help people escape the steamy heat. But the Victorian-era trend toward more picturesque architecture—combined with a passion for more naturalistic landscaping—had made the "rocking-chair porch" an American icon by the end of the late nineteenth century. Which was how Seth was able to get the additional design element past the review committee.

Although the sign in the window read Closed, all the lights were on and the Scandinavian-blue door opened before Jolene could even get out of the car.

Not appearing the least bit ill, Gloria Wells ran out of the house, down the porch steps and embraced Jolene in a mama bear hug as if she were a prodigal daughter returning home after decades, rather than a few months.

"I'm so glad you're here. That's too bad about the bridge closing. But how wonderful is it that the navy welcomed you home?"

Her mother had always been the most positive person she'd ever known. How else could she have put up with her husband all those years? He may not have cheated or, as far as Jolene knew, lifted a hand to his wife, or spoken a cruel word to her. But as much as he'd proclaimed to love Gloria, and as often as he promised that someday she'd be living in a big house up on the bluff, overlooking all the people who'd ever snubbed her, he'd been a terrible husband.

"Do you remember that time the carrier came past

the harbor? And Giovanno Salvadori, came out and played 'Anchors Aweigh' on his bugle?"

"I was thinking about that when I was watching the sub." When she'd returned home for the wedding, she'd learned that Giovanno's son Luca, whom his parents had taken back to Italy his senior year of high school, had returned and opened his own restaurant, Luca's Kitchen, and had catered Kylee and Mai's wedding luncheon.

"Your father should have joined the navy," Gloria surprised Jolene by saying. "This town was never big enough for him. He always dreamed of seeing the world, but never had the money. The military would have paid for it."

"That's a thought," Jolene said mildly, not mentioning that she doubted her father would've gotten through boot camp without being court-martialed. While he could be charming and funny, he'd also never been one to follow the rules.

"Sometimes I really miss him," Gloria said.

No way was Jolene going to touch that statement. "I love your hair," she said as she got her overnight and cosmetic bags out of the car. The duffel could wait. It wasn't like in the city, where she might have worried about leaving it in the car overnight. Besides, who'd dare break the law with Aiden Mannion as chief of police?

"Thank you." Her mother preened and fluffed her shoulder-length layered bob that she'd changed from streaky light summer blond to a deep brunette base with bright magenta highlights. "It's my new color. I'm calling it chocolate and cherry."

"Your new color for now."

As the daughter of a hairstylist, Jolene had gotten used to her mother's continual change of colors. She'd always thought it made her mom literally more colorful. Except for that time when Gloria had double bleached for an entire day to strip out a raven black that hadn't worked at all with her coloring, causing much of her hair break off just inches from the roots. It had been at least two months before she could pass a mirror without crying. Jolene assuring her that Rod Stewart rocked much the same look hadn't helped.

"True. It won't be that long until I'll want to go lighter for spring." The color changes were as much a part of her mother as her huge heart and optimism. And, Jolene thought with a new concern that hadn't occurred to her, along with her fear of hospitals, she had to be worrying about potential baldness.

No. Don't think about that now. You can face it tomorrow, she told herself as she walked into the building and breathed in the rich, mouthwatering aroma of a braising beef and vegetables.

"I've fixed up the guesthouse for you," her mother said as they walked through the salon. "I thought we could move you in after you have dinner."

Although Gloria had asked Jolene to help her with the decor, which is what had originally brought her back for the wedding, she hadn't really been needed. Sarah Mannion, Aiden's mother, who was studying for her interior design certificate after years of helping friends decorate their homes for free, had chosen a palette of whipped buttery yellow walls with indigo-and-white furniture and accents. Although designed to bring sunshine to the Pacific Northwest's gray winter days, the decor was casual enough for local clientele, while sophisticated enough for the occasional wealthier bride who'd come from Seattle. It also would have fit right into Jolene's previous Rodeo Drive neighborhood.

Sarah had used cohesive beach-glass blues and greens that she'd described as "secret garden meets seaside" to encourage relaxation. Michael Mannion, whom Jolene had met at a showing of his paintings at the Gallery Rodeo she'd attended with Shelby last year, had chipped in a mural of a tropical beach on the reception room wall of the spa. Other of his prints decorated the private massage and skin care rooms.

"That would be great since I'd planned to try out some new skin care formulas and wouldn't have to take over your kitchen. But you didn't kick out any guests for me, did you?"

"No, not that I wouldn't have in a heartbeat for my daughter." She opened the door leading up to the second-floor apartment. "Bookings are always down this time of year. The Lighthouse View Hotel and Herons Landing are getting the majority of the business. So, I simply took the guesthouse off the rental calendar until after the new year."

A second door at the top of the stairs led into the apartment that had only been unfinished Sheetrock the last time Jolene had been here. She and her mother had stayed in the small apartment Gloria was living in between houses. Seth had created it as an open concept, with kitchen, dining and living room all in a large space. It reminded her much of Shelby and Ètienne's, but more casual and cozy. Jolene put down her bags, turned and hugged her mother, hard, blinking back the threatening tears.

"I love you, Mom."

Gloria hugged her back. "I love you, too, daughter." She leaned back and gave her a long, searching motherly look. "Are you sure you don't have a broken heart over the breakup?"

"No. It's just that I think the reality of the fire is finally hitting home." That much was true. But it was the thought of losing her mother—people could die young, look at her father and her mother's parents—that had caused the unexpected tears.

It was going to be all right, she told herself. Hopefully the lump would turn out to be merely a false alarm. That happened all the time, right? And even if the worst did happen, they'd get through it together. As they had all storms.

They fell easily into old routines, Jolene setting the table, her mother dishing up the meat and vegetables into deep plates.

"So," Jolene said, with a casualness she was a very long way from feeling, "Aiden Mannion has come home to stay?"

Gloria looked up from where she was slicing a round loaf of crusty rosemary bread on the kitchen counter. "Didn't I tell you that?"

"I don't think so." Definitely not something Jolene would have forgotten.

"His dad talked him into taking the job of police chief after Axel Swenson had a stroke."

"Oh, no! Chief Swenson had a stroke?"

"It wasn't all that bad, as far as strokes go. Everyone pitched in to help, with meals and pet-sitting and such while he was in the hospital and rehab. I gifted Ethel with some massages and a mani-pedi, so she could relax because she'd definitely been spending too much time at the hospital and hovering over him like a mother hen. Tory Duncan, a lovely young masseuse who left a spa in Sequim to work for me, said that when Ethel came in, her muscles were like boulders."

"I can imagine." Jolene's own shoulders had felt like

rocks since Sarah Mannion's call. There was currently a knot the size of a baseball at the back of her neck that hadn't been helped by her encounter with Aiden.

"But Tory has magic hands, so Ethel was doing much better when they left town on that Alaskan cruise they'd always promised each other to take." She held up a bottle of pinot noir. "Wine?"

"Thanks."

Her mother looked around, brow furrowed.

"Something wrong?"

"I know I got out the wine opener. But I don't see it." She rubbed the line between her brows. "I've been so forgetful lately. I walk in a room and have no idea what I'm there for. Last week I ran to the market for cereal and filled up a cart with groceries and got home without any cereal. I hate the idea of getting old."

"You're not old. You're just busy." And, Jolene suspected, stressed out from worry.

She went around the island and checked the counter. The only two things on it were a coffee maker and the vintage sunshine yellow Pyrex canisters that Gloria had inherited from her mother. A set designer, who'd bought a similar set for a TV pilot Jolene had worked on, had told her they were back in vogue, and it had cost a bunch to buy a set on eBay.

"It happens to me all the time. What were you doing right before you came out to see me?"

"I was getting the bread out of the pantry…" Gloria opened the pantry door, and there, next to a wire bin of loaves of sourdough and English muffins, was the wine opener.

"I tell you, my thoughts are like soap bubbles lately. They just come into my head, then either pop or float away. Which is frustrating, because I've always been so organized. I nearly forgot to check on Mildred Marshall's perm. Fortunately, I'd remembered to set the timer, so she didn't leave the salon looking like a Brillo pad."

"It happens to everyone. I'd be a mess without my planner and iCal."

"Thank you for the reassurance." After opening the wine, Gloria poured it into glasses etched with a picture of Herons Landing. The weekend of the wedding, Brianna had mentioned that she'd had them specially made for the small gift shop she'd created in her B and B so guests could buy souvenirs of their visit to the town. She'd told Jolene she'd gotten the idea for the store from the guys at Cops and Coffee, and the pair of elderly twins who owned the boutique where Kylee and Mai had gotten their wedding dresses.

"So, anyway," Gloria continued, "the chief retired and after a few weeks of physical therapy, which apparently he can continue to keep up on his own, they took the Alaskan cruise they'd always been promising themselves, and are down in Costa Rica right now house hunting."

She set the wineglasses on the table and they sat down as if it were any other night. At least any more special night that called for pot roast. "I heard from Donna—you know, who essentially runs the police office?—that Don James is angry about Aiden because he felt, as deputy chief, he should have been automatically promoted."

"I never understood why he was given the deputy job in the first place."

"Because he's Ethel Swenson's brother. But Donna says that he's been stupidly butting heads with Aiden, so he may be looking for new employment down the line now that his sister's no longer here to protect him."

"I remember him being a bully."

"He is. He's also lazy. The department's delivering Thanksgiving dinner boxes from the food pantry, and apparently he feels that's beneath him."

Personally Jolene didn't think even a slug was beneath Don James. She remembered him once sucker punching Aiden in the ribs after he'd pulled him out of the car when they'd been parked out by Mirror Lake, then shoved him in the back of the patrol car. He hadn't put a hand on Jolene, but he'd kept his flashlight aimed at her breasts, which were covered in a pretty flowered demi bra she'd bought with Aiden in mind, for far longer than necessary allowing her to button her blouse.

She was honestly afraid of what he'd do until a call came over his radio sending him to the harbor, so he'd literally yanked Aiden out of the patrol car, wrenching his elbows and throwing him to the ground, kicking him one last time for good measure before driving away. Looking back now, she realized that they should have reported him to the chief, but they'd been too worried about retaliation. Perhaps even on their family members. So they kept silent.

The following night, while out on his boat in Serenity Cove where the deputy chief couldn't spot them, Jolene had kissed each and every bruise until Aiden had begged her to stop, warning her that he was on the brink of losing control.

She still remembered the power she'd felt, knowing that she could make him feel that way. Knowing that she'd created that bulge beneath those five metal buttons of his Levi's. She'd felt exactly the same way, but had been grateful that he'd kept his promise not to start fooling around below the waist. Because he understood her fear of ending up a teen mom like her mother. And he'd assured her, becoming a dad at eighteen wasn't something he aspired to, either.

It had gotten harder as the weeks went on. She'd often thought that keeping their relationship secret had added both to the romance of their situation, and upped the sexual tension, because, after all, the forbidden was always a siren call.

"That's nice," she said, dragging her mind back to the present. "Not that Don James is causing a problem, but that the department is helping out like that." She remembered when her family had received a frozen turkey, yams, a can of cranberry sauce, potatoes and dressing in a bag from the pantry for Thanksgiving dinner.

Gloria had invited the two women who'd delivered the meal into the house, made them tea and gotten out some Oreos she'd arranged on a flowered plate that had belonged to Jolene's grandmother, who'd inherited it from her mother. It might not have had some fancy hallmark on the bottom, and it had probably originally been bought at the Newberry's that had long since closed, but to Jolene it had always represented a family of strong women. Her father, she recalled, had spent that weekend in jail for a DUI after driving his pickup off the dock into the harbor.

He'd survived. The truck, already rusty from years of rain, had been totaled.

"It was Aiden's idea." Gloria placed the bread on that same flowered plate, handed it across the table to Jolene, then dished up the roast. "And he didn't just assign it to the deputies. He's been out and about himself delivering boxes all week. I don't care what people used to say about him, that boy always had a kind heart."

And didn't Jolene know that firsthand? She wondered, as she always had, what would have happened if she hadn't gotten mad at him for stealing that damn beer and getting arrested the night they'd both decided to go public as boyfriend and girlfriend.

Even after he'd broken up with her, she hadn't given up on him because she'd believed he'd only been thinking of her. As was totally his way. Which was why she'd planned to finally tell him the night before he left for basic training that she loved him with her entire heart and soul and wanted to go all the way, because, well, Marines got sent to war and he could be killed before they'd ever made love.

Then that very afternoon Jennifer Cherry had told her, with a suggestive smirk, that she'd seen Aiden and Madison Drew all cozy together at the Big Dipper ice cream shop, and in a fit of teenage pique, Jolene had made the mistake of her life.

Shaking off the painful and unsettling memories seeing him again had caused to come flooding back, she took a bite of the bread. "Wow. This is really good."

"It's from Ovenly. The new owner made Kylee and Mai's double Wonder Woman cake. And those delicious cookies on the buffet dessert table. I'm sure you must've met her at the wedding. Desiree Marchand?"

"I did. She's stunning." And having spent so many years making beautiful women stunning for the camera, Jolene didn't use that word lightly.

During their brief conversation before the wedding, Jolene had learned that Desiree was the daughter of a famous pastry chef whose name even Jolene recognized, and a Haitian mother who made hats for a living.

Apparently, after she'd finished culinary school, Desiree's father had expected her to return to his restaurant, where she'd started rolling dough as soon as she could reach the marble counter by standing on a stool.

But instead, wanting to escape his star power, after applying for pastry chef positions in both Portland and Seattle, while she was waiting to be offered a job, she'd visited Honeymoon Harbor and felt an inner click. Less than a week later, she'd turned down three offers from prestigious restaurants, and had bought out Fran, who'd owned Fran's Bakery seemingly forever, and immediately renamed the business.

"I've been stocking her cookies," Gloria said. "They sell like hotcakes… No," her mother corrected with a smile that didn't give any hints that anything might be wrong, "like the best madeleines ever."

"Is she another member of the business club?"

"She's the one who got me into it. Our lunch yesterday was wonderful. It was catered by Leaf, a wonderful new vegetarian restaurant I'm going to have to take you to."

The conversation moved on to other news, who was getting married, who was getting divorced, who'd left town and who'd arrived. Unimportant topics they hadn't had time for during the hustle and bustle preparing for the wedding. Not only had they done hair and makeup for the wedding party, but they'd also insisted on doing hair and makeup on all the women from Mai's extended family, which had turned out to be a crowd. Hawaiians, Jolene had discovered, were very big on family.

"That was fun," Gloria said. "Making everyone beautiful for the wedding."

"It was," Jolene agreed. "I've been doing makeup

for so long, I'd forgotten how much I enjoyed working with hair."

"I have some brides coming in Christmas week. Maybe you'd like to take a couple? Though I warn you, they're probably going to want upsweeps."

"The dreaded prom hair." She laughed. Then thought took her back to that day her mother had banned Madison Drew, the senior class queen bee, from the salon after she'd said snarky things to Jolene while she'd been washing Zoe Robinson's hair. Zoe had allowed her shiny black curls to tumble down her back, that, along with the Empire-waist Grecian-style gown she'd just picked up from the shop and put on at Gloria's request, had made her look like Aphrodite descended from Mount Olympus—and not the one a few miles away, but the one in Greece where the gods and goddesses all lived.

Jolene sighed, thinking of Zoe's too-young death. But, fortunately Seth had moved on and last year had fallen in love with Brianna Mannion.

"Brianna's wearing her hair loose for her and Seth's summer wedding," Gloria said, as if reading Jolene's mind. "They're going very casual and comfortable, with just close friends, so I think it'll suit both her and the occasion perfectly."

"What's her dress like?"

"She hasn't decided yet. Doris and Dottie, who own the Dancing Deer dress shop, ordered three different dresses she admired in one of their catalogs. They've been doing quite the business with their You Bring the Groom—We'll Supply the Dress slogan."

Jolene laughed. Back in the early 1900s, the town had voted to change its name to Honeymoon Harbor to celebrate a visit from the king and queen of the European principality of Montacroix. They'd been friends with President Teddy Roosevelt, who'd declared what was now Olympic National Park a monument and recommended that the newly married royals add it to their honeymoon tour of America. The name change had created the uptick in tourism the townspeople had hoped for, including a bustling wedding destination business.

"Well, that's not very subtle, but it makes a point," she said. "I suppose they're also part of the women's business group?"

"They are and I can only hope I have half their energy when I reach their age."

Jolene had met the elderly twins at the pre-wedding suite in Herons Landing. They'd been bustling around the B and B, ensuring that the two brides would be turned out perfectly for their big day, smoothing skirts, buttoning buttons, zipping zippers, finishing each other's sentences as she suspected they'd been doing since birth. They'd been a new addition to the town, bringing in clothing women had once had to travel to Seattle to find.

Although she'd planned to wait until tomorrow to have this discussion, her mother had just given her the perfect opening. Reaching out for the bottle on the table, she topped off both their wineglasses.

"I can't imagine you not being equally energetic at their age," she said mildly, taking a drink, hoping it would soothe her suddenly jumping nerves. It didn't. "After all, you're still young with a lot of living left to do."

"Knock on wood." Her mother rapped her knuckles on the table. Then, eyeing Jolene over the rim of her own glass, asked, "Who told?"

CHAPTER EIGHT

There was no need for Jolene to ask what they were talking about. "I can't say."

"I had to be Sarah. Or Caroline Harper, she was in the salon, too, when I got the call, but Sarah and I have become closer since Caroline began traveling." She ran her fingers through her hair, which had always been a tell, something she only ever did when she was nervous. "My doctor wouldn't have breached confidentiality, even though I did list you as my emergency contact and checked the privacy box allowing her to discuss my medical condition with you. But there's nothing to discuss."

"Isn't there?"

"No." Her mother had never been a very good liar. She shrugged. "It's no big deal. And Sarah had no damn right to interfere."

"I'm not saying it was Sarah. But whoever it was only told me because she cares about you. You need to get that ultrasound."

"I can't."

"They don't hurt." Jolene had accompanied a pregnant, fellow makeup artist whose husband had been working as a carpenter on a movie in New Zealand. "I'll go with you."

Gloria's eyes narrowed. "That's why you're here, isn't it? It's not because you need a break. Or even because of the fire, because surely it wasn't the only apartment in Los Angeles you could rent. You think I'm dying."

She'd never known her mother to be dramatic. Indeed, Gloria Wells had always been steady as a rock, able to handle all storms life had brought her way.

"Of course I don't!" Which was true. Jolene didn't have any idea of the seriousness of her mother's situation, but on the drive from LA, she'd decided to reject that option. "And I honestly do need a break."

She opted not to mention also hiding out in case any press tried to descend on her after her signing that public statement that she saw on CNN at the airport was beginning to get some coverage. There was also the breakup. Though she and Chad hadn't had anywhere near the star power as Brad and Angelina—a power couple breakup that continued, after all these years, to stoke new rumors—both Chad and Tiffany loved the spotlight.

"But yes, I also want to be here for you. As you've always been for me." Including that night her mother had rushed to the hospital after Aiden's call, hugged Jolene, who'd been hooked up to a rehydration IV, and assured her that everything would be all right.

"I'm scared," Gloria admitted.

"I doubt there's a woman in the world who wouldn't be."

"Not of the cancer. The treatment."

"Again, it's only natural to be scared, but if treatment is necessary, that's why I'm here. And I'll stay as long as you need."

"You don't understand." Her mother's green eyes, so much like Jolene's, brimmed with tears that spilled down her cheeks. The wine sloshed over the rim of her glass and caused a crimson puddle on the white wood table. "I don't want to lose my hair." It came out as a wail. Drawn from the very depths of her being.

Jolene knew many people would think she was being foolish. Even vain. Who worried about hair when you were fighting for your life? She was also sure that her mother wasn't alone. For Gloria, hair, especially her own, had always been her life. And she'd been blessed with hair that any supermodel would envy. Hair she'd passed down to her daughter. Hair Aiden had once loved to comb his fingers through while she laid her head on his bare chest that was as physically perfect as the rest of him.

"I get it," she said, reaching across the table and taking her mother's hand. "I really do. I've done makeup for stars who've asked me how I get my hair to look like this. I always tell them I inherited lucky genes from my hairdresser mom." She'd often thought that's why her mother had gone into hairdressing in the first place. Because, looking back through fading Polaroid photos, Gloria Wells, née Rogers, had begun trying out new styles before she'd started kindergarten.

"But here's the thing. Even if we get to that point, which we have no reason right now to believe we will, hair grows back. But I honestly can't bear the thought of losing you."

"If I die, I'll miss having grandchildren," she sniffled. Jolene stood up and got a box of tissue, reminding her of that camo handkerchief Aiden had given her.

"You're not going to die."

"Now you have a crystal ball?" Jolene blew her nose and tucked the tissue into the pocket of her sweater.

"No, but I volunteered to do the makeup for last year's LA pink ribbon campaign and learned that the five-year survival rate for patients with cancer in one breast is 99 percent."

"Which means there's still that 1 percent who don't survive."

"Mom, listen to me." She sat down, took hold of her mother's hand again, this time tighter, and held her damp gaze. "I'm not going to let you die. Because I can't imagine going through life without my mom."

Gloria took the tissue from her pocket and again dabbed at her moist eyes. "I wouldn't want to miss my grandchildren," she said again.

"See?" No way was Jolene going to rain on her mother's parade by telling her yet again that she had no intention of getting married and having children. She'd witnessed firsthand how hard it was to be a single mom. Women did it every day. With success. She just didn't want to be one of them.

She lifted her glass. "And never forget, we're the Wells girls. Whatever we tackle, we conquer."

"I've never wanted to burst your bubble, Jolene, darling, but real life isn't the *Gilmore Girls*."

"It isn't?"

"Not even close."

"Well, it should be." Jolene sobered. "Whatever happens, dammit, Mom, we tackle, we conquer. Together. The same way we've always done. If the situation were reversed, wouldn't you be telling me the same thing?"

"Of course. And I'd still make the pot roast."

"See?"

Her mother blew out a long breath. Ran a hand through her hair. Then lifted her glass. "Whatever we tackle, we conquer."

Relief, mingled with a very real fear she refused to reveal, flooded over Jolene. "So," she said, stabbing a piece of beef so tender she doubted Tom Colicchio could top it in a quick-fire challenge, "we'll call Dr. Jones in the morning and make an appointment."

"He retired."

"Him, too?" What with Seth's father, Ben, retiring, then the police chief, and now the doctor who'd treated nearly everyone in Honeymoon Harbor, the town had definitely changed during her years away. Not that she'd expected it to stay frozen in place, like *Our Town*, that the Theater in the Firs seemed to do nearly every year, but it was still a little unsettling. And Aiden being police chief was at the top of the list.

"Dr. Laurenne Lancaster bought out his practice. She's a former Doctors Without Borders physician who inherited her grandmother's old house and set up her office in it. She lives above the store, so to speak. The same way I do. Do you remember Olivia Lancaster?"

"Wasn't she one of the summer people? From somewhere in the desert? Phoenix, or Las Vegas, or something, right?"

"Close. Palm Springs."

"I remember her being mega rich."

"An heiress, so the story goes. *Her* father, who'd be Dr. Lancaster's great grandfather, was an inventor who held hundreds of patents. One of the later ones had something to do with a machine that cut identical size French fries and onion rings, which helped fast food restaurants become so popular."

"So the doctor inherited the inventor's fortune?"

"Just the house. Apparently Olivia donated the rest of her estate to charity. Her own daughter Katherine, Laurenne's mother, turned out to be one of those poor little rich girls who partied too much and went through multiple husbands and, to hear Olivia talk about her whenever I did her hair, threw her life away. She didn't want to risk any of her future heirs growing up the same way."

"Sounds as if she needn't have worried about that with her granddaughter." A Doctors Without Borders physician was the polar opposite of an heiress party girl.

"True. I met Laurenne once when she was about fourteen, she came to spend the summer with her grandmother while her mother was on an extended honeymoon in the Greek Islands. She'd spent most of her life with nannies and in boarding schools, and was a pretty, but very serious girl then."

"I don't remember her."

"Her grandmother kept her on a very short leash. She was too old-school polite to say it, but since she was a terrible snob, I always suspected Olivia didn't want Laurenne mingling with small-town riffraff. She did allow Brianna Mannion to visit for a sleepover a time or two."

"Given that Brianna was essentially the princess of Honeymoon Harbor, I suppose she was deemed socially acceptable," Jolene said without a hint of envy or malice.

Brianna Mannion could have used her family's standing and historical importance in the town to have been a real bitch. But she'd been the kindest person Jolene had ever met. She'd never behaved as if she were above anyone and she'd certainly never treated Jolene as if she'd been below her. Jolene bet all her guests at the newly opened Herons Landing loved her. Her fiancé, Seth, had spent most of Kylee and Mai's wedding day gazing at her as if she hung the moon and he couldn't believe his luck that she'd accepted his proposal. Which, Brianna had admitted during the hair and makeup session, hadn't come easily and had involved some groveling on his part.

Still, if anyone could have helped him recover from losing Zoe, who he'd loved since middle school, it would have been Brianna.

"So, getting back to the subject at hand, we'll make an appointment for the recheck—"

"I don't need an appointment. Dr. Lancaster called in the referral and the radiology department at the hospital is open seven days a week. All I have to do is show up for an ultrasound. Which I was assured doesn't involve any more boob squishing. She also promised that as soon as I got it done, she'd fit me in to her schedule the moment she got the results back. It might take a day or two since the film probably has be sent to a radiologist in Seattle for a second opinion. But apparently they can do it over the internet now."

"Terrific." Tomorrow gave her mother less time to back out. "We'll get it over with, then how about going up to Lake Crescent and having lunch in the Roosevelt dining room?"

Lake Crescent, located in Olympic National Park, was famous for Franklin Roosevelt having hosted a political dinner in the lodge dining room, then spending the night in one of the cabins. Many tour books considered the lake the most beautiful in America.

"I need to work."

"It's my first day home," she pressed. "And when I was here for the wedding, you'd already hired two stylists, and manicurist, and that massage therapist you mentioned from Sequim. With the summer people gone, you can't be all that booked up, so surely your staff can handle things for one day." Jolene paused for effect.

"Did I mention my apartment burned down just two days ago and I really need some self-care of my own?"

"That's emotional blackmail."

Jolene wasn't about to deny it. "Is it working?"

Gloria shook her head. "You knew it would."

"It's been forever since I've been up there." Jolene pulled out her phone, ignored all the texts and emails waiting, undoubtedly all still gossip-breakup related, and tapped into the lodge's website. "Oh, wow. They've updated the menu. How does a cup of Quinault clam chowder, with bacon, fresh thyme, red potatoes and white wine sound for a starter, then an organic Dungeness crab mixed green entrée salad with sweet grape tomatoes, carrots, red onion, spiced pecans and a lemon lavender vinaigrette sound?"

"Delicious. And expensive."

"Nothing like what it would cost in LA, even if the fresh oysters and crab were available. Besides, we're worth it. Wait, I have a better idea."

"I was just looking forward to the chowder."

"We'll have that. But tomorrow's Saturday."

"So?"

"So the salon isn't open on Sunday. And you've already said they'll probably send your ultrasound to another radiologist for a second read." She'd read up on various possible procedures the night she'd gotten the call from Sarah Mannion. "So, since we'll go with no news is good news until we can meet with Dr. Lancaster on Monday, why don't we spend the night? And come back late Sunday afternoon?"

"Because..." Gloria paused. Frowned. "I honestly can't think of a reason."

Other than the fact that Jolene couldn't remember her mother ever doing anything for herself. Either she'd been trying to keep her husband out of trouble, or smoothing things over when he had gone on a tear, or doing her best to ensure that Jolene's life was easier than her own had been.

"It's settled." Jolene tapped some more on the phone's keyboard. "Fortunately it's off-season so they have vacancies. You want separate rooms or do you want to share?"

"Why would we want separate rooms when we've been apart for so long and can catch up. Unless, of course, you'd prefer the privacy."

"A single it is." Hearing the hesitation in her mother's voice Jolene wondered if she thought she'd stayed away because she didn't want them to be together. Whenever her mom had visited her in California, Jolene had packed the time with so many activities she thought her mom would like, but now realized that while she'd been showing off her exciting big-city life, they'd never really had that much quiet time together.

Though she had seemed to enjoy the Emmy Awards and lunch. They'd sat at a table with a hairdresser who'd once done Meryl Streep's hair, and had immediately hit it off, launching into a discussion of the actress's chameleon looks, able to take on the persona of whatever character she was playing. Which, as they both agreed, was helped by hair and makeup, including Streep eschewing Anna Wintour's trademark brunette bob and insisting on imitating Helen Mirren's real-life hairstyle for *The Devil Wears Prada.* A bit of movie trivia even Jolene hadn't known.

"Here's a great first-floor room with two queen beds, a private bath and a porch, views of the lake and mountains, and it's only a hundred feet from the shoreline." Jolene turned her phone so her mother could see the photo.

"It looks perfect."

"It doesn't have TV."

"That's fine with me."

"Terrific." In truth, ever since she started working in the business, Jolene found it hard to lose herself in a movie or TV story when she was constantly checking out and—yes, she'd have to admit—often criticizing the actors' makeup. "It'll be like a grown-up slumber party."

Two clicks, her credit card charged, and they were set. After which Jolene stood up, went around the table and gave her mother a hug. "We've got this," she promised.

"I remember telling you the same thing when I picked you up at the hospital after Aiden Mannion's call that night."

Aiden. There was no escaping the man.

Then her mind jumped to that moment, just for a second, when she'd remembered all too well how those silky black curls had felt against her breasts. And how his beautifully shaped lips could be both strong and soft at the same time.

Nope. Not going there.

"I remember." Jolene shook off memories that had escaped the box she'd tried to lock them away in. "And you were right."

With her mom's support, hard work and a lot of luck, Jolene had moved on. As they'd do with whatever that suspicious lump turned out to be. *Whatever we tackle, we conquer.*

CHAPTER NINE

IT HAD BEEN a quiet, uneventful morning. Just the way Aiden liked it. After starting his morning with coffee and a Danish from Cops and Coffee, he'd checked into the office and found that Don James had called in sick.

"If you ask me, he's faking," Donna said. "Just to get back at you for yesterday. And for the record, he's out of personal leave days."

Aiden shrugged. Honestly, if it wouldn't be a waste of taxpayers' dollars, he'd be more than happy to have the guy stay home forever. "It's not worth fighting over."

Although the former chief's brother-in-law had always been a bully, when Aiden had first accepted the job, he'd been willing to give James the benefit of the doubt. After all, he, himself, was proof that people changed. Unfortunately, from the scattering of unofficial complaints he'd been told while having dinner at his brother Quinn's pub, or picking up bread and milk at the market, it seemed that James had never evolved.

It wasn't that James had been reported using excessive force on anyone, though Aiden knew from personal experience that the deputy chief of police had done that on at least one occasion. And every kid in high school knew he got sadistic kicks harassing teens he'd caught making out, though as far as Aiden knew, he'd been the only one physically harmed. But even if his deputy chief didn't go around beating up Honeymoon Harbor's citizens, his swagger, and the way he often rested his hand on the grip of the pistol holstered on his hip, undoubtedly spoke volumes to those who didn't want to cross him.

Donna passed him a small handful of message slips, which had him smiling, remembering the huge stack that would usually greet him in LA. All marked "urgent." And any day he hadn't had to start a new murder book was a good day, right?

He glanced over and saw Bodhi checking out the flyers for the upcoming Christmas festival on the community board, including the Holiday Court princesses wearing evening gowns and red sashes.

"They're too young," he said when one of his partner's blond brows rose at a particularly nubile student from the community college.

"What did you say?" Donna asked, looking up from her knitting. Even as he scrambled for an answer, it occurred to Aiden that this was another thing about small towns. What jurisdiction in Los Angeles County would have a 911 operator spend a good portion of her day knitting blankets for Project Linus, a volunteer group that provided blankets for seriously ill or traumatized children?

"I was just saying how young the princesses look compared to when I was in school."

"They look younger as we get older," she said, her needles clicking away. This latest blanket was blue with yellow stripes. "That's the way of life. I still remember the first time the boy bagging my groceries at the market called me ma'am. I cried all the way home."

"You'll never be old," he assured her, shooting a side eye at Bodhi who'd moved to sitting on the edge of his desk. "Because you've got a young heart."

She laughed. "And aren't you the same silver-tongued devil you always were."

"Do people think that?" He asked what he'd been wondering since before he accepted the job. "That I'm the same smart-ass kid who was given the choice between juvie and the Marines?"

"Some expressed doubts when they heard you'd come back from California." Donna believed in speaking the plain truth, Aiden appreciated that. It might be a small force, but he'd still been tasked with protecting and serving the people of Honeymoon Harbor. Which he couldn't do if his team, such as it was, shielded him from the facts. "After all, you were certainly a handful growing up. I recognized your behavior because my baby brother, a preacher's son no less, behaved much the same way."

"I'm almost afraid to ask how he turned out."

She chuckled. "After sowing his wild oats, finishing college and getting his divinity degree, he settled down as a Methodist minister down in Oregon. Grants Pass, to be specific. He married the woman who led the church choir and they've got two smart, well-behaved kids who are in college themselves."

"That's great."

"It's a true happy ending, sure enough, though my mother always blamed her gray hair on him. Anyway, when you disappeared out to the coast house, there was talk about what might be going on out there."

"Really?" At first he was surprised anyone would even care, but then again, entertainment being what it was in the harbor town, he could see why there'd have been speculation.

"You know how it is. Same gossip that let you know right off the bat that it was the Rogers boy who tagged the railroad trestle with that red spray paint last weekend keeps folks buzzing about local happenings."

It hadn't taken all that many detecting skills to learn Ryan Rogers had been the one to paint "Marylou Jennings is a heartbreaker," since apparently half the town and probably all of the high school knew that Marylou had broken up with Ryan for flirting with Jessie Reynolds at the Big Dipper. After a great deal of groveling, and a pair of dangly shell earrings from the Dancing Deer, Ryan had won his way back into Marylou's good graces.

Meanwhile, Aiden had made him clean the paint off the trestle and write an official apology to the Jennings family that was printed in a box in the *Honeymoon Harbor Herald*, right next to the weekly police report.

"But Seth cleared things up when he told people that you were just recovering from getting shot and losing your partner during a top secret Homeland Security mission. Which, tragic as that was, impressed a bunch of people, especially the guys down at the Veterans, Elks, and American Legion halls."

"Hey, I gave you creds," Bodhi said, blowing on his knuckles, then rubbing them over his heart. Or where it would be, if he was still alive.

"Given Seth's recommendation, along with the fact that Homeland Security trusted you, the town council decided to appoint you chief. To be honest, it was a no-brainer since the only other person who wanted the job was Don James."

"Yeah, I figured I got this badge by default."

"It doesn't matter how you got it because you're doing a good job. The only holdouts are mostly ones who grumble about nepotism, but then again, they're old goats who wouldn't have any reason to get up in the morning if they didn't have something to complain about. They're the same ones always griping in the comments section of the online *Herald*, so no one pays them any mind."

"Anyone ever tell you that you're a treasure, Donna?"

Her plump cheeks colored. "Not that I recall. At least since I lost my Alton."

"Well, you are. And while I might still be learning how this department works, I could spot the first day that you're the one who really runs the place."

"Oh stop that. You may have gained responsibility, but I'll bet there are a lot of women here in Honeymoon Harbor who are going to be glad you didn't lose your charm. I swear, you remind me of your uncle Mike when he was your age."

"I meant it," Aiden said seriously, before turning his attention to the messages.

There was one reminding him of the monthly chamber of commerce meeting he'd been scheduled to give a speech at, another asking him to represent the department for career day at the elementary school, one from his mother asking whether he'd rather have oyster or sausage dressing with the Thanksgiving turkey and a final one from his father, letting him know that although the fire department was responsible for hanging the town's Christmas street ornaments, the police department traditionally had a decorated boat in the annual harbor parade.

"We have a boat in the parade?" he asked Donna.

"We always do," she said. "Guess it's been a while since you've been to one."

Probably not since he was twelve and decided it was for kids, Aiden thought, but did not say.

"Don't worry. Chief Swenson didn't do all that much. Just strung up some lights and put up an artificial tree, which, truth be told, has gotten pretty ratty if you look at it up close, on the bow. We've already got the decorations we've used for the past few years in storage. Though if you'd like to change things up—"

"No, whatever we've done will be fine."

"Seems a new administration should have a new, updated look," Bodhi suggested. "Just saying." He held up his hands when Aiden shot him a narrow-eyed look. "It's a good way for you to put your own stamp on the department's image."

And wasn't that why they'd been such good partners? Because they'd each looked at things so differently, together they'd been almost invincible.

"Maybe we'll change things up," he said.

Donna beamed, obviously pleased with that idea. "That's a good idea. Not that I'd want to complain, but, like I said, the old stuff is getting a bit ratty and dated. And everyone's seen it for at least a decade. Perhaps—"

She broke off as the 911 phone rang. "Honeymoon Harbor Police Department," she answered. "Is this an emergency? It is?"

Aiden's shoulders immediately stiffened.

"Oh, hello, Mrs. Gunderson. Yes, he's here. Yes, I understand. I'll send him right out. No problem. That's what we're here for."

"Do you need to call fire or an ambulance?"

"No, it's just Mrs. Gunderson. Ever since she was widowed, she calls in with a problem every so often because she's lonely. You might remember her. She taught English at the high school."

Unfortunately, Aiden did remember. She'd also sent him to the principal's office on more than one occasion. Which was weird, since the principal was—hello?—his mother.

"What's her problem this time?"

"Someone's stolen one of her gnomes."

He knew the bungalow well. It was part of a development that had been built as housing for mill worker's families back in the 1930s. Not wanting to move into his family's farmhouse, Aiden was currently renting an almost identical one three blocks away. A major difference was that his had a harbor view and the front yard didn't look like a gnome forest. "How can she tell?"

"She's named them all. Apparently Nisse isn't guarding the gate where he belongs. She needs you to, and I quote, 'lock up the scoundrel who kidnapped him.'"

"Make sure you bring your dusting kit to check for fingerprints," Bodhi said.

Knowing when his chain was being yanked, Aiden didn't bother to roll his eyes. "Tell her I'm on my way."

THE ELDERLY WOMAN, who had to be eighty if she was a day, was standing by the front gate waiting for him, despite the fact that the rain was beginning to turn to sleet as the wind sweeping off the Olympics caused the temperature to drop dramatically. It wouldn't be long before the roads began to ice up. Another problem he'd never had to deal with in LA.

"It's about time you got here," she said as he got out of the SUV, although it had been all of three minutes since she'd called the station.

"Sorry, Mrs. Gunderson," he said. "So, Donna tells me you called in a property crime?"

"A kidnapping. Or, I suppose, to be technical, you'd consider it a theft," she said. "Nisse was guarding the yard and house. It's obvious someone stole him to make us—" she waved her mittened hand around to encompass all the other gnomes and her house "—vulnerable to a more dangerous crime. Like breaking and entering." She pressed her hand on the outside of her puffy jacket over her heart. "Or even worse."

"Can you give me a description of the missing gnome?"

"He's about this high." She put her hands about three feet apart, that would have made him one of the larger of the community she'd created. "With a white beard and a red hat." Her voice broke and he thought he saw her eyes moisten behind her thick glasses. "My Lars gave him to me for our first Christmas sixty-two years ago next month."

Okay. Damn, he hated waterworks, which had always been part of the job. Apparently even here in Honeymoon Harbor. He was going to have to find the damn gnome if it took all day. "Why don't you go into the house, Mrs. Gunderson," he suggested. "While I look around for him."

"I already have," she insisted.

"I'm a professional," he assured her. "I've been trained to locate missing objects."

"He's not a mere object. There's a spirit inside him. A spirit that tends to have a temper if things don't go exactly as they're supposed to. Whoever did this is in for a terrible time."

"All the more reason to find him," Aiden said in his official *Don't worry, the police are on the job* voice. "Now, please, go in before you catch pneumonia."

"I wouldn't mind," she said as she nevertheless turned back toward the little house that didn't have lights up yet. It was still early, not yet being Thanksgiving, but if she didn't have them up in the next week or so, he'd stop by and put them up himself.

He walked the yard, row by row. At least she was

Scandinavian tidy and had them all placed in straight lines like a gnome army waiting for inspection.

"This is a little creepy," Bodhi said.

"She's right," Aiden said, after making his way up and down each row. "It's not here... But..."

He headed over to the thick blue spruce that had grown considerably since the last time he'd been here back in middle school. While the Rocky Mountain tree wasn't native to the peninsula, many people planted them for their Christmas tree shape and eye-catching grayish-blue year-round color. "Bingo."

"How the hell did you find that?" Bodhi asked.

"Didn't the afterlife give you super detective powers?"

"Apparently not."

"It wasn't detecting," Aiden admitted. "But a good guess. I hid one of the smaller gnomes in the tree back when I was twelve."

"Why?"

And wasn't that the million-dollar question? "Because I was a shithead who hung out with other shitheads who thought it was cool to mess with people." One of those people being Mrs. Gunderson. Which was one of the reasons he was going to put her lights up.

"Because your dad was mayor."

"You were paying attention in those community policing seminars," Aiden said mildly, replacing the gnome where she'd pointed it belonged. The lace curtains at the windows twitched, and a moment later the door opened.

"You found him!"

"I think he was sending out vibes," Aiden said, hoping her memory didn't go back that far to when he'd stuck a gnome in that same, much smaller tree. He hadn't gotten caught for that bit of delinquency.

"I feel so much better. I made cocoa. You must come in and have a cup to warm up before you go back on patrol."

"That isn't—" He began to assure her that wasn't necessary, then thought of her being alone during a time that was for families. She and Lars Gunderson had never had children, he remembered. But they'd always added skeletons and witches to the yard for Halloween and although they'd given out apples from their backyard trees instead of candy, he now realized that they'd been good people. The kind who had built Honeymoon Harbor and cared about their neighbors. Even ones like him, who hadn't deserved it.

"I'd appreciate that, Mrs. Gunderson," he said, resisting glancing at his watch. Time, after all, moved more slowly in Honeymoon Harbor.

Which was how he ended up drinking a mug of homemade cocoa, the real stuff, cooked on the stove with milk, and not out of a package and nuked with water, garnished with miniature marshmallows while he looked through a scrapbook of photos, each depicting some occasion when one of those gnomes had joined the family. So many Christmases, birthdays, anniversaries.

The former teacher might be old, but her memory, at least when it came to personal events that mattered to her, was still as sharp as a tack. She reminded him of his grandparents, who still bickered occasionally, but whom he'd caught sharing a kiss on the front porch, watching the sunset one night last week he'd gone out to the farm for dinner.

"This is Hallows, the gnome Lars bought me for Halloween one year." She pointed toward a plastic gnome with a black hat, flaming orange beard and a hollowed-out stone mushroom for a basket. "That was the same year you and your friends papered our tree with toilet paper."

Because of those damn apples. Which were only a step above a box of raisins in his asinine twelve-year-old mind. "I'm sorry about that."

"So you said when your father brought you to the house to apologize. I'll be honest, Aiden Mannion. I didn't have a lot of hope for you. Especially since your behavior became even more delinquent in high school. But the Marines seemed to have made quite an impression. I read in the paper that you received a Purple Heart."

"It wasn't that big a deal. Just a flesh wound." From flying rock when his team had come under fire.

"And some other medal. For heroism, I believe?"

"More for losing my temper," he admitted. He'd run from behind the Humvee, blasting away like Audiey Murphy in one of those old black-and-white Westerns his grandpop liked to watch. "And it wasn't that big a deal."

"The older you get, the more you realize how precious life is," she said. Damn. Here came those effing tears again. "That fact that you saved one was a very big deal. I'm sure your father was very proud."

"Probably more relieved I'd gotten my act together," he said, knowing otherwise. He handed her a handkerchief.

"My Lars always carried a handkerchief," she said as she dabbed at her tears. "But his were always white. I'd iron stacks of them so he'd always have a fresh one. I don't think I know any men who still stick to a gentlemanly tradition like that.

"We were never blessed with children, Lars and I, but I know I'd be proud if I were your mother. Truth be told, the entire town was proud of you, Aiden Mannion. And I know I'm not alone in being glad that you're our chief of police."

"Thank you, Mrs. Gunderson. That means a lot to me." More than she could ever know. Finishing off the cocoa, he stood up. "And thank you for the cocoa and cookies."

"Take a cookie with you," she said. "For later."

She walked him to the door, and as he climbed back into the SUV, he saw her patting Nisse's red hat who was back to standing sentry.

"You really were a shithead," Bodhi said.

"I told you I was."

"I didn't know about the medal."

"It wasn't a big deal."

"Yeah. So you said. What was it?"

"So, there's not some big permanent record of my life you can look it up in?" Aiden asked.

"If there were, I wouldn't tell you because you're not supposed to know."

"Why not?"

"Because, duh, you're still alive. It's all a mystery. Even to me sometimes, but I figure that'll change eventually… Or maybe not. Anyway, why don't you tell me so I don't have to waste time grilling you."

"It was a Silver Star. A sniper shot a couple of my teammates. Since I was the closest, I ran out from behind cover—"

"Under fire."

"Like I told Mrs. Gunderson, I was mad. So, yeah. I dragged them back. One made it. The other didn't." But fortunately, he hadn't been physically haunted by the young Marine who'd been killed on his third day of deployment. *He* only showed up in dreams reliving the event. Often in slow motion. "Then I got a shot off that got the shooter. But not before getting a bunch of gravel stuck in my leg after the grenade he'd been holding blew the area around us to hell. And earned an automatic Purple Heart. End of story."

"Now you've got me wondering if there are other times you lied to me," Bodhi said.

"Why?"

"Because you're obviously lying now. I seriously doubt a day like that ever really ends. I lucked out and never had to kill anyone. But I'd bet I'd sure as hell never forget if I had."

Aiden was saved from answering when a black Porsche Cayenne SUV roared past in the opposite direction. Although he hadn't done traffic duty in California, he'd gotten good at estimating speed and this guy had to be going seventy. On a road with a thirty-mile-per-hour limit that was beginning to dangerously ice up.

He pulled a U-turn, floored the gas, turned on his flasher and caught up with the SUV when his speedometer passed seventy-five. Fortunately, traffic was light, and only four cars had needed to pull over. Unfortunately, the driver of the car either didn't notice or didn't care about the flashing red, white and blue lights he must have seen in his rearview mirror.

"You're going to have to use the siren."

"Yeah." His call to Donna, to find out if there'd been any black Cayennes stolen, had come up with zilch. Which made sense. Although they weren't uncommon in LA where a lot of soccer moms bought them because they were flashier than the former top-runner kid-hauler Mercedes, and you might see one up here on the peninsula during summer tourist season, it wasn't a vehicle many locals could afford to drive. Since the guy didn't rabbit, just kept driving the same too-fast speed, he probably wasn't fleeing a crime scene. Which, again, meant he wasn't paying attention, that could be as dangerous as the speeding. Or he was simply an asshole.

He went with a short yelp of the siren. Nothing. Another. Still nothing.

"Hell." He had three options, another shorter yelp, a longer wail, that he doubted the driver would pay any attention to, or a hi-lo sound. In the city, he also had a PA system he could use to blast out kids grooving to their gazillion-watt sound systems. Because studies showed drivers don't hear sirens after a short time, he knew a few patrol officers who had up to twenty-five sounds to choose from.

As they approached a hill, he flipped back and forth between the wail and the hi-lo, that would hopefully get the attention of any approaching vehicle that couldn't see the Porsche and him coming.

Next to him, Bodhi started singing the opening "Bad Boys" theme song from *Cops*.

"Not funny."

Finally. The guy pulled over. Without signaling, but at this point, Aiden was just relieved to get him off the road. He ran the license plate and recognized the name immediately.

Thane Covington IV was the son of a Realtor whose father had bought out the blocks of bungalows that had been company housing before the closure of the mill. The same ones Mrs. Gunderson, and Aiden, lived in. Covington III had done as little as possible to bring them up to code, but was now making a big profit as the market for Craftsmen-style homes had gotten hot thanks in part, Seth had told him, to all those TV reno shows.

Back when Aiden had been in high school, Thane's father bought a waterfront Folk Victorian just outside the historic district, tore it down to the shock of everyone in town and replaced it with a three-story, five-thousand-foot McMansion that blocked the water views of the houses behind it. Since he'd seen some Covington real estate signs scattered around town, Aiden figured Thane Covington IV had taken over the family's firm. Or, at least, joined it.

Aiden reached the driver's side door that boasted an extra dark gangbanger-style window tint that wasn't only impractical in this land where sun was welcome, but also illegal under state law. Although too dark tinting was a primary offense that could get you pulled over all by itself, Aiden wasn't in the mood to get into explanations with a guy who'd been on the debating team with his older brother Quinn. He also recalled how Quinn, the most easygoing of the four brothers, had been furious when the entire team had been disqualified after Thane Covington IV had falsified evidence in the Lincoln-Douglas division of the state finals.

He made the motion for the guy to roll down his window, instructing him to stop when it was halfway down. It took longer than necessary for compliance, but then again, he didn't have to worry about getting shot. Of course he'd made that mistake once before.

"Hey, Aiden," IV said. "I heard your dad got you appointed chief of police. Congratulations. That's quite a plum, given that the most crime you're probably going to run into is mailbox-bashing and jaywalking."

Aiden thought about wanting to get Amanda Barrow out of danger before her obviously sociopathic husband killed her, and how Jolene had been so emotionally and physically wounded by assholes like this guy, but didn't bother debating the topic of big-city versus small-time crime.

"Do you have any idea how fast you were going?"

"No, but I'll bet you're going to tell me."

"I clocked you at seventy-three. In a thirty-mile-per-hour zone. And that's in good weather. Which this isn't."

"Wow. I hadn't realized." White teeth that would've fit right in with the Hollywood crowd flashed. "This Porsche has more horsepower than I sometimes realize. I promise to watch my speed more closely, *Officer*." The last word was heavy with snark.

"That would be my suggestion. May I see your license and registration, please?"

"Come on, Mannion. I really don't have time for this. I'm late to meet a client for a listing, you probably know the house. The Victorian old lady Lancaster left to her granddaughter."

"Your identification?"

"Hell." Impatience radiating from him, Thane reached into the center console, pulled out the registration and an alligator wallet with his initials stamped in it and held them out.

"Please take your license out of the wallet."

"Hey, you don't have to get all official on my ass, man."

"This is an official stop. Therefore, I'm going to behave officially." And dammit, not let the dick get under his skin. Aiden had dealt with a lot worse slime in vice and the gun racketeering team. But at least they'd fully acknowledge they were bad guys. It was the ones who pretended otherwise who chapped his hide.

Huffing out a breath, Thane yanked the license out

the wallet and handed it over. Along with a well-worn cardboard card.

"A courtesy card?" Aiden read the bold dark blue print at the top of the card.

"I contribute to the Friends of Police fund," Thane said with what appeared to be a sense of pride. Or more likely entitlement as the meaning of the card sunk in.

"Which happens to be headed up by you?"

"Nah. I just contribute. You know, it's a way of supporting the police, while the police, in turn, support the citizens. One hand washes the other."

"Do you see that SUV behind you? The one with the bar lights?"

"Of course."

"That's my rig. Along with the lights and siren, it also happens to have *Protect and Serve* written on both doors below the town seal. Nowhere on that vehicle does it specify which citizens get protected or served."

"Well, sure, I mean, if someone gets their house broken into, of course you're going to show up to dust for prints, or whatever other CSI stuff you do. But, maybe no one told you when they gave you this job, the courtesy card is more like a—"

"Get out of jail free, or in this case, get out of a ticket card."

"Exactly." Another flash of smile, as if to reward Aiden for having gotten the right answer. It also reminded him of another time two rich guys got out of jail free because their rich daddies got them out of town before the police could make the arrest.

"Well, I hate to be the one to break it to you, but there's a new police chief in town. And my department doesn't run a protection racket." He ripped the card in half, then tucked it in his jacket pocket.

"Hey! You can't do that. It's an official department card."

"Not my department. Not in my town. But, you can try telling it to the judge." Although he normally hated traffic stops, Aiden was beginning to enjoy this one. He pulled his light transmission meter out of his belt and held it up to the window. "I'm also ticketing you for the window."

"What the fuck?"

"The legal limit is 24 percent tint for the front side windows of an SUV. You're considerably over that." He turned the meter so Thane could read it.

"I never heard of that. I'll bet it's a bullshit charge you just made up."

"It happens to be the law. You might want to pick up a booklet at the license bureau. They hand them out free. However, since you managed not to kill anyone, I'm going to let you off without tacking on a reckless driving charge that could have gotten you a year suspension and added an extra five thousand dollars into the city's budget. Not to mention jacking up your insurance costs."

"You always were a son of a bitch, Mannion."

"You'd think a debater would choose his words more carefully," Aiden said as he wrote up the ticket. "I may have been a delinquent. But unlike some people who'll go unmentioned, since this is an official stop and I don't believe in insulting citizens, I was also known for my charm. Which helped me get out of my own share of trouble without having to carry around a fake courtesy card."

It was his turn to smile as he tore off the ticket and handed it back through the window, along with IV's license. "Have yourself a nice day. And drive carefully.

You wouldn't want to wrap this shiny black Porsche around a tree on the way to your listing."

"You should've hit him with the reckless driving," Bodhi said as Aiden turned the police SUV back around.

"Not worth it. His dad would've shown up at the next city council meeting and tried to get me fired, and my dad, too. Then he'd probably take on the school board to go after my mom. Besides, I'm handling the situation." He radioed the office. "Donna, please contact everyone on the duty roster. We're having a meeting tomorrow morning at zero seven hours sharp."

"Even the volunteers?"

"Even them."

"Wow."

He knew she was dying to ask. He also knew that she was probably one of the few people in town who didn't gossip, that was why he'd kept her on as 911 operator and office manager. Because people went through a lot of stuff they deserved to keep private. Like Amanda Barrow, who was going to stick in his craw until he figured out what to do about that situation.

"Yes, Chief. I'll sent out texts now. Anyone who doesn't respond right away, I'll call."

"Thanks."

"What are you going to do?" Bodhi asked, looking interested for the first time since Aiden had called his dad to accept the job.

Aiden grinned. "I have a hunch, but if I told you, it wouldn't be as much fun to watch. Right now I have some calls to make, and if I'm right, we're visiting a judge, then my family's bank."

CHAPTER TEN

THE FOLLOWING MORNING all ten full- and part-time members of his police force filed into his office carrying tall cups from Cops and Coffee and doughnuts that Donna—who'd been the first to arrive, taking over from the Salish county 911 operator contracted to handle the night shift—had brought. They filled the room to the walls, which showed how small an office had come with the job. Aiden wasn't surprised when the deputy chief was the last to show up.

"Since we've all got things to do, I'm going to cut to the chase," he said. That stopped the various murmured conversations in their tracks. "I've called you all in to talk about courtesy cards."

The silence was deafening. He also noticed that not a single officer looked at any of the others.

"Here's the deal," he said. "I don't care how things were done in the past. This is now, and this department doesn't take bribes."

"They're not bribes," James shot back. "They're exactly what they say they are. Courtesy cards."

Aiden folded his arms. "So, would that mean you give them out to everyone in town? Maybe throw them from the Fourth of July police float like Mardi Gras beads?" His voice was mild; the iced anger in his eyes was not.

"I'm saying that if someone in town wants to support the police department, then the police department is going to appreciate them back."

"Appreciation might be a ticket to the annual fire and police fund-raising spaghetti dinner," Aiden said. "But courtesy cards don't just represent bribery, they're embezzlement."

More looks. "You just hit a nerve, dude," Bodhi said. "You've got those two guys in the back sweating."

It was James's turn to fold arms beefy from weight-lifting over the beer gut that strained at the buttons of his blue uniform shirt. "No. Fucking. Way."

"Way," Aiden said. He waited a moment, aware that the next two minutes would define his tenure as chief. "Give me the fine amounts for each increment of speeding infraction."

"Why the hell should I know? I'm not a damn judge."

"The town can be grateful for that." Aiden, who'd studied the fines preparing for his first day, rattled them off. "That's not chump change. It means that every time you hand out a courtesy card, you're possibly costing the town hundreds of dollars. You may not have your hand directly in the till, James, but you and anyone else who hands them out in lieu of ticketing actual infractions is stealing from the coffers that fund every single agency in town.

"When there's less money to apportion, less gets spent on roads, the library, the school, the harbor, fire department, every single bit of business. Including funding us. Which is why you all would've had to buy your own bulletproof vests last year if the schoolkids hadn't come up with the idea to have an online fund-raiser."

"No shit. The kids did that?" Bodhi said.

"You don't get it," James said on dangerous growl. "You think you can come here from *California*—" he heaped an extra helping of scorn on the state's name—and bring your big-city ways to our town."

"Since you're taking this personal, we're taking the conversation into the back room." Which served as a supply and coffee room.

"Hell, no. You have anything else to say to me, you can damn well say it here in front of witnesses so you can't go spreading lies around town." It was obvious, as his hard gaze swept over the others, he was counting on them supporting him over the guy from LA whose father got him the position James believed was his right. "Your choice."

Aiden shrugged. James wasn't going to be able to say he hadn't been warned. Like all bullies, he believed that bluster was a sign of power. He was about to be proven wrong.

"I was born here," Aiden reminded him. "My family were early settlers. So, that makes it my town, too."

"You left. While the rest of us stayed. The job of chief damn well should've gone to me when Axel retired." There was a pause. "He promised it to me right before that stroke."

Experience had taught Aiden to read a lie. But since it wasn't relevant, he wasn't going to call the other man on it. "I left to fight for and defend my country. As a US Marine. And let me tell you here and now that one thing you don't want to do is mess with a Marine. But that's not why I'm firing you."

"What?" His mouth gaped open like a landed trout. "You can't fire me!"

"I can. And I am. Not because you spent a good deal of your shift hanging out at the casino. And not because you've been using your courtesy cards as Christmas presents to all your relatives—"

"That's a lie." But it did have some of fellow officers, who'd remained as mute as stones, exchanging looks.

Aiden arched a black brow. And waited. Apparently the deputy chief was as bad at interrogation as he was everything else because as the silence stretched out, he caved. Sort of.

"You have no damn way of knowing what the hell I give my relatives for Christmas."

"I called your wife's cousin. Who happens to be one of the cafeteria ladies at the high school and belongs to my mother's book club."

Small towns, Aiden thought. No wonder they always had higher crime-solving statistic rates than cities. There were no secrets. Since news spread in Honeymoon Harbor faster than it took to drive from one end of town to the other, what happened here in the office definitely wasn't going to stay here. Which was why, although it damn well hadn't been the way things had worked in LA, he was glad James didn't take him up on his offer to have this conversation in private. This way there'd be less speculation and lies woven in with the gossip, and the facts about what happened would be right out there on the table.

"She told me she and her husband each get one every year," Aiden said. "She also told me they toss them out because they don't approve. Maybe she doesn't keep them because she's a good, law-abiding woman. Or maybe because she gets paid from the town coffers and hasn't had a pay raise in three years. Partly because of the money you and the others handing them out have cost the town. Whatever her reason, you're busted."

A wave of low muttering moved through the ranks. He could tell from the ones whose complexions went gray who else he was dealing with.

"I could check with more relatives," he told James, "but we both know that'd be a waste of my time and theirs and there's no point in causing family dissention. The reason you're fired is because you've skimmed from a fund that was set up to help both serving and retired officers and their families."

"That's a lie."

"You may have forgotten, my family founded the bank that financed most of the town's early buildings and still does. And although my grandfather's mostly retired, he keeps a hand in the business. Enough that once I got a warrant yesterday, he was more than willing to go through the fund's account. And guess what? Some of those payments for services went to dummy accounts set up in the names of various online businesses, all that list your wife as the owner."

And didn't that cause more muttering? None of it seeming to go James's way.

"I donated fifty dollars we couldn't afford to that fund," one of the retired volunteers offered. "Supposedly to help a fellow cop who needed transportation to the VA hospital."

"And my wife insisted we donate because it said on the website officers' kids needed school supplies," another said.

The dam broke, with a lot of troops complaining, listing one or more of the reasons they'd chipped in. Being public servants in a small town, the salaried cops didn't make all that much and the volunteers had dug into their own savings and retirement accounts.

"This is a waste of time. I'm getting out of here and going the hell back to work." James turned and began marching toward the door. Aiden could feel everyone else in the room holding their collective breaths to see how this was going to play out.

"You're not going anywhere, because I'm placing you under arrest."

Don James spun around and fisted his beefy hands on his broad hips. His face was as red as a boiled Dungeness crab. "You can't do that."

"I can and I am. And since I don't have much confidence you've bothered to memorize them, I'm going to read you your rights."

"I fucking know them."

Aiden ignored him. "You have the right to remain silent and to refuse to answer questions. Anything you say may be used against you in a court of law. You have the right to consult an attorney before speaking to the police and to have an attorney present during questioning now or in the future. If you cannot afford an attorney, one will be appointed for you before any questioning if you wish. If you decide to answer questions now without an attorney present, you will still have the right to stop answering at any time until you talk to an attorney."

"This is bullshit."

"Like I said, tell it to the judge. I called the DA, who called Judge Baker, and your bail hearing is at ten tomorrow morning. Since you've more or less served the community for sixteen years, I suspect the DA might be willing to cut a deal with your attorney that keeps you out of jail. Meanwhile you'll be staying here as a guest of Honeymoon Harbor."

The room had gone as quiet as St. Peter the Fisherman's Church on a Monday morning.

"I want a lawyer."

Aiden shrugged. "Your choice. Meanwhile, I'll need your weapon. And your badge."

James slammed the Glock down on the desk, and threw his badge hard enough to send it skidding over the top of the desk, where it landed on the floor.

"Owens." Aiden turned toward one of the newer recruits, a recent graduate of Clearwater Community College, who he assumed didn't have a personal history with the former deputy police chief. "Would you please escort our guest to a cell?"

If James's face got any redder, his head would've burst into flames. Aiden wondered about his blood pressure, and realized he was going to have to assign someone to watch him during the night.

"Okay." He blew out a breath as the two men walked through the door to what was laughingly referred to as the cellblock, which held all of three cells. Which had never been filled since he'd been here, and so far had only been used for a couple of drunk-to-the-gills fishermen who'd gotten into a fistfight at the harbor over crab traps.

"Here's the deal. I'm not going to investigate who's been handing out the cards. But that practice stops now. And if you know any person who happens to have one, then you'd better retrieve it. Because I'm not going to look on it at all kindly if I hear of anyone trying to use one. And in the event a citizen does hand you one, you're to confiscate it and politely explain that they've expired."

He paused, and glanced around, noting a few shifty, back-and-forth glances that gave him an even better idea who'd been taking advantage of the situation.

"Now, let's get back to work."

As everyone filed out, one officer, Jennifer Stone,

lingered behind. According to her file, she had been on the force for the five years, since graduating from UW with a degree in criminal justice. Her dad had been a cop who'd had the dubious distinction of being the one and only Honeymoon Harbor officer ever killed in the line of duty. Sergeant Ken Stone had been shot during what he'd expected to be a routine traffic stop.

Tragically, that event occurred only six months after his wife had died in a ten-car pileup when a truck had dropped a load of logs on a wet and slick mountain road. Although Jennifer had already started law school, she dropped out, returned home and joined the force while parenting her then eight-year-old brother.

"May I say something without you thinking I'm sucking up?" she asked after everyone else had left.

"Sure."

"I think you're doing a great job," she said. "And you make me proud to be a police officer."

"Thank you." Even if she was sucking up, it was good to hear.

"I'm relieved you did something about those cards," she said. "I've stopped people who've complained when I wouldn't accept them. That hasn't gone over real well with some of the guys."

"I can imagine. You could have come to me."

"I didn't know Don was skimming," she said. "So, it seemed like a gray area. Plus, you've never said anything about them, so I thought maybe you approved. And quite honestly, because of my home situation, with my brother and all, I really need this job. So, I didn't want to rock the boat."

"Did you know your father arrested me?" Aiden asked.

Color bled from her face, but her brown eyes stayed steady on his.

"No. I didn't know that, sir."

"More than once. One time for papering Mrs. Gunderson's house on Halloween."

"Small towns," she said, with a bit of a smile quirking at the corner of her lips. "Did he officially charge you?"

"No. But he did bring me in and make me sit in the cell while I waited for my dad to come pick me up. I was in my rebellious stage at the time, and he said he wanted to show me where I might end up if I didn't straighten out."

"That sounds like Dad." The smile broke free for a quick moment. "We had our own clashes during my teens. His first-date lecture scared off a lot of potential boyfriends." Her eyes softened with a faint sheen. "There may or may not have been some slamming of doors over house rules."

"He was tough," Aiden agreed. "But always fair. He was also the one who got me sent to the Marines for boosting the beer."

"Oh." When her brow furrowed, Aiden wondered if she was worrying about the stability of her job again. "I guess I should say I'm sorry?"

"Not necessary. I deserved it. Judge Burns, who'd gotten sick and tired of seeing me in front of his bench gave me a choice. The military as soon as I turned eighteen and graduated, or juvie. I chose the Marines, which taught me a lot about discipline. And honor, that's only one reason why those cards pissed me off."

"My dad was a Marine."

"That's partly why I chose to be one. Because it took me a while to realize it, but in a way, along with my dad—who I'd been rebelling against mostly because with my dad being mayor and my mom the school principal, my brothers, sister and I were expected to be better behaved than the other kids in town—your father was a role model."

This time the smile warmed and for a fleeting moment they could have been two friends reminiscing about a special person they'd lost.

"So, getting to the point, I'm appointing you deputy chief."

"Me?" Her hand flew to the front of her uniform, over her heart, as if to settle its wild beating. "But I'm only twenty-six."

"True. And that's going to earn some grumbles from the old retired guys who, deep down, may not have evolved enough to have fully accepted women into the ranks. But you're older than your years. And due to your upbringing and how you've handled all life's thrown at you you're the most responsible member of the force. Donna agrees, by the way."

"She does?" The new deputy chief Stone glanced toward the glass door, where Donna Ormsbee was doing a piss-poor job of pretending not to watch them.

"In forty years working here, she's seen a lot of cops come and go. She said that in your case, the apple didn't fall far from the tree, and you're one of the best who's ever worn the Honeymoon Harbor uniform. You're also the only member of the force I get emails about. Not a single one is a complaint, just appreciation for having gone out of your way to help them in some situation."

"I was just doing my job."

"We agree on that. But not everyone takes it as seriously as you do." As Aiden himself did. Which surprised him. He'd taken the Marines seriously. And his days working for LAPD. But he'd honestly never expected to feel that same sense of responsibility, and even pride, heading up this force that wasn't big enough to even need a fancy organizational flowchart.

"So, it's settled? You'll take the job?"

"Yes, sir. If you're sure I'm up to it."

"If I wasn't sure, I wouldn't have offered it to you. It also comes with a raise. Not as much as you'd get in Seattle, Tacoma, or even Olympia. But every bit helps, right?"

"It does. My brother wants to play baseball again this summer. He's going to need a new uniform because he outgrew his old one."

"A complaint I remember hearing from my mother a lot. My oldest brother, Quinn, and my sister, Brianna, were the only kids in our family who always got new clothes."

She laughed. Then sobered. "I'll do my best to live up to your confidence, sir," she said.

"I've not a single doubt. I'll have Donna put in a requisition for a new badge," he said. "Meanwhile, I'll make the announcement at tomorrow morning's roll call."

"Good call," Bodhi said as they both watched her walk out of the office. "Of course, now you're not going to be able to date her."

"That wasn't even in my mind."

"Of course it wasn't. Because you're a straight arrow who'd never end up on a #MeToo social media outing. But, in case you didn't notice, she's damn fine."

"All I'm interested in is that she'll be a damn fine deputy chief."

"You do realize, that while talking to that douche with the Porsche, and those cops, that you referred to this little burg in the remote corner of the country as *your town*."

"Yeah. I heard that, too." Which had been a surprise. Aiden had taken this job to humor his father, get his mother to stop cooking all that damn food and worrying about him, and for something to fill his days for the next few months while he decided what he was going to do with the next stage of his life.

Sometime, when he hadn't been paying attention, apparently being chief of police of his old hometown had become the next stage.

CHAPTER ELEVEN

After a light breakfast of Greek yogurt and blueberries, Jolene drove Gloria to Honeymoon Harbor General Hospital. Having downloaded a map of the hospital the night before, she felt as prepared as she could be. What she hadn't been prepared for was Aiden, who arrived at the double glass doors the same time they had.

"Small world," he said. "Hello, Mrs. Wells."

"Your mother's a close friend, Aiden. You've certainly called me by my first name whenever I've cut your hair."

"Sorry. I'm here in my official capacity. So, it's automatic." He glanced over at Jolene. "Good to see you again."

Gloria's eyes narrowed as they went back and forth between the two. "I hadn't realized you two had run into each other so soon."

"Chief Mannion pulled me over for speeding when I first arrived."

"Oh, dear."

"But I didn't give her a ticket since she hadn't known the limit had been changed."

"Well, that was very nice of you. I hope what brings you here today isn't due to family trouble."

"No. Like I said, it's official business."

"I'm glad to hear that. I also hope it's not very serious."

"That makes two of us." Although he was polite, Jolene noticed him taking a surreptitious glance at his watch.

"Well, we'd better get going," she said. "Mom's just here for a routine test. I came along to keep her company."

"That's good." Another glance at his watch, this time revealing a tinge of impatience. Which was just as well, since Jolene wasn't in any mood to be chatty. Especially with Aiden Mannion.

"It's nothing." Gloria waved a hand that had been tightly clenched with her other all the way to the hospital. "Just routine." She smiled. "A pesky woman's thing."

"Okay, then. I'd better get back to work." He gave Jolene what appeared to be an almost sympathetic look. "Good luck."

Then his expression hardened in a way she'd only ever seen from him once before as he headed toward the ER on a long, determined stride nothing like the reckless bad boy swagger that had drawn such long sighs from nearly every girl in high school. He'd definitely changed over the years he'd been away. Just as she had.

But, dammit, he still strummed chords she didn't want strummed. And that powerful tug of attraction was something she didn't want. It could only lead to something even more dangerous.

Following the downloaded map and the signs on the walls, they went through another door into the radiology department, where the receptionist took Gloria's information, then directed her to a waiting room in the Breast Cancer Center.

"I did some reading about the hospital last night," Jolene told her mother, who was once again clenching her hands together so tightly her knuckles whitened.

"It's public and part of a large state coalition. It's rated higher than some of the bigger named ones."

"That's good to know," her mother said absently as she watched the Pioneer Woman slicing up an orange butternut squash for a Thanksgiving side dish on the flat-screen TV attached to the wall.

"It's not only a critical care hospital, it has top-rated surgical services. And an oncology clinic."

"Which I won't be needing because I don't have cancer."

Pioneer Woman had begun peeling the outer layer off a mountain of brussels sprouts. "I wasn't suggesting you did. It was just one of the clinics highlighted on the website. It also has an orthopedics unit, a wellness program and has been diagnosed baby friendly by the World Health Organization."

"I don't plan on having any more babies, either," Gloria said, her eyes glued to the TV as if the most important thing in her world was this dish. Which looked pretty good.

"I was just saying."

Since she could tell she wasn't going to get anywhere, Jolene gave up trying to reassure her mother as they both watched Pioneer Woman put the squash and sprouts on a baking sheet with sliced red onions, sprinkle with chili powder, salt and pepper, then drizzle it all with olive oil before sticking it in the oven.

The TV personality chef had moved on to mashed potatoes two ways when her mother was called into a back room.

"Do you want me to come with you?" Jolene asked.

"I'll be fine," Gloria said, color returning to her cheeks as she stood up and squared her shoulders as Jolene had witnessed her doing so many times in her life. Some might view Gloria Wells as a victim, both of circumstances and an unreliable, criminal husband who'd made her a widow thanks to his unwise choices.

Jolene knew that inside, her mother was Wonder Woman. If the tests did find bad cells, her mother would kick cancer's butt. As she watched the TV cook stirring enough cream cheese and butter into the potatoes to clog all her guests' arteries before they even they got to dessert, Jolene said a silent prayer that she and her mom would have something to be thankful for this Thanksgiving. Then she texted Shelby to update her on the situation and received three high fives and five multicolor hearts in return. There were times Jolene idly wondered what her best friend had done before the invention of emojis.

ALTHOUGH THERE WERE still four more days before Thanksgiving, Honeymoon Harbor General Hospital was getting a head start on Christmas decorating by putting up the artificial tree in the lobby. For as long as Aiden could remember, the ornaments were all cards and pictures made by children who'd been former patients over the year. They were all sent home with craft kits, then their parents would either mail or, more likely, drop them off at the reception desk, where they'd be added to the collection.

Aiden remembered Brianna helping his then seven-year-old brother Burke make a construction paper red-nose reindeer after he'd broken his arm jumping off the barn roof in an attempt to fly. After Christmas, like all the ornaments, the reindeer had been returned to his family to use in future years on their own tree. Despite the grim task he was facing, as Aiden exchanged a wave with the woman behind the reception desk, he idly wondered if his parents still had Burke's reindeer.

Dr. Lancaster was waiting for Aiden as he reached the ER.

"What's the story and where is she?"

"Amanda Barrow is in treatment room four. She has a periorbital hematoma that's going to turn into a killer of a black eye, a probable concussion, since the neighbor, who'd been raking leaves and called 911, said that she was unconscious for at least a minute. Maybe longer. He wasn't close enough to tell when it first occurred."

Aiden cursed under his breath.

"Her shoulder was wrenched out of the socket," Dr. Lancaster continued, "but Dr. Honeycutt, the ER attending, injected Ketorolac for pain and maneuvered it back into place. She has another hematoma the size of my spread hand on her hip that undoubtedly occurred when she hit the concrete driveway. And probably a cracked rib, but we won't know for sure until we get an X-ray.

"Because the patient was insisting on going home, Dr. Honeycutt called me knowing that I'm her family doctor, hoping I'd be able to talk her into staying. Unfortunately, I got nowhere. Hopefully you'll be able to get her to see the light." She paused. "According to the neighbor, her husband kicked her in the ribs before driving away. Apparently she managed to roll out of the way before he ran over her."

Aiden ran his hand through his hair. "I've already talked with her about this. It's going to be a lot more difficult for her to cover up for the guy now that we have a witness. I'll have someone take the neighbor's statement right away."

"Good." She gave him the name and Amanda's address, adding that she didn't know which house was the neighbor's. "But the EMT said it was the brown rancher with white trim. Ms. Barrow's house is the blue split-level with white shutters. The witness, a Mr. Cooper, is waiting for someone to come by. Meanwhile, Dr. Honeycutt assigned a nurse to stand guard outside the door in case she tries to leave before you got here, or in the unlikely event her husband has the balls to show up."

Despite the circumstances, her lips curved in a half smile. "In a way I wouldn't mind if he did. Since the nurse just happened to have played fullback for UW and it would be a shame if anything happened to the husband while trying to take her out of here."

"You're not alone in that thought."

After trading hellos with the nurse, who looked like he could hold his own with Dwayne "The Rock" Johnson, Aiden tapped on the door.

"Who is it?" a shaky voice asked.

"Chief Mannion." Although he'd told her to call him Aiden, he needed her to understand the seriousness of this official police visit. He opened the door and went in.

Despite being in what had to be a great deal of pain, Amanda had ditched her hospital gown and dressed again in her jeans and a blue T-shirt sporting a red wheelbarrow full of flowers that read *I'll be in my office.* Apparently she still fully intended to go home.

"Hello, Chief Mannion." She didn't look surprised, which told him what he'd already figured out the first time they'd talked. This wasn't her first rodeo.

"Hello, Ms. Barrow," he responded. "Would you rather I call you Ms. Barrow, or Amanda?"

"It's still Amanda. And, as you probably already know, Barrow is my maiden name. Since my business was already established when I got married, I kept it for name recognition." Her hands were clasped tightly together, and beneath what was obviously a struggle for composure, she appeared embarrassed, fearful and a host of other emotions Aiden had witnessed too many times before during his patrol days.

"Dr. Lancaster told me you'd like to go home."

"I want to leave," she qualified. "After that..." She shrugged, and he could tell, that despite the local painkiller, the movement hurt her shoulder. "I haven't decided."

"You do know you're not safe at home right now," he said gently.

A single tear overflowed her eyes and trailed down her cheek. "I know, but—"

"No *buts* this time, Amanda. I read the file from the Palo Alto police department. How many other cities would have similar reports?"

Her dark lashes glistened with moisture. She shook her head, and flinched, giving credence to Laurenne Lancaster's suspicion of a concussion. "Does it really matter?"

"Not at the moment." It might when it came time for prosecution, if whatever judge pulled the trial would allow past incidences, but this wasn't the time to push too hard. "I suspect it's been a few."

"He can't help it," she said. "Eric's not well."

And didn't that have Aiden hoping Eric hadn't gotten his hands on a gun?

He didn't ask why she'd stayed. He'd learned that reasons were complex and individual to each circumstance. To each battered spouse. He'd also learned, from a seminar he'd attended given by the police psychologist along with women who'd escaped their situations and had gone on to live happy, productive lives, that asking that question implied guilt and could inadvertently suggest that the wife, partner or girlfriend had somehow encouraged the violence.

"How not well?" he asked.

"He's bipolar. In the beginning, when he was taking his meds regularly, everything was fine. He was sweet and funny, in a nerdy kind of way. In fact, it wasn't until after we married that he even told me about having the disease. I hadn't suspected a thing.

"We met in California when he was working at Lawrence Livermore National Laboratory. I was installing landscaping outside a restaurant where he'd go for lunch. His job was so top secret, we'd dated a month before he even admitted he worked there. To be honest, I had to Google it, where I learned that it's a premier research and development institution whose principal responsibility is ensuring the safety, security and reliability of the nation's nuclear weapons." She put air quotes around the description.

"I've heard of it." Aiden also wondered how a bipolar guy who obviously had a trigger temper had landed a job dealing with nuclear weapons.

"Then, shortly before our first anniversary, he was working on a project and kept complaining that he was missing a vital point in the equation. I didn't realize it at the time, but that was when he'd decided that the very same medicine that was keeping his mind—and our marriage—stable, was also taking away the mental edge that had always made him brilliant.

"He didn't eat. He didn't sleep. For a while I thought maybe he might be on drugs. Or, since he'd also started going to the gym in the mornings after only three or four hours sleep, maybe anabolic steroids. I'd come downstairs in the morning and find formulas written all over our dining room walls."

"He'd gone off his meds."

"Yes. That was when he started becoming impatient with me, and all the rest of us with our 'moronically dull minds.' It started with sarcasm. Then temper." She paused. "Then one day, when I didn't have dinner ready when he got home, he slapped me. I'd gotten hung up at the nursery waiting for a delivery of azaleas." She lifted a hand to her bruised cheek as if remembering that previous pain.

"I was stunned. And didn't know what to do. But he immediately apologized and promised me he'd never, ever hurt me again. That the pressure at work was too much, that it was breaking him. He had quit that day."

She drew in a breath, flinched from the pain in her ribs. "I found out later he'd actually been fired. But he went back on his meds and I supported us for a time until he found another job in El Segundo working as a propulsion engineer for the NRO. The National Reconnaissance Office. Again, I had no idea what he was doing, but it had something to do with rockets to send spy satellites into space."

"Your husband is an actual rocket scientist?"

"A brilliant one," she said. "I've always felt inferior, which I suppose is partly how I landed here." She waved a limp hand around the room. "He's also into controlling everyone around him, who would be me, which is laughable when you think about it, because he can't even control himself." She laughed, but the ragged sound held no humor.

"Anyway, the cycle's been going around and around for eight years with the time between episodes getting shorter. Finally, when we were in Palo Alto, I'd decided to file for divorce. But then he came home and said he wanted to move here, because he decided that he was being held back by working in those rigidly controlled labs where everyone behaved like robots programmed not to ever think outside the box.

"He thought that living in a small town, in such a beautiful place, would calm his mind and give him the opportunity to achieve what he was meant to do. He literally got down on his knees, promised to stay on his meds, even go to counseling, and begged me to give him one more chance."

"Which you gave him." Aiden had heard that story too many times.

"He showed me Honeymoon Harbor's website and it looked like a wonderful place for both of us. And for a while it was. I'm always closed on Mondays, so we'd spent the day hiking, taking sailing and canoeing lessons, and even went over to the coast for a long weekend. He was unusually quiet during that trip, but when I asked if anything was wrong, he said he was just thinking about his work.

"Then this past summer, he announced that he'd decided to set up his own research company."

"To send satellites into space?"

Aiden didn't know anything about rocket propulsion or satellites or nuclear weapons, but with all the scientists around the world engaged in a war to be the biggest, best and first, he had trouble imagining anyone creating a unique, never-been-tried system in the dining room of a 1930s bungalow on Washington's Olympic Peninsula.

"No. To send *people* into space. His intention is to have the first colony established on Mars by 2025. He's now decided he can only plan that off the grid in Alaska. That was why he got furious at me this morning. I love it here, I have employees depending on me, and who fires people at Christmas? So I refused to go with him this time."

"Wise call." Aiden didn't believe she'd stay alive that long if she allowed him to isolate her somewhere in the wilds of Alaska. "You do realize you have to get out of that cycle," he said. "Because it's only going to escalate."

"I know. But I—"

"We can help you," he said quietly. But firmly. He looked at his watch. "We only have a four-hour arrest window in Washington State from the time of the abuse, and the clock is ticking, so we'll need to do that now." Whether or not she agreed, but she'd already given up so much power in her marriage, he didn't want to tell her that she had no choice in this situation.

"All right." Her eyes were still glazed from pain and, he thought, regret for all that had gone wrong in a marriage she'd undoubtedly entered with such high hopes.

"We'll pick him up, then, because you say he's brilliant—"

"He is."

"Our jail is pretty much like what Otis used to sleep off benders in Mayberry, so I'll have the county sheriff's department take over from there. They have the facilities to keep him incarcerated until the trial. And he'll have a psych evaluation, and I expect the doctor assigned to his case will get him back on meds."

"What if he gets released on bail? Or on his own recognizance?"

She'd either looked up the process of arrest to trial previously, or watched a lot of *Law & Order: Special Victims Unit.*

"When I leave here, I'm taking copies of your medical files and photos, along with other information I managed to collect, to the DA, who I called on the way here after talking with Dr. Lancaster. He'll be ready to press charges this afternoon. Which in this state gives us seventy-two hours before he has to appear before a judge for the bail hearing.

"Both Dr. Lancaster and Dr. Honeycutt will be there to testify, if necessary, and the prosecutor who's going to be appointed to the case just happens to be a woman whose mission in life is to put bad guys away and she has a particular distaste for husbands who beat their wives. Probably because her sister was one of them, who didn't escape in time to avoid being killed."

He felt bad about causing what little color she'd had in her face to fade to white, but he'd feel a lot worse having her end up on a slab in the morgue. Not in his town, Aiden thought again. "If you can give us other towns where the police have been called, the DA can start creating a case. Then, if he doesn't plead guilty on the spot, we'll gather even more for the trial."

"You still have to catch him. As I said, he's brilliant. And has gotten really good at survivalist stuff." She dragged a hand through her hair, which was stiff from dried blood. She paused and he watched as realization dawned in those sad, tired eyes. "All that time we were hiking and camping, he could have been practicing for this. Maybe to escape and hide after he killed me."

"You may be right, but we'll find him. Meanwhile, after you're released, we'll take you to a safe house run by a former Portland homicide detective and her Navy SEAL husband."

"But the nursery… As I said, this is a busy time for me, and although I could absorb the loss, I have employees who would be hurt by a closure."

"Can they run the place for a few days?"

"Emily and Jen can handle the inside business," she said slowly. "And most of the seasonal greenery will probably be sold at your family's farm anyway. Jesus, Emilio, Greg and Tom take care of stock and planting, which we don't have that much of this time of year, except I expect we'll get some calls to plant some of the potted Christmas trees. Your dad offered to hand out my cards to people who buy them."

"So, you're set on that front."

"I guess I am. At least for a few days."

"Okay. Good. I'll let them know what's going on. You're not going to be able to keep what happened a secret in this town anyway. It makes sense to give everyone the Thanksgiving weekend off, since, honestly, from Friday to Monday, my family's going to get most of the floral decorating business and that way none of the will have to deal with an angry husband looking for you."

"I wouldn't want any of them to get hurt." Her eyes filled at the thought.

"That's not going to happen." He hoped. Hell, he'd put one of the volunteer cops on nursery duty if they hadn't apprehended the husband by Monday.

"I'll handle the police business while Dr. Lancaster takes care of the tests you need. After that, she'll take you to up to the surgery recovery floor. That way, even if your husband decides to show up here, he won't find you in the ER. As soon as the doctors say you're good to go, we'll move you. If you give me a key, I'll have Jennifer Stone, the department's new deputy chief, get some personal things out of the house for you. Anything special you need?"

"Just my purse. And some clothes and underwear."

She blushed a bit at that. "And shampoos and toothpaste and stuff."

"Consider it done. They're good people. I think you'll like them. And I know they'll like you. And keep you safe."

The tears she'd been trying to hold back broke free and streamed down her face.

"I'm sorry." She wiped at the tears with the back of her hands. As a cop, he'd gotten used to tears, but they still tore him up inside. He decided the day he got so numb to the results of crime that they didn't, it'd be time to get into another line of work.

"You've nothing to feel sorry about," he assured her, handing her a handkerchief.

She dabbed at her eyes, then looked up at him "I've never met a man who carries a handkerchief."

"Yeah," Aiden said. "I hear that a lot."

CHAPTER TWELVE

GLORIA'S HANDS SHOOK with nerves she'd been trying to hide from Jolene as she unhooked her bra after taking off her shirt behind the closed curtain of the dressing stall. The lab tech had given her a little pep talk about she didn't have to worry, and explained that the ultrasound was safe and painless, that she'd have some gel placed on her skin, then high frequency sound waves would be transmitted from a probe through the gel into her body, which would bounce back to allow a computer to view them as sound waves to create an image. No different from the kind every pregnant woman received.

Yada yada yada. As if Gloria hadn't already read every article she could find online. She might be the empress of denial, but now that she'd started on this unwanted path, she intended to be prepared for whatever might happened.

Despite her outwardly brave words, she'd learned early in life that it was better to expect the best, but prepare for the worst. Like the old saying went, if you're going through hell, just keep on going. That was how she'd always lived her life, and she had no intention of changing. As the machine started beeping, which the tech assured her was merely the Doppler evaluating blood flow (again, something she'd already learned online), she also vowed that she was not going to die. At least not anytime soon.

Not when she still had her daughter's wedding to attend someday. And hopefully, grandbabies to look forward to down the road. She was imagining a future festive family Christmas with stockings hung from the mantel when the tech broke into her daydream by cheerily announcing that they were all done. And that the radiologist would read the images and have them at her physician's by Monday morning.

After dressing, fluffing out her hair that had been flattened while lying on the table, and touching up her lipstick in a mirror beneath a fluorescent light that wasn't the least bit flattering, Gloria returned to the waiting room where Jolene was reading a romance novel. Ironic, she thought, for a woman who insisted she didn't believe in true love or happily-ever-afters.

"All done," she announced.

On the TV Jolene had been ignoring, Pioneer Woman had given way to Trisha Yearwood, who was making a pecan pie for the upcoming holiday. Gloria hadn't been counting on doing much for Thanksgiving herself. Perhaps picking up one of those already made dinners Mildred Marshall sold at the market. Or, since there wasn't going to be anyone to share it with, nuking a frozen turkey dinner and baking a Sara Lee pie. But now, with her daughter home, she was going to have to rethink that plan.

"Great." Jolene stuffed the book in her bag and stood up. "We've plenty of time to make brunch."

"THIS IS WONDERFUL," Gloria said as she and Jolene sat in front of a stone fireplace tall enough for a grown man to stand in. After brunch, they'd taken their wine to a pair of chairs overlooking the lake that was just misty enough after today's earlier rain to look like the entrance to a magic watery kingdom. "I'm so glad you thought of it. Despite the reason."

"We should have done it earlier," Jolene said. "I should have come home more often."

"I always knew why you didn't. And understood. I also can't deny that I enjoyed those fancy LA restaurants and that Emmy party. Who would've thought that I'd ever be in the same restaurant with George Clooney?"

"That makes two of us," Jolene said. She'd never been fortunate enough to do the makeup for the superstar who always arrived with his own entourage, but had heard from friends who'd worked on his movies that he was as warm and funny as he appeared in interviews. But a terrible practical joker.

"I am worried I'm keeping you from work," Gloria said.

"Don't worry. I'd honestly already planned to take the time off to work on my skin care line. I have some new things I want to try."

"I thought you were just making that up so I wouldn't feel guilty."

"Well, I wasn't. And let's make a deal. Whatever happens Monday, we're going to be honest with each other. We're not going to hold back any thoughts or feelings and we're definitely not going to lie just to make the other person feel better."

"So, if I get bald you'll tell me that I'm beautiful."

"Let's not get ahead of ourselves. But you're already beautiful. Besides, lots of movie stars have buzzed their hair. Cate Blanchett, Natalie Portman, Charlize Theron—"

"For a postapocalyptic movie set in a desert. Even she couldn't have kept her hair looking good in a situation like that."

"Toni Collette."

"Who played a woman with breast cancer in that movie with Drew Barrymore."

"Oh. Right. Okay, that might not have been the best example… Demi Moore."

"In *G.I. Jane*. This may surprise you, but I've never wanted to be a Navy SEAL."

"See, you're keeping your sense of humor. That's a good thing. And let's not forget Jada Pinkett Smith. Will certainly seems to find her sexy."

"Since I'm not interested in any men finding me sexy, that's not an issue."

"You're being stubborn."

"I'm entitled. I may have cancer. I shouldn't be mocked by my own daughter."

"Sneaky how you're now using the outside possibility of cancer to your advantage."

"One uses the tools one has. And this is where I point out that I do know how to use the internet enough to Google stars with bald heads. As you undoubtedly did after Sarah told you about my mammogram. No one, even a woman who works in Hollywood, could have rattled off that list so quickly."

"I was preparing to be supportive."

"I know… I need to admit something I never told you," Gloria said, looking out over the lake. A man was in a wooden boat, fishing from the bow. With the mist over the lake and the lushly wooded mountains looming up in front of him, he could have been a watercolor painting.

Jolene glance over at her. "Okay."

"When I found out I was pregnant, I was so scared. I didn't know what to do. I didn't want to be pregnant at sixteen."

"Who would?"

That was why those vicious, mean-spirited rumors about her mother were so hurtful. Also, knowing how difficult life had been for Gloria, there was no way she was going to make the same mistake. Of course, keeping her virginity wasn't that difficult when there wasn't any guy in school that she wanted to have sex with. Except Aiden Mannion. But they'd both had reasons to keep their secret relationship…romance…whatever it had been, from ever going that far.

Except for that day…the last time she'd seen him before he left for basic training. When she'd clung to him like moss on a tree and begged him to make love to her. He'd turned her down flat, devastating her.

"I didn't know what to do," her mom, unaware of Jolene's thoughts, continued. "My parents had just been killed and I was all alone, which was probably why I had sex with your father in the first place."

"Comfort sex," Jolene murmured. "That's understandable."

"I suppose so." Gloria sighed. "Social services sent me to live with my grandmother. Who'd be your great grandmother on my mother's side."

"You never talk about her."

"Because I don't want to think of those days. She didn't live long enough for you to meet her, but believe me, you didn't miss anything. She was a harridan who treated me like an indentured servant. I probably wouldn't have minded that so much if she hadn't spent all our time together complaining about how my mother and father eloped because my mother turned out to be a slut who got herself ruined by a smooth-talking boy."

"I didn't know that." Jolene only knew her grandparents had eloped. To save the money and all the fuss of a wedding, her mother had always told her.

"I never saw any point in sharing it," Gloria said. "Because my mother was certainly no slut and it was obvious that they were madly in love, and even if the reason for the elopement was true, which I doubt because I could do the math and my mother would've had to get pregnant immediately, they still would've gotten married.

"My father was the sweetest, most romantic man. I wish you could have known him. He was taking Mama to a lodge on the coast, not far from where the Mannions have their summer home, to celebrate their anniversary. He'd run all his plans by me first to make sure she'd really love it. Including having chocolate-covered strawberries waiting in the sea-view room with a bottle of champagne and an anniversary cake after dinner in the restaurant with *Dennis Loves Janice* piped on in pink frosting. Pink was her favorite color.

"The only thing that kept me from falling apart when the trooper came to tell me that they'd been killed was the fact that they'd been on their way home from the trip when the accident had happened. Mama had called me from the lodge that morning, telling me how beautiful everything was, and how they'd just come back from beachcombing and she had a bag of shells and another of agates and sea glass. She'd decided that we could buy one of those rock tumblers to polish the rocks and glass and make jewelry together. She was so excited and happy. That was the last time we ever talked."

"That's so sad. But it's a nice memory." Yet so bittersweet.

"The car was totaled. I never got the shells. Or the rocks."

"Is that why you make your jewelry?" Necklaces, rings and bracelets from stones and sea glass her mother found on the beaches she'd once sold on eBay for extra money. She'd continued to make them but now they were sold in her salon, a boutique in the Dancing Deer dress shop and at the Herons Landing gift shop.

"It is. Every necklace or bracelet I make has me feeling as if a part of her is with still me. It helps keep her memory alive."

She quieted, as if lost in thoughts Jolene didn't want to intrude on.

"What do you think happens when we die?" she asked finally.

"You're not going to die."

"We're all dying, darling. You, me, that good-looking young man who waited on us in the dining room. Who, I noticed, had his eye on you."

"I didn't notice."

"He did. As did Aiden when we ran into him at the hospital."

"He did not."

"He did, too. He looked at you the same way he did at Kylee and Mai's wedding. Like you were a frosted cupcake he'd like to eat up. But you kept moving as far away as you could from him."

"Maybe you should have had a brain scan while you were in radiology," Jolene said. "Because you were obviously hallucinating."

"I know what I saw. And I saw that Aiden was more than a little interested. And you were trying not to be."

"Mother..."

"There were sparks," Gloria insisted. "And I wasn't the only one who saw them. Sarah and I discussed it afterward, and she agreed there was definitely a mutual attraction."

"Even if there was, and I'm not saying that's true, there's no way I'd get involved with Aiden Mannion."

"Surely not because of that night?"

"Partly."

"But he was the good guy. The one who rescued you."

"I know. But you weren't there. A lot of that night is blacked out, but I definitely remember throwing myself at him, begging him to have sex with me." Years later she'd looked up Ecstasy and learned that increased libido was one of the reasons some seriously scummy guys used it to drug girls' drinks. Which had happened at that party she never should've gone to.

"Oh… Well. You *had* been given drugs, so you can't feel responsible for what you did under the influence. And the doctor who did the rape exam at the hospital told me you were still a virgin."

"Only because Aiden and Seth arrived in time. And after beating those boys up and chasing them off, Aiden turned me down."

"Of course he did. Because, despite all the trouble he'd get into, he was, at heart, a good boy. Who grew up to be a good man."

"He was always a good boy. He just hid it well." He'd also been the only person she could talk with back in those days. She still had no idea why he'd kept sneaking out with her, since she'd made it clear that he'd never get past second base, when she knew other girls in town who'd brag about having gone all the way with him.

"Though I have to admit that I never, in a million years, would have expected him to become Honeymoon Harbor's police chief."

"He's turned out to be an excellent one." Gloria

sipped her wine. "He only agreed to take the job temporarily, but Sarah says she thinks he'll stay."

"All the more reason for me not to get involved with him. Because it couldn't go anywhere."

"Why not?"

"Because I don't do long-term relationships."

"That's because you've never been with the right man. The one you can't imagine a life without. Your relationship with Chad just ended. I'd say you're entitled to have a have a rebound fling to get over the cheater."

"I don't need to get over Chad. Because I was never emotionally invested. Although this is probably not something to share with a parent, our relationship was mostly sex and a way to avoid becoming one of those women who takes some strange guy she's just met home from the bar for the night because she's lonely. I happen to be a serial monogamist."

"We're both adults. I hope there's never anything you feel you can't share with me," Gloria said mildly. "So, be a serial monogamist with Aiden while you're here. You are leaving after New Year's. Meanwhile, it could brighten the holidays."

Jolene had already considered that idea after a particularly hot dream involving Aiden, and those handcuffs he wore on his belt. And had rejected it as being nothing more than an adult version of her youthful fantasies.

"I don't think it'd be possible to have a fling with him. Maybe once, back when he was wild, but he seems so grounded now. He might not even know it yet, but my guess is that he's going to stay here in Honeymoon Harbor, keep his job and choose himself a woman for the long term. One he can marry and have kids with." And, of course, they'd undoubtedly get a dog.

"While I was getting my ultrasound, I imagined

a family Christmas at the lighthouse, with children's stockings hanging from the mantel."

"Not happening." Jolene took a longer gulp of her wine.

"I'd been thinking of taking a lover," her mother volunteered.

The unexpected statement almost had Jolene spitting out her wine. Then she remembered that her mother was still in her forties. And had been widowed for years. "I think that's an excellent idea." And, although some people might consider thinking about their parents having sex as icky, she'd rather talk about that than her own sex life. Or, more specifically, lack of it.

"Oh, I can't now. At least not until we get the tests back and they're all clear. Because what man would ever want to go to bed with a bald woman with only one breast?"

"Overreacting much?" Jolene asked her mother. "And to answer your question, I'd say maybe a man who doesn't reduce women to body parts? Also, I've never known you to be such a negative thinker."

"I've never looked cancer in the face. Or, to be more accurate, in the breast. Though you're right about the negativity.

"Caroline told me that negativity only draws negative forces and suggested meditation and imagining white lights and such. It was all a bit woo-woo for my taste, but I appreciated the gesture and I am trying to think positively. I tried meditation, but my mind wanders."

"It takes practice." Jolene felt a sizzle run through her as she thought back to the image she'd conjured up while waiting for her ticket. The one where Aiden had replaced her Hawaiian beach boy.

"That's what she told me. But, it's hard." She dabbed at her eyes with the corner of the linen napkin. "Not just the meditation, but this feeling of having my life swerve so out of control."

"I know." Jolene took her mother's hand in hers. "And we'll get that control back as soon as we know what we're dealing with. So, returning to the original far more interesting topic, who did you have in mind for your lover?"

"You'll laugh."

"Scout's honor, I will not."

"You were never a Girl Scout."

"Lucky thing. I never would've sold any cookies because we'd have eaten them all ourselves."

"Good point. Okay… Michael Mannion."

"Brianna's uncle?" Jolene barely remembered him. Michael Mannion was a painter and a world traveler, who'd breeze through town every few years, the closest thing Honeymoon Harbor had to an actual celebrity. She'd seen his paintings during a gallery showing she and Shelby had gone to. She remembered him looking a lot like Pierce Brosnan, with his dark hair and those riveting blue eyes most of the Mannion men seem to have inherited.

"He came back to town a year or so ago. I cut his hair, and sometimes, I get the feeling that he might be a tad bit interested, but then again, he's such a charmer, it's hard to tell."

"You told me he painted that mural on your spa wall for free."

"He was probably just being nice," Gloria said. "Because his sister-in-law and I are friends."

"A sketch is being nice," Jolene argued. "That's one big-ass wall, Mom." A wall that now took spa guests to a visual Tahiti. Or Hawaii. Which, dammit, caused that fantasy to flash back again.

"When you put it that way… For a while he and Caroline looked like they were going to be a thing, back when Ben and Caroline were separated—"

"Seth's parents were separated?"

"For a short time earlier in the year. But Ben got his act together and Caroline went back to him and they've been traveling the country in a motor home. She swore to me that she hadn't let her relationship with Michael go any further than friendship and him teaching her painting, but it was obvious to a lot of us who were watching that he wouldn't have minded if she'd chosen him."

"Wow. Talk about a soap opera."

"I really felt for her. She didn't want to leave Ben, but he'd become such a negative old stick-in-the-mud. She'd just gotten to her breaking point. Then she had her heart attack—"

"Brianna mentioned that at the wedding. That must've been what scared him into doing whatever it took to win her back."

"It probably made him realize what he'd lose if he'd lost her," Gloria agreed. "But she told me he'd already been working on fixing things before that. They even had a date. In Port Townsend. And he brought her flowers."

"That's sweet."

"It was. I was so happy for them. But that's when I started thinking that maybe it was time to get back out there. Although I haven't been on a date since I was fifteen, so I've no idea how it's done these days."

"It's probably not a movie and milkshakes afterward at the Big Dipper. Michael Mannion's a world traveler. He might take you to Seattle. Or even Hawaii. Can you imagine spending January lounging on a tropical beach instead of wind, rain and gray skies?"

"I said I'd been thinking about the idea of a lover," Gloria said. "Not that he'd probably ever ask me."

"So, ask him. It's a new world, Mom. I realize you haven't dated since you were a teenager, but women can initiate things now."

"So Caroline and Sarah keep telling me. And easy for them to say, since they're both happily married... Sarah keeps offering to set us up. But it's a moot point now."

"Why?"

"I told you. Because I may have cancer."

"And you may not."

"But still, even having a suspicious lump means that it may be lurking inside, just waiting to break out."

"I don't remember you ever being so pessimistic." Even all those years with Jolene's father, her mother had always believed he'd change.

"I know. I just don't feel at all like myself anymore. I've been overly emotional all year. Dr. Lancaster diagnosed it as probable perimenopause, and put me on a low-dose estrogen. I asked her about the risk now, with the lump, but she suggested we just wait for the tests, then we could discuss taking me off the pills gradually, or quitting cold turkey."

"She sounds sensible."

"She is. And very nice. Did I tell you she has a daughter? There doesn't seem to be a husband in the picture so I'm guessing that she's divorced, but of course, it's not the type of conversation that comes up in a well woman checkup."

"Well, my vote is that you should move Mike Mannion to the top of your list of potential lovers."

"I don't have a *list*! This is a small town. There aren't

that many eligible men. At least not that I'd be interested in."

"Certainly none as good-looking as him."

"He has a haircut scheduled next week. He said that Harriet Harper, Sarah's mother and the matriarch of the family, informed him that his shaggy—and, personally, I think sexy—hair might be appropriate for a bohemian European artist, but he's in Honeymoon Harbor now and she expects him to look respectable for their family Thanksgiving."

Jolene laughed, her mother joined in, and for that frozen moment, sitting here together, watching the sun set into the lake in a fiery blaze as the fishing boat puttered back to the dock, life was as perfect as it had been in a very long while.

CHAPTER THIRTEEN

THE WEEKEND AWAY turned out to be everything Jolene had hoped for. By mutual, unspoken consent, neither she nor her mother talked again about the cancer scare Saturday night or Sunday morning. Nor when they made a side trip to Port Townsend, where they stopped at a craft store where they bought several sample-sized bottles and jars Gloria could use in her Christmas booth. To add to the presentation value, Jolene tossed a roll of gold-edged labels, two gold calligraphy gel pens—since all hers had been lost in the fire—and, thinking optimistically, she put a hundred gold organza drawstring bags for the sample collections into their cart. Then on impulse, threw in another hundred.

"Surely that's too many," Gloria protested.

"We're in optimism mode, remember?" Jolene reminded her mother. "So we're thinking large."

After staying long enough for a lunch overlooking the water, real life started to intrude on their drive back home to Honeymoon Harbor when Sarah Mannion called Gloria's cell, inviting her and Jolene to Thanksgiving dinner.

"I should get a result from my ultrasound tomorrow," Gloria mused. "I don't know if it's going to end up a biopsy, or surgery, or—"

"Or nothing." Jolene heard Sarah say through the car's Bluetooth speaker. "I have a cousin in Denver who had a biopsy, and I flew over to be with her although it's not like a full surgery, and was fairly painless for her. She was sore for a few days due to bruising. It wasn't terrible, and she was able to go back to work, but I wouldn't have wanted her cooking a holiday dinner."

"I have Jolene to help."

Jolene wondered if her mother remembered she didn't know how to cook. Her hours had been so erratic in the past few years, if her meals didn't come off a catering truck on set, they were takeout or frozen Lean Cuisine, except for those glorious gourmet days when she'd go over to Shelby and Ètienne's.

"I'm so glad she's come home to be with you. But seriously, if you do end up needing a biopsy, I know you well enough to know that you won't stay lying down. You'll be up trying to do it all."

"Hi, Mrs. Mannion," Jolene broke into the conversation. "You don't have to worry. I'll make sure she stays put."

"I'm sure you would, dear," Sarah Mannion said in her velvet bulldozer voice, the same one she'd used for years to maintain order with a school full of teenagers. "But Brianna would love a chance to see you. Everyone was so busy at the wedding, the two of you didn't get much time to talk.

"It's not that big a crowd. Just family. Quinn's closing the pub that day, but unfortunately, Thanksgiving isn't the calmest of days for some families and there's more drinking, so Aiden will be on duty. Then, of course, Brianna and Seth, and his parents, Caroline and Ben, my mother and father, John and me, and John's brother Michael, who'll be joining us for the first time in years, which is a treat—"

"We'll come," Jolene said quickly before her mother

could reject the invitation. "What can we bring?" She was thinking along the lines of wine or a veggie plate from the market.

"Just yourselves," Sarah responded.

"We insist," Gloria said, ignoring her daughter's sharp look. "I'll bring my cranberry apple pie. And Jolene would love to bring a side dish."

Jolene felt a stab of panic. Although potatoes were a vegetable, she doubted a bag of chips counted as a side dish.

"Wonderful. We'll count on you coming. We'll eat at three, so why don't you plan to show up anytime after noon? That way we'll have plenty of time for chatting while the turkey's roasting. And don't worry, Caroline and Ben, and John and I will be the only ones there who'll know about your heath situation, so it won't become part of the conversation."

"Thanks and we'll see you then," Jolene said, holding up her hand before her mother could try another objection. She hit the phone icon on the steering wheel, ending the call.

"You did that because she said Michael will be there," Gloria accused. "And put me in a box because if I'd refused after you'd accepted, I'd sound rude."

"I cannot lie. I absolutely did accept on purpose. It'll be like a first date, but you'll be surrounded by people, so you won't have to worry about keeping up your end of the conversation the way you would if you were out to dinner alone. It'll also let you see if there are any sparks."

"There is the slight problem that except for my pot roast, which would be superfluous given the roast turkey, neither of us can cook anything up to Sarah's standards." Sarah Mannion was a home cook whose fried chicken always won both county and state fair blue ribbons year after year.

"At least you can bake."

"My mother taught me to make that pie the Thanksgiving before she died. When I make it every year, I feel as if she's in the kitchen with me."

"That's lovely."

It also made Jolene realize again what her life would be like without her mother. Which had her feeling guilty for not returning home all these past years, but that was going to change. She was no longer a girl who could be taunted, bullied, drugged and assaulted. She was a kick-ass Emmy nominee who was on her way to having her own cosmetics business. Look out Paltrow and Kardashians, Jolene Wells is coming for you. But even if her business took off like a rocket, next year when her mother made that pie, no matter where she was, or what she was doing, she'd be back in Honeymoon Harbor in the kitchen with her. And every Thanksgiving after that.

"I'll text Shelby and have her ask her fiancé for a side dish recipe that I can make without risking poisoning everyone."

"Isn't he the one who owns the restaurant you took me to last time I visited?"

"That's him."

Her mother shot her a skeptical look. "There was nothing on that menu either of us could make. I didn't even know what half of it was."

"I know. He could probably be an Iron Chef if he wanted. But he likes me. And he'll come up with something I can handle because he loves Shelby, who's my best friend, and will do anything to make her happy."

"We can only hope," Gloria said, as Jolene hit the

phone symbol again on the steering wheel and called Shelby, explaining her situation.

They were just turning onto Lighthouse Lane when Shelby texted back a recipe she swore Ètienne said had sold like hotcakes when he'd had a food truck, saving his money to open Epicure.

"That was fast," Gloria said, after the phone read the text.

"It was. Maybe we should go shopping for the ingredients for it and the pie now. Just in case life gets complicated."

"See, you think my test is going to go badly, too."

"No. I truly don't. But it's good to be prepared and by shopping ahead of time we'll miss the Thanksgiving eve market wars."

"That's a treacherous day at the market," Gloria agreed. "I remember one time Helen Jackson and Ruth Hunsaker nearly got in a hair-pulling battle over the last can of cranberry sauce."

"Perhaps we should buy double the ingredients for the cheesy corn in case I screw it up the first time."

"Like a test run."

"Exactly." Jolene nodded. "And if it works out, we can eat it for dinner."

"I always knew I'd raised a brilliant daughter," Gloria said as Jolene turned the car around and headed toward Marshall's Market.

"ÈTIENNE SAID THAT he used grilled corn," Jolene said reading from the text again. "But that I can get away with canned." She put four cans into the cart that already held a box of panko bread crumbs, bacon and three different types of cheeses.

"Good. Since this isn't exactly grilling weather."

"I still need garlic and a jalapeño. What do you need for the pie?"

"I already have the flour, salt and butter at home. So, I only need four different kinds of apples and a bag of frozen cranberries. The frozen foods are just two aisles over so we might as well get them first."

"Okay. Where's the wine?"

"The far wall."

"We'll pick up two bottles. One for us and one to take."

"You can never have enough wine at a dinner party," Gloria agreed. "And it just may give me enough courage to speak to Michael."

"Surely you two speak when you're cutting his hair."

"True. But that's professional. As you pointed out, this will be almost like a date." Her eyes widened. "Oh, my God. What if he thinks it's a fixup?"

"It's a family dinner." Jolene wasn't about to admit that she'd had the same conversations with Shelby over the years about ways to fix each other up for test meetings without appearing too obvious.

That hadn't been a problem in high school, given that Jolene had never dated. Except for Aiden. And those weren't exactly dates, but secret rendezvous. Which, at the time seemed wonderfully romantic, like a young noblewoman sneaking out of the family country house for a tryst with the stable master in a romance novel. Though, to be more accurate, given the social structure of Honeymoon Harbor, Aiden would've been a duke, and she'd have been a scullery maid.

She'd just turned the corner at the frozen food aisle when she nearly ran into the man she'd been imagining in his bedchamber—his royal blue silk Regency period dressing gown open to the waist, revealing a mouthwatering ripped chest—about to ravish her. Rather than embracing Jolene in his manly arms, he was taking a stack of Hungry-Man dinners out of the freezer.

"Why, Aiden," Gloria greeted him with a warm smile. "What a coincidence! Your mother just invited us for Thanksgiving, so we're gathering up ingredients for my pie." She opened the freezer and took out a bag of cranberries. "Jolene's bringing a side dish."

He turned his attention to Jolene. "Really?" Was that skepticism she heard in his tone?

"She's using a recipe she got from a famous Los Angeles chef."

"Sounds fancy," he said, giving Jolene an accessing look.

Yes, that was definitely skepticism. What, did he think she ate out at Spago, the Chateau Marmont or Epicure with movie stars every night? She could cook. Sort of. In a pinch. Like the blue box of bright orange mac and cheese Ètienne had instructed her to never again mention in his presence. She'd gotten the feeling he wasn't kidding.

"It looks pretty easy," she admitted. "But Ètienne, he's my best friend's fiancé, who worked his way up from a food truck to an insanely popular restaurant on Melrose, assures me everyone loves it."

"Does it have bacon in it?"

"As a matter of fact, it does."

He smiled. That slow, easy smile that brought out those dimples he used to use to his advantage back in high school and made Jolene glad she was holding on to the cart handle because she could feel her knees going weak.

"Well." Her mother glanced back and forth between them. The same way she had at the hospital. "Since your mother says you won't be able to be at Thanksgiving dinner because you have to work, why don't I leave you two to catch up while I get the apples for my pie and jalapeño for the side dish? Oh, and the wine."

Jolene blew out a breath as her mother headed off with the cart. "That wasn't obvious or anything."

"If there's one thing I've learned, it's that once their kids hit a certain age, all mothers start thinking of marrying them off. And having grandchildren."

"Tell me about it," Jolene muttered. "She told me she'd be lucky to get a grandpuppy. Which, to be honest, is probably closer to the truth, given my work." And her decision to stay single like other women who'd redefined old maid spinsterhood. Like Diane Keaton. Oprah. Queen Latifah. Her brain scrambled for another example. Mother Teresa probably didn't count since she'd also remained celibate all her life.

"Brianna's taken a little heat off my brothers and me," he said. "For now. But if she and Seth don't get married and pop out a kid really soon, we'll all be back in Mom's bull's-eye."

"That's understandable from a woman brave enough to have five children herself." Jolene suddenly realized what a crowd of Mannion grandchildren that one family could produce. "Wow. If each of you were to have five children, then each of them had five..."

"Yeah. I've done the math. But I wouldn't hold my breath on any of us going that overboard. Though it would give Seth a lot of work expanding Mom and Dad's farmhouse for family sleepovers."

Jolene glanced down at the six-pack of his Winter Blizzard Brew, a nonalcoholic beer from his brother Quinn's microbrewery, and the boxes of frozen meals.

"FYI," he said. "Despite how this looks, I do eat real

food. In fact, Luca has a pepperoni and sausage pizza waiting for me when I finish up here."

"Your meal choice suggests you're not staying at the farm." She couldn't see anything in that cart his farm-to-table mother would approve of. Even Sarah Mannion's famed fried chicken was sourced from a local organic farmer. She did wonder about the non-alcoholic beer.

"As much as I love my family, that's more closeness than I'd care to have. I did spend some time at the coast house when I first got back."

Jolene had been to the coast house once, right before their breakup. They'd each told their parents the clichéd teenage lie that they were staying with friends, and had escaped for an overnight to the coast. It was a beautiful house set on the cliff overlooking the sea. Even then, they hadn't really done anything but some petting with their tops off.

In fact, he'd given her the master bedroom and slept in his room down the hall. To avoid temptation, he'd said at the time. Part of her had been relieved. Another part had wanted to make love with Aiden Mannion so badly, she could practically feel her hormones shouting at her to just get out of bed and walk down that hall.

"Do you think they knew about us back then?" she asked. It was one thing to avoid the topic at the wedding. Another for it to be between them if they were going to keep running into each other, which was inevitable in a small town.

"I thought we were being brilliantly surreptitious at the time, but yeah, looking back, my mom, at least, probably suspected, since she spent all day at the school, and I swear had eyes in the back of her head because no one ever got away with anything. So she probably would've told your mom. As for Dad, he can be typically guy-clueless about that kind of thing, so who knows?

"This is a tough place to keep secrets," he said what she'd learned long ago. "Seth told me he'd thought he and Brianna were keeping their relationship under wraps until he discovered that nearly half the town knew about them before they went public. And not casting any shade, but you made it even more obvious something was going on between us when you went out of your way to ignore me at Kylee and Mai's wedding."

"You ignored me first."

"Me?" he shot back, with what appeared to be honest, baffled male frustration. Dark curls her fingers literally itched to touch fell over his forehead when he shook his head. "Hell, Jolene. I was only following your lead. I'm not the kind of guy who pushes myself on a woman who's throwing out a don't-you-dare-to-get-within-a-hundred-yards-of-me vibe."

"Okay." Jolene blew out a long breath. "Maybe I *was* trying to avoid you." There'd been no *maybe* about it, and they both knew it. "But not because I was mad about you breaking up with me, but because I was embarrassed."

"Seriously? Not about that night?"

"This isn't any place to talk about that night," she hissed as Madison Drew, who had supposedly been being publicly "cozy" with Aiden that day that had changed her life, paused down the aisle at the ice cream section.

From the toddlers seated in the cart, it appeared that she, at least, had provided her mother with grandkids. Jolene remembered Madison had always had to be better than anyone else. That she'd somewhat accomplished that with twins, had some small, snarky (and obvious insane) part of Jolene, who remembered the bullying all too well, wanting to give her own mother triplets, just to one-up Madison.

"I agree this isn't the place. But don't you think you should just let it go after all this time?" His face was nearly as serious as she vaguely remembered it being that night. "Believe me, I've learned that some stuff will eat away at you if you hold on too long."

She glanced over at Madison, who wasn't even trying to pretend she wasn't watching them. Where was her mother with those damn apples?

"I hardly ever think about it. Except..."

No. She was about to mention those nightmares, that too often turned into erotic dreams with Aiden, like Hugh Jackman's Wolverine but without the claws, arriving to save the day. Which was weird because she hated the damsel in distress romance trope. Then again, she had been in serious distress, and he had saved her day. Or more specifically night.

"Except when you're here in Honeymoon Harbor," he finished for her. "That's why you've always flown your mom down to California for visits instead of coming home."

"How did you know that? If you've only recently been back yourself?"

"I always came home for Thanksgiving or Christmas. Except when I was in Afghanistan. I think Seth may have mentioned you never coming back."

"Proving yet again that guys gossip, too."

"It's not gossip. It's sharing information."

Information about her. Why? Had Seth volunteered the information? Or had Aiden asked? And didn't that send her right back to high school? Next she'd be passing a note to Brianna to ask Seth to ask Aiden if he liked her.

"It's not all that easy being back," she admitted, remembering that he'd been the only person in town she could talk with. She hadn't shared the cruel conjectures about what might have been going on in that trailer with her mother, because she hadn't wanted to hurt her. She'd later realized Gloria had undoubtedly known about the gossip for years. "Especially with you here, too."

"It'll only be hard if you make it that way. And my vote is for moving on, since I'm not going anywhere and you said you're staying until New Year's."

"Or longer, if Mom… Well, I'm trying not to go down a scary road I don't even know might be there."

"I know that feeling. But here's the thing, we need to talk."

"I really don't want to relive that night with you."

"Not that night. Well, maybe some of it. But the other thing that happened."

"When you stood me up for the prom?" And didn't that sound silly all these years later? But it was going to be the first time they'd have gone public, and when the night had gotten later and he still hadn't shown up at the trailer, she'd become convinced that he hadn't wanted to be seen with her.

"Because I got arrested."

"For stealing that beer. Then the next day you broke up with me. But we were just kids. And now we're not. Like you said, I've moved on. I don't ever think about that. In fact, before you brought it up, I'd forgotten all about you dumping me." *Liar, liar, pants on fire.*

"We need to talk," he repeated. "Clear the air. Because life doesn't tell you your end date ahead of time."

"Talking about end dates isn't very helpful when my mother's possibly facing a cancer diagnosis."

"Yeah, okay, so that wasn't my best example." He dragged his hands through those curls again. "But the Marines and the cops have taught me that life can be cut short and sometimes you don't get a chance to say the things you've been wanting to say for a long time."

And suddenly, out of nowhere, that wickedly familiar smile flashed its dimples. But as charming as it was, it didn't reach his eyes. "You wouldn't refuse me a chance to try to explain and grovel for past misdeeds, would you?"

"You don't have anything to grovel for." Teenagers tended to have relations that lasted as long as spindrift blown from the crest of a wave. They broke up every day. So did adults, as she and Chad proved.

"Sweetheart, we couldn't begin to count the ways." A bit of the light she remembered so vividly appeared in his eyes like storm lighting on the water. Hot, dangerous and gone in seconds. Jolene also assured herself that *sweetheart* hadn't been a true term of endearment, but something guys said automatically.

"All right." She threw up her hands. "You're probably right. Because it's obvious we've both moved on." She wondered if he was seeing, aka having hot sex, with anyone, but wouldn't her mother have mentioned that? "But Mom's getting the news about her ultrasound tomorrow. I can't even think of anything else until at least after that."

"I totally get that." He handed her his phone. "Put in your number. And, unless you think I'm going to harass you with dick pics—"

"Don't even *say* that." She'd already had more than her share of those. So many men in Hollywood, it seemed, were prone to want to share their junk. That was one of the reasons she'd signed that petition. Then, surprising herself by laughing at the idea of Aiden, of all people doing such a repulsive thing, exchanged phones.

"See," he said as their fingers touched, sending off such a shower of sparks and heat she was surprised didn't set off the store fire detector sprinklers. "We still have it. Whatever the hell it is."

"I really have to go," she said.

"Okay. And although your mom will probably call mine after her doctor's report, give me a call or text and let me know how you're both doing. Because I care."

It couldn't be this easy, Jolene thought as she walked away, unable to resist pausing in front of the frozen vegetables. While she pretended to ponder whether to get the mixed carrots and peas or stir-fry veggies, Madison had apparently finally decided on her ice cream and steered her cart directly to Aiden. The way she was looking up at him through her lashes as she avidly chatted away, seemed inappropriate for a mother of twin toddlers.

"Hussy," her mother said, who'd just returned as Madison brushed his arm with the side of her breast as she leaned into the freezer to retrieve a box of Lean Cuisine spring rolls. Gloria dumped a plastic bag of apples and another with jalapeños into the cart. "I've never liked her."

Neither had Jolene. Not only had Madison Drew led the mean girls' taunts, she'd been the one to declare who was *in* and who was *out*. During those years the only two people who'd sit with Jolene at the cafeteria had been Brianna, who might have only been doing it because her goal in life seemed to make everyone feel comfortable, and Kylee, who still hadn't come out of the closet, which made her an outsider. Jolene had always considered Kylee fabulously talented and ridiculously gorgeous in a Ginger Spice way, but individuality wasn't exactly embraced in high school.

"Isn't she married?" For some reason, the editor of the alumni newsletter had unearthed Jolene's email address after she'd gotten nominated for the Emmy and had sent her a copy. Although the last thing she wanted to think about were her high school days, curiosity about how people's lives had turned out had her occasionally skimming it. Madison's twins had been big news. Along with the fact that she had—natch—gotten down to her pre-birth size two in just six weeks.

"She is. She married Thane Covington. You know, his family owns that real estate company and he was only around in the summer because he went to prep school back East somewhere. Until then, she'd been working as a teller in the Mannions' bank. But marriage doesn't always stop people from fooling around. And no," she tacked on as Jolene's eyes narrowed with a question, "your father, for all his flaws, never ran around on me. He had incredibly poor judgment and not the best group of friends, but he was always faithful."

"I'm glad. Aiden would never hook up with a married woman." She recalled him telling her about being hit on by a housewife whose lawn he'd mowed one summer.

"Of course he wouldn't. He was never the bad boy he wanted everyone to think he was. Back then he rebelled against what everyone expected him to be because of John being mayor. These days, they'd just call it acting out."

They made their way to the checkout stand, where Winnie Cunningham, who'd been checking out Honeymoon Harbor customers in the market for as long as Jolene could remember, was still behind the register.

"Why, look who's back home," she said, looking at Jolene over the top of her trifocals while not stopping scanning the items. "I'm so sorry about your breakup."

"Thank you." Jolene was getting tired of telling people she really didn't mind. She also wondered what the reaction would be if she told the absolute truth. That'd he'd been a bust in bed.

"You're lucky to be rid of that bum who was cheating on you with that actress. Is it true you might be pregnant?" She skimmed a look over Jolene, who had an urge to suck in her stomach.

Damn. Perhaps she should have checked more of those texts. "Absolutely not."

"I told Hazel—you remember, hon, she waited tables at the diner. Still does for that matter. Anyway, after she read it in *The National Enquirer*, I told her that was fake news probably made up so the story would read more sensational. Like that Bat Boy years ago. Because if your mama was going to be a grandmother, she would've been shouting the good news from the rooftops, wouldn't you, Gloria?"

"I wouldn't go quite that far," her mother said, exchanging an *I'm sorry* look with Jolene. "But my daughter would have told me, so I can attest to the fact that she's definitely not pregnant."

"I knew that," Winnie said. "I swear, I, for one, am never going to go to another of either of those two's movies. In fact, I was going to hide all the magazines with you on the cover, but Mildred, who still owns the place, though I've been trying to buy it from her for a decade, insisted it stay up in front where everyone could see it. Given that you're a hometown girl and all, it's been selling like crazy. Though some people just read it in line and put it back, which annoys me no end."

As Winnie scanned in the cheeses, Jolene glanced at the rack and saw her photo on a tabloid magazine in a little circle below the large one of Chad and Tiffany showing off her iceberg ring. The tagline beneath the main photo promised the inside scoop. The one below her, caught wearing her oldest sweater and leggings, with her hair up in a messy bun, simply shouted out her name and JILTED!

"We were already separated," she hedged. It was almost the truth. They would have been if they'd stayed together long enough for her to break up with him. "It's not easy keeping up long-distance relationships."

"I've been down that road, honey pie," Winnie said sympathetically. "My husband, Earl, was a long-haul trucker. Even after he keeled over from a heart attack after a run to Fargo, there were times I'd almost forgotten he'd died, I was so used to being alone."

Not knowing what to say to that, Jolene said nothing, but with that Spidey supersensitivity she'd always had toward Aiden, she felt him come up behind her in line.

"But Earl certainly had nice turnout at the memorial service," her mother helpfully filled the small silence.

"That he did," Winnie agreed. "The man never met a stranger."

She began bagging the groceries into the canvas bags Jolene always kept in the trunk of her car. "We were all real proud when you got nominated for an Emmy. Now *that* should have been on the cover of *People*."

"I didn't win."

"Burke didn't win the Super Bowl last year, either," Aiden volunteered from behind her. "But that doesn't mean that he shouldn't be proud of playing a damn good season."

"That's exactly what I told her," Gloria said. "I always knew my girl was destined for great things. Attending that awards ceremony was one of the highpoints of my life. Second only to giving birth to my girl." She shot a dismissive glance at Madison, who'd joined the checkout line. "All the girls at the salon had a party watching the show stream online. I was told everyone booed when that other makeup person won. Who needs another Tudor movie anyway?"

Jolene laughed, since it was exactly what she'd thought. "I love you, Mom."

"Well, isn't that handy, since I love you, too, daughter." Gloria glanced over at Aiden. "You have a good evening, Aiden, and maybe we'll see you on Thanksgiving if you have time to drop by the farm for a piece of my cranberry apple pie."

She swept another quick glance over at Madison, whose twins were beginning to squirm and scream to get out of the cart. "Poor babies," she said. "They're probably hungry. Best you get them home real quick."

Then she smiled at Aiden. "And, of course, we'll make sure to save you some of Jolene's famous celebrity chef's cheesy corn and bacon. After all, a man can't live on frozen dinners all the time."

That said, ignoring the way Jolene rolled her eyes, she swept regally out of the store like the dowager countess leaving Downton Abbey.

"Mom," Jolene complained as she pushed the cart across the parking lot to the car. "Stop trying to set me up with Aiden. Because it isn't going to happen."

"Fair's fair," Gloria said with a toss of her hair, looking like a woman who'd fear nothing. Like the woman

Jolene had always known. "After all, the only reason we're going to the Mannion farm for dinner is that you accepted in order to throw me together with Michael."

Jolene wasn't going to deny it. "Great," she said dryly. "Maybe we can double date."

Either her mother chose to ignore her sarcasm, or it flew right over her head. "Now, isn't that something to think about?"

Jolene flatly refused to look back to see if Madison had managed to catch up with Aiden as they left the store. Even knowing that he wouldn't be tempted to sleep with the married mother of two toddlers didn't prevent an uncomfortable prick of jealousy. Especially since she remembered them being a couple for a week or two junior year.

Madison had told everyone that she'd broken up with him because he wanted her to do things she just wasn't prepared to do. Jolene hadn't believed that for a minute, since everyone knew she'd already slept with Thane, who'd been playing the field in those days. But if Aiden had been the one to call their short-lived high school romance off, he wasn't talking. That was another problem with coming home. You couldn't seem to escape high school.

Especially when she was with Aiden. Even when he'd stopped her for speeding, she'd been too aware of those neon blue eyes. And the mouth that had once had the power to shoot sparks straight from her lips to her breasts, then down to her parts that would begin to hum.

He was right. Whatever they'd had was still there. She'd thought at the time it had been love. Had desperately *wanted* it to be love. But just as he'd learned that life could be short—which had her wondering about if Aiden had ever killed anyone, or known anyone who'd been killed—she'd learned that while happily-ever-afters were wonderful to read about, if they weren't impossible (Kylee and Mia, and Brianna and Seth, certainly looked as if they'd be forever), they were definitely elusive. And as ethereal as sea foam.

CHAPTER FOURTEEN

"YOU ARE SO TOAST," Bodhi said as they watched the Miata leave the parking lot.

"I don't know what you're talking about."

"I'm talking about that connection thing. It's not just the sex stuff, which, from the vibes must be off the chart—"

"I wouldn't know."

"Seriously? How could you resist that when you were seventeen?"

"There were reasons, okay? Complicated reasons." And now there were new ones.

"She's the real deal, isn't she?"

"Hell, I don't know." Instead of taking the groceries straight home to put them in the freezer, he headed toward Cops and Coffee. The last thing he needed after seeing Jolene was more caffeine and sugar, but it beat picking up a bottle of Jack Daniel's. "It's complicated."

"Love's complicated."

Aidan gave him a side-eye. "Says the guy for whom two weeks was a long-term commitment."

"I preferred to compartmentalize," Bodhi said. "I saved the complications for work. In my personal life I preferred to just go with the flow."

And he had. Until work and his personal life had come crashing together like a tsunami, and he'd gotten caught in a riptide.

"Is there anything you wish you'd said or done before..."

"I took that bullet that killed me?"

"Yeah."

It occurred to Aiden that he wasn't exactly the one to lecture Jolene about letting things go. But while he'd probably never be able to erase that night when they'd been ambushed and outgunned, he'd climbed out of the pit he'd been in and gotten himself on a path. Was it the path he'd planned? Hell, no. But, to be honest, while the Marines had taught him some much-needed discipline and the ability to plan ahead and execute that plan, he'd pretty much gone with the flow, same as Bodhi.

The judge had sent him off to the military, which wouldn't have been his first choice back then. Then, after basic training, because apparently he had twenty-fifteen vision, they'd sent him to sniper school. Then on to Afghanistan. Again, definitely not his first choice. If someone had asked him to make a list of preferred assignments, Hawaii would've hit the top of the list, followed by California, then Florida. Bodhi had always joked that his mistake was hoping for a beachfront base, while not specifying that he'd prefer an ocean to go along with the miles of sand he'd landed in.

Then, when he was about to leave the military and return to civilian life, he got an email from his former instructor from sniper school who'd ended up at the LAPD. They were looking for experienced snipers for their SWAT teams, and hey, since that was what he'd learned to do, why not?

He hadn't enjoyed the police sniper gig because, in one way, it was like being back in the military, but there was a difference. In a war zone, you and your spotter could walk miles, searching out the enemy like a pair of lions stalking prey. Or could lie, concealed, for hours, even days, looking for a target. A goat herder taking a grenade out of a burlap bag as he approached a military unit, a guy planting an IED on a roadway. War was war, it sucked, but the plan was for you to take out the bad guys before they killed you. Or that team of Marines you were scouting for.

One man; one shot; one kill. But that single shot was taken a long distance away in order not to risk giving away your presence.

Being a police sniper turned out to be very different because his battleground was located within normal society. A neighborhood of tidy houses, outside a nightclub or, in the worst-case scenario—that thank the baby Jesus he'd never had to face—a school. The upside was that you could save a hostage, or a classroom of kindergartners. The downside was that after you'd taken the shot, killed another human in such an intimate way (because unlike in the military, a police sniper wanted to get as close as possible), once the threat was neutralized and you were debriefed, you were expected to act like a normal guy. Go back to your family if you had one (because snipers had one of the highest percentage of divorces), or stop by a rib joint for takeout on your way to your apartment, where you lived alone. Or, more often, to a cop bar, where even then you put off a vibe most of the other guys stayed clear of.

The details of the job, and the pressure it put on you, definitely wasn't something you wanted to share with your wife and kids, or even your priest. Not that Aiden, whose time as an altar boy had been very short-lived, had attended church in years.

So, realizing that he was walking a very dangerous razor's edge, he'd wandered through a few other assignments and squads, liking some better than others, and had been headed toward trying to help kids stay out of trouble when all hell broke loose, and his Marine sniper ability to hit a target at a thousand-plus yards hadn't been worth squat in a street fight.

Although there'd been the mandatory requirement to talk to a police psychologist (after Internal Affairs had gotten through grilling him), Aiden didn't want to share private feelings with someone who could never know where he was coming from. Who'd never killed anyone. Probably never seen anyone die. Especially someone who'd become as close as your own brothers.

"You're doing it again," Bodhi broke into his thoughts.

"What?"

"Wallowing in misplaced guilt. It wasn't on you, bro. It was just my time. So, why don't we talk about how you're going nail that hot curvy redhead. Who, by the way, looks like she should be painted on the side of a WWII bomber."

Aiden had never made the connection before, but Jolene did look like an old-time pinup girl. And not just because she was still dressing in those vintage clothes she wore in high school. Back then, she'd worn them to avoid having to wear the clothes wealthier parents had donated to the thrift shop. Clothes that had drawn such derision from mean girls like Madison, who'd felt the need to tell the other kids that they'd once owned them and tired of them.

He never told anyone, but that was the main reason he'd broken up with Madison. That and the fact that she'd kept pushing to have sex, and while he might not have been all that wise of the ways of the world, he'd recognized that she wasn't above getting pregnant on purpose.

Which would've ended with him becoming a teenage father. Hell, ending up fighting terrorists in Afghanistan had been easier than he'd figured parenthood would be.

"If you want to talk about her, I'm here to listen," Bodhi offered. "And by the way, if you do go to bed with her, you don't have to worry. I know how to be discreet."

"We're not talking about her," Aiden said. "And while I've never known you to have an ounce of anything resembling discretion, thanks for giving me some privacy in my personal life." Not that he had much of one, other than making sure he at least dropped by his mother's Thanksgiving dinner. He'd missed too many while in LA and although she'd never complained, he knew she'd prefer to have her entire family seated around the table.

"I can keep secrets," Bodhi argued.

"Name one," Aiden said as he pulled into the coffee shop parking lot.

"If I told, then I'd prove your point about my lack of discretion."

Did he have to argue every damn thing? "I'm nearly as removed from my old life as you are. So, who am I going to tell?"

"Good point. Okay. But you might want to wait until after you get your caffeine and sugar hit to hear it."

"That bad?"

"Worse."

"Great." Aiden opened the door. "Just effing great," he said. It wasn't often that he'd seen his partner serious. The fact that he was now looking as serious as he had when they went out on that last case wasn't encouraging.

After getting a triple shot of espresso in a twenty-ounce cup and a glazed doughnut, they were back in the SUV.

Aiden took a long drink, felt the caffeine jolt his system and began to understand why AA meetings reportedly went through gallons of coffee. "So. Let's hear your proof of discretion."

"Okay… Here goes… I may or may not have been sleeping with the wife of the deputy chief of Counter-Terrorism and Special Operations."

That had been Aiden and Bodhi's unit. "The hell you were."

"Says the saint and moral conscience of the unit."

"I'm no saint." He took a hard bite of doughnut, cracking the sugar glaze all over the front seat. There was just enough rebel remaining in Aiden to resent that label. "Ask anyone in town and they'll tell you I was Honeymoon Harbor's sinner."

"*Was* being the operative word. And it's been my experience that reformed sinners make the most obnoxious saints."

Aiden shot him a hard look. "I am not obnoxious."

"You're not that bad, I guess," Bodhi allowed. "Though you can't deny that you played strictly by the book."

"That's the whole idea of a book in the first place. Once you start sliding on the rules in order to make a bust, you land on a slippery slope and pretty soon you can turn into one of those rogue cops who give us all a bad name. And getting back to the topic of you and the DC's wife, is the reason you didn't tell me was because you couldn't trust me not to turn you into IAD?"

Considering whom Bodhi had recklessly chosen to sleep with, that would've had Internal Affairs going straight to his superior. Who'd just happened to be the guy whose wife was playing around with Bodhi. Yeah, that would've gone well.

"I may have been a stickler for rules, but I never would've turned you in. But I would definitely have told you that you were a damn fool for thinking with the wrong head. Hell, stuff like that could cost you your job. Or worse yet, get you killed."

A thought occurred to Aiden. One so outrageous, he brushed it off as impossible. "How did you meet her, anyway?"

"For some reason she'd noticed me at one of the press conferences where the DC was blowing his own horn about how his unit was working hand in hand with the feds to keep the homeland safe from terrorists. While we rank and file were required to stand there at attention."

"Technically he had us standing at parade rest," Aiden corrected. "Which isn't relevant to this conversation. Please tell me you weren't dumb enough to hit on her afterward in front of him?"

"Of course not. She sort of smiled in my direction, so it seemed the only polite thing to do was smile back, and I figured that was it… You know…a moment."

"So, how did you get from this *moment* to sex?"

"About a week later, I was surfing one evening at Hermosa Beach. By the pier. She later told me that was a beach she liked to run on. Turned out she was a lawyer in Century City."

"That's a half an hour from the beach. Then, since the deputy chief lives in the Valley, which is, on a good traffic day—which doesn't exist in LA—another hour home from Hermosa Beach. My bet is that she was stalking you."

"Do you trust anyone?"

Aiden had to think about that for a moment. "My mom and dad. My brothers and sister. And Seth. And you, though it appears you did turn out to have a loose acquaintance with the truth."

"If you'd asked, I would've told," Bodhi said. "And yeah, her stalking me sort of occurred to me, too, since I hung out there a lot and would have definitely remembered seeing her. Anyway, I'd been working on aerials and was pretty much through for the day, when I came onto the beach and there she was."

"Nice coincidence," Aiden said dryly.

"Whatever." Bodhi shrugged. "We talked a bit, then she asked me if I wanted to have a drink at the beach dive bar. Since, like you said, the DC lives in the Valley, and instead of that dark, proper gray lawyer suit she'd worn that day of the press conference, she was wearing short shorts, a tank top and running shoes, with her hair in a ponytail through the back of a Dodgers ball cap, so she didn't stand out enough to ever be recognized. And hell, I was a regular around there anyway, so people were used to seeing me with a new woman."

"It was still damn risky."

"Yeah," Bodhi allowed. "That was admittedly part of the appeal in the beginning. And you might be right about thinking with the wrong head, but hell, Aiden, you should've seen her legs. They were this amazing golden tan, not the sprayed-on Cheetos stuff, and they went on for a mile."

"When was this?"

"It started about six weeks before we were sent out to do that gun deal. And ended when I took that bullet. And died… Sort of."

"Six weeks? Wasn't that a record for you?" Aiden had never known Bodhi to last past a second date.

"She was going to leave her husband."

"I suspect that's what most cheating spouses say."

"No, I believed her. She told me things had been bad for a long time and had gotten physical. She texted me a picture of her with a black eye and bruises on her arms and shoulders. I wanted to go confront the bastard there and then, the hell with the fucking job, but she begged me to stay away because it would only make her situation worse.

"She was going to wait until the next morning when he went to work, then call the police and have the locks changed on the house."

"And she sent you that when?" Aiden had always been a stickler for timelines and he was getting a bad gut feeling about this one.

"The night before we were sent out on that guns for drugs trade."

"When we walked into an ambush." Another coincidence. Aiden didn't like coincidences. Hell, he didn't believe in them. Except, he allowed, maybe Jolene coming back to Honeymoon Harbor so shortly after him. "And you were killed." Fury, more ice-cold than hot, surged through his veins.

"Yeah. Like I said, sort of killed, since part of me seems to be still around. But that would be my take on it," Bodhi said with apparently far less anger than Aiden was experiencing.

Maybe being dead gave you a more pragmatic view of life? Or maybe because you couldn't do anything, the need for revenge wasn't as strong?

"There's more."

"Of course there is."

"Six weeks after that, she drowned. Her body was found in the ocean not far from the Hermosa Beach pier.

At night. Dr. Denise, the coroner who drew the case, declared the death undetermined. Since there was salt water in her lungs, but she wasn't dressed for swimming, there was some conjecture that she may have been hit by a sneaker wave. Her husband said she'd been drinking at dinner, which guests confirmed, but her blood alcohol level wasn't enough to have her going down to the tideline."

"Why not?"

"Because it turned out she really did run every day, just never on the beach. She confessed that she'd done that only to meet me, because she was afraid of the water. Even in the daytime. There was a full moon that night, but she still never would've been out there that close to the tide on her own."

Aiden had already left LA by then. But, that didn't mean that he'd ever stop being a cop. Even now that he was a small-town one.

"Interesting timing."

"Yeah. It was a helluva coincidence," Bodhi said, his tone heavy with sarcasm.

"Where was the DC at the time?"

"At home."

"Alone?"

"Of course. He did admit they'd had an argument because he hadn't made it home for a dinner party. He said he called her from the station during the dinner to tell her he was caught up in an operation and couldn't get away.

"Dinner guests remembered the call. He said he came home late, after everyone had left, she was furious, threw a crystal vase with flowers that had been the dining table centerpiece, then stormed out. He figured she'd drive around and cool off like she did most other times. According to him, they'd been fighting a lot because of his extra hours on the Homeland Security deal since his promotion. He told the investigating detectives that she had a helluva temper, tended to get overemotional and had threatened suicide more than once. But he figured those were just threats to get him to cut back on his hours."

"Did you ever notice a temper? Did she seem suicidal, or ever mention thoughts of taking her life?"

"No. She wasn't happy in her situation, but she'd never mentioned suicide and she'd certainly never shown any indication of being a risk. In fact, the last time we talked, she was determined to leave and was looking forward to her new life...

"And granted, if I were interrogating me, I'd point out that ours wasn't exactly a domestic situation, so we hadn't had that that much reason to argue—"

"Unless she'd been planning to stay with her husband. Who outranked you, so made more bucks. A fact that could have made him the more attractive choice to stay with, while you were younger, better-looking and more fun to play around with as the guy she kept on the side."

"Yeah. Since investigations always start with the husband and/or boyfriend, under normal circumstances, I'd have been a person of interest, if I hadn't already been out of the picture by then. And for the record, she didn't care about money or position. She'd wanted to leave because of the abuse. I told you about the bruises."

"What did the coroner's report say about them?"

"That she could have gotten them by her body hitting the pier or rocks. She was wrapped in some kelp. But like I said, she was looking ahead. We were planning on making it permanent."

He turned, looking out the window at the harbor where a white-and-green ferry was chugging toward the dock. "I loved her, Aiden. I'd been through enough hookups to know this was the real thing. And I know it was real for her, too. I also suspect that us falling in love might have been the impetus for her getting up the nerve to leave. So, that puts her death on me."

Aiden was about to point out that Bodhi hadn't been responsible. Maybe he'd been part of the reason she'd upped her timeline, but the simple fact was that if she hadn't left, her husband could well have killed her. Aiden suspected he had. Women had also been known to be killed after getting an order of protection, something he was determined not to allow to happen to Amanda Barrow on his watch.

No longer hungry, he rolled down the window far enough to toss out the rest of the doughnut that the seagulls—who'd been flying hopefully over the harbor, waiting for ferry to churn up fish—immediately attacked. As the noisy birds began fighting over the sugary fried dough, Aiden raised the window again. "And you never told me anything about all this back then, why?"

"Like I said, I knew you'd warn me about being crazy, and I didn't want to get in an argument about it because I wasn't going to quit her. I figured, once we moved in together, I'd probably get kicked off the team—"

"You think?" Aiden's tone was as dry as the sand on Hermosa Beach. "But you could have told me afterward. When you showed up here."

"I was planning to. When the right time came along. But at first you were so fucked up, I didn't want to risk you running down to LA to confront the DC, avenge my death like the straight-arrow guy you are, and get yourself killed."

"That wouldn't have happened. Because I'd have fucking killed him first."

Aiden had killed before. Twice in the line of duty as a Marine, then once as a sniper during hostage situation, to save a life. And again, that night he and Bodhi had been ambushed he'd blasted away at the bad guys in an attempt partner and him from being killed.

But, although he didn't want to think of himself as being capable of murdering in cold blood, Bodhi had been like a brother. Sometimes even closer than his own, given what they'd gone through together. If he'd found out about this while he'd been trying to drink the state dry, with his brain all messed up, he damn well might have done exactly that.

"You just proved my point," Bodhi pointed out.

"I probably wouldn't have killed him. But I damn well would've wanted to." Aiden took another long drink of coffee and made a decision. "I'm calling a couple guys I know in LA." No way would he go back there. Not unless he wanted to do something that got him arrested. And cops never fared all that well in prison, which could've made it a suicide mission.

"Guys in IAD?"

"No. Homicide."

"What makes you think they'd be interested?"

"Solving murders is what they do. They're also former Marines, who take that Semper Fi thing as serious as all of us do. So, they'll look into the case for me. But also, because they believe in upholding the law. The idea of any cop—especially one with the power the deputy chief has—making deals with drug dealers and gunrunners would majorly piss them off.

"That's not the part of America they risked their lives for on seven combined tours. If there's anything there, they'll find it. And probably bring Internal Affairs into it. I'm going to also call the coroner, since we both know that once IAD gets started, they aren't going to tell me anything during the investigation."

"Dr. Denise always liked you. Didn't you go out with her for a while?"

"Not that long. A few weeks. Then I started noticing wedding magazines on her bedside table and she asked me if I liked kids."

"You don't?"

"Sure. It's just marriage I wasn't into. We both know cops make lousy husbands. Undercover cops have the worst divorce rate on the force because the only people we meet are scumbags and women who tend to be junkies, strippers or hookers. Or all of the above. I liked Denise too much to put either one of us through the hell that relationship could have been. Meanwhile, you need to tell me everything you know. Including how the hell you know that the DC's wife—"

"Jessica. That was her name. But I always called her Jess."

"Sorry." Of all people, Aiden, being a cop and talking with too many victim's family members should've remembered how important it was to use the names of loved ones. "But how the hell do you know that Jess supposedly drowned after you'd already been killed?"

"I haven't a clue. I guess that's another one of those eternal mysteries."

"Fuck that woo-woo stuff. We're going to break this case and bring that murderous son of a bitch down." Aiden pulled out of the parking lot.

"Now that," Bodhi said, "is worth coming back for."

CHAPTER FIFTEEN

DR. LAURENNE LANCASTER'S office was located in one of Honeymoon Harbor's big old historical Victorian homes, much like the one Brianna had restored for her bed-and-breakfast. There had obviously been a great deal of interior wall moving, allowing for a reception area and waiting room, that led to various treatment rooms that probably would have been parlors back in the day.

Although Jolene had never been invited into the older heiress's home, the office appeared to have once been a library. The doctor had kept the jury-paneled bird's-eye maple walls lined with bookshelves. Many, Jolene noticed, were medical tomes. Other volumes covered history, art and nature, including several books on the Pacific Northwest.

"Hello, Gloria." The doctor rose, came out from around the desk, paused to pump some sanitizer on her hand from a container over a sink and greeted her mother with a handshake. Then turned to Jolene. "You must be Jolene. I'm pleased to meet you. Your mother has told me so many wonderful things about you. Including how hard you work, always flying around the country or the world to work on movies and TV shows. It must be a very exciting life."

"It's one of those jobs that sounds more exciting than it is," Jolene said, grateful that her Emmy nomination hadn't come up. She had a feeling that loss might end up being the first line in her obituary. And wasn't that depressing?

"I totally understand. From some of the comments I've received at social events, I get the feeling people expect my life to be like *Grey's Anatomy*, with me having a grand love affair with Dr. McDreamy."

"He died," Gloria said. Then literally covered her mouth. "Oh, my God. I'm so sorry. I'm just really nervous and I wasn't thinking."

"It was quite a few years ago." Dr. Lancaster turned toward Jolene to explain her mother's dismay. "I'm a widow. My husband, who was an ER doctor and quite dreamy, at least in my opinion, died of sudden cardiac arrest at forty-three while running on one of the park trails."

"I'm sorry," Jolene said.

"Not as sorry as I am," Gloria murmured.

"You truly have nothing to apologize for, Gloria. I understand why you'd be nervous. So, let's get down to business. Would you like some water? Coffee? Tea?"

"Your receptionist already asked," Jolene said. "We're good." *Just impatient.*

"The ultrasound showed a cyst."

"Oh, that's positive, right?" Jolene asked. "I had a friend who had one of those and they just keep an eye on it."

"It's fairly good news," Dr. Lancaster said cautiously. "But in this case there are some concerns because it also contains some solid factions that could just be fat necrosis. Or blood cells that died." She brought out the film and pointed them out.

"There's no reason to be terribly concerned because I sent a copy to another radiologist, and he agrees with me that since the shape is very regular and the low odds of cysts being cancerous it's very encouraging at this point. But we all agree that you should have a biopsy to be sure we don't miss anything."

"Fine needle?" Jolene asked.

"You've been doing your homework," Dr. Lancaster said. "Some of my fellow doctors get annoyed when patients get medical information from the internet, because there's a great deal of misinformation out there, but I find it helpful if a patient does have some idea of what can often turn into medical speak.

"So—" she turned back to Gloria "—the needle used in a fine-needle aspiration is a very fine needle, hence its name. It's a smaller gauge than the needle normally used to draw blood."

"I hate having blood drawn," Gloria said.

"I doubt many people enjoy it. This is a simple outpatient procedure that you'll have in the same department where you had your ultrasound. Your file doesn't show you taking any herbal supplements or blood thinners. Have you avoided aspirin products like I asked you to when we made the appointment for the ultrasound?"

"I haven't taken a thing," Gloria said. "But I did have a glass of wine at Lake Crescent this weekend with my daughter."

"That sounds lovely. I envy you. My daughter's still too young for wine, but the two times we've been there we had a wonderful time. I spoke with the radiologist first thing this morning and he can fit you in for the procedure tomorrow morning at seven. How does that work for you?"

"Fine," Jolene answered for her mother. "I'll go with her."

"Good." She turned back toward Gloria. "You'll be

locally anesthetized beforehand. Like the deadening a dentist injects before filling a cavity."

"Another one of my not-favorite things," Gloria muttered.

"You won't get any argument from me on that case," the doctor said.

"Do you put me to sleep?" Gloria asked, with a swipe of her hand through her hair. "Like for surgery?"

"No, that's not necessary. It's a percutaneous procedure, medically meaning through the skin and, as I said, shouldn't be painful.

"The procedure itself usually only takes a few seconds, but you should count on being in the room from fifteen minutes to twenty minutes. If the fluid extracted is clear, the lump is most likely merely a cyst and not cancer and should deflate. Bloody or cloudy fluid can mean either a cyst that's not cancer or, very rarely, cancer. If the lump is solid, the radiologist will pull out a small pieces of tissue, as well.

"Once the biopsy is done, the area will be covered with a sterile dressing. The main advantages of FNA are that the skin doesn't have to be cut, so no stitches are needed and there's usually no scar. Also, we get a faster turnaround on the diagnosis."

"How long do we have to wait for results?" Jolene asked.

"For FNA, we should have it back in two to three days. Probably, in this case, since we're dealing with the Thanksgiving long weekend, a bit longer."

"And if it's benign, that's it?" Gloria asked hopefully.

"It's not that cut-and-dried, unfortunately. Even if the biopsy reveals normal results or if the lump is benign, the radiologist who took the sample and the pathologist who also will study them have to agree on the findings.

"While an FNA biopsy is the easiest type of biopsy

to have, it *can* miss a cancer if the finer needle misses the cancer cells. Even if an FNA does find tissue that suggests cancer, there may not be enough cancer cells to do some of the other lab tests that are needed. So, the short answer is that if the results of the FNA biopsy don't give a clear diagnosis, or if your medical team still has concerns, you might need to have a second biopsy."

The doctor folded her hands, nails neatly manicured and tipped with a clear polish, on top of the medical file. "In the unlikely event your pathology report finds cancer is present, it'll include what type you might have, and a great deal of other information, including whether it's hormone receptor positive or negative. We've learned a lot in the past years. Together you and I, and your team, and it *would* include a team, would develop a treatment plan that best suits your needs."

"This is my busy time of year," Gloria complained. "What I need is to put the biopsy off until after the New Year."

"There's no way either of us are going to be able to enjoy the holidays with this hanging over us," Jolene said. "If necessary, I can take those clients. I kept my licenses active in both states. If you need that second biopsy and you're worried that I won't do their hair up to your standards, you could come downstairs for short times and observe."

Gloria shook her head. "I don't remember you being so strong willed."

"Yes, you do. You just never minded because we almost always agreed on everything."

The doctor laughed at that. "I'm going to remember this conversation when my daughter grows up," she said.

"Are there any questions you might have that I didn't cover?"

It was hard to know what to ask with so much still in the air. Jolene and Gloria exchanged a look.

"I don't think so," Gloria said finally.

With instructions to wear a bra to the radiology clinic in order to place a cold pack inside afterward to help reduce swelling, they were on their way back to Lighthouse Lane, stopping at Luca's for some takeout fettuccini Alfredo and garlic bread Jolene ordered from her phone.

"It's a heart attack on a plate," Gloria said. "But at this point, I'm not going to worry about that."

"We're not going to worry, period," Jolene said.

"Liar," her mother returned. But with a resigned half smile.

"We've been through a lot, Mom," Jolene said. "We'll get through this, too. With flying colors."

She hoped.

AIDEN EASILY SPOTTED Jolene sitting in the waiting room outside the day surgery unit in the radiology department. Her hair was pulled back and tied at the nape of her neck with an elastic band and she hadn't bothered with makeup. Not that she needed it, but it did make those freckles across the bridge of her nose and the bones of her too-pale cheeks stand out. He'd loved her freckles. She'd hated them. Today, he figured, she probably didn't give a damn about them.

She glanced up as he entered. "What are you doing here?"

"Keeping you company. Mom was going to come, but the school had a surprise lockdown drill."

"I know. She called, but how did you know?" He

watched her process that. “Never mind. You would’ve known about the drill ahead of time. Somehow, even wearing that patch on your jacket, I have a hard time remembering you’re chief of police.”

“I had the same problem a few weeks ago.”

“And now?”

“It’s starting to feel like not such a bad fit. I brought you something.” He held the white oversize Cops and Coffee bag out to her.

She opened it, finding a cup of coffee, but instead of the doughnuts she was expecting, there were two small flowered boxes. She opened the first and drew in a breath.

“Oh, wow. You brought me chocolate croissants.”

“Yeah. I got one for you, and another for your mom when she gets out of her test.” He shrugged out of his jacket and sat down on the plastic chair beside her.

“That’s so sweet.” She took a bite. “Even though it’s probably got a bazillion calories that will go straight to my hips.”

“I’ve always liked your hips. And their sassy swing when you walk.”

“I am not sassy.”

“Yeah. You are.” He smiled and leaned over, giving her time to back away, before brushing a flyaway hair from her cheek to behind her ear. “And, for the record, I’ve always liked the rest of you, too.”

“I’d accuse you of coming on to me, but I know that even at your wickedest, you wouldn’t hit on a woman waiting for her mother to finish a breast cancer biopsy.”

“Just stating the facts, ma’am,” he said in his best Joe Friday voice. Although, admittedly he was hitting on her. She’d always proven irresistible. And it appeared time and distance hadn’t changed that. At. All.

"There are cookies in the other box. I didn't know which kind to get because there were so many, but Desiree said your mom likes the lemon-glazed madeleines, so I figured they were the safest way to go for her. And I got coconut ones for you."

"Damn you." Her eyes were misting up again. He prepared to pull out the fresh handkerchief he'd put in his jacket pocket this morning, but she resolutely blinked the moisture away. "Stop being so nice. You're making it harder and harder for me to keep my distance."

"Any special reason why you should?" he asked before taking a drink of his own cup of coffee.

"More than a few. But Mom's the main one."

"Are you referring to that same mother who tried to fix us up in the freezer section of the market?"

She blew out a breath between those lips he'd tasted last night in a damn nice dream. "You don't fight fair."

"Here's the thing," he said. "I don't want to fight, Jolene. I never did." He'd just wanted to love her. Even after he'd screwed everything up because he was young, impulsive and trying to do the right thing.

And how had that turned out? Aiden asked the question Bodhi probably would've asked if he'd been in the room. Apparently being true to his word, he was staying out of Aiden's personal business.

"And just because I hadn't seen you in years before Kylee and Mai's wedding, I never stopped thinking of you."

"Huh." She bit into the croissant and moaned like a woman on the verge of an orgasm. Then her eyes cleared enough to shoot him a skeptical look. "Brianna never told me you'd joined a monastery."

"I never claimed that. I just said that I hadn't stopped

thinking of you." He paused. If there was one thing years of being a cop had taught him, it was that were times to talk. Times for silence. Then times to go in big with the exact words that nailed your point. "Ever."

He watched her process that. First came surprise. Then cynicism. Then, an even deeper surprise as his words fully sank in. That even when he'd been with other women, there'd too often be a flash of Jolene's expressive eyes, a taste of her lips, a touch of her hands that were the smoothest he'd ever felt. Hands that he wouldn't mind feeling everywhere over his body.

She shook her head, causing more of those streaked strands to fall free of the band. "Once again, this is neither the time nor place to talk about this."

She was right. But accustomed to listening to what people didn't say, as much as they did, because omission was often the important parts, he was encouraged.

"You'll want to be with Gloria today. And tonight."

"Of course I will."

"And however long it takes for results to get back."

"I can't even think beyond the moment right now, Aiden." Her eyes darkened with concern and stress, and, he thought, the same need that appeared even stronger than it had been back when they were kids. Maybe, he thought, because now they were both adults who'd experienced enough to know that the feelings they'd shared weren't merely teenage hormones. But something deep. Something more.

"I get that." He reached out to touch her cheek again, then pulled back when she suddenly drew away and put a restraining hand on his chest.

"Wait a minute," she said. "How did you know to bring me coconut madeleines?"

"You ate three at the reception. And snuck another two into in your purse."

"Wow. You really are a cop. I cannot tell a lie, Officer," she said, even as she appeared bemused that he'd been watching her that closely. Bemused and a bit unsettled. "I shoplifted madeleines from the dessert table."

Because, although she might not have noticed, her fingers had started stroking the front of his shirt, he covered her hand with his own. And hot damn, it felt good. But only made him want a whole lot more. "Since it's only petty larceny, I could let you off the hook."

For a moment, the years spun backward, and they could have been back on the deck of his boat, struggling for control, discovering that pleasure, could indeed, also bring pain. They were, he'd thought at the time, probably the only couple in school who weren't jumping each other's bones every chance they got.

"So, no arrest?" She lowered her lashes. Paused a beat, making him wonder if, just maybe…

No. The same way he shouldn't be hitting on a woman while her mother was in getting a vital test, there was no way she'd be flirting with him.

Then she looked up at him through thick lashes nearly the same dark red as her hair. "That seems like a waste of handcuffs."

No. Make that *hell, no.* There was no way Jolene Wells would be suggesting they play policeman in this situation.

Their gazes held so long that Aiden wasn't sure if he was still breathing. Not that he cared. Though he'd rather wait to die until he'd finally gotten to make love with her.

"All done," a cheerful voice broken the tension that had strung between them like a taut electrical wire.

They both looked up at the nurse who was returning Gloria back to the waiting room.

Surprisingly, Jolene's mother didn't look like a woman who'd just had a needle shoved deep into her breast. And yes, he had looked up the procedure last night when he'd gotten his mother to tell him what the scheduled test was.

"Mom." Jolene jumped up. "That didn't take long. How are you feeling?"

"Surprisingly, just dandy," her mother said. "Everyone was so nice, though my breast is still numb right here, which feels really strange. Like it's asleep." She rubbed the spot in question, then looked past Jolene to Aiden. "Well, hello, Aiden," she said. "I'm sorry if I embarrassed you. I've never been very good with drugs. That Xanax seemed to have made me feel a little tipsy. Or floaty."

Both the nurse and Jolene caught her as she weaved like a drunk on a bender.

"There's a wheelchair just through that door," the nurse said. "It's in an alcove on the left. Would you mind getting it, Chief Mannion?"

"Sure." He helped the two women ease Gloria into the chair. "I'll take her out," he told the nurse, with whom he'd spent one hot date not watching the movie at the Rainshadow drive-in one summer night back in high school before he and Jolene had become a couple. Her smile suggested she wouldn't turn down a repeat. "As a first responder, I'm the obvious choice."

"Well, having someone on staff wheel a patient out is hospital protocol," the nurse said. "But being as you're the chief of police, and apparently a friend of the family...?" She glanced questioningly at Jolene.

"Aiden's mother is a friend," Gloria said. "And although that makes Aiden young enough to be my son, no way I'm going to turn down such a gallant offer." Looking up at him, she fluttered her eyes in an even more exaggerated way than her daughter had. The Wells women were damn dangerous, Aiden decided, wondering how Jolene's mother had managed to stay single so long after her small-time crook husband's untimely death.

"Thank you," Jolene said stiffly, with none of the flirtation she'd treated him to moments ago. She handed him the fob with the car door remote on it. "I'll just get the discharge instructions and meet you outside."

"Fast work. So, are you and Officer Hot Buns a thing?" he heard the nurse ask as he wheeled Gloria out of the waiting room.

He paused. Waiting for Jolene's response. "He's just an old friend of the family," Jolene said. "His mother was going to come, but the high school had a lockdown drill. So, she sent him."

"Meaning he's free?"

"You'd have to ask him," Jolene answered. "But I'm going back to LA after New Year's unless my mother's test shows problems. So my life's too complicated for any holiday fling."

"Good to know," the nurse—Emily, Aiden remembered—said. "I hope everything turns out okay. With her test and with her plan for Officer Hot Buns's uncle."

"How did you know about that?"

The nurse laughed. "Your mom's right. She's a Xanax lightweight. She told everyone in the room that she couldn't possibly have cancer because she'd decided to take Michael Mannion as her lover."

It was good to hear Jolene laugh. The sound was

like a clear glacial brook tumbling over rocks beneath a summer sun.

As Aiden wheeled Jolene's mother, who'd dozed off, to the Miata, he decided that he was definitely going to change Jolene's mind about a holiday fling. And more.

Gloria roused long enough for him to get her into the car. He'd just safely buckled her in when she'd dozed off again. After checking her pulse, he leaned against the car, watching the door. When Jolene finally came out, her hips weren't sassy. In fact, she reminded him of a Marine marching on a drill field.

"I don't know what we helpless little womenfolk would have done without you," she said, not offering a single word along the lines of *Gee, thanks, Officer Hot Buns*—and okay, he was vain enough to kind of like that name.

Not that she'd ever been helpless. But he wasn't the one who'd brought up the handcuffs, which he now was going to be thinking about all day, dammit.

"Officer Hot Buns?"

"You weren't supposed to hear that. But, you'll note, I wasn't the one to come up with it. The nurse, who, by the way is interested if you are, did. Though it admittedly fits. You and your brothers were always the hottest guys in town. And your uncle's not bad, either. At least Mom chose well this time." She glanced past him. "How is she?"

"Conked out. Don't worry, I checked her vitals after buckling her in. She wasn't kidding when she said she doesn't do drugs."

"Her limit's always been a glass of wine," Jolene said. "Thanks. I do appreciate the help."

"No problem. I'll follow you home."

"Why?"

"Because there's no way you're going to be able to get her up the stairs into her apartment."

"Good point. She can stay in the guesthouse today and tonight with me. That way I can keep an eye on her without her getting away and falling down those stairs."

"You still need to get her into the house. That isn't all that easy when the person you're trying to move can't stand up."

Damn. He saw the flash of embarrassment and wondered if she'd thought he was referring to her dad's drinking, which he wasn't.

"Thanks," she said again, with a slump of the shoulders that had him feeling like Officer Asshole for having caused. His only excuse for the lapse was that Jolene Wells had always messed with his mind the same way the Xanax had fogged her mother's.

He followed her to the lighthouse in his SUV, then carried the still sleeping Gloria into the bedroom, where Jolene got her undressed and into a pair of pajamas while Aiden waited in the living room of the cozy cottage.

That Jolene's mother had turned into an entrepreneur didn't really surprise him all that much. She'd proven her strength and ingenuity by supporting her family all those years first when she'd been married, then widowed.

"Thanks again," Jolene said when she returned from settling her mother in. "And about what I said...about the...you know..."

He lifted a brow. "The handcuffs?"

"I don't know what came over me. It must've been nerves. And sugar overload."

"I'm not letting you get off that easy," he said. "It

came from the same place we've always been. That's why we're going to talk about it. On Thanksgiving."

"Your mother said you have to work," she said, walking toward the door. Having been a hotshot detective until his life had blown up, he recognized that as a clue it was time for him to go.

"I'll make time. For you." Humoring her for now, he went along with her ploy, then stopped at the door and grinned down at her, flashing those God-given dimples he'd that discovered sometime before preschool seemed to work wonder on females of all ages. Who'd figure? "And that supercheesy corn-and-bacon side dish."

She shook her head. Slowly. A bit regretfully, but Aiden figured he could get past that. "It can't work..."

"You don't know that. We'll talk."

"Everyone will be there. Your family is a crowd by itself. And now adding Seth's means there isn't going to be anyplace to talk privately." Except one of the many upstairs bedrooms, that he noticed she didn't mention.

"Then we'll go somewhere. Someone always forgets something and has to go to the market. We'll volunteer." Because he couldn't resist, he run his thumb along her lower lip that was turned down in a frown. "And then we'll see where we go from here."

"If Mom's okay, I'm going back to LA right after New Year's," she reminded him.

He laughed. "If you think a few hundred miles is going to stop me this time, you're got another think coming." He bent his head. Waited a whisper away from those lips he'd been wanting to taste again. When she didn't move away, he finally touched his mouth to hers.

CHAPTER SIXTEEN

HIS LIPS WERE as silkily as thistledown. He tasted like coffee. And, as much as he kept the kiss tender, he skimmed the tip of his tongue around the arch of her upper lip, before nipping at the bottom one, the Aiden she remembered. The wild boy who was, in reality, all alpha male, but, at heart, a patient caretaker, rather than the hellion he'd tried so hard to portray. As she heard herself whimper for more, he drew back for an instant and she found herself drowning in those blue eyes that could always see inside of her, past the rumors, beyond her insecurity, her pain, deep down to her very essence, that teenage girl, who, looking back on it, had had a desperate need to be loved.

That almost X-ray vision must have served him well as a cop. She wondered if it was as unnerving for suspects as it was at this moment for her.

He blew out a breath. Lowered his forehead to hers. Surely he wasn't going to stop? But wasn't that what she wanted? *No.* Even as her head told her it would be better if they stopped now, her heart, and other vital parts that were being bombarded with lust, had different plans.

"Please, sir," she said, deciding to play it cool, even as heat flooded through all those parts. "May I have some more?"

He lifted his head. His lips quirked as those all-seeing eyes let her know that he knew she was feeling it, too. That he hadn't forgotten how they'd been together. His hands turned her around, his body pressing her up against the door, the winter wool of his uniform shirt rubbing against her achingly sensitive nipples.

He was gloriously hard. Everywhere. And she wanted to rip off that uniform, and do what she'd never allowed herself, or would have dared to do back then. Lick him all over.

A low sound escaped from deep in his throat as he captured her mouth, tangling her hair in one hand, pulling it free of the elastic tie she'd put on at the ungodly hour of five this morning, holding her head as he kissed her, deeper, harder, hotter, until her toes were curling in the high green boots she'd worn today. Knowing how flammable nail polish could be, she wouldn't have been at all surprised if her toes, polished in Unrepentantly Red, burst into flames.

His other hand was roaming everywhere, down her side, slipping between the wood door and her butt, squeezing her cheeks, pressing her up against that part of his body she'd never allowed herself to touch. But oh, how she'd looked at the way it was so temptingly cupped in those five-button Levi's he'd worn back in the day.

She twined her arms around his neck, pressing tighter against him, as if she could imprint him forever on her own body. Between the kiss and all that male hardness, being bombarded with all those feels, Jolene was quickly losing her ability to think. Like her mother, who was hopefully sleeping, she was drunk. Not on any pills, but on pure—or, impure, more likely—unadulterated lust.

Did he feel it, too? His hard body and crushing mouth certainly suggested he did. As her tongue tangled with his and her hips swayed—definitely, purposefully sassily—she wanted Aiden, for once, to lose control. And take her with him.

Since she'd left Honeymoon Harbor, there had been other men. Many equally good-looking, because you couldn't throw a stone on any LA beach without hitting some wannabe actor hunk. All with the same parts. But none had ever made her feel like Aiden made her feel. None had ever gotten past her emotional barricades enough to allow her to completely let herself go. But she knew, with a female knowledge as old as Eve, that Aiden could break through those carefully constructed walls. And take her there. To places she'd only ever gotten close to in her dreams.

She wasn't frigid. She enjoyed sex, although early on, when some, more insecure, males had blamed her for her inability to climax, leading to some very uncomfortable moments, she'd become the best actress in Los Angeles. If there'd been an Oscar for fake orgasms, she would have gone home with the gold statue every year.

But she'd always known, deep down, that it wasn't her fault. Nor theirs. Well, except for those few duds who'd spent too many years being stoned or coked up to perform. The problem had always been that they were the wrong men. They weren't Aiden Mannion.

Just as she'd come to that realization, he broke off the kiss and—no!—backed a few steps away. "Not here," he said on a voice roughened with the lust still zinging through every atom in her body. "And not now."

"Where have I heard that before?" she said.

"Damn." He dragged both hands through his black hair. "I'm sorry. I didn't mean to put us back in that place. I was just thinking about your mother." He nodded toward the short hallway to the bedroom. "Because, when I take you, and because I'm a modern guy who believes in equality, when *you* take me, I'd prefer not to have an audience."

The fog of lust was starting to lift from her brain. "That would probably be a good idea," she said, noting that he said *when*, not *if*.

As if the universe was against them, the radio on his open jacket called out a code. "Gotta go," he said. Then bending down, instead of the sorry-but-duty-calls-so-I-have-to-take-my-boner-and-and-leave, curl-her-toes-again kiss she was expecting, he dropped a light one on the tip of her nose. Her nose?

"See you Thanksgiving. I've been really hungry lately," he said as he opened the door and let a gust of cold wind in.

With a wicked bad boy wink he was gone, leaving Jolene to wonder if that had been a metaphor for something entirely different.

"You have a dirty mind," she muttered, as she went off to check on her mother.

GLORIA HAD MOSTLY come out of her Xanax fog as soon as the cold air had hit when Aiden had lifted her out of the little car. But she wanted to give him and Jolene time to talk, and yes, so what if she might, just possibly, be eavesdropping, just a bit? A daughter was still a mother's little girl whatever her age and it was a parent's duty to watch out for her.

At least that was what she conveniently chose to believe. But it was true. While Aiden and Jolene had been too young when they'd first fallen for each other, she'd known they'd had a serious relationship they'd tried to keep secret. As far as she knew, the only other person in town who hadn't missed the signs was Sarah, whose day job was watching teenagers like a hawk.

Gloria had never told Jolene that, afraid they'd do something foolish, she'd had a talk with Aiden that spring before he'd gone off to the Marines. And, from what she could tell, he'd never told, either. Looking back, she'd made a tactical mistake, but how could she have known that her daughter would have ended up suffering such dire consequences? She hadn't, after all, instructed Aiden to break up with her. Just try to hit the pause button while he was away.

But as bad as it had been, it all seemed to be working out all right. And if her health problems were the universe's way of evening things out by getting her daughter and Sarah's son back together again, well, she'd take it.

She heard the footsteps coming down the hall. The door opening. She yawned, stretched, and opened her eyes. "I'm sorry," she lied. "I've no idea what came over me." That much was true. She couldn't remember anything from the time she'd laid down on that table in the surgical room to when Aiden had carried her into the house. If she were twenty years younger, and he wasn't obviously still in love with her daughter, she might have found that gesture wonderfully romantic. As it was, she'd found it convenient.

"The Xanax," Jolene said. "Remember when you had your tooth crowned? We had to call Mr. Wagner to come pick you up in his taxi at the dentist because I didn't have my permit yet." Earl Wagner had been the only taxi in Honeymoon Harbor. She wondered if he was still driving.

"I do remember that. I passed out as soon as I stood

up from the chair. I hope I didn't make a fool of myself today." She noticed Jolene's flinch. "What did I do?"

"Nothing."

"Try again. I can always tell when you were lying."

"You didn't know everything," Jolene said.

"Like when you and Aiden spent that night at the Mannion's coast house?"

"What?" Her daughter's eyes widened. "How could you possibly know that? And for the record, we didn't do anything. At least we didn't have sex."

"I knew because Sarah and I talked. And kept track of things, which wasn't that difficult in that case because Aiden didn't come home that night, either. And no, before you bother to give me a lecture about the right to privacy, I'm not going to apologize. Someday you'll be a mother and realize that giving a child total privacy and free rein can prove dangerous. As for how I know you didn't have sex, Aiden promised me that you wouldn't."

Damn. A bit of the Xanax still must be in her system. She hadn't intended to say that.

"You. Talked. With. Aiden?" Jolene narrowed her eyes and crossed her arms over her chest. "Back then? About us having sex?"

"I did. He assured me that I hadn't needed to worry."

"He never said a thing. Even in the market."

"You talked about that in the market? In the freezer section while Madison Covington was listening in on the two of you?"

"She wasn't there yet. And we didn't talk about *that*. Just about whether or not you and his mother knew we'd been seeing each other."

"Darling, I'm a hairdresser. I can tell the difference between a curling iron burn and a hickey."

"Well." Jolene blew out a breath. "Since we're having this mother-daughter sharing thing, I think this is where I warn you that you told everyone in the room during your procedure that you'd decided to take Michael Mannion as your lover."

The bedroom that had been warm despite the cold November rain falling outside, suddenly chilled. "I did not," Gloria gasped, appalled. "You're just saying that to get back at me for not being entirely honest with you back then."

"You really, truly did say that. And you weren't dishonest back then. Exactly. However, if you'd asked, I'd have told you that we weren't having sex. Not because I didn't want to, because I did. So much it hurt. But because I didn't want to ruin my life."

Jolene's cheeks flamed. It seemed they were both having trouble with safe words during this minefield of a conversation. "Not that I was talking about your life being ruined."

"Of course you were. And I'm glad, in a way, that my situation, as rocky as it admittedly was, seems to have proven instructional. Besides, as I said, getting pregnant turned out to be a plus because I have you."

"And I have you."

"And Aiden? What are you going to do about him?" Gloria was more than happy to skim over the subject of Aiden's uncle.

"I don't know. It's complicated."

"Life's complicated," Gloria said. "Love even more so. But you're both reasonable, logical adults now. You'll figure it out."

Jolene sat down on the edge of the bed and gave Gloria a hug, careful not to touch bodies so she didn't cause her mother any pain. "How are you feeling?"

"Still a bit woozy. And I think I could use another package of peas. Dr. Lancaster was right about my breast being a little sore."

"You've got it. You've also got your TV. And I see you already have books on the table. And your iPhone for music. Oh, and Aiden got you a chocolate croissant and some madeleines."

"He did?"

"Lemon glazed, because Desiree told him that's the kind you liked."

"That's so sweet of him."

"It was." Gloria could tell Jolene was a bit conflicted about that. Which was okay. They had time to work things out.

"He also bought coconut ones because he noticed I ate so many at the reception."

"See." Gloria settled back on the pillows Jolene had plumped up. "He's perfect husband material. I certainly would love him as a son-in-law. He's ever so much better than the others."

"You never met any other men I went out with."

"Which tells the tale. If they'd been worth being serious about, you would've introduced me to at least one of them when I'd come visit."

"You're not wrong. I never made it to the Meet the Mom point in a relationship with any of them."

"I already know Aiden. So, you don't have to go through that uncomfortable situation."

"Why don't I make you some soup and tea," Jolene suggested, dodging the issue, "and get you a tiny but annoying bell in case you want to summon your daughter house wench who'll promptly come fetch whatever the countess may require."

"It's contessa," Gloria said, recognizing the *Gilmore*

Girls episode where Rory was feeling both emotionally and physically bad and her mother had taken care of her. "And I'll start with the croissant and tea, please. Then you can get into pajamas and we'll watch that episode together."

"It's a date."

Jolene kissed her mother's forehead, and had just reached the door, when Gloria called out, "I love you, my darling daughter."

She turned. "I love you more, my bestest mom."

"Ah, but I've loved you longer."

Unable to debate that point, Jolene left the room to fetch the contessa's croissant and tea, leaving Gloria to imagine walking her daughter down a white runner toward Aiden Mannion in the lovely Herons Landing garden Amanda Barrow had created for Brianna's B and B. She'd have to ask both Brianna and Amanda when the gardens would be the most glorious. Because her daughter deserved everything to be perfect.

CHAPTER SEVENTEEN

"So," Bodhi said, as they drove away from the lighthouse, "how did things go?"

Aiden slanted him a look. "You don't know?"

"I told you I could be discreet. And that includes not being around the two of you. Besides, you make a guy realize what he's missing."

"Hell, I'm sorry."

"Like I said, it is what it is. That doesn't mean I have to like it all the time, though."

"I thought paradise was supposed to be perfect."

"Maybe it is. After what you left unfinished is settled."

"You get to do that?"

"I don't have a clue. But, again, if not, why else am I here?"

"You really weren't told?"

"Sorry." He shrugged in a "who knows" gesture. "The big guy isn't exactly in my circle of acquaintances."

"You realize your little glimpses of what appears to be an afterlife can be damn frustrating." If they weren't hallucinations. Or echoes of Aiden's own thoughts.

"It's not that easy for me, either, dude. So, did you hit on the redhead?"

"A guy doesn't kiss and tell." Yet, if Bodhi had only told him about his affair with the DC's wife, both he and Jess might still be alive. *Unintended consequences.*

"Then you *did* kiss her," Bodhi said. "You'd be a fool

if you didn't. She's hot. And definitely one of a kind. Hell, if you didn't want her I'd go for her if I were still alive."

"Apparently you've never seen *The Ghost and Mrs. Muir.*" Another old movie his mom had made him watch.

"Nah. I wasn't into that old stuff. And before you try to claim it's a classic, may I point out that *you've* never seen *The Endless Summer.* That really *is* a classic."

Since there was no response to that, Aiden said nothing.

After refereeing a fender bender between two harried shoppers in the parking lot of Marshall's Market that ended up with both calling their insurance agents and delivering the last of the turkeys from the food bank to local families down on their luck, Aiden decided to stop by Mannion's for lunch.

As they drove through town, the fire department was getting a head start on Christmas, using their cherry picker truck to hang tinseled garlands of lights across the street and snowflakes on the old-fashioned Victorian lampposts. All the storefronts had decorated for the season, as well, getting ready for Honeymoon Harbor's version of Black Friday.

"It's beginning to look a lot like Christmas," Bodhi said. "By the time they finish, this place will have turned into Bedford Falls."

His mother had decreed that movie a Christmas Eve tradition. Wondering how, while he and his siblings had been drinking cocoa with marshmallows and watching Jimmy Stewart's transformation, Jolene and her mother had spent their Christmas Eves, Aiden realized yet again how fortunate he'd been.

They'd nearly reached the office when his cell rang. With news he could've done without.

The sniper business had taught Aiden patience.

Being a detective had been much the same. Hours of tedious waiting. And hell, making out with Jolene back in high school, and now, not just taking what he knew they both wanted, wasn't helping because just because he could be patient, didn't mean he'd ever learned to like it.

Jolene was worth waiting for, especially now that she had this complication with her mom. But getting the news that the two detectives he'd wanted to talk with about Bodhi's cold case had both taken time off to spend a long Thanksgiving weekend with their families sucked.

"Perks of seniority," Bodhi said. "We would've done the same thing."

That was true. Bodhi would've hit the beach for the weekend, while Aiden probably would've come home to Honeymoon Harbor because his mom always made a big deal about all holidays, but especially this time of year. She was like a walking, talking Hallmark commercial.

He'd grown up surrounded by people he knew would always have his back, while Jolene had that mess of a dad and a mother who worked long hours to make ends meet. No wonder they were so close. Often more like sisters. He didn't want to think how hard it would be on her if anything turned out to be seriously wrong with Gloria. It had to be hell for Jolene, waiting for test results. And there wasn't a damn thing he could do but stand by and be there for her. It didn't seem enough, but…

Damn, he thought as he pulled into the pub's parking lot. He wasn't used to not being able to control events. Sure, as a Marine, things could always and would go wrong. They didn't call it the fog of war and snafu for nothing. But at least there were actions to take, protocol to follow.

The same in the police department, which had felt comfortable because it was the closest thing you'd find to a civilian military. It had rank structure, organization, guidelines and rules designed to get you the results you were looking for. Being a detective had involved a lot of boring door knocking and digging up informants, but at least you weren't sitting on your butt waiting for someone else to handle the situation.

White fairy lights framed the mirror behind the bar, and a tree decked out with colored lights and shiny balls brightened the corner over by the pool tables and dartboards.

"Wow, you've turned into Martha Stewart," he told Quinn as he took it all in.

"Ha ha. Mom and Brianna came in loaded with boxes of stuff like they were storming Omaha Beach. There was no stopping them."

"That's not quite true," Seth, who'd apparently had had the same idea, said. "He did manage to man up and refused to let them put Christmas music on the sound system."

"Thank God." Aiden slid onto a stool next to Seth. "Speaking of Brianna, where's your bride-to-be?"

"The B and B is fully booked for Thanksgiving with lots of people here to celebrate with their relatives. The noise level of all the catch-up cross-talking rivals the decibels at a Seahawks home game, and they'd all booked a dinner, so I decided to make my escape."

"Rather than help out my little sister?" Quinn's eyes narrowed in a way that looked as if they could laser right through a guy.

"Hey, she told me I'd just be in the way. She's hired

some students from the college's culinary program. It lets them experience a real time situation. Win-win."

"That's good. I'd hate to have to ban you for deserting her. After all, for a long time you were my most loyal customer."

Quinn had told Aiden that for the two years after Seth's wife had died, he'd come in every night, order a burger to go, drink one beer, then go home to eat in an empty house. Until Brianna had returned to town and saved him from himself.

"Since you still make the best wings in the state, I'd never risk banishment," Seth said. "I'll take an order of the maple-whiskey-bacon ones. And the blue cheese burger with fries."

"You know, we do have things other than burgers on the menu," Quinn said.

"I know. You've even added salads, which still mystifies me. But there's something to be said for tradition."

"You'll get no argument from me. I happen to know that women are the ones who choose where they're going to eat on a date. And apparently they often like salad as well as burgers and fries." Quinn turned to Aiden. "How about you?"

"The same wings. But pulled pork on a kaiser bun with beans, coleslaw and the hot spiced fries."

"A man with an appetite. I like that," Quinn said approvingly.

He put the orders on the clip in front of the open window leading back to the kitchen, where Jarle Bjornstad, a Norwegian who'd given up cooking on fishing boats when he'd gotten tired of freezing his ass off during Alaska's crabbing season reigned supreme. Fortunately he was one helluva cook because at six foot seven, with shoulders as wide as a redwood trunk and arms—one that boasted a full sleeve tattoo of a butcher's chart of a cow—Aiden doubted anyone would ever dare send anything back.

"What'll you have to drink?"

"That Winter Blizzard Brew. That is, by the way, really good."

"I didn't give up the big legal bucks to brew shit beer," Quinn said. "Bottle or tap?"

"Tap."

"So," Quinn said, "how's Jolene's mom doing?"

"She was sleeping when I left." Seth hoped. "She didn't seem in any pain."

"So I heard," Seth said. "Apparently she told one and all that she's got her eye on your uncle for a lover."

"Where the hell did you hear that?" Aiden asked.

"It was on the town's Facebook page."

"Damn. What, exactly, did it say?"

"It wasn't that specific. It was something about what merry widow had staked her claim on Honeymoon Harbor's resident artist? It didn't take a genius to figure it out."

"I didn't realize you read the Facebook page," Quinn said to Seth as he put the pint glass in front of Aiden.

"I don't. Brianna checks it a couple times a day to check for comments about Herons Landing. She doesn't want to miss a complaint. She's never received one, but you know what a perfectionist she is."

"Sort of like the guy she's marrying," Quinn pointed out. "I watched you redo this place. I didn't realize it was possible to measure to one sixty-fourth of an inch."

Seth shrugged. "I didn't take over a century-old family business to build shit," he said, tossing Aiden's words back at him. "Mildred Marshall posted it."

"If that woman had lived back East in the Revolutionary War days, Paul Revere could've saved himself that midnight ride," Quinn said. "So, how's Jolene holding up?"

"Fine," Aiden said. "She's tough. Like her mom. She's naturally worried about the cancer thing, but the breakup with that actor doesn't seem to have fazed her. Except for maybe seeing herself on those magazines in the market."

"Well, at least it opens the field for you," Quinn said as he filled an order for two glasses of wine a waitress had brought over. "About time."

"Did everyone know about us?"

"Hey, I shared a bedroom with you growing up. I knew what time you got in. And the shaving lotion in the bathroom sure as hell never smelled like gardenias. But Jolene did."

"She's got a lot on her plate right now," he said. "We're taking it slow. Besides, she's going back to LA after New Year's."

"And you're going to let that stop you?" Seth asked.

"Geez," Aiden complained. "What are you now? A sorority girl?"

"Now that Seth's proposed to our sister, he's turned into an expert in love and marriage," Quinn said. "He's nearly as bad as Mom when it comes to trying to fix people up. I've warned him if he even tries to turn his evil powers on me, he'll be banished from here for life."

"You're going to be my brother-in-law," Seth said, appearing unafraid. Probably because he knew Brianna would never let her eldest brother get away with that threat. "I just want you to be as happy as I am."

"I am happy. As a clam."

"So, you don't miss being one of Seattle's rising young lawyers?" Aiden asked.

"Not for a minute. I'm doing what I want, where I want to, which is all that matters. Life's too short not to make the most of it."

"Your big brother speaks truth," Bodhi, who was standing behind the bar, checking out the top-shelf labels, said.

"Jolene came back here to work on her organic skin care business," Aiden said. "But this thing with Gloria threw a wrench into the works. Apparently she's got a good customer base down in LA, but doesn't have enough money to expand. Or the expertise because she's been too busy with her TV and movie makeup gig."

"It's a learning curve," Quinn said. "I spent a long time studying microbrewing and running a restaurant before I jumped into this place. Fortunately, I was able to find the perfect brewmaster to make it happen. Brendan O'Keefe, who graduated from UC Davis brewing program, worked in a few places in San Francisco and Eugene before he found my ad for a master brewer on a brewbiz site. Having established a reputation for using local ingredients in his beers, he's been inspired by all that we have available here.

"You know, after a couple years in litigation, which I didn't enjoy because it reminded me of high school debating—"

"Speaking of debating, I stopped Covington IV for going over seventy in a thirty-five zone the other day," Aiden broke in. "He was his usual narcissistic self. I also nailed him for the tint on his window, but left off the reckless driving because I didn't want him to sic his father on Mom and Dad."

"Good call. But I would've been happy to see him behind bars," Quinn muttered, still apparently pissed over that state disqualification.

"It still worked out. I learned about the courtesy cards—"

"Courtesy cards?" Both Seth and Quinn said at once.

"Yeah. A get-out-of-a-ticket-free card."

"I've heard of departments that use those. Lots of times sheriffs' departments because that's an elected position and it builds goodwill at election time. Ten years or so ago, Seattle PD had a sticker off-duty cops could put on their family cars that pretty much did the same thing. But I had no idea the HHPD had them," Quinn said.

"We don't anymore," Aden said.

"Is that why you fired James?" Seth asked.

"A good lawyer could've gotten him out of that," Quinn said. "And last I heard, you also arrested him."

"For embezzlement, setting up a fake charity and a bunch of other stuff the DA is going to toss at him. He'll probably end up doing some time."

"Karma's a bitch," Quinn said with a wicked smile. Oh yeah, he was still pissed about that debate. "Where I was going until you made my day with that newsflash," he continued, "is that I switched to mostly doing business law, including some start-ups. I could help Jolene with the incorporation and other legal tax stuff. If she plans to ship to different states, it could get complicated."

"I think that's her long-term goal. But it's a case of the chicken and the egg. If she can't afford to expand her line and produce enough products, she can't afford to expand. And there's no point in trying to expand, if she doesn't have the inventory to sell."

"I'll try to talk to her at Thanksgiving," Quinn said. "If she's interested, Gabe could help her with the growth and scale part of the plan."

"He buys and sells bazillion-dollar businesses," Aiden said, of the brother who'd left the state after graduating UW, gotten a masters in finance at Columbia, and gone on to make a fortune. "Why would our very own Wizard of Wall Street even consider such a small deal?"

"Because he's in the weird position of having too much money, so along with contributing a lot to charity, he's also started investing in businesses that interest him."

"My heart, if I had one, would be bleeding for him," Bodhi said. "Talk about your first-world problems."

"I didn't realize he was doing that," Aiden said.

"Well, you kind of went off the grid for a while," Quinn pointed out.

"More like off the rails," Bodhi corrected. "But same thing."

"The past couple years he's invested in smaller businesses. Like an eco-toy company based in Rochester, New York. And a mobile pet grooming business over in Tacoma that he's helping to start selling franchises."

"You're kidding."

"Hey, do you know how much money Americans spend on their pets?"

"No." Neither did Aiden care. But apparently Gabe did.

"Neither did I until he told me. Last year Americans spent nearly seventy billion dollars on their pets."

"You mean million."

"That's what I said. Nope. It's *billion*. With a capital *B*. And it's growing."

"Wow."

"Yeah. He took that one on last year. I wrote the franchise agreement. It felt good to use my law degree for good rather than greed."

"Um, not to knock your brother, because I've always liked him a lot, but billions sounds a bit greedy," Seth suggested.

"Not when you're easing people's minds by having their animals groomed at home. The groomer who started the company only uses made-in-the-US allergy-free products that haven't been animal tested. Gabe seems to enjoy being an angel investor more than he does the big-bucks stuff. Made in America, going green, as Seth managed to do when remodeling this place, and organic are all hot topics, right now. I could see him being interested in Jolene's skin care line."

"Is he coming to Thanksgiving dinner?"

Quinn laughed. "Gabe take a day off? Not happening. No, he'll probably be at the computer, wheeling and dealing, and trading dollars for euros, yens, pounds, rupees or whatever the hell else he does. But you might want to give him a call and see what he says. Hell, her mother's proven to be a good entrepreneur, and since Jolene in no way takes after her father, I'd say the apple probably didn't fall far from the tree."

"Thanks. I'll do that."

First he'd have to think of some way to pull it off without having her think he was trying to take over and tell her what to do. Because the one thing he had figured out was by leaving Honeymoon Harbor when she did, and not only making a living in Hollywood, but as the Emmy nomination proved, achieving some serious recognition, she was every bit as independent as her mother.

"You wouldn't last a week with a woman who wasn't," Bodhi said, showing an apparently new, spooky ability to read his mind. "Whatever happens with the investigation, which I'm starting to wonder if making sure you two end up together is really what I'm here for, I may just stick around for your wedding."

As Jarle came out of the kitchen with a huge aluminum tray laden with food designed to keep cardiologists in Beemers for years, Aiden couldn't decide whether to take that statement as a promise or a threat.

CHAPTER EIGHTEEN

JOLENE HAD LEFT her mother napping after watching their *Gilmore Girls* episode and went into the kitchen to test the recipe Ètienne had sent her.

A mere fifteen minutes after putting the casserole dish in the oven, Jolene took a tentative taste. Wow! The cheesy corn and bacon side dish turned out as insanely good, as promised. Even better than she'd hoped. She immediately called Shelby.

"Tell Ètienne that I love him. If he wasn't already engaged to you, I'd have his children."

"You don't want children," Shelby reminded her.

"I would for this dish. No wonder it sold out when he had his food truck. Hell, maybe, since you've staked your claim on him, I'll just marry this side dish."

"I'm glad it worked." Jolene could hear the smile in Shelby's voice.

"It totally did. And the best part is that he's saved me from poisoning anyone on Thanksgiving."

"Always a plus. So, how did things go with your mom?"

"The test went well. And it was quick. About half a Pioneer Woman and ten minutes of Trisha Yearwood."

"I never will understand why you watch so many of those shows when you don't cook."

"It's food porn. I have very imaginative taste buds. Anyway, if we don't get the results back tomorrow, we won't hear until after Thanksgiving. Though the part of me that's worried sick it'll be positive is thinking it might be better to wait until afterward to hear the news."

"You'd just be anxious and unable to enjoy the day anyway," Shelby said. "You can compartmentalize it in one of those infamous mental boxes of yours and concentrate on celebrating the day."

"That's a point. I don't have a single doubt that Mom can handle whatever comes up. One of the hardest parts will probably be hiding the fact that I'd be terrified. But right now I have all this anxiety because I don't know what to expect. I should've asked the doctor for a Xanax when she prescribed one for Mom. Oh, funny story..."

Jolene paused and listened to the bedroom TV that was now playing a Christmas romance movie, one that her mother loved. There were times that she suspected that her having worked on three of them meant more to her mother than her Emmy nomination. Especially since, when hearing what a fan Gloria was, the director of the third one had invited her to Vancouver, BC, to watch a day of filming where the July green grass was all covered with fake snow and the actors were sweating profusely in their wool caps, puffy jackets and boots.

The best part had come when the female director had surprised Jolene's mother with a role as an extra in the ice sculpting contest scene during the town's Christmas festival. Having proven that years-old, mean-spirited gossip about what she might have been doing out in that trailer dead wrong, Gloria had already become an accepted part of the community. Being in that film had elevated her to the closest thing Honeymoon Harbor had to a movie star.

Last holiday season, the Olympic theater filled their

red velvet seats over three consecutive nights and a Saturday matinee with a showing of *The Little Bakery Around the Corner*, a story about a cynical food industry billionaire—think Richard Gere's character in *Pretty Woman*—who comes to a small town to convince the heroine to sell her Christmas cookie recipe so he can add it to his company and make it a worldwide brand. When he finally learns the magical secret ingredient none of his many food chemists have been able to unearth, turns out to be, of course, the love put into each cookie, he discovers the true spirit of Christmas. And, as the viewers knew would happen all along, fell head over his Gucci boot heels in love with the sweet and all-American pretty baker.

Jolene had long ago figured out that the movies swept viewers into a magical snow globe where all the stress and family drama the season can create turned perfectly pretty beneath those falling snowflakes, where families reunited, people were kinder to each other, and it was possible, for two magical hours, for even a cynic like Jolene to believe in happy endings.

"Sorry," she said to Shelby, "I just wanted to be sure Mom wasn't eavesdropping." Which she'd already admitted to doing once today. "But the doctor gave her a Xanax before the procedure—"

"I'd want a bucketful if it were me," Shelby responded.

"Yeah. Me, too. Anyway, she's a substance lightweight. So, under the influence, she informed everyone that she was taking Michael Mannion—remember, he's that artist I introduced you to at the gallery on Rodeo Drive that night?—as her lover!"

Shelby broke into giggles. "She did not!"

"She did."

"I wish I'd been there for that. I love your mom. And you know, I don't really blame her. Michael was too old for me, but he was hot. Like Pierce Brosnan."

"That's him."

"Oh, talk about small worlds, maybe you and your mom can double date. Didn't you tell me that he was your Aiden's uncle?"

"He's not *my* Aiden… But, okay, here's another not so funny thing. I kissed Aiden. Or he kissed me. I'm still not sure exactly how it happened. I'm blaming the pastry for the momentary lapse."

"Back up a minute. What pastry?"

"He showed at the hospital with coffee, chocolate croissants and lemon-glazed madeleines for Mom and coconut ones for me."

"That's your favorite kind. You always have them with the fresh peach ice cream when peaches are in season. But how did he guess that?"

"Apparently he saw me eating them at the wedding."

"The one where you kept running away from him?"

"I wasn't so much running. Just avoiding."

"And apparently missing a great opportunity if he was watching you that closely and thought to buy them for you. That's so sweet. I love him already. How was the kiss? On a scale of one to ten?"

"It wasn't that long. And there wasn't really any grabbing or tearing of clothes going on."

"One to ten," Shelby reminded her.

"Twelve."

"Oh, wow. I wish I was a scriptwriter instead of a caterer. I can just see it now. Workaholic heroine on rebound from breakup to horrid, self-centered, cheating cad returns to the small town she grew up in, where hot high school boyfriend is now the police chief. Problems arise, kisses ensue, romance blooms, then hot hero proposes to heroine at the town Christmas tree as big, fluffy snowflakes fall around them."

"You know how Mom and I watch *Gilmore Girls* together, even when she's up here and I'm in LA?"

"Sure. I don't know any daughters and moms that are as close as you two are. You're lucky."

"I know. But my point is that you two should sync your Christmas movie channel watching together. Because that's exactly what she's doing now."

"What can I say?" There was a shrug and a grin in Shelby's voice. "They're more addictive than Ètienne's croissants. Kind of like Xanax for holiday stress. And here you are, living one your own self."

"Did you forget my mother may have cancer?"

"Or may not. But that adds needed conflict to the story. And sweetie, Aiden brought you croissants and cookies! That could *so* be in a movie. Street-toughened Marine-slash-cop showing his softer side to his high school sweetheart he's never stopped loving. That'd definitely go to the top of my Christmas movie faves list."

It had been years since Jolene had thought about Aiden like that. But as she found herself falling into Shelby's fictional scenario, she was torn between wishing it could be true, and wanting to run as fast and as far away as she could.

"Life isn't a feel-good Christmas movie," she paraphrased her mother's earlier words about her favorite TV series.

"Well, the world would be a lot better off if it was. You're not going to pass up this chance for your own happy ending, are you?"

"You have romance on the brain because you're engaged to get married to a hot chef who has glittery little stars in his deep brown eyes whenever he looks at you."

"That is true," Shelby allowed. "But two things can exist at the same time. Just because I'm over the moon in love doesn't mean you can't also allow yourself to be."

Allow. Was that the definitive word? Jolene had sworn, since leaving Honeymoon Harbor, to never put her heart at risk again. But here she was, back in the same place with the same man, with all those same feels.

"It's not the same," her friend argued when she admitted to that. "You've both changed. You're not that damaged girl who escaped, and may I point out, survived, a terrible situation. And he's not the boy who loved and protected you."

"After he broke up with me."

"Did you ever think that might have been because he was going off to war?"

"Honestly, no." In their years apart, he'd grown from a rebellious teenager to an adult responsible for the safety of an entire town. Granted, they hadn't had much private time together to talk about their lives during those years apart, but now she was wondering about what all he might have experienced to cause that change. "He said he never forgot me."

"See. There you go. Didn't I say that? It's right out of a script that hardly ever gets written because guys in Hollywood just never get romance movies right." Her voice turned serious. "Fate's given you a second chance, Jolene. You'd be a fool not to go for it. And, being your best friend, I can attest to the fact that you're no fool."

"He wants to talk. On Thanksgiving."

"I thought when you texted me last night you wouldn't be seeing him because he has to work that day."

"He said he'd make time. After he kissed me." And she'd kissed him right back.

"He's stealing time away from protecting Tiny Town for you." Jolene heard the long sigh. "Be still my heart."

"It's not as if the town won't be protected. It's not that small. There *are* other officers on duty. He's just working to give the day off to those with families."

"My heart is melting here. How can you possibly resist a man who'd not only do something that generous, but bring you and your mom chocolate croissants and French cookies?"

"I'm afraid."

Impossibly perhaps more so than she was about her mom's health scare. Even if the tests did show positive for cancer, as Dr. Lancaster had said, there were plans to make and protocols to follow. But what she was feeling for Aiden was like being adrift at sea, on a moonless midnight, without even a lighthouse or buoys to prevent her from crashing onto the rocks.

"Of course you are. Don't forget, I threw up while getting ready to go out the night I knew would be the night Ètienne and I first had sex."

"I remember that well." Probably partly because Shelby had refused to eat all day for fear of ingesting as much as an apple would require a body shaper, that was probably the unsexiest piece of underwear ever. "You were a wreck. I think you tried on everything in your closet. Twice." They'd been roommates at the time and Jolene had been amused by Shelby's nerves because it was obvious that Ètienne was The One.

And damn if that wasn't exactly how she was feeling now? Not the for sure part. The hovering on throwing up part. "How did you know?" she asked seriously. "That you'd end up where you are now?"

"That's easy. I'd gone out with my share of guys. Just like you have. But Ètienne was the only one who ticked every one of my boxes. Even ones I hadn't realized I had. And don't forget, he was still doing his food-truck thing at the time, so I wasn't even thinking about him going on to win all those awards and getting on the covers of all those foodie magazines as one of the hottest new chefs in the country."

"You'd never marry a man for his money."

"Of course I wouldn't. Even if I hadn't seen so many of those marriages go on the rocks…

"I just knew that he was the man I wanted to spend the rest of my life with. The one with whom, may I point out, I'm considering having three children with, something that if you'd even suggested a year ago, I'd have asked you what you'd been smoking. When it's real, it gets even better than in those first giddy days."

"I'm happy for you."

"I know you are. And because you're my best friend and I want you to be happy, I wish the same for you. Speaking practically, what would it hurt to have yourself a holiday romance? The worst that'll happen is that you'll get tired of him and move on like you did with Chad and every other guy who came before him.

"Then you'll come back here after New Year's, or if your mom does turn out to have cancer, once she gets better, you'll either launch your new business to smashing success, or continue working in the industry, or both. And be beloved Aunt Jolene to my offspring."

"When you put it that way it sounds reasonable."

"That's because it is. Promise me one thing."

"What?"

"That you won't let your past get in the way of your future."

From the bedroom, Jolene heard the closing music of the movie her mother must have caught just in time for the happily-ever-after in the fictional snow globe town.

"I've got to go," she said.

"Promise me," Shelby pressed.

She heard TV click off. "Okay, I promise."

"There. Was that so hard? Just remember, you had a front row seat to my grand romance. So I'm going to expect to be updated on all the deets about yours." She ended the call before Jolene had a chance to respond.

Touching a finger to her lips, Jolene could've sworn she could still feel Aiden's on them. Then, shaking off the lingering need that her conversation with Shelby hadn't helped at all, she went to dish up some cheesy corn for her mother.

CHAPTER NINETEEN

WITH HER NERVES jumping nearly out of her bruised skin, Amanda stood at the window of the parking lot, watching for the white sedan Aiden had told her would be arriving to pick her up. She'd never before realized how many white cars there were in Honeymoon Harbor, but finally one parked in the zone that had been reserved for patient pickup and watched as a woman matching the description Aiden had given her climbed out while the driver waited inside the car. She was wearing a blue parka, jeans and ankle-high boots.

Stephanie Dunn entered the building without so much as glancing around, carrying a small duffel bag with her. Which, Aiden had assured her wouldn't look suspicious in the event Eric, who, despite a bulletin sent to out to all the police and sheriff departments in the state, and neighboring Oregon and Idaho, still hadn't been located, might be watching. After all, he'd said, many people need fresh clothes coming home from a stay in the hospital.

Ten minutes later, she was looking at herself in the mirror, unable to recognize the woman in the long brunette wig, a Seahawks sweatshirt and skinny jeans, something she'd never worn because they definitely weren't designed for planting gardens.

"Is all this necessary?" she'd asked as the former detective had begun taking the disguise from the bag.

"Probably not," Stephanie replied. "If your husband was hanging around the hospital, waiting for you to leave, he'd have been noticed. There are cameras focused on every part of the parking lot. And the doors. But there's no point in taking any chances. Do you have your phone?"

"Yes, it's right here." She held up the burner phone Aiden had brought her because Eric could probably track her old one even if it was turned off or dead. Her old one was now smashed and in the town's electronics recycling bin.

"Good. Here's your ID. I don't expect you to need it, either, but you never know and if we get in an accident on the way to the house, we'd want emergency personnel to know who you are."

"That's something I wouldn't have thought of."

"You're not supposed to have to. My husband, Scott, and I are professionals. And one of the things he learned in the SEALs was a failure to plan was a plan for failure. So, if we seem overly cautious, it's just because we've never lost a woman yet, and don't intend to.

"We have gained a new resident since Aiden called about you." Stephanie changed the subject. "A young mother with a six-month-old baby and a four-year-old. I hope you're okay with kids."

"I love children." Amanda had always pictured herself as a mom, reading *Goodnight Moon* to her children, celebrating birthdays, and most of all, at this time of year, she imagined staying up all night putting together bicycles and dollhouses for them to find from Santa on Christmas morning. "But I didn't dare." She'd never fully admitted that. Not even to herself.

"That makes it easier to relocate you. Fortunately, these kids are young enough that we don't have to worry about enrolling them in a new school. So—" she handed Amanda a brown parka with a hood "—let's get going. I picked up some fresh oysters at Kira's Fish House and have oyster stuffing to make. And don't worry if you don't like oysters. I'm also making sausage dressing in a casserole dish for my husband and Emma, the four-year-old."

"We're having Thanksgiving?" The holidays had always been a bad time with Eric. Too many parties, too much drinking, which, from what she'd researched, was a form of self-medication. As much as she grieved for the man she'd once loved, Amanda also knew that Chief Mannion was right. Her marriage had reached the point that if she'd stayed, she might not have made it alive to Christmas.

She hadn't been surprised that they hadn't found Eric right away. He was so smart. But, as she'd been reassured so were all the law enforcement officers, and the police at Sea-Tac airport looking for him. He was outnumbered and would be apprehended. And, because it turned out that he'd also stolen property from his work computer at the National Reconnaissance Office by downloading on a thumb drive, the FBI was now involved. That, the chief had assured her, would keep him away in a federal prison for a very long time.

"Of course we are," Stephanie said. "Everyone pitches in. It's like one big family. And best of all, Tara, that young mother I mentioned, learned how to make pies when she was working at a chain restaurant in Spokane while going to WSU. We usually have frozen, which are simpler for women like me, who are baking challenged." Her smile was warm, making Amanda feel as if she'd been wrapped in a warm woolen blanket. "So this year, we're lucky."

"Lucky," Amanda murmured, as she glanced around the hospital room, then walked out the door. She was in the car, driving away from the hospital when she recognized the emotion she'd felt as she'd left the room. It was one she hadn't felt in a very long time...hope.

THE DAY AFTER being assured that Amanda Barrow was safely ensconced in the safe house, Aiden drove out to the farm where the Mannion farmhouse was bustling with activity. The air was filled with the mouth-watering aroma of roasting turkey, fresh baked pies, yeasty rolls and all the other items that were filling the table large enough, when the leaves were added, as they were today, to seat eighteen. In the center of the lace tablecloth Sarah's parents had given them for their wedding so many years ago, was the centerpiece Amanda had sent from her nursery.

As glad as he was that she was temporarily settled and safe, Aiden was frustrated that her husband had disappeared, giving credence to his wife's belief that he'd been planning his escape for weeks. Along with the country sheriff's department and the state troopers, he'd been working with the FBI and US Marshals, because Eric Palmer had allegedly stolen sensitive government rocket secrets from the National Reconnaissance Office.

After entering the rental house where Amanda and Eric had lived, they'd discovered the manic-created chaos she'd described, including the laptop with the thumb drive on the desk beside it, but no Eric. A credit check showed he'd spent over a thousand dollars at a sporting goods store in Port Angeles.

"I remember the guy." Joe, a bearded giant that looked a lot like Jarle, had helped Eric at the store. "We were busy that day, with Christmas shoppers, but you don't forget a guy who says he's going to go live off the grid in Alaska. That happens a lot, but sure as hell not this time of year. He bought snowshoes, poles, a ski jacket, pants, a balaclava and gloves. And an ice pick, in case, he said, he needed to build an ice cave, and said he'd watched a video on how to do it on the internet.

"He did say he had a tent, and the ice cave was just a backup plan. It was obvious he didn't have a clue what he was doing, but hey, he didn't want to listen to any advice about this being a bad time of year, so what are you gonna do?" He shrugged his massive shoulders. "I expect he'll be found sometime around spring thaw between here and Alaska."

"No way is he going to get to Alaska," the lead FBI guy said as they left the store. "He'd have to cross into Canada. We can pick him up at one of the checkpoints whether he drives, takes a train or a ferry. And the police at the airport and TSA have his name and a photo."

"He's not thinking clearly," Aiden pointed out. "But from what his wife said, he's traveled internationally for conferences in the past, and they've been through the Peace Arch, which is the busiest, so he might go for that one, since it's familiar. Though even during manic episodes, he'd probably be smart to realize he'd need a passport. He'll also figure out that his lack of access to credit, now that his cards have been cut off, is going to prevent him from a long road trip."

"Thus the camping equipment," the FBI special agent said.

"Exactly. He's probably still aimed for Alaska, but my guess is that he's going to wait around here until he figures out an escape plan. Or swings back to normal."

Or at least what was normal for him, which had been

enough for Amanda Barrow to keep trying to make her marriage work.

"One problem is that we're talking about a lot of geography. Olympic National Park is a million acres, larger than Rhode Island. And then you've got Rainier, and Baker, and the forests. Washington State encompasses forty-three million acres, half of which is forested."

"So, we've got a needle in a haystack situation," one of the FBI guys said.

"It's coming on winter," Aiden said. "Even with all that gear, he's probably not going to last all that many days."

But they'd find him. Eventually. Unfortunately, the longer he stayed on the run, the slimmer the chances of finding him alive were getting.

"WOW, DUDE," BODHI SAID, taking in the scene as they'd entered the house. "If I'd known your family made such a big deal of the holidays, I might've come home with you one year. This could be right out of a Norman Rockwell painting that should be corny, but it's pretty awesome."

Thanksgiving was the last day until Christmas that the Mannion family could all gather together for a meal. Because first thing tomorrow, come rain or shine, even before the sun rose, everyone would be setting up for the festival they'd been preparing for most of the year. Beginning with the spring tree planting, then later, the summer trimming to ensure all the trees were a perfect Christmas shape. The running joke among all the Mannion kids were that their parents had had five children in order to get so much free labor.

Gallons of cinnamon-spiced apple cider were waiting

in a huge walk-in commercial refrigerator ready to be warmed, cookies that had been baked all fall had been taken out of the freezer to thaw, and wreaths and swags and sprigs of mistletoe tied with red velvet ribbons for hanging were waiting in one of the three barns to be put out for both decoration and sale. Seasonal employees hired from around the peninsula would continue to create more over the next month, and cut and wrap trees to secure onto the tops of cars or backs of trucks, and colored lights had been strung on the barn, fence, and farmhouse.

The old sleigh that John Mannion had bought at auction and equipped with tractor wheels, since snow was a rarity in this corner of the world, had been painted, as had the train that would take children and parents for a ride around the front part of the lot.

The farm offered three choices: choose your tree and have one of the workers cut it for you, cut your own, or buy one of the potted living trees meant to be planted once the season had ended. Over the years many parents would buy one for each child, and now the Mannions were seeing a second generation, with those children returning to buy a living Christmas tree for their own family.

Partly due to the fractious history between the Mannions and Harpers, his mother's parents had originally forbidden her to date John Mannion. But over the years they'd carried on a secret romance and had even separated for a time to different corners of the world, but had eventually reunited, returned to Honeymoon Harbor, bought the farm and established the holiday tradition they'd both dreamed of back when they'd been younger than Aiden was now. The similarities between his parents' romance and his and Jolene's story gave Aiden hope that theirs would turn out the same way. If it didn't, he was determined it wouldn't be for his lack of trying.

Wanting, no *needing*, to see Jolene, if only for the few minutes while the FBI and Marshals went shopping for some heavier weight jackets and boots, he'd managed to arrive home before everyone had sat down to eat, so braving the kitchen filled with women, his eyes immediately found Jolene, who, even without standing out with her dark auburn and burgundy hair was even more of a beacon in a green-and-blue tartan pleated schoolgirl skirt, a dark blue turtleneck sweater, purple tights and a pair of black ankle boots. Hunger hit in his gut, and not for the enormous turkey that his mother had resting on a cutting board.

He was so concentrated on watching her mash a huge pot of potatoes, that she was the only person he saw until he heard his mother say, "Why, Aiden, what a wonderful surprise! We hadn't expected you."

"I can't stay long," he said, as he returned her hug. "I was in the neighborhood and thought I'd drop in and see if maybe you needed me to get something from the market."

Given that the farm was on a dead-end road outside of town, that was definitely the lamest excuse he could have thought up. If he'd been that brain-dead while working undercover, he wouldn't have lasted the first day. His only excuse, as his eyes locked over his mother's shoulder with Jolene's, was that every rational thought in his head had been washed away by the sight of those legs that, as Bodhi had said, went on forever.

The chemistry sizzling in the air didn't escape Sarah. "No, we seem to have everything we need."

"You sure?" he said. "No rolls, butter, peas, anything? Because I could run down to the market to pick them up for you."

"We're fine," she repeated. "But Jolene, why don't you dish up a bit of your amazing side dish for Aiden? It's so delicious I'm not sure any will last for leftovers. And why don't you take it to the sunroom, so no one can complain that you're getting a head start on dinner."

His mother was as obvious as he'd been about supposedly dropping by. But Aiden didn't care. And neither, apparently, did Jolene as she spooned some of her corn into a porcelain bowl with a scene of a snowy old bridge on the bottom. His mother had brought out that same set of dishes for Thanksgiving and used them every day through New Year's Day dinner for as long as Aiden could remember. Following Jolene out of the kitchen into the sunroom Seth had added during the last remodel, he enjoyed the sway of that plaid skirt.

"Sassy," he said.

"I feel that way," she admitted as he closed the door behind them. "I think you'll like this. It's three kinds of cheese, corn, bacon and chopped-up jalapeños. But of course you already know that, since you were in the market when we were buying the ingredients."

"It looks great," he said, taking the spoon and bowl and putting them on a side table next to the towering Christmas tree he'd helped decorate two weeks ago. The Mannions had always put their own trees up early because the weeks leading up to the day after Thanksgiving to December twenty-sixth were the farm's busiest time of year. "But I've only got a couple minutes, five, tops, and want to taste you."

She smiled and, without hesitation, walked into his outstretched arms.

As he gathered her against him, her female curves

melded into his hard male body as if they'd been created to fit together in just this way.

Jolene lifted a hand to his cheek, her fingers brushing against the dent that would become that dimple that always pulled something elemental in her whenever he'd smile. "I've missed you," she said.

"It's only been two days."

She looked up at him as he looked down at her and realized that he could see her unguarded heart gleaming in her eyes. The remarkable thing was gazing into his blue eyes was like looking into a mirror.

She'd once loved Aiden Mannion. Truly, madly, deeply. But it had been young love, created from a teenage girl's dreams of what romance should be. As his beautiful dark hands with their long fingers cupped her face, she reminded herself that she was a grown woman. Sane. Realistic. And, okay, maybe Shelby was right about her being a bit cynical. A reasonable, adult woman couldn't fall in love this fast. But even as her rational mind warned her of that, her newly opened heart felt neither rational nor cautious.

"Longer than that," she said. "For years. And years."

There. She'd said it. Those years she hadn't dared fully admit to herself. A silence hovered between them, as he seemed to be taking that risky statement—that could once again cause her to end up with a broken heart—in. No one had ever looked at her like Aiden was now. So deep. And so long.

Just when she was no longer sure whether or not she was still breathing, it happened. His beautifully cut lips curved in that slow, wonderful smile that had always held the power to tangle her emotions and weaken her knees.

"You're sure as hell not alone there," he finally said, his gaze turning so tender, she nearly wept with relief.

Then, proving that actions spoke far louder than words, he dipped his head, touched his lips to her, and in that moment, a wonderfully blue sky that had opened up over the rows of Christmas trees outside the glass walls of the sunroom, the stunningly decorated tree from the family's farm, this house, Honeymoon Harbor, the entire world and everyone in it magically vanished and there was only this man.

He tasted of sweetened coffee he must have picked up at Cops and Coffee. He smelled of that woodsy soap she'd remember him using all those years ago, of the rain that had been falling when he'd first arrived and the brisk aroma of fir trees and salt water.

Her lips parted on a pleased, inviting sigh at the touch of his tongue, which didn't thrust, but instead skimmed along the arch of her top lip, then the bottom, nipping a bit. He took his time, drawing out the pleasure, as if they had all the time in the world, his mouth both soft and warm against hers, a quiet kiss, but still possessing the power to cause her heart to hammer and her head to spin.

How could he possess such patience, she wondered as he drew the kiss out, keeping it so exquisitely soft? So gloriously long?

Finally! He angled his head to deepen the kiss, when the ringtone of his phone shattered the moment and sent her crashing down to earth with a bang.

He drew his head back at the same time he pulled the phone out of his pocket. "Mannion." When he heard the voice, he mouthed, "I'm sorry."

She shrugged and gave him the resigned look that she figured cops' significant others had been giving since the first prehistoric human had picked up a club and left the comfort and safety of the cave to protect their group. Their community. All those who couldn't protect themselves.

His conversation was curt. Short. His expression had turned from tender to ice in less than a minute. "I'll be right there. For now, just keep an eye on him. I'll call the others. And have the sheriff's department helicopter stay close enough to come in, but not so close it tips him off."

"You found him?" she asked, reminding herself that not just Amanda's safety, but the safety of anyone who might accidentally stumble across the man was more important than a mere kiss. Not that there had been anything *mere* about it. But still.

"That was the head law enforcement ranger in the park. He spotted Eric's SUV inside the Hurricane Ridge gate last night, but there was no one in it, and some snowfall wiped out any footprints. One of the other rangers spotted smoke from a viewpoint."

"In the campground?" She remembered that particular campground was open year-round. She also remembered from one less than successful Girl Scout skiing trip there, it was really, really cold this time of year. "You'd think he'd want to stay away from people."

"In a way, if he'd been focused enough to check out the ridge ski calendar, that would've told him it doesn't open until next week, there'd be enough campers, snowboarders, skiers and tubers up on the ridge that a lone guy might be able to fit in while he figures out his next steps. From the fact that he left his laptop behind, he's probably running on instinct and adrenaline. He's not in the campground, but the smoke wasn't that far away."

"He could be dangerous."

"Amanda said they don't have any guns," Aiden said as they left the sunroom. "Let's hope that's still true."

"Sorry, folks," he said as he went through the dining area, where people were starting to sit down at the table. "Duty calls. Have a great Thanksgiving."

Jolene followed him to the front door. Then, in full view of everyone, she reached up, pulled his face down to hers and kissed him fast and hard. "Stay safe," she said. "And come back to me."

He gave her a wink, as if this was like any other day. Which, to him, perhaps it had once been. "Don't worry. I'm not in the habit of leaving things unfinished."

With that he was out the door and down the steps. Jolene stood there, watching him speed down the long driveway toward the road. And, although she knew it was impossible, she thought she heard a whisper, like the wind in the trees.

"Don't worry that pretty red head, Gidget. Everything will turn out excellent."

CHAPTER TWENTY

THE DINNER WAS delicious and the company wonderful, but it was hard for Jolene to keep her mind off Aiden. What was he doing? How was he doing? She assumed if they'd found Eric, Aiden would have called, if for no other reason than to let her know he was okay. That could mean one of three things. They hadn't found him, they'd run into trouble after finding him, or he was too busy doing police things to call his girlfriend in front of the FBI.

Girlfriend. Wasn't that an odd word? She'd been his girlfriend in high school. Brianna had been a different type of girlfriend. And Shelby was her best girlfriend. So how did she and Aiden, as adults, fit in? She was too old to have a boyfriend, that sounded more like someone you shared shakes with at the Big Dipper than sex.

But he wasn't her lover (yet), not that she'd ever introduce him that way. He could become a friend with benefits. That was more what she was accustomed to.

But it was different with Aiden. Because he was different. They needed a new word, she decided because *significant other* sounded like something you'd call a person you were signing a bank loan with. She glanced across the table at Brianna, who was sharing a private laugh with Seth. Now see, she had it easy. Seth was her fiancé. Who told one and all that he was the man she was going to marry.

That got Jolene thinking that the lack of a word for a monogamous, romantic/sexual/committed relationship seemed to say that society was all centered around marriage. A boyfriend, to perhaps partner, then fiancé, then husband. Easy peasy, if you followed the path set out for you. But what if you weren't sure that's what you wanted?

Relationships were difficult, which is why she'd always tried to avoid them. Until she'd come home to Honeymoon Harbor, and was back with the only man who'd ever had her even thinking of possibilities.

She was relieved to be able to put the dilemma aside as Sarah asked about her skin care line, which had totally gotten put on hold yet again. Then Quinn brought up the idea of incorporation, and telling her that he'd talked to his brother Gabe, who'd thought the idea sounded like something he'd be interested in investing in.

And if that wasn't enough of a surprise, Seth joined into the conversation. "Remember Roosevelt School?"

"Of course." Jolene had gone from first to third grade at the school that had served the community since 1907 until all the students had been moved to a shiny new building.

"It's empty."

"I thought it had been condemned," she said. She remembered the older kids telling horror stories about students who'd been burned to death in the building during a fire that had charred the cafeteria and continued to haunt the place. The images had given her nightmares for weeks until her mother found the reason for her night screams and had assured her that the only things that had died in that fire were possibly the rodents who'd chewed the electrical wiring.

"It still is," he said. "But I was checking it out last

month with the idea of doing something commercial with it. It could make a good workplace. It's ten thousand square feet, all on one floor. It'd be a serious gut job, and when I took off a piece of cedar siding, there were a lot of carpenter ants, so they'll have to be dealt with, then it'd need new siding. I'd use fiber cement, that's a mix of wood pulp and Portland cement, that'd gives you minimal upkeep, is rot, termite and fire free, and gives you the look of painted wood clapboards, stone, or even brick. It also costs less than wood or masonry."

"You've been thinking about this," Jolene said.

"I have. Like I said, I was thinking of buying it myself as an investment property. I did, by the way, use the same siding on the carriage house Brianna and I are living in at Herons Landing. You could divide the space up any way you'd like. Obviously Gabe and Quinn could handle the financing while I took over construction. And I'd give you a fair price."

"I'd never think otherwise," she assured him, still trying to wrap her mind around this conversation. "I've seen what you've done with Herons Landing. And Kylee and Mai's darling Folk cottage."

"Thanks. Though the interior of the carriage house is still a work in progress. Fortunately, Brianna's taking living in a construction zone in stride."

"I'm living there with you," Brianna said. "Which is all that matters."

The smile she shared with her fiancé caused an ache deep inside Jolene. It wasn't jealousy. Or envy. But an emptiness. She still didn't believe you needed to be married to be happy, but to have the kind of relationship Brianna and Seth, and Shelby and Ètienne had was obviously very special. And rare, the last bit of romantic cynicism she was clinging to with her fingertips reminded her.

"And while the town's grown in popularity with the arts community, and the wooden boat business is still going strong, and the college has brought in a lot of new people, Honeymoon Harbor is still lacking in good, solid job opportunities to keep young people from moving off the peninsula," John Mannion spoke up. "You could be helping the economy while growing your business."

The idea of Quinn, Gabriel and Seth all having gotten together and discussing a way to help her was amazing. Jolene glanced across the table at Brianna, who lifted her hands. "It wasn't me who thought of it, although I wish I had because the products I put in Herons Landing's bathrooms sell off the shelves in the gift shop. But I have to give credit to these guys who came up with the idea over beers and burgers at Mannion's."

She felt moisture stinging at the back of her lids. Since Aiden wasn't here with his camo handkerchief, she blinked then away. "Well," she said, "as it happens, I have an idea for a new brown-sugar scrub. If it's okay with Mom, you three can come in for a free facial at the spa."

"What a wonderful idea. And I'll throw in a pedicure," Gloria offered.

"I'll chip in for a waxing," Sarah called out cheerfully.

"And a seaweed wrap," Caroline Harper, Seth's mom, home from Yosemite, offered. "I had one in Phoenix that was absolute heaven."

When the two Mannion brothers and Seth, alpha males all, looked as if they'd rather face a charging grizzly, the table erupted in laughter, and for that brief moment, Jolene's fear for Aiden was replaced by a rush of love for these friends who epitomized the small-town spirit of generosity and caring for your neighbors.

Not that she was technically still a Honeymoon Haborite. But she'd grown up here and was Gloria Wells's daughter. And for them, that was all that mattered.

After dinner, as Jolene and Gloria insisted on helping clear the table for dessert, Jolene's mother pulled her aside into the small butler's pantry next to the kitchen.

"Are you okay?" her mother, seated next to her, asked quietly.

And isn't that what she should be asking her mother, Jolene thought. Who was the reason she'd come back to Honeymoon Harbor. "I'm fine," she assured her with what felt like a stiff smile. "I was just worrying about Aiden."

"He's an experienced Marine and big-city detective." Her mother patted her leg in reassurance. "And it's not like he's out there alone."

"He wasn't alone when he was wounded in Afghanistan." Mrs. Gunderson had reminded everyone of his medals while praising the new police chief for having found her missing gnome on Facebook. "And he wasn't alone when he was shot in an ambush with drug dealers in Los Angeles."

Gloria arched a brow. "How did you know about that?"

"I Googled him. And you look as if you already have."

"Sarah told me. Apparently he spent several weeks at the coast house recovering." She paused, as if debating her loyalties. "Both physically and emotionally. He lost his partner that night."

"The article I read hadn't mentioned that part."

She hadn't wanted to dig deeper. If he wanted to tell her, he would. The same as she would tell him about the text from Shelby letting her know there were beginning to be repercussions from that letter she'd signed. Nothing specific, just rumors. But she wanted Jolene to be prepared in case anyone contacted her.

"John wouldn't have proposed him to be police chief if he hadn't believed he was capable of doing the job." She took hold of Jolene's hand beneath the lace tablecloth and squeezed it reassuringly. "Remember what you told me about the powers of negativity and positivity?"

"Of course." It was harder to believe it now while she was the one with her nerves screeching even as she'd attempted to join into the table conversation.

"Good. Because I'm positively thinking of a wedding. June is so predictable, don't you think?" she asked. "How about July? Perhaps even you and Brianna could have a double ceremony. Wouldn't that be lovely? That's why I've decided I don't have cancer. Because I want to be healthy enough to help you plan your most special, happiest day."

Jolene's mind scrambled from concern over Aiden to trying to come up with an answer that wouldn't dent Gloria's regained positive outlook. And also she knew that deep down, her mother, who'd been a pregnant bride married at the courthouse, and was always doing hair for so many women who came to Honeymoon Harbor for their own ceremonies, had undoubtedly always looked forward to the day she could give her daughter a beautiful, perfect wedding.

"Not that I don't believe you're going to be well and healthy next summer, but I think Aiden and I have some issues to work out before we even get to a point where we're talking about weddings," she said carefully.

"I know, darling." Gloria ran a hand over Jolene's head and down the back of her hair, a reassuring maternal gesture going back to those simpler childhood days. "But it's fun to think about."

"Why don't you think about you and Michael instead? And what you two were talking about?" It had not escaped Jolene's notice that Sarah had seated her brother-in-law next to Gloria. Nor had she missed what sure felt like attraction sparking between them.

Her mother ran a hand through her hair, revealing tangled nerves. "We were talking about his wine and painting nights. He thought I might enjoy one."

"That sounds like fun."

"It does."

"Maybe you should take it."

"I'm considering it. I've been worried that he might have heard what I said during my procedure, but if he did, he's too much of a gentleman to bring it up."

Jolene knew that there was no way Michael Mannion could have escaped hearing about her mother's declaration to take him as a lover. "Perhaps that's why he mentioned the class," she said mildly. "To let you know that if you meant what you said while under the influence of Xanax, he's interested."

"I said I'm considering it." Her mother's tone also declared the subject closed.

IN THE END, after two days of searching for Palmer, it didn't prove difficult. He turned out to be where the ranger had noticed him, but when Aiden called for him to come out of the tent that had heavy snow on the roof, he'd called back that he couldn't. Because his feet weren't working.

"Do you have any weapons?" Aiden asked, knowing that people lied all the time.

"No!" The pain sounded real. "I j-j-just need someone to come rescue me before I d-d-die."

"He sounds authentic," the FBI special agent said.

"Does to me, too," the marshal agreed. "I grew up ice fishing in Wisconsin, but I sure as hell wouldn't have wanted to spend two days and nights in a tent obviously not made for winter out here in this temperature."

Unholstering their weapons, the three men tromped through the snow to the closed flap. "I'm going in," Aiden said, knowing that the FBI guy could play the fed card to claim authority. "He attacked someone in my town."

The other two men, along with the Salish County sheriff, exchanged looks, then shrugged. Unholstering their weapons, the sheriff stood back, as if he would do going through a door where a gunman might be on the other side and Aiden charged through it, pistol drawn.

And saw a man who looked as if he hadn't been exaggerating about possibly dying. Eric Palmer was shivering violently. Having climbed to the glaciers enough times in his teens, Aiden knew shivering was the body's way of generating much needed heat. His ski mask and sleeping bag were wet with condensation from breathing that had caused it to rain, or even snow during the colder hours of the night. His hands were tucked inside the damp bag that was lying on the ground rather than a thermal mat. Palmer was obviously a guy who'd only done California or summer camping.

"I n-n-need you to g-g-get me out of here," he managed.

"We're going to do that," Aiden said as the ranger

accompanying them called for an Air Force Rescue Coordination Center, that in turn contacted the Coast Guard station in Port Angeles to send a medevac copter. "But I'm going to need you to take your hands out from that sleeping bag." No way was he going to risk the guy having a pistol under there.

Although it took an effort, with his arms so stiffened, Eric Palmer pulled his hands out. They were gloved, but held no weapon. His face, when Aiden managed to pull the wet fleece mask off was a dangerous pale gray.

They unzipped the damp sleeping bag and wrapped him in the emergency Mylar blankets Aiden always carried. He also managed to get some water down him, despite his cracked lips because dehydration increased hypothermia. They didn't take off his boots or gloves, because at this stage it could do more harm than good. Warming up skin that might freeze again, which was possible in the copter, then warming it a second time would cause more damage, including the risk of amputation, and better left to medical professionals.

Even having to go through three layers of government services Air Force Rescue arrived within five minutes and Aiden and the others loaded him up onto the litter and watched it go up into the copter that would transfer him to Olympic Medical Center in Port Angeles. The last thing he said to Aiden was to tell his wife he was sorry.

"I'll bet she's heard that before," the sheriff said.

"You'd win that bet," Aiden said.

"We get first dibs on him," the FBI special agent said. "Given we're talking a serious homeland security breach and you've only got him for spousal abuse."

"Perhaps if you'd seen his wife you would've left the *only* out of that sentence," Aiden said. "But yeah, I'm fine with you having him first. But I'm still going to charge him and arrest him before you take him off to wherever it is you feds take people. Because I want an official record of the assault and attempted homicide."

"You're going to go with that?" the sheriff asked with an arched brow.

"Yeah." Aiden knew he probably couldn't win that one, since any defense attorney would argue Palmer nearly running over his wife would be accidental, but since it would probably be a very long time before the feds released Palmer for trial in Salish County, he wanted to stack the deck as much as he could to keep the guy behind bars for as long as possible. They'd undoubtedly get him back on his meds while in custody, but he'd already proven incapable of staying on them without strict supervision.

They trudged back through the snow to their vehicles. "Well, since he's yours for now," he told the FBI agent, "I'm going to go have some turkey and cheesy corn and bacon with my family."

But first he had to call Amanda and let her know that her husband had been found and was reasonably safe. He informed her she could receive his condition from the hospital after a while, but he advised not going there. Because he'd probably soon be moved. He'd keep her updated.

After she'd thanked him profusely, he drove out to the farm. Because he had a dinner to eat and a kiss he needed to finish.

CHAPTER TWENTY-ONE

AIDEN HAD CALLED Jolene as soon as he was on the way, so his mother already had a plate fixed up and waiting for him. Everyone else had moved on to Gloria's warmed cranberry apple pie topped with the vanilla-bean ice cream Aiden knew his father would've made that morning. John Mannion had always been the ice cream maker in the family, that had him thinking again of his family traditions and how he'd want to create his own, along with adding his past ones with his own family one day.

He'd always believed that cops had no business being married because the job became your life, you only hung out with other cops, and the hours, stress, and not big bucks pay could take a toll on a family that never got the time they needed to fully bond.

He bent down and gave Jolene a quick kiss, effectively revealing to probably no one's surprise that they had a relationship. And, although Aiden knew it was undoubtedly sexist and Jolene would probably call him a Neanderthal, he was effectively staking his claim.

Which she didn't seem to mind all that much, because, when he sat down beside her, he could see in her eyes that her smile came from her heart.

He gave a quick rundown of the Eric Palmer situation, since he knew everyone would be wanting to know the details, then, realizing he was starving, dug into his dinner. Beginning with the cheesy corn. "You're right," he said to her. "This is insanely good."

"Thank you. That means a lot. Especially since it's the only thing I can cook besides frozen pizza."

"Aiden can cook," Sarah offered from the end of the long table. "I made sure all my boys could. Some of them, especially Aiden and Burke, complained that cooking was a girlie thing, but I pointed out that every man should be able to feed himself." She smiled down the table at her husband. "John cooked me the same dinner we'd once had at a famous Boston hotel," she told Jolene and Gloria. Everyone else in the family, and Seth, had heard the story every year. Especially when their dad recreated the meal every year on their anniversary. "The next day he proposed right here at the farm."

"And you made me the happiest man in the world," he said, lifting his glass to toast his bride of so many years.

"Thank you, darling." Her warm smile assured him it was the same for her. "Proving," she said, "that men cooking is not a girlie thing. But a very manly, even sexy thing." Her smile suggested that her husband could get lucky once everyone had gone home for the night.

Even as Aiden cringed a bit inside at the thought of his parents having sex, he decided that he was going to cook Jolene dinner. He hadn't done any cooking for a very long time, but he figured the same way she'd gotten the cheesy corn recipe from her friend's husband, Quinn and Jarle could undoubtedly come up with a recipe he could pull off.

"That's true," Brianna said. "I love all those food shows and have a mad secret crush on Tyler Florence."

"You never told me that," Seth said, seeming surprised, but unperturbed.

"I suppose it never came up. But don't worry. I have

an even bigger thing for hot guys wearing a tool belt with a big hammer."

Aiden, who'd just taken a drink of water, nearly spit it out. "Isn't there some rule about sisters not discussing their personal lives with family over dinner?"

"Just saying," Brianna replied with wide-eyed innocence no one at the table believed for a minute.

"I like Tyler, too," Jolene said. "But Michael Symon is my chef crush."

"You like bald guys?" Aiden asked. It wouldn't be his first choice, but he'd be willing to shave his head if it made Jolene happy.

"Not especially, although he rocks it. Most of all, I love his laugh."

That kicked off a conversation among all the women comparing the various celebrity chefs. Aiden thought about suggesting they may just be objectifying males, but not wanting to risk blowing up his plans for the evening, decided to just keep eating.

"You know," his grandfather said, "it's good to have two of my grandsons back home again. Especially when they're both proving to be as smart about choosing their women as I was with my Harriet." Who was, Aiden knew, his second wife, after he'd been widowed young. Just like Seth.

"You've always been such a sweet talker," Harriet fussed, obviously enjoying the comment after decades of marriage.

"It's easy when I'm talking about my sweetie," he returned. "And good thing I was or you might've married Frank Jensen."

"I've told you time and time again that I never had any intention of marrying Frank. I just let him dance with me at the Snow Ball to make you jealous so you'd finally get around to proposing." She shook her head. "I swear, that stroke did something to your memory."

"It was a TIA," he corrected. "And it didn't do anything to my memory. I just like hearing you tell the story of how I was always your true heart's beau."

"Stop that," Harriet said, her remarkably still-smooth cheeks turning nearly as red as the cranberry base of Gloria's pie. "You're embarrassing everybody."

"Nothing embarrassing about loving your wife." He narrowed his eyes first at Seth, then Aiden. "As you'll both be finding out soon enough." That said, he shot a look at Quinn. "And you'd get busy finding yourself a girl. Because you're not getting any younger and heaven knows I'm not. And I've every intention of dancing with my bride at each and every one of my grandchildren's weddings."

"Okay," Sarah said in an obvious attempt to rescue her sons and the man who would soon be marrying her daughter. "Who'd like to help clear the dessert dishes off the table?"

After everyone pitched in to clean up, the evening ended early because the family had to get up before dawn to set up the festival. Fortunately, the forecast was chilly but sunny. Which was the way of life in the Pacific Northwest. As their bodies touched, one of them trembled. It could have been her. Or him. Or maybe, since they'd always been so in sync, until he screwed it up, both of them.

Aiden kissed Jolene again, with a tenderness that he'd never felt for anyone else. "There's something I want to get out of the way. So, we might as well do it, now. Fast and quick. Like pulling off a Band-Aid."

"All right." She glanced over her shoulder back toward the main room.

"Your mom's fine with waiting a moment more."

"How do you know that?"

"Because I saw her talking to Uncle Mike."

"Oh." He felt her relax again in his arms. "Do you think they're going to get together?"

"I wouldn't bet against it. Mike can be very persuasive when he puts his mind to it."

"I don't want her hurt. She told me he dated Seth's mother this past spring."

"I've heard it wasn't the kind of relationship we have. It was more of a friendship. Though, he may have been testing the waters."

Admittedly, that's exactly what they were doing, too, because Aiden didn't get the feeling Jolene was all in yet. *Yet* being the definitive word.

"But he never would've done anything with Ben Harper still in the picture. From what Seth told me at the wedding, his parents had some things to work out. Which they did. And Mike, being a pragmatic guy, isn't the kind to carry a torch."

"Perhaps, because he doesn't get committed, so it's easier to move on."

And wasn't that like what she'd told him about herself? Until she'd admitted, today, that he'd been the exception. That was enough to give Aiden hope. "But I don't get the feeling he's a player, because there have been lot of women suddenly taking his art with wine classes and, according to Mom, he hasn't dated any of them."

Jolene laughed. "Maybe my mom and I should go to the next one."

"It'd probably be fun. I was watching him talking with her while I was eating your seduction side dish, and he sure seemed focused in on her."

"That's the feeling I got, too." She slapped his shoulder. "And it is *not* a seduction dish."

"Hey, it had bacon. For a guy, that'll work every time."

He stopped her midlaugh by kissing her again. Longer, deeper, a kiss that went straight from their lips to below his belt. Damn. He had no control over himself when it came to this woman. And never had. He couldn't count how many times he'd gone home from being with her and jacked off in the shower because that old saw about cold showers had never worked for what she'd done to him.

"We're going to have to wait a minute," he said. "Before I go out and embarrass us both."

Her eyes drifted down. Her lips curved in a smile that was definitely meant to seduce. "I'm not sure I'd have anything to be embarrassed about. Actually, I should feel pretty smug about my female power."

He touched her cheek that was as soft as silk. If this was what her skin cream did, she was going to make a bundle. "All those women's magazines that tell you about how to satisfy your man's burning need, and men ranking their top fifty favorite sex moves would go out of business if you knew that you women have always had the power.

"How about this? If your mom gets an all clear tomorrow, we go out to dinner."

"Like a date?"

"Yeah. Dinner, drinks and whatever."

"We never had a real date." There had been a reason for that, but it had dawned on him that she might have gotten it backward.

"I know, that's the Band-Aid I intended to rip off. But I always seem to get sidetracked when I'm with you."

He kissed her again a warm, lingering kiss filled with promise. "We'll save it for tomorrow."

Gloria and Mike were deep in conversation as Aiden and Jolene returned to the main room.

"Ready to go?" Jolene asked.

"Oh." Her mother looked up, appearing surprised to see her. That wasn't all that surprising since they'd seemed to be in their own private world. Gloria's cheeks were as flushed as a teenage girl's. "Yes, we should let everyone get to bed."

After more exchanges of goodbyes, and thanks, they were out the door and on their way back to the lighthouse.

The phone rang while Aiden was driving away from the lighthouse, following Jolene and her mother down the long, tree-lined driveway. It was the FBI, calling from the hospital.

"So," said Bodhi, who had been absent during the search and dinner was back riding shotgun and had obviously heard the call through the speaker. "I guess everything was copacetic."

"Yeah. It was frustrating not being able to find him right away, but Palmer was camping out in the snow, got hypothermia and is currently at the hospital in Port Angeles." The agent had reported that once they got him warmed up, they'd be moving him to Seattle because it looked as if he could lose a couple of toes. And maybe the tips of some fingers.

"Good deal. How did things go with Gidget?"

"Jolene," Aiden reminded him. "And right now it's push-and-pull baby steps while waiting to see what happens with her mother." He glanced over at his former partner, lifted questioning brow and waited.

"I haven't a clue," Bodhi said. "Hell, if I knew anything, I'd have told you earlier on. But for what it's worth, I hope she gets an A-OK. Not just for her sake, but for yours and Gidget's—Jolene's," he corrected.

"Me, too." Patience, Aiden reminded himself. It had been fourteen years since they'd been together. He could wait a bit longer.

But not much, he thought as he headed back toward town. While usually Honeymoon Harbor night police calls transferred to his cell or the deputy chief's cell phone, he decided to patrol a couple more hours, because Thanksgiving dinners, with the mix of alcohol and family members forced together on holidays, were always trouble waiting to happen. Then, if the night stayed quiet, he'd head for home himself.

ALTHOUGH GLORIA HAD closed the salon from Thursday until Monday, the day after Thanksgiving she insisted she was well enough to start getting ready for Saturday's merchants day at the farm.

"It could be an exhausting day," Jolene warned. "Maybe you should rest up."

"Dr. Lancaster said I could go to work the day after the procedure," she pointed out. "It's been longer than that. Plus, I still need to work to get my samples ready to give away tomorrow."

"All right. We'll do them together. I was planning to try new blends while I was here, but for now, we should probably stick to the tried-and-true." She went over to the closet where she'd stored the boxes.

"Wow." Gloria's eyes widened at all she'd brought with her. "You're thinking big."

"*Titanic* big," Jolene said. It had occurred to her, as she'd left the supply store that by planning for such a commercial success for her mother, she could well be sending vibes to the universe to prevent her from having cancer. Because if her products could help generate new spa customers, then Gloria would *have* to be well.

"While I make some new batches, why don't you start opening the larger jars you have in stock and putting products into these sample sizes," she suggested. "Lotions in the bottles, creams in the jars."

"I could have figured that out for myself," Gloria said dryly.

"I know. I'm sorry. That was condescending. But I've never really been an employer before. So I can make all my mistakes with you if I take Quinn and Seth up on their idea."

That would first require Gabe Mannion to be her angel investor. And Quinn to help her set up a business plan. She'd also probably need an accountant for that because this was going way beyond her current self-employed small business.

"Do you think I'd be biting off more than I can chew?" she asked as she could feel anxiety hovering out there just beyond horizon, like Jaws, waiting to attack. "I won't even be living here. How will I keep track of what's going on?"

"That's what planes are for," Gloria said. "And phones. And I'm sure you can find someone to manage production for you."

"It's always just been me and occasionally a couple of part-time beauty school employees to help fill a larger order," she said.

"You've got the college here," Gloria pointed out. "And enough salons around that you'd undoubtedly be able to find an experienced manager. Maybe even from one of the cities, someone looking for a slower pace of living. I see those couples all the time on *House Hunters International*."

"But ten thousand square feet?"

"It *is* a lot," Gloria allowed. "But not that much larger than this place."

"You started small."

"So did you. You're just skipping some middle steps. Besides, you have a secret weapon."

"A magic wand? Wonder Woman's bracelets?"

"No." Her mother's smile was wide and warm and gave Jolene the impression that this conversation had momentarily taken her mind off waiting for the doctor's call. "Me. I'll be here to oversee things. Hold down the fort, so to speak. Because I'm your mother and I love you."

A rush of love almost too large and strong to contain swept through Jolene with the power of a tsunami. She threw her arms around her mother and hugged her tight. The way she had that night Aiden had stood her up for prom. "I love you more."

"But I've loved you forever," Gloria repeated their familiar lines. Then laughed, stepped back and said, "For the win!" She'd just high-fived Jolene when the phone rang.

And although it was probably just her imagination, the room turned chilly. As if a ghost had just entered.

AIDEN HAD JUST walked into the police station with a large cup of coffee, a sugar-dusted doughnut and a lingering bit of sexual frustration from last night's dream of Jolene when Donna stopped him at her desk. Today's sweater signaled the change in holidays with an ice skating penguin wearing a red scarf.

"I have the plan," she greeted him.

"Plan?"

"For the boat. In the parade."

Damn. He'd forgotten all about that. He took the piece of paper she thrust at him. "You want to make the boat look like a police car?"

"Exactly." She tapped the eraser of her yellow pencil on the top of the outline. "Then you could put red, white and blue flashing lights on the top. Right here."

"I like it," Jennifer Stone said, coming over to look at it. Her shiny new deputy chief name tag must have arrived from the engraver while he'd been out looking for Palmer. "It beats the plain old boring lights and poor Charlie Brown tree we've been doing forever."

"Not forever," one of the older deputies said. Jim Hooper had retired two years ago, but continued to volunteer three days a week because his wife told him he was driving her crazy. "Don't forget the year of the jail."

"Oh, Lordy, don't remind me of that," Donna said.

"Would you care to fill me in?" Aiden definitely needed more caffeine. Like in an IV.

"Don decided we needed something different. So he came up with the idea of a jail cell."

"A cell?"

"Yep," Jim said. "It was essentially a steel cage. With a door. He also thought it would be a riot to have some deputies dress in black-and-white prison uniforms."

"How did that go over?"

"Because nothing says Christmas like imprisonment," Bodhi said. Aden couldn't disagree.

"Like a fart in church," Jim said.

"A few drunks thought it was a riot," Donna added. "But the *Herald* got a lot of negative letters about it. It was, thankfully before Facebook was real popular so folks couldn't yell about it on that. I told the chief it was a mistake, but bucking James too much was a sore subject in his marriage, so he mostly shrugged it off. Next year we went back to the lights and tree."

"How hard would this be to do?" he asked Donna.

"My Hank's real handy. He said he could make a frame in an afternoon. One where you wouldn't even be able to see the boat under it. It'd look just like a car floating on the water. Though he did recommend blue lights for the bottom and white for around the windows and the top. He says heavier colors look better on the bottom."

"Sounds like he knows what he's doing," Aiden said.

"Oh, he certainly does. He's done all the lights on both the town's Christmas trees since before you were born. And he's built all the animated lighted figures in the park. This year's theme is penguins. Though we'll always have the angel at the start of the walk-through, because she's real popular and, of course, Santa... Speaking of which, you *do* know you're going to be driving the boat in a Santa costume."

"That would be a hell no."

"The police float always ends the parade. Then Santa gets off and hands out candy canes to all the kids. It's a tradition."

"Maybe I'll hang around to see this," Bodhi suggested. "Because so far that sounds like the second-best highlight of my visit, after bringing down Jess's killers."

"Can't anyone else do it?" He looked pointedly at Hooper.

"Don't look at me," the retired officer said. "I may have packed on a few extra pounds since Cops and Coffee brought their doughnuts to town." He folded his arms over his doughnut belly. "But I damn well never volunteered to play a jolly old elf."

Hooper had been a good cop who'd come from Phoenix before looking for a slower life in the Northwest. Aiden thought that if he hadn't retired, he would've probably made a great chief.

Donna lifted both her chins. "Like I said, it's a tradition. And it connects the police with the people you're protecting and serving."

"I thought that was what I was doing when I went out and found Mrs. Gunderson's gnome."

"It was. And she appreciates that. And what you did for that poor girl Amanda Barrow was wonderful. But this is a big deal, too, Chief. It'll also show those few naysayers out there that you're the real deal."

"And me wearing a Santa suit will do that?"

"It's public relations. It'll work," she assured him.

"Do I have to wear padding?"

"Well, all I can say about that is that you have a damn fine body, Chief." She swept an appreciative look over him. "I imagine you've also got a fine washboard beneath that shirt. But what do we tell the little kids when a skinny Santa shows up in Honeymoon Harbor?"

"Don't forget what happened when the chief didn't listen to her last time his brother-in-law suggested the lame cell idea," Bodhi said. "I say go for it."

"I'll do it," Aiden caved.

"Ask if we get to run the siren," Bodhi suggested.

"I suppose I'm expected to run the siren."

"It ends the parade," she confirmed.

"Ask Hank to start building," Aiden said. "And ask him if he needs a down payment to buy materials."

"Oh, he never takes any money." Donna waved his words away. "He's got three barns full of stuff on our property and building Christmas displays is his hobby. Like some guys fish or hunt. He's got displays on all five of our acres hooked up to a computer this year. He figures he'll be ready to get on *The Great Christmas Light Fight* TV show in the next couple years."

"Well, tell him thanks, and I hope he makes it on the show."

"Oh, he probably will. Hank can do just about anything when he puts his mind to."

A lot like his wife, Aiden considered.

After approving the plan, he received a call from the DA that Don James was paying back the money he'd stolen from the fund and pleaded guilty to embezzlement and criminal charity fraud. Because of his years of service to the town, he'd been given a sentence of two years' probation, credit for the night he'd served and a schedule to pay back the debt with interest. If he missed a payment, he'd be immediately arrested and incarcerated in the Salish County jail.

The best news, as far as Aiden was concerned, was that he'd been allowed to serve his probation time across the state in Spokane, where his younger sister's husband owned a body shop and had offered to give him a job. Which meant that he wouldn't be around to stir up trouble in Aiden's town.

"Hot damn," Bodhi said, as they drove out to respond to a stray dog that had been reported to look as if it'd been hit by a car. The caller had tried to catch it, but it had run away. Honeymoon Harbor was too small for its own animal control team, so usually those were handled by the fire department or police. Unless it was something bigger, like a bear wandering through town getting into trash cans. After breaking into a house and tearing apart a pantry, one had been taken back out into the woods by the county wildlife control.

"The trouble with working undercover was that we didn't get to use the siren all that much."

"But we did get to drive a Ferrari and a Lamborghini," Aiden reminded him. The second had been wicked cool, but took too much time to climb out of, so they hadn't even driven it out of the impound lot.

"There was that," Bodhi agreed. "So, when are your detective friends going to get back?"

"Monday. I'll call them first thing... Damn. I should've thought of that."

"What?"

"You said Jess sent you photos."

"Texted them."

"So where's your phone?"

"I don't know." Aiden could see his partner's mind working. "Since I was dead, and not a suspect, the cops on the scene weren't paying as much attention to me as to trying to figure out who all the bad guys were. It's probably sitting in an evidence box with all my clothes."

They'd been removed in the coroner's office while Aiden was getting the slug dug out of his thigh, where, the doctor on duty had told him, if it'd had hit two inches to the left, he would've bled out before he'd gotten to the ER.

"Then moved to a box in the evidence room," they both said in unison.

They exchanged looks.

"Great minds," Aiden said.

"We still got it, dude," Bodhi said. "Just like Crockett and Tubbs."

Aiden couldn't disagree.

They stopped by Mannion's, where Jarle cooked up a plain burger to go for dog bait, and headed out to the location he'd last been seen, Aiden spotted the black, white and copper Australian shepherd limping along on three legs down the railroad tracks that ran through the edge of town. Coincidentally, it had been the lack of a railroad that had kept the once bustling seaport from becoming the state's capital city as early dreamers had lobbied for.

She was down to skin and bones, her coat was matted, and, as he'd suspected, she was hungry, because she swallowed down the burger in one bite after he'd lifted her into the back of the SUV, where she'd settled down with a huge moan.

He drove the dog to Cameron Montgomery's veterinarian office where Cam, who suspected either a bad sprain or a break, was going to X-ray the leg. She whimpered as Aiden left, as if she'd already decided he'd do just fine as her new human. As he drove away, Aiden thought that might not be such a bad idea. He'd been thinking of getting a dog. Maybe fate had stepped in and given him this one.

As he went back on patrol, Bodhi drank in the trees outside the windows, as if committing them to memory. Aiden wondered, once they put the DC away for a very long time, hopefully life, if his partner would be taking off to continue his journey to wherever the hell he was going next. If he did, he'd miss him like hell, but at least this time he'd be prepared.

CHAPTER TWENTY-TWO

"IT'S DR. LANCASTER." As Gloria read the caller ID, she turned as pale as snow and sank down on one of the shampoo chairs, as if her legs had given out on her.

"Put her on speaker," Jolene advised. Her mother's head had to be spinning even worse than hers was, so it was important for both of them to hear. Whatever the news was. She grabbed the old-fashioned appointment book that her mother used as backup in case of a computer crash, and pulled a pen from the pretty round box next to the book so she could take notes.

"Hello?" her mother answered tentatively.

"Good morning, Gloria," the doctor said with a professional warmth that gave nothing away. Jolene wondered if they taught that tone in medical school. "The results of your biopsy just came in and I've good news. It's benign."

"That means no cancer, right?" Gloria said.

"None. Though, since you did have this abnormality, we'll want to keep a close eye on it. While the odds are against any additional problems, I'd like you to have another mammogram in six months."

"I will. Thank you!"

"You're very welcome. Passing on good news is the one of the best parts of my job."

Jolene took out her phone. "I'm writing a date down six months from today on my iCal and make sure you schedule one, then I'm going with you when you have it done."

"What if you're in Los Angeles? Or Ireland?"

"It doesn't matter if I'm in Timbuktu. I'll be here."

"I'm sorry I caused you to come up here."

"You didn't. Not really."

"I could always tell when you were fibbing."

"All right," Jolene allowed. "You're right. If Sarah hadn't called me, I probably would've just rented another apartment in LA. But she did call me, so I came, and I'm so glad I did. Because even though it was sometimes hard and scary, I wouldn't change this time together for anything. And I'm so looking forward to working the booth with you tomorrow and meeting all your friends."

"You're going to work the booth?"

"Of course. It's my product, I should be pushing it. And it's a chance to work with my mom again. Just like the old days."

Gloria looked around at the beautiful salon and spa. "We've come a long way from the trailer."

"We have. But back then we were closer. And it's been my fault."

"You had your reasons for moving on," Gloria said. "I always understood that. And look how well you've done. And the same way I was your date for the Emmys, you can be mine for the annual showing of my holiday movie."

Jolene laughed. "I wouldn't miss it. I was only nominated for an Emmy for makeup. You, on the other hand, are the only person in Honeymoon Harbor who's appeared in a movie."

"Well," Gloria said, patting her colorful hair. "I wouldn't want to boast, but everyone in the theater did point out that the camera did seem to focus more on me than the other extras."

"As well it should," Jolene said. "Because you outshone the stars. Now, let's take this over to the cottage and you can make up the gift bags on the kitchen table, while I make up more samples on the counter."

To her surprise, her mother's eyes misted. "This is," she said on a voice that wavered with emotion, "the best holiday season of my life."

"Mine, too," Jolene said, feeling her own tears threatening. Damn. Where was Aiden with his camo handkerchief when you needed him?

THE DAY OF the festival dawned gray and foggy with intermittent sprinkles that were not enough to keep visitors away. While the Mannions were selling trees and other greenery like crazy, the barn was also crowded with Honeymoon Harbor locals as well as people from neighboring towns on the peninsula.

Jolene, who'd honestly been a bit uneasy about talking with people, especially those she'd gone to school with who'd either ignored or bullied her, found herself enjoying the day. The barn was packed, with everyone going from booth to booth, spending their money while picking up stamps for a chance at the grand prize.

"Why that makes my hand just as smooth as a baby's bottom," Donna, who typically had weekends off with 911 calls either being sent to Aiden's cell or the sheriff's department, said. "I'll take one of those pretty gold sample bags, but I'll be in next Wednesday to buy a jumbo-size bottle." She grinned wickedly. "Give my Hank a holiday surprise."

While Gloria was happily chatting with Winnie from the market and going through all the things that were in the bag with her, another woman about Jolene's age came up to the booth. She looked vaguely familiar, but Jolene couldn't quite place her.

"I'm Ashley Winters," she introduced herself.

Ah. A member of Madison's beehive. Reminding herself that those high school days were long behind her, Jolene managed a smile. "I remember you," she said, reaching into the basket behind her and taking out a gold bag. "Are you interested in a sample kit, or would you just like a stamp?"

"I intend to buy one," the petite, slender brunette in the red parka, black jeans and tall plaid boots, which, if they weren't Burberry were a good knockoff, said. "But I mostly came over to ask if you had a moment to talk privately."

"Um. Sure," Jolene said with a glance at Gloria, whom she noticed was watching them with an eagle eye. Or that of a mama grizzly prepared to protect her cub.

"I can handle things," Gloria said. "The crowd's thinning out a bit while everyone goes over to the tent to get some lunch."

Along with the Mannion's grilled burgers and fries, Taco the Town had set up its truck; Kira's Fish House was selling bowls of clam and potato chowder; Sensation Cajun had opted to go with po'boy sandwiches; Leaf was proving vegan can please even the carnivores in the crowd with their loaded vegan nachos by topping tortilla chips with rice, beans, juicy tomatoes, spicy chilies and corn; while Luca's Kitchen drew in the dessert crowd with a crispy cannoli that had chocolate chips, seasonal allspice and cinnamon added to the cream filling, then was dusted with powdered sugar. One thing was for certain, no one would be leaving hungry.

Not knowing what she was letting herself in for, but hoping it wouldn't be horrid, Jolene followed Ashley outside and over to where she'd parked, and prepared herself for the worst.

"It's been a long time," Ashley said.

"Several years," Jolene agreed.

"Congratulations on your Emmy."

"It was a nomination. Not a win."

"But still, there are so many shows, and so many episodes every year, that's an amazing accomplishment. You must be very proud."

"I am."

"I always wanted to be a reporter. You know, like Barbara Walters. Or Diane Sawyer. Maybe Katie Couric, though I hate early mornings." She sighed. "But I ended up here writing for the *Herald*, that probably gets fewer readers than the town's Facebook page."

"You're still doing what you love, right?" Jolene said. "How many people get to be reporters at all? Especially women."

"That's true. I read about you signing that letter. I was impressed."

"Thank you." Jolene was still wondering when she was going to get to the point. None of this couldn't have been said at the booth. Especially since, as her mother had pointed out, the crowd had moved in a herd over to the food booths.

"I was wondering if I could interview you. About your work, and how you broke into the business, and, of course the Emmy..." She paused. "And, if you'd be willing to talk about it, maybe why you signed that letter."

"Sure." It was beginning to sink in. "Have you always been at the *Herald*?"

"Um. No. I started out working for *UWTV* in college. Where I may have had more viewers than readers here. After graduation, I got a job in Boise, then worked my way across the Midwest for a while until landing in Phoenix, then some California stations, but New York or DC were my ultimate goal."

"But?"

Her smile held no humor. "I'd always had to put up with jokes, and stuff, because, you know…guys."

Jolene nodded "I do know. All too well."

"Yeah. I suppose you would, from what's come out about the movie industry. Anyway, at one place, things got, well, nasty and physical. But it came down to a he said/she said thing."

"So nothing ever happened."

"Well, I guess something did. Because since he'd been voted best anchor in the city for ten years running, and I was the new girl, I got fired and here I am. But I'm sorry, that's not what I wanted to talk to you about. I just got sidetracked. Sometimes it just gets in your head. Like a flashback."

"I've been there." One reason Jolene had stuck to men that she didn't care all that much about was that they mostly served as a buffer. A male who might be seen as being in her corner if anyone tried things. It didn't always work, but she had found it made some difference. Especially when said boyfriend worked in the industry.

"The reason I wanted to talk with you was to apologize."

"Okay."

"About the way I acted. I was a shy kid when I moved here from Spokane, not knowing anyone. But I was pretty—not that you weren't, in fact you were gorgeous and didn't look like anyone else in town, which was why so many girls were jealous, but—"

"I get it," Jolene lied. *Seriously? The mean girls had been jealous?*

"Anyway, Madison invited me into her clique. And I felt like I belonged somewhere so being new was easier. But I never felt good about the way you were treated. I was just afraid of being kicked out of the group. Of being on my own again."

As she'd been. Except for Brianna, who'd already had her own circle with Kylee and Zoe. Jolene thought back and couldn't remember any bullying Ashley had participated in. That didn't make her blameless. But Jolene also realized that it was past time to shake off the last of those days. Still, although it might be petty and cruel, she still would've loved to have blended some poison ivy into Madison's avocado face cream sample.

"So." Ashley let out a long breath. "I'm sorry. I should have been a better person and I hope you'll forgive me for not being braver and standing up for you."

"It was high school," Jolene said. "It's a wonder any of us survive those years."

"Thank you. And thank you for not making this any harder on me. Which you had a perfect right to do."

"Believe me, Ashley, you haven't met mean girls until you've worked in Hollywood."

"There was an anchorwoman in Phoenix who was much beloved by viewers and always voted their favorite who'd often had stomping-high-heel temper tantrums during commercial breaks," Ashley said. "Once she threw a heavy glass paperweight and hit a cameraman in the head. She just barely missed his eye. Then, without missing a beat and ignoring the blood streaming from his cut, while one of the assistant producers was madly dabbing at his wound with a paper towel, the bitch of an anchorwoman sat back down at the desk, smiled broadly and welcomed the next guest as if nothing had happened."

As bad as she felt for the poor cameraman, Jolene laughed. "Well," she said, "now that we've bonded over work horror stories, want to go get a couple burgers? I have an in with the owner, who'll probably let us jump the line if you interview him while he's grilling."

Ashley grinned. "Though I've truly turned over a new leaf and frown on line jumping, I am starving. And, as it happens, I have an in at Mannion's, too. I'm dating the chef."

"Jarle?" Jolene tried to picture this petite brunette with the former fishing boat cook who any casting director would've loved to cast as a wild Viking marauder.

This time it was Ashley's turn to laugh. "I know. We're definitely an odd couple, but although Jarle looks as if he could break The Rock in half like a matchstick, he has a marshmallow heart. Maybe the four of us could double date sometime. You and Aiden, Jarle and me."

"There's not an Aiden and me," Jolene said.

"Of course there is," Ashley said easily. "And believe me, Madison is not at all pleased about that."

And didn't that revelation please Jolene? Talk about being high school petty.

As they reached the grills where Jarle and Quinn appeared to be having an *Iron Chef* challenge to show off their burger-flipping skills to an appreciative crowd, Jolene linked arms with Ashley. "I think," she said, quoting Bogart's famous last line from *Casablanca*, "this is the beginning of a beautiful friendship."

BY THREE O'CLOCK that afternoon, Jolene had felt as if she'd worked for days. She'd forgotten how it had felt to stand on her feet all day. And she'd been behind the booth for only five hours, with a short break for lunch. Her mother, on the other hand, was still going like the

Energizer Bunny, which Jolene suspected was partly a burst of adrenaline energy from relief at the good news.

She began to pack up the empty boxes. The fact that they'd sold out of sample bags before the drawing for the grand prize—won by a third grade teacher at the new and improved Roosevelt Elementary school—had Jolene thinking again about Seth's suggestion regarding remodeling the old school building into a workshop for her products. Which was difficult to do when every coherent thought whooshed out of her head as Aiden approached the booth.

"Hey there," he said, glancing over at the boxes. "Looks like you did okay."

"We did. I'd wondered if I'd been overly optimistic when I bought so much packaging before coming up here, but we could have sold a lot more if we'd had another hour. Of course, I'd probably be dead by then. I thought my job was hard, always making sure everyone looked good and the same for every take. But I don't believe I've ever talked so much and for so long ever in my life."

"That explains the husky voice." He did that slow smiling thing with his mouth and his eyes that she imagined could still hold power over her when she was rocking on the porch in some old folks' home for retired makeup artists. "Here I was hoping it was for me."

"Goodness," Gloria said suddenly. "I forgot to put the chicken in the Crock-Pot for the chicken and dumplings I'd planned tonight." That was the first Jolene had heard about any chicken dinner. "Why don't I just run over to the food booths before they all close and pick us up some takeout?" She was off before Jolene could say a word, causing Aiden's dimples to deepen at her total lack of subtlety.

"Don't do that," Jolene complained. "I'm too exhausted to handle all those killer pheromones you're throwing at me."

"Sorry." This time his grin was quick and just as dangerous. "I dropped in to see if you wanted to go out tomorrow night. You did agree to a date."

"You asked me out," she teased. "I don't remember agreeing."

"I was hoping you wouldn't remember that part. We can have dinner, anywhere you want, then go to the tree lighting in the park."

Honeymoon Harbor always had two official tree lighting ceremonies. One the Sunday night after Thanksgiving in the park, and a second one down at the harbor the night of the boat parade. The Mannions always supplied the park tree. The one at the harbor was created by crab fishermen from crab pots stacked in a pyramid shape.

"I'd like that. But I wouldn't want to leave Mom to go to the lighting alone."

"Look over there," he said, nodding to the far side of the barn near the food booths where Mike Mannion and her mother were talking. Jolene suspected it was not the heat from Mannion's grill that had Gloria's cheeks flushing. "My uncle is asking your mom the same question I just asked you and I have a feeling he's getting much the same answer."

Damn. He was right again when her mother looked across the emptying barn. Her mother deserved this, Jolene told herself as she nodded and gave a thumbs-up. Blowing her a kiss, Gloria turned back to Mike.

"You Mannion men just doubled-teamed us," Jolene said.

"Tell me you're sorry about that."

She shook her head. "I can't."

"So, that's a yes?"

"I guess it is."

He rubbed his jaw. "I can't remember when I've received a more enthusiastic response to an offer to take a woman to dinner," he said.

"I didn't mean it to sound like that. It's just..." *What?*

Having had such a roller-coaster life growing up, Jolene preferred to be the one in control. Both in her personal and business lives. She'd never felt that way with Aiden. Yet, for some reason, as her hormones were screaming "What are you waiting for?" She couldn't think of a logical answer.

"You just realized you don't have any reason to turn me down."

"I could turn you down for being so damn smug."

"But you won't. Because you want to be with me as much as I want to be with you. And you're too smart to cut off your cute nose to spite that lovely face."

He'd taken off his leather gloves and stuck them in his pocket, allowing him to trail a warm finger down her cheek. Then he bent his head, kissed that cheek, her nose, and finally her mouth, which, responding right on cue, clung to his.

It wasn't that long a kiss. Not long enough to embarrass a couple in public. Not that they were a couple. But, she knew, that by going to dinner and the tree lighting tomorrow night, by the time that switch was pulled to turn on the lights, every person in Honeymoon Harbor would have decided they were together.

And would that be so bad? It wasn't like their relationship was going to be permanent.

She'd be leaving Honeymoon Harbor January second. And besides, there was always the chance that she'd exaggerated what having sex with Aiden Mannion would be like. Perhaps, when they did go to bed, as they both knew they would, it would turn out not to match her heightened expectation.

As if that could happen, she thought, as she found herself drowning in his blue eyes. Just like maybe it'd snow on Christmas this year. As a girl, she'd always hoped for a snow day from school. Unfortunately, the odds of a white Christmas in this rainy, Northwest part of the country tended to range from 6 to a very rare 10 percent.

"So," he said, "now that you can't put me off any longer, where would you like to go?"

It took only a minute. "Mannion's," she said. The pub might not be the fanciest first date place, but it was where anyone they knew who was going out tomorrow night would probably end up, so she'd no longer be Aiden Mannion's secret girlfriend. Another thing it had going for it was that, short of Taco the Town, it was the most casual place to eat, meaning she wouldn't have to worry about dressing up.

"Mannion's it is," he said. "As it happens, I've already reserved a waterfront window. Just in case you said yes."

"And if I'd said no?"

"I'd have sat alone at the bar and moped into my nonalcoholic beer."

Once again she wondered about his reason for that nonalcoholic beer, but as his head swooped down again, this kiss hard and quick, but still possessing the power to curl her toes, she decided this wasn't the place or time to ask if he had a drinking problem. She certainly hadn't seen any sign of that. Maybe, she considered, it was because he seemed to be on duty 24/7 and needed to stay sober.

"Since it gets dark early, and kids have school the

next day, they're going to light the tree at seven on the dot. I realize it's probably earlier than you're used to in LA, but we're not all that movie-biz trendy here, so how about I pick you up at the lighthouse cottage at five thirty?"

"I've never been movie-biz trendy," she said. Those few weeks with Chad and his ever-present, camera-flashing paparazzi had taught her that she wouldn't want to be. "I'll be ready."

This time his fingers traced around her lips. Lips that could still taste the coffee and a sweetness that must have come from the cannoli he'd eaten before coming up to the booth. "Me, too," he said.

And with that promise of dinner and a whole lot more lingering in the air, he strolled away, whistling.

CHAPTER TWENTY-THREE

AMANDA'S KNEES WERE literally shaking as she walked down the hallway of the University of Washington Medical Center burn unit floor the Sunday after Thanksgiving. The doctor she'd spoken with had told her that burn units usually had more experience and facilities to treat frostbite because the procedures were much the same.

Although she'd talked to Eric briefly on the phone, she'd waited until today to visit him, telling herself that she was allowing his parents and sister, Jan (whom she'd called as soon as Aiden had called her, letting her know he was being brought to Seattle), to have family time with him after his surgery. She'd never shared what their life had been like with them, but from the resigned tone of his mother and father on the phone, it sounded as if they weren't all that surprised. That had been a relief, suggesting what Aiden Mannion, the counselor at the hospital, and the woman at the safe house she was still living in had already told her. That she hadn't done anything to trigger his episodes.

She hadn't seen his family since the wedding, but they still greeted her with hugs, then left the room.

She hesitated inside the doorway. Eric looked terrible. Gauze wrap covered the middle of his face, his legs were elevated with his feet wrapped, as were his hands. The doctor had also explained that while once surgery had been advised sooner than later, they'd discovered that led to complications. So now they waited until the dead skin sloughed away to decide on a further course of action.

"Hi," she said. She washed her hands with the antibacterial foam from the container hung by the door, then held tight to the handle of her purse, as if it were a life preserver keeping her head above water in a stormy sea.

"Hi, yourself." He sounded tired, which could be from the pain meds the floor nurse had explained were running along with fluids and antibiotics thought his veins. "Guess I really screwed up this time, didn't I?"

"It was a whopper," she agreed. "You had us all scared."

"I didn't mean to hurt you."

"I know." The medicated Eric, the one she'd loved, had always meant that. The same way the unmedicated Eric always forgot it. "I talked to the doctor. He believes you won't need surgery."

"Yeah. They've got me in a warm whirlpool bath twice a day to help the dead skin slough off." His eyes misted, making her own sting. "It reminds me of that hot tub we had at the house in Palo Alto. Remember?"

"I do. We had some good evenings there." With music playing quietly and wine at the end of their workday.

"Bygones," he said with a sigh. "It'll take a couple to three weeks to know. But I could be in here as long as a month."

"I'm sorry." *So, so sorry.*

"You're not going to be there when I get out, are you?"

All the emotions swirling in his eyes were echoed in her own heart. "I'm sorry." She shook her head, swiped the tears that had begun to overflow onto her cheeks. "I just can't. Not anymore." She plucked a tissue from the box on the table and dabbed at her cheeks.

"I could tell you that I'd stay on my meds."

She bit her bottom lip and closed her eyes.

"But we both know that's not true," he continued. "It's like a drug. I need the highs. I suspect my sister, who appears to have escaped that particular gene, got her medical degree in psychiatry because of Dad and me."

His father was a brilliant neuroscientist, who, her mother-in-law once admitted, when they'd moved into his parents' basement for a month between jobs, had the same outbursts. But, she'd assured Amanda, they'd lessened as he'd gotten older.

"I suspect it's a decrease in testosterone," she'd said, taking Amanda's hands in both of hers. "So it does get better."

"That's good. Not about, you know, your dad and your disease, but that Jan got that medical degree."

"She thinks I'd do better in a controlled environment. She's also looking for an attorney who's won cases such as mine to keep me out of prison and in something like a resident home. But gated."

Like a prison, Amanda thought. But so much better than the one the government would send him to. "I think that sounds like a good idea," she said. "And I know you never believed it, but you really did think better when you were more stabilized."

"That's what Jan's been telling me, having watched me all through school. But it's not what my mind's telling me. You know?"

Amanda nodded. Oh, yes, she had a wall covered with mathematical equations attesting to that.

"There's something you need to know," he said.

"Okay."

"I always loved you. And despite what I've said and done over the years, I always will."

"I know." Her heart was breaking, her eyes were burning, but the rational part of her brain, the part she could hear everyone who cared about her saying, was reminding her that love wasn't worth dying for.

She stepped closer to the bed and, not wanting to hurt him, with a touch as light as a feather, brushed her fingers against his cheek. "Good luck, Eric. I'll always remember our good times. And you need to remember that you have so many people, including me, rooting for you."

Then before she said anything that might give him hope, like telling her soon-to-be-former husband that a part of him, that funny young man who made her laugh and told terrible jokes and spun wonderful tales of the future they'd have together, would always hold a part of her heart.

She made herself walk, not run, from the room, then closed her eyes and leaned against the wall, the handrail digging into her back. It was all she could do to keep from sliding down that wall onto the immaculate clean tile floor.

"You did the right thing," she heard a familiar voice say. Opening her eyes, through the blur of tears, Amanda saw Eric's sister. "The only thing you could do. Now, I'm going to tell you something my parents never will, so you won't weaken. My uncle, my father's brother, killed his wife when I was eight years old. Then shot himself. On Christmas Day, which is why I hate this season and have always volunteered to work overtime so I don't have to remember those twin caskets. I'd be in Oregon working today if this problem hadn't sprung up. And it turns out Uncle Henry wasn't the only suicide in the family. I love Eric. How could I not? He's my brother. But I will never entirely trust him. Ever. And neither should you."

That said, Jan surprised Amada with a quick hug, and said, "Get out of here. Go make a wonderful life for yourself because you damn well deserve it."

TWO HOURS LATER, Amanda was back in Honeymoon Harbor, having taken the ferry because she'd needed the time to separate from what she'd just done. Time to breathe. To stand at the rail, the cold wind of Puget Sound whipping at her hair and stinging her cheeks, clearing her head.

Now that she was going to be single, she could, she realized, go anywhere in the world. She could throw a dart at a globe and just take off. Go to Italy. Peru. Maybe even Iceland, which was supposed to be beautiful, although the growing season wouldn't be very long there, which would prevent her from keeping a business she'd built literally from the ground up and loved.

As she saw the lighthouse come into view, followed by Brianna's beautiful Herons Landing, Amanda watched the boats bobbing in the marina near the ferry landing and realized that she didn't want to go anywhere. That she'd found her home. Or, more accurately, Eric had found it, but despite what had happened, it didn't diminish the inner pull she'd felt when she'd first seen the town online. That she belonged here.

After driving off the ferry, Amanda still wasn't quite ready to go back to the shelter residence where everyone would undoubtedly want to hear how her visit went. She wasn't ready to talk about sad things yet. She wanted to savor this moment of freedom. Of coming home.

On impulse, she decided to stop at Mannion's, intending to treat herself to a glass of wine. Quinn was behind the bar as she walked in. He greeted her with a slow easy smile that didn't look as if he had any idea where she'd been or what she'd been up to, but she suspected he did know. There were no secrets in Honeymoon Harbor and Aiden was, of course, his brother and Quinn had also been at that interrupted Thanksgiving dinner.

"Well, welcome back," he said as she climbed up on a stool. It may be foolish, but she always felt uncomfortable sitting alone at a table. "I saw you drive off the ferry and was wondering if you were going to come in here or Cops and Coffee."

"Caffeine is that last thing I need after the last few days. I'll take a white wine. A chardonnay." She glanced around. "I like what you've done with the place. I hadn't realized your talents extended to holiday decorating as well as microbrewing."

"Cute, but unfortunately not all that original. I've been getting ragged about it from nearly every guy who comes in. And I know that you know all this sparkly stuff was put up by Mom and Brianna because they bought those berries and ribbons for the tree from you."

"I cannot lie. That would be true. But I did talk them out of the gold-and-white tulle draping around the bottom. And glitter."

"That makes you a saint in my book. One chardonnay coming up."

He opened a new bottle, a label that had her arching a brow at the price. Eric had almost ordered it once for a table of six in a Napa restaurant they couldn't afford if it'd been just the two of them until one of the other men, who knew about wine, had suggested a less expensive merlot.

"It's on the house," Quinn said. "A rep from the winery dropped off a trial case the other day and you're the first to weigh in on whether or not I should buy more."

"I don't know anything about wine tasting."

"Neither do I. But you drink wine, so that makes you more of an expert than me."

He poured the wine into the stemmed glass, then placed it in front of her on a white bar napkin.

She held it up. Studied it as if she knew what she was doing. It shone like sunshine in the light streaming in from the waterside window. "It's got a good color."

"That's a start," he said.

She swirled it around, sniffed. "I smell fruit. And vanilla."

"Sounds good."

She took a little sip. "There's a hint of apple. With a touch of pear. And..." She tilted her head, took another sip. "Maybe a touch of passion fruit?"

"I'll definitely push that on New Year's, date nights and Valentine's Day," he said.

Yet a third sip. "And a finishing of crème brûlée from the oak."

He lifted one of those Mannion Black Irish brows and said, "I thought you didn't know your wines."

"I don't." She surprised herself by bursting into laughter. How long, she wondered, had it been since she'd laughed? "I just remembered that being part of a description from a pretentious sommelier with a fake French accent in Napa."

He grinned. "It still sounds impressive. How does it taste, really?"

"It's really good. Even though I don't have a clue what went into it."

"The rep also gave me a fancy multipage binder with lots of photos explaining the process," Quinn said. "I'll check it out for any foodies who'll want to know. In case you feel like a late lunch or early dinner, one of the Harpers brought in some fresh Dungeness crab an hour ago. Jarle's planning to make chowder, and some other stuff, but tonight's special is going to be crab fettuccini."

"Sold," she said. She hadn't had an appetite for a week, but suddenly she was hungry. Even if that meal was a heart attack on a plate. The chef at Leaf, the vegetarian restaurant down the street where she more often ate, would probably keel over on the spot, just looking at it.

"Comfort food," he said approvingly. "And, by the way, before you pass out at the price on the menu, it's also on the house."

"I can't let you do that."

"Hasn't anyone told you? Everyone gets a dinner on the house for their birthday."

"But this isn't my birthday."

His smile faded and his gaze gentled, touching her face like the lightest of butterfly kisses. Not a hitting on her or sexually suggestive way. But the kind meant to comfort a broken heart Amanda wasn't certain could ever be fully put together again.

"Yeah. It is," he said. Then turned and took her order into the kitchen.

CHAPTER TWENTY-FOUR

DECIDING THEY DESERVED a day off after yesterday's busy market and all the stress they'd been through, Jolene and Gloria had started off a lazy Sunday morning in the apartment above the salon in pajamas, eating decadent chocolate chip pancakes that might have come from a box mix, but they *had* added the chips, chocolate sauce and canned whipped cream topping themselves. Afterward, they crawled back into bed where they indulged in a *Christmas in Connecticut* and *Miracle on 34th Street* double feature and agreed that for some reason movies seemed the most Christmassy in black-and-white.

Then, as the clock struck four, they realized they needed to start thinking about getting ready to go out.

"Did I mention I've forgotten how to date?" Jolene's mother asked as she stood in front of a tall standing mirror Sarah had found for the bedroom at Treasures, the local antiques shop.

"You have. But by the way Mike looked at you at Thanksgiving, I seriously doubt that'll be a problem, Mom."

"I'm too old."

"Don't be ridiculous. Haven't you heard? Fifty is the new thirty."

Gloria put her hands on the hips of her pink silk pajamas, that were a stark contrast to the comfy green tartan flannel ones Jolene had bought in Ireland. "I am not fifty." She tossed her gloriously colored head in a diva-like way Jolene couldn't pull off in a lifetime. "I happen to be in my midforties. As you well know."

"Isn't that when women are supposed to be in their sexual prime?"

"I'm not having sex with Michael Mannion." She walked over to her closet and stood there, just looking at her clothes as if seeing them for the first time. "At least not tonight… I may be in my sexual prime but I'm old-fashioned enough not to sleep with a man on the first date. Which I may not even be going on, because I don't have anything to wear."

Said the woman with walk-in closet filled with clothes. "It's going to be cold. You'll be all bundled up. Dress warm. He already likes you. You don't need to dress to impress."

"I'm nervous."

"You're not alone. Want to sit together? Like a double date?"

"No. Because I don't want to take private time away from you and Aiden. I'll just put on my big girl panties, which are thankfully not granny panties yet, not that he's going to see them, and let him take the lead."

She sighed. "Caroline Harper is such a Southern belle. Even after all these years in the Pacific Northwest. Whatever her and Michael's relationship was this past spring when she was separated from Ben, she probably always sparkled like Scarlett O'Hara charming the Tarleton twins at that barbecue before all those foolish men raced off to war."

"Don't be dramatic. Just be yourself. That's the woman he asked out." A thought occurred to Jolene. "Where are you going?"

"Luca's. How about you?"

"Mannion's."

"They've divided to conquer."

"You could be right about that. But I chose Mannion's."

"Seth and Brianna will no doubt be there. And, of course, Quinn. And a lot of people your age. My guess is he's publicly staking his claim. The same way he did when he kissed you in front of everyone at Thanksgiving."

"No one stakes a claim on me," Jolene said.

"Why don't you keep saying that," Gloria suggested sweetly. "Perhaps one of these days you'll believe it."

IT WAS ALREADY dark when Aiden arrived at the cottage less than five minutes after Gloria, who'd opted for a fluffy white angora sweater and a pair of red wool slacks beneath a lipstick red parka and atypically flat-heeled suede boots, had departed the lighthouse apartment with Michael Mannion, headed to Luca's Kitchen. From the way his blue eyes had lit up at the sight of her mom, she needn't have worried about sparkling.

Jolene, who'd hadn't had the time to get to the Dancing Deer to fully replenish her wardrobe, decided that the white fisherman's sweater she'd bought in a little shop in County Clare, a pair of skinny black jeans and her Ireland boots with two pairs of wool socks, would have to do. Knowing the wind could come sweeping off the mountains, she put her hair up in a messy bun before spritzing a bit of cologne she'd created for herself while playing around with scents, into the air, then walking through it. It was technique she'd learned from Kyan Douglas the grooming guru of the original *Queer Eye* whose makeup she'd once done for an appearance on a morning talk show. At the last minute she'd reached into a small box she'd carried with her all over the world for years, took out a necklace and fastened it behind her neck.

She couldn't remember the last time she'd been so nervous waiting for a man to pick her up. Then again none of those men had been this one, she thought as she'd opened the door to the sight of Aiden with those beautiful black curls, neon blue eyes and those lips that she wanted to feel all over her. His parka was open, revealing him casually dressed in a blue-and-black checked Pendleton wool shirt that accented the blue of his eyes, over a black T-shirt, dark indigo jeans, and brown leather lace-up boots that made him look a bit like a sexy lumberjack.

"You look gorgeous," he said, taking her into his arms as if it were the most natural thing in the world. Since it certainly felt that way to her, she went willing.

"You look pretty good yourself."

"You look a helluva lot better." He nuzzled her neck. "You smell great, too. Like summer. You wore a gardenia cologne that summer, too."

How had she forgotten that? And even more surprising, how had he remembered? She also realized that was undoubtedly why, while playing with oils, she'd come up with a scent that was far more over-the-top old Hollywood feminine than the fruity and green notes used in most perfumes today. But it had always made her feel sexy. Just as it did tonight.

Talk about giving a man mixed messages.

"It always reminded me of the glamorous, gilded age of Hollywood movie stars wearing a white gardenia in their hair with those backless and beaded body-hugging dresses with the plunging necklines." His smile turned reminiscent. "Which is why I didn't mind watching all those old black-and-white movies Mom liked so much. Looking back, they were sort of like training porn before I turned thirteen and Burke showed me where Quinn hid his *Playboy* magazines. Who knew back then that you'd end up in Hollywood?"

"In a much different era and behind the scenes."

"I'll bet you could've become an actress if you'd wanted to. You were always the most glamorous girl in town."

How strange that this was the second time in the past two days someone had used that description on her. In that vintage look she'd taken on to avoid wearing those other girls' castoffs, she'd always felt like a Martian landing on a planet populated by confident girls wearing Juicy Couture, bedazzled jeans, words written across their butts (she never had figured out why anyone would want to do that) and UGGs.

"That was Kylee."

"Kylee was the most noticeable because she was so extroverted, while you always seemed to want to hide away. Your scent reminded me of a gardenia. Exotic and mysterious.

"That's the real reason all those rumors swirled about you. All the girls were envious and wanted to be like you. All the boys wanted you. And when they couldn't, they thought it raised their stud quotient by lying and saying they had."

They'd never spoken about it back then, but while Jolene hadn't a clue the girls might have felt that way about her, it was impossible to miss the knowing leers from boys who'd known nothing about her.

"I always understood that false rumors were why you didn't want to be seen with me," she admitted. That had been hard, but having given her teenage heart to him so fully, Jolene had been willing to keep their relationship secret. Also, if it had gotten out, the other boys, and many of the girls would've dirtied what they'd had.

"Hell." He surprised her by scrubbing his hands down his face. "I was so clueless back then, it never occurred to me that you'd think I was trying to protect *my* reputation. I will admit to wondering if you possibly had thought that since you got back to town."

"You came from an important family," she pointed out. "One of the earliest families in town."

"So did you."

Despite the seriousness of the topic, she had to laugh at that. "My family—neither on my mother's side nor my father's—was ever up to your level. The Mannions were town mayors, and even a state congressman."

"None of that meant anything to me. Hell, I was such a smart-ass juvenile delinquent wannabe, I was trying to protect *your* reputation. I was the last person in Honeymoon Harbor you needed to be seen with."

And wasn't that a revelation?

Jolene wondered how things would have turned out differently if they'd talked about this misunderstanding back then. They had talked. A lot. He'd tell her about how hard it was to be expected to live up to a Mannion family reputation gong back over a century. How people had expected him to be a choirboy and even his parents had wanted him to focus on the future.

Quinn, the eldest, had always had a big-city law career in his sights and was so focused, he'd done all that debating in high school to prepare for litigation. Burke seemed to spend every spare minute throwing footballs through a tire in the backyard behind the farmhouse, developing skills that would take him to the NFL. Gabe's aim had been to become the family's first millionaire living in a penthouse in Manhattan. The family's only daughter, Brianna, had, of course, appeared perfect. Like Honeymoon Harbor's own Princess Di.

But before the Marines had shaped him up, Aiden had always drifted, unable to find his place in his family, or in life.

"You weren't really a juvenile delinquent," Jolene said. The story she'd read on the Facebook page today about him searching for that poor, stray, wounded Australian shepherd and then taking it to the vet for treatment when he'd finally found it, reminded her of that owl he'd saved.

And while he'd admittedly played typical teen boy pranks, like papering the Gundersons' tree on Halloween, the worst he'd ever done before stealing that beer had been to drive too fast and get in fights. But they'd always been to protect the underdogs, kids that were routinely bullied, couldn't stand up for themselves and had no one else to fight for them. Except Aiden Mannion.

A thought struck like a bolt from the blue. "Some of those fights that got you sent to Saturday detention had been about me, weren't they?"

He shrugged. "There were so many, I forget. Mostly they were because I was a dick."

"I wouldn't have fallen in love with a dick."

"You realize you just said the *L* word."

"Young love," she pointed out. "Which, like that old song says, is filled with deep emotion."

Jolene might not have known much about herself in those days, but she had been determined not to get stuck in a too early bad marriage like her mom. Although, for all his problems, Aiden had been nothing like her father.

Or, another thought suddenly occurred to her, perhaps both men had both just been rebelling at seventeen.

Unfortunately, unlike Aiden, her father had never managed to grow up. Could that be why her otherwise intelligent mother still claimed to have loved him until the end? And why she'd stated she still missed him at times.

"Dad made my mother cry a lot," she mused aloud. "But he also made her laugh. There was this one special Christmas Eve, when I was about five, and we all went skating during a rare cold snap that had frozen Mirror Lake. Apparently Dad had played youth hockey growing up, and although I'd been terribly wobbly on the thin blades of the white skates he'd rented for me, he'd held my mittened hands and had led me around and around in circles.

"Then he bought us all cocoa with pastel-colored mini marshmallows from a tiny cabin decked out in bright lights and greenery from your family's farm… I'd forgotten all about that until now." How easy it had been to focus on the difficult aspects of her father while overlooking the good times.

"I knew guys like your dad," Aiden said. "Some couldn't get with the Marine program and got booted out of basic training. Others, when I was a cop, were repeat offenders. They'd rotate in and out of the system, but weren't really bad guys. They just, for one reason or another, couldn't seem to get their acts together… And hey, isn't this a fun date night conversation?"

"It is a good one," she decided. "We cleared the air about what seemed like a major misunderstanding back then on both our parts, and you reminded me of a wonderful family evening." She smiled at the memory.

"Speaking of memories…" He reached out and touched the necklace that was lying just below the spot where her pulse kicked up in response to that lightest of touches. "You kept it all this time?"

It was simple heart made from a piece of aqua sea glass found on the peninsula that hung on a white gold chain with a fastener that looked like a mermaid's tail. He'd given it to her one summer night at the cove in July.

"In the beginning I was afraid not to wear it. Because I thought you might be killed in the war if I took it off."

"And I thought we Irish were superstitious. But hey, maybe it worked. Because I survived."

"You've no idea how glad I am about that," she said. "Because I would've felt so guilty if I hadn't, and you'd died."

"It doesn't work that way. And believe me, guilt can eat away at you."

"Feelings aren't always logical."

"Believe me, I know that."

"I stopped wearing it after I'd heard you'd left the Marines," she said. "But I could never make myself get rid of it. Because that may have been the best night of my life."

"Let's see if we can give you an even better one." He took her back in his arms for another lingering kiss that had her toes curling in her boots and if probably everyone in Honeymoon Harbor didn't know they were having dinner tonight at Mannion's, she'd just pull him into the bedroom of the cottage and have her way with him.

He laughed when she shared that thought as they walked out to his SUV. "This time we don't have to worry about misunderstandings, because we're both definitely on the same page."

MANNION'S PUB AND brewery was located on the street floor of a faded red building next to Honeymoon Harbor's ferry landing. The tragic story of the devastating

1893 fire that had swept across the waterfront, consuming all the original wood buildings had been chronicled and was now in the Honeymoon Harbor historical museum. Jolene knew that one of Seth Harper's ancestors had rebuilt the replacement for Finn Mannion, who'd reopened the pub until Prohibition had put the place out of business. It had remained an abandoned eyesore until Quinn had come home from Seattle and hired Harper Construction to reclaim the place.

There were five choice tables next to the windows offering a dazzling view of both the harbor and the mountains beyond. A second row on risers behind the first row also allowed a prime view. Other heavy wooden tables Quinn had custom-built from reclaimed wood took up a good part of the floor, with a long wooden bar that Seth had found at a reclamation place in the old gold rush town Virginia City, at the end of the room across from the door. Behind the bar, out of view except for a rectangular window, where Quinn hung the orders, was the kitchen.

White fairy lights framed the mirror where the glass shelves for liquor bottles were set, and a tree, decked out with colored lights and shiny balls brightened the corner over by the pool tables and dartboards.

"Wow," Jolene said, looking up at the stamped tin ceiling. "Quinn's really brought it back to life. It looks like it must have looked back when it was rebuilt after the fire." She hadn't had the time nor inclination to go to a Mannion restaurant when she'd been in town for the wedding.

"Seth kept it as close to the original plans as he could. The Harpers apparently never throw anything regarding their work away," Aiden told her. "So Quinn told me he was working with those original plans. He did put in the windows. Originally, all four walls were brick."

"Probably for men hiding from their wives," Jolene guessed.

Aiden laughed, which despite the warmth of the fire burning in the gas fireplace caused her nipples to harden as if a cold wave had swept through.

Apparently everyone in town was eating out tonight because the tables and bar stools were filled to capacity. A cardboard Reserved sign rested on the center four top, boasting the best view.

Quinn, who was pulling a draft pint of porter, waved a hello, as he took a drink order from one of the servers.

She shrugged out of her coat, and instead of hanging them on the rack by the door—in Honeymoon Harbor, people still didn't worry overly much about theft—he draped them over the back of the empty seats. The server who'd just left the order with Quinn came over to the table. She was in her early twenties, which had Jolene wondering if she might be a student picking up extra money while attending the college.

"Hi," she said, putting a leather-bound book with a few choices of wine, and more of beer, that Jolene decided made sense given that Quinn hadn't entirely given up the law to run a pub, but to have his own microbrewery. "I'd like the chardonnay," she said.

"Good choice," the young woman said with a warm smile, despite the fact that the place was crazy busy. "We just got a case of a really great label." She pointed to the name on the list. "It's a bit higher priced, but worth it. Quinn's also handing out cards, asking people who order it, if they don't mind, to tell them what they think, taste and pricewise. It's just a one to five scale. You don't have to write a research paper," she said with a grin.

"That sounds fine," Jolene said.

"How about you, Chief?" she asked.

"I'll have a draft pint glass of the Winter Blizzard Brew," he said.

"Dandy. I'll go get those while you look at the menu and decide what you'd like." She took a small plate from her tray. "Meanwhile, here are some fried clam strips pulled fresh out of the water today. On the house."

"Being family definitely has its privileges," Jolene observed.

"Don't knock it. Jarle's spice mix, the recipe that he swears he'll take to the grave, is amazing."

"Speaking of Jarle." Jolene tilted her head toward the bar, where Ashley sat at the end closest to the kitchen door. The giant cook was looking down at her as if she was the most fabulous dessert he'd ever seen.

"Wow, he really cleans up nice," Aiden said. Jolene decided that only love would have gotten him to cut his long flaming hair, which was rocking a man bun. And he'd trimmed his bushy beard neatly close to his face.

"He's quite handsome." She'd met him only two days ago, but he'd definitely toned down the Viking marauder look. She squinted. "Is that a full-sleeve tattoo of a butcher's chart?"

"Of a cow," Aiden confirmed. "He takes his carnivore cooking seriously. To show how he's into full courting mode, he's traded his usual Embrace the Lard T-shirts for a plain black one. Quinn originally tried to put him into a black chef's jacket, but he refused, so the topic was dropped.

"I'm not surprised. Although Ashley claimed he had

a soft heart, I doubt anyone would want to get in an argument with him."

"He looks scary. Seth had to cut two rows of bricks above the door because he's six foot seven. But he really is a softy. Quinn told me he gets crushes on all the women that come in—which might have something to do with spending years on fishing boats up in Alaska—but he's always respectful and has never made a move on one.

"Until Ashley. He fell for her. Hard. To hear Quinn tell it, he messed up nearly every dish that came out of the kitchen that night. It cost Mannion's a full night's profits, but apparently it was so cute, Quinn felt the entertainment value alone was worth it. Halfway through the dinner serving, customers caught on, and started just ordering wings."

Jolene laughed. "I suppose that made it on the Facebook page, too?"

"How could it not? Someone took a photo of his charred to shoe-leather rib eye, and posted it with another of Jarle bringing out a salad with flowers on it and placing it in front of Ashley as if he were presenting a token to a queen."

"I've never been to a pub that serves flowers on salads. That sounds more like Leaf."

"That's where he got them. He abandoned the kitchen to Quinn for long enough to run over and beg for them."

"Aww." Jolene pressed her hand over her heart. "I adore him."

"Too bad. He seems to be taken, so you'll have to settle for me."

She took his hand in hers atop the table. "I'd never consider that to be settling."

The wine proved to be excellent, not that she was any

expert, so she gave it a five on the card the server had brought with it. Jolene never got into the wine snobbery that was so popular in the movie business. She'd once been at a wrap barbecue at a producer's house, and while being given a tour, had seen a stone-walled, temperature-controlled wine cellar that held a thousand bottles.

"Someone who needs to show off," Aiden decided when she told him about it. "I've been called to homes in the hills." He took a drink of the dark ale. "The people aren't all that different from anyone else. Just richer, with a sense of privilege, so they also tend to treat cops like employees."

"I can imagine. May I ask you a personal question?"

"Sure."

"Do you drink nonalcoholic beer because you're always officially on duty, being chief of police in a small town?"

"That's a careful way of asking if I'm an alcoholic and, given your dad, I can see why you'd want to know up front," he said. "I drink nonalcoholic beer because I spent a few months drunk to the gills when I first came back here. Before I took the job of police chief."

"You didn't seem impaired at the wedding."

"I was suffering from the mother of all hangovers, but I quit drinking the night before so I wouldn't disrupt Kylee and Mai's big day. Believe it or not, weddings are up there at the top of drunk-and-disorderly police calls."

"I guess I can see that," she said. "But why did you go in the first place? I don't remember you being close with them."

"No, but Brianna was close with Kylee. And Seth's always been my best friend, his mom was officiating, and Bri had pointed out to me that I'd been ignoring him since returning to Washington. There was also the fact that if I did get drunk there, my sister would have murdered me on the spot."

"I think that's an overstatement."

"Probably. All right, totally. But I had some issues I needed to deal with. Since I mostly have moved past them I don't need to use alcohol to hide from them. But now that I've stopped, cold turkey, I just decided not to start again."

"That's probably wise. Not everyone can do that."

"It's my guess that your dad had a disease," Aiden said gently. "I just had issues. There's a difference." He bestowed one of those dimple-creasing, blood-warming smiles on her again. "So, now that we've gotten past that hurdle, let's get on with the date part of the evening."

Jolene returned his smile. "I'd like that."

After a dinner of steak and potatoes for him, a cioppino of right-off-the boat crabs, shrimp, and fresh clams for her, they left the pub, which was quickly emptying. As they headed toward the town square, anticipation of the rest of the night, after the tree lighting, hummed warmly in Jolene's veins.

CHAPTER TWENTY-FIVE

THE THIRTY-FOOT Douglas fir was donated by the Mannions, as it was every year. It had been brought into town on a trailer last week, then lowered into the concrete and metal holder by the town's utility company crane. Several dozen volunteers had spent the past week—giving up their own Thanksgiving dinners for a potluck in the town hall—to put on the lights and decorations. Last year, on December 26, the committee had decided to do a riff on Disney's It's A Small World ride and during the year, woodworkers, including Aiden's grandfather, had carved dolls wearing painted native costumes, celebrating immigrants from many of the countries that made up America. Members of the high school band accompanied the school's choral singers who stood in the lacy white Victorian bandstand serenading the gathering crowd, many who sang along, with Christmas songs.

Placed in a way that created a walking path, were the large lighted Santa, an angel, and all the animated penguins skating, skiing, and leaping over igloos that Donna's husband, Hank, had made and spent a rainy day setting up.

"I've always thought Honeymoon Harbor outshines Stars Hollow at Christmas," Jolene said. Since Brianna had never missed an episode of *Gilmore Girls*, Aiden immediately got the connection. "It does," he agreed.

"Especially since Stars Hollow didn't have a boat parade." Which he still wasn't all that enthused about. Especially the Santa bit.

"Damn." Bodhi appeared at their side. "This place really *is* Bedford Falls." Rather than scoff at the small-town celebration, he began to sing along. He was flat, as always, but sang as enthusiastically as he'd done everything in life. Aiden almost felt sorry that he was the only one who could hear him.

The town hall tower clock, viewable from all four sides everywhere in town and spotlighted extra bright for the occasion, ticked its way toward seven o'clock. When there were ten minutes left before the lighting, Aiden spotted Amanda Barrow standing with a young woman holding a child with either hand, and an older woman with a blue streak through her silver hair. Accompanying them were Stephanie and Scott Dunn.

"Would you mind if I run over and talk with someone?" he asked.

"Not at all," Jolene said. "And if you can do it without embarrassing her, would you tell her I'm so glad she's safe." There was no pretending that she didn't know what had happened. Even if she hadn't had Thanksgiving at the Mannions, and been there when Aiden had come home to tell the outcome of the story, the search for Amanda's abusive and possibly dangerous husband had made TV news from Portland to Seattle. "Not that she has anything to be embarrassed about," she added.

"That's exactly what I told her." He kissed her quickly, causing a loud "eww" from the five-year-old boy standing next to them. Followed by a loud "Hush!" from his mother with an apologetic laugh from Jolene.

"Merry almost Christmas," he said as he reached the group. Amanda's bruises were now in the process of changing from the green stage to a healing yellow-brown.

"Merry Christmas," she said, already looking a great less nervous and worried from the emotionally battered woman she'd been only last week. He knew it would take longer and more than a Christmas tree lighting to repair the damage Eric Palmer had done, but he also knew she was in good hands and receiving counseling. She introduced him to the mother and children and the older woman, who, she informed him, had knit her hat.

"Linda does amazing work," Stephanie told him. "I've been suggesting she talk to Dottie and Doris at the Dancing Deer. I'd bet they'd love to feature her sweaters, and this time of year, hats, scarves, and gloves."

"I'll bet they would," Aiden said. "Do you happen to have any?"

"I have quite a few stocked up," Linda Marvin told him. "Knitting relaxes me."

And he suspected she'd needed relaxing to have landed up in the Dunns' home. "Would you mind if I dropped by sometime next week?" he asked. "I'd like to buy some for my mother, grandmother and sister."

The woman blushed. "Not at all. But I wouldn't know what to charge you. I always wanted to open a little boutique, or maybe just a booth at some of the local craft fairs, but Wayne, he's my husband, always said I didn't have any head for business. So, like I said, I have a lot to choose from."

"Why don't you call the Dancing Deer," he suggested. "Doris and Dorothy would be able to give you some suggestions on pricing. Do you have any small sized women's sweaters? My gram says her bones get cold during our cold rains."

"I do." A light brightened in eyes the same color as the streak in her hair.

"Terrific." He glanced back up at the clock, which had ticked down to less than five minutes. "Well, it was good meeting you all," he said to the mother, kids and Linda. "And I'll also be in for some of those poinsettias," he told Amanda. "Since this is our busy time, Mom and Gram didn't get into town to buy any for the house."

"I'll put the best ones aside for you," she said.

With another quick glance at the clock, he mouthed a "thank you" to the Dunns, then returned to Jolene. He'd gotten accustomed to Bodhi's presence enough to know that he'd taken off to wherever ghosts go when they're not haunting their former partners.

"How is she doing?" Jolene asked.

"A lot better, I think. I bought three scarves and a sweater from the elderly lady with the blue hair. She knits. But Wayne—that'd be her husband—apparently didn't want her to earn any of her own money. So, she's got them stockpiled. Since I need to buy presents for Gram, Mom and Bri, I figured this solved my shopping problem while giving her some income."

Jolene went up on her toes and kissed his cheek.

"What was that for?" he asked.

"Because you're the nicest man I know… Oh, look!" She pointed toward Mike and Gloria, headed toward them. They were holding hands. "Isn't that sweet?"

"Seems they clicked," Aiden said.

"It does."

Jolene couldn't ever remember seeing her mother so happy. Her face was glowing as if she'd had a honey, olive oil and baking soda facial. She was laughing up at something he'd said, and in that moment, she could have been starring in her own holiday romance movie.

"She's happy."

"She's not alone." Mike was gazing down at Gloria as if he was about to lasso the moon for her.

"Darling," her mother said on a musical lilt as she hugged Jolene as if it had been years, rather than an hour since they'd been together. "Isn't this the most perfect night?"

"We were lucky with the weather," Jolene said as Mike and Aiden exchanged a one-armed man hug.

"That, too," Gloria agreed. She dimpled in a way Jolene couldn't ever remember seeing. "How was your dinner?" she asked Jolene.

"It was lovely. How about yours?"

"Wonderful. My bucatini carbonara was like being whisked away on a magic carpet to Rome. Luca said his secret is adding lemon to it to balance out the richness. I'd never been there for dinner before. It's very upscale for Honeymoon Harbor, with white tablecloths and candles on the tables."

"Sounds romantic."

"It was." Her mother glanced up at Michael again, hearts dancing it her eyes.

"The food was great, as always," he said with a slow smile guaranteed to melt the most guarded heart. "And candles are always a nice touch. But it was the company that made it special."

For a suspended moment, they could have been the only two people in their world. Aiden lifted a brow as he and Jolene exchanged a look. Jolene loved that he seemed to be enjoying the couple's obviously shared attraction. *Go, Mom!*

Then it was time for the event everyone had come

out on the chilly winter night to experience. John Mannion, acting in his role of mayor, walked to the dais that had been erected that morning and handed the switch over to a little blonde girl, who looked to be about eight. She was wearing a green parka and an elf hat and was seated in a wheelchair.

She pressed the button, and as the tree burst into bright multicolored flashing lights, the band and choral singers broke into an enthusiastic rendition of "We Wish You a Merry Christmas."

Diamond bright stars spun in a black velvet sky as Aiden pulled Jolene close. His public kiss was brief, but nevertheless made her feel as if she were floating. As she kissed him back, Jolene wished she could freeze this moment forever.

"I KNOW THIS is our first date," Aiden said, when they were back in his car. "So, under typical circumstances, I'd be out of line, but there's never been anything typical about what we have together. So, I'm going to come straight out and ask…your place or mine?"

No, Jolene thought, there'd never been anything typical about Aiden and her. "Mom's going back to work full-time tomorrow," she said. "And for the prework crowd, she opens at seven. Although there's probably no one in town who doesn't know about us this time around, I really don't want her clients to see the chief of police parked outside my cottage in the morning."

"My place it is."

He drove a few blocks through the rain that had fortuitously held off during the lighting, past Mrs. Gunderson's house. "She has her lights up," Jolene murmured. "With those projector things making it look as if snow's falling on her gnomes. She couldn't have managed it herself. Gee, I wonder who in town might have done it for her?"

"You've been reading the Facebook page, haven't you?"

"Yes, and I thought it was sweet how she posted how lovely it was that Honeymoon Harbor's prodigal son was back home after having to reform himself."

"I hate that page," he muttered.

"I probably would, too, if I were in your place," she said. "But I was relieved that what happened with Amanda and her husband didn't show up."

"Donna, my officer manager and 911 officer, moderates the page," he said. "But she didn't have to block anyone because no one said a word. One thing about this town, it's always cared for its own. And I'd guess a lot of people feel bad about not recognizing the signs right away."

"You did."

"Because I've seen it before."

"In your police patrol work, I imagine."

There was a significant pause, giving her the impression that she'd hit an uncomfortable topic. "Yeah," he finally said. "I was a Marine sniper scout. When I was getting out, I was contacted by one of my old instructors, who offered me a job on the SWAT team, which sounded like it'd be a good transition."

"But it wasn't?"

"No. My first call was a hostage situation. The husband was barricaded inside with his wife."

"I'm afraid to ask."

"She got out alive." A longer pause. "He didn't."

"You saved her."

"I guess. And can we change the subject, because I may be a little rusty when it comes to seducing a beautiful woman, but I don't think this counts as the best foreplay conversation."

"Probably not," she agreed. "Unless I was a cop groupie." When he gave her a sharp-eyed glance, she said, "I did makeup on a few episodes of *Blue Bloods*. One was a bit like *Fatal Attraction* meets *Law & Order*. And, to set your mind at ease, I'm not hot for you because you're a cop. I'm hot for you *despite* your job. And I promise not to boil your bunny."

"That's good to hear. Though I don't have a bunny. But it looks like I might have a dog." He told her about the stray he'd rescued.

"Oh!" This time she clutched both hands to her melting heart. "You're going to keep her?"

"It seems so. She's not chipped, so there's no idea who her owner is, and Cam Montgomery, he's the vet, says she looks and acts like she's been on the road for a long time. The shelter's at full capacity, so he was hoping to find her a foster family."

"And you stepped up to the plate."

"Someone had to," he said with a shrug.

Oh, God. Jolene realized that she didn't just *want* Aiden Mannion. She could well be falling in love with him all over again. And how much would that complicate her life?

No. She wasn't going to think about that now. This was simply going to be a holiday affair. Like all those Christmas movies her mother marathon-watched. Without the forever-after ending.

He pulled into the driveway of one of the 1930s bungalows that looked like most of the rest of the houses that she knew had been once been homes for mill workers.

"It's darling," she said. "It reminds me of the *Gilmore Girls* house."

"Bri says the same thing. She found and rented it for me while I was still at the coast house."

"She did good. Which is to be expected since she's perfect."

"Wait until you see the inside," he said dryly as he cut the engine. After going around and opening door, he took her hand and they dashed through the rain that had begun falling in earnest.

"I love front porches," she said. "You don't see that many in Los Angeles because people seem to prefer the privacy of their backyards, whatever the size."

"Yeah. I noticed that. I guess when you're living in a beehive of a big city, privacy becomes more important. A place to decompress from all the noise and craziness around you."

"I suppose so. I always breathed a sigh of relief when I got home, even though it was an apartment."

"Mom told me about the fire. I'm sorry about that," he said as he unlocked the door, reminding her how, when she'd grown up here, no one had locked their doors. Despite Honeymoon Harbor not being the big city, she noticed he did have security cameras set up.

"It was just stuff," she said what she'd told everyone else. The difference was now, after going through that cancer scare with her mom, she believed it.

The exterior of the bungalow was a typical cute 1930s Arts and Crafts style. She could completely imagine herself living there. Until she walked inside.

"Oh, wow," she said, staring at the blue carpet and wallpaper printed with huge peonies, as she sat down on a bench by the door to pull off her boots so as not to track water. "You're living in a grandma's house."

"Yeah." After taking off his own boots, he looked around, as if seeing the pink velvet couch with the gold tassels and room crowded with tables, which in turn were taken up by enough old knickknacks to stock Treasures antiques shop several times over. "I guess I've gotten so I don't notice, because mostly when I'm here, I'm sleeping."

"If the bedroom is anything like this, I'm surprised you get any sleep." Clutter had always put her own nerves on edge. She would have guessed that as a Marine, accustomed to traveling light, he'd be much the same way.

"When you're in the military, especially as a scout sniper, out ahead of your team, you learn how to sleep anywhere, and quick." He gave her just a hint of a sexy smile. "And hopefully you won't want to sleep. Or I'll be doing it wrong."

She doubted that was possible. He hung her coat on an antique coat tree covered with iron birds and leaves while she tried to find table space for her purse, gave up and put it on the pink Victorian sofa. Like most of the furnishings, it didn't fit the plain and simple concept of the house. At. All.

"Would you like something to drink?" he asked.

"No, thank you."

"Is this going to be awkward?"

He definitely got more to the point than the men she was used to. In her world, everyone, even nonactors, seemed to be playing roles. Her agent had explained that her brand was quirky, creative, cheerful, easy to work with and unrelentingly dependable. She'd never miss being on the set on time because she was hungover, overslept from partying too late, or suddenly decided to take off to Cancún for a few days of Me Time.

"It's a little," she admitted.

"Because of the wallpaper?"

"No." She laughed because the question sounded serious. "My eyes are going to be so much on you, I won't even notice it."

"You probably will," he said on a long sigh. "The bedroom is cats. And not the Broadway play kind. The furry ones. Apparently whoever owned this place last must have been a cat lady."

"I like cats," she said.

"Good. I just didn't want to risk you freaking out at them all staring at you." He frowned. "I should've thought of that and booked a room in Port Townsend."

"It'll be fine. The only reason I'm feeling a bit awkward is that it's been so long. And we're such different people now."

"True." He ran his hand down her hair, across her shoulder, down her arm and laced their fingers together. Then lifted their joined hands and pressed a kiss against the center of her palm, causing her pulse to pick up. When his thumb touched the inside of her wrist, she knew he could feel it jump. "But the chemistry, attraction, connection, is still exactly the same."

"More so," she said.

Back then she'd been a virgin who fought against sexual feelings for fear of a pregnancy that could ruin her life. And Aiden's life, as well, because, despite his bad boy reputation, she'd always known that he'd want to do what he'd consider the right—and only—thing. Marry her. And then they'd be two struggling teen parents trying to raise a child when they weren't yet adults. She put those thoughts aside because they were far the past.

"And because of that, I have no doubt that tonight is going to be memorable. In all the best ways." She went up on her toes and kissed him. Lightly, at first, then let it linger.

They walked together, hand in hand, down the hall, lined with overly Romanized Victorian paintings of children she'd always found a bit creepy, into the last of the three bedrooms.

"Okay," she said, when he turned on the light. "This is a bit weird."

Ceramic, porcelain and blown glass cats were on the top of the dresser and one of the side tables. The other was bare, save for a normal brass lamp that suggested he one, slept on that side of the bed and two, didn't bring company home. This wallpaper was covered with cats wearing oversize white feathered wings and halos, floating in a blue sky and sitting on clouds in what she assumed was supposed to be heaven.

"That's either a Victoria's Secret runway show, cat edition, or the former owner was a cat serial killer who wanted to memorialize the poor kitties she sent to heaven."

"Cat killer was my first thought," he laughed. "I suggested to the owner that I wouldn't mind repapering on my own time and dime, but she wanted to keep it just the way it is. It's her great grandmother's house and apparently some of her happiest memories were summers here. Her bedroom is across the hall. It's all unicorns and rainbows."

"Maybe you could get that removable wallpaper and cover over the cats while you're here."

"My lease came with an option to buy, which Seth and Mom want me to do. But meanwhile, how about we just open the blinds, turn off the light, let the moon shine in, and get back to what we're here for?"

"I like the way you think," she said as she moved

over to him and began to undo his shirt with hands that were far from steady. She let out a frustrated breath as she fumbled with the buttons.

As if deciding it could take all night before they got to the good part, Aiden pulled her down onto the bed, where they fell in a tangle of arms and legs. Jolene could feel his heat as their clothes landed piece by piece on the carpet, leaving them erotically hot skin to hot skin.

Even after all this time, and despite their rigid control all the other times they'd been together, the man knew her body as clearly as if he possessed an internal sensual GPS. He remembered that licking her breasts would make her arch her back for more. And that taking her hardened, sensitive nipples in his mouth and sucking on them would cause her to whimper. He knew that moving his tongue from her aching breasts to her navel could make her press her lower body closer, harder, against his.

Beyond that point had always been unexplored territory. Yet somehow he nevertheless knew that nipping the back of her knees, first one, then the other, would create delicious ripples of pleasure. That stroking the inside of her thighs, over the hot flesh she'd smoothed scented lotion on before leaving the house, would cause them to fall open, and that burying his face against her heat, sucking, licking, tasting would bring out a wild recklessness she'd never realized was hiding inside her.

The first climax of her life not caused by her own hands or batteries was mind-shattering as it tore through Jolene. How could he have known that this was exactly what she'd been waiting for, dreaming of, ever since that long ago summer of their secret love? She came alive, little explosive charges going off everywhere he touched.

Feeling wickedly, wonderfully wanton, she touched, then tasted, his sweat-slicked bare skin. Everywhere. As he'd done, and continued to do, to her. She took his erection in her hands, then, when he groaned, her mouth, then murmured a complaint when he buried his clever, wicked hands in her hair and lifted her head.

"Not yet," he said in a deep, husky, pained voice that vibrated through her body. "We've waited too long for this. We deserve it to last."

Jolene wanted to beg. As he continued to tease, torment and thrill, she heard herself begging as he unlocked that secret part of her that no other man had ever found. Because it had always belonged only to him.

She lost track of how many times she came, like stormy waves crashing against the western cliff where they'd spent that long ago clandestine night. Outside the house a white crescent moon moved across the sky, the wind moaned in the tall firs, rain pelted like stones thrown by a giant hand against the windowpanes. But neither noticed nor cared.

There was only now. Only him. Only her.

He paused only long enough to reach into the bedside table drawer for protection. Watching him roll that condom over his rock-hard erection was the most erotic thing Jolene had ever seen. Then, finally(!), he gripped her slick hips and lifted them, entering her as if they'd been created to fit together, so perfectly only with each other, in just this way. He never took his eyes from hers as he began to move. Even when she lifted her legs around his hips and he went deeper, harder, faster, he watched her face with an intensity that claimed her—body, heart, soul. Just as he'd promised he would. Just as, he'd also promised, she'd claimed him.

Suddenly they were catapulted into a swirling dark

universe of shooting stars and fiery comets streaking around them, and despite being truly lost, Jolene felt safe because she wasn't alone. She was with Aiden, whose name she cried out as the universe exploded.

CHAPTER TWENTY-SIX

"WOW," SHE GASPED sometime later, as she lay on her back, looking up at the ceiling that she hadn't originally noticed had some sort of glitter sprayed on it. Or maybe it was left over stardust. "I've been dreaming for years how making love with you would be."

"Well?" Lying on his side, braced on an elbow, Aiden ran a hand down her cheek, across her shoulder, continuing on to circle each breast with a fingertip. "Did it live up to your expectations?"

She turned toward him and put a leg over his. "Better," she said. "So much more than I'd ever imagined."

"Same for me." He pulled her on top of him and nuzzled her neck. "But maybe it was a fluke."

"Do you think?" Her body was warming, softening, fitting so perfectly against his.

"It's a possibility." This time his stroking touch moved down her back and over her bottom. "I think the only way we'll know for sure is to try it again."

"That was pretty intense," she said, even as she felt him hardening against her again. "Are you sure we could survive?"

"Hell, I haven't got a clue about much of anything right now." She felt his laugh against her breasts, the same way she could feel his heart, which had coordinated its rhythm with her. "But I want you again, and I think you want me—"

"I do," she said on a long, fluid sigh of pleasure as his hand slipped between them.

"Well, then. I say we risk it."

It was her turn to laugh. Another thing she'd never done while having sex. "As it happens, I'm feeling reckless tonight," she said as she lowered her mouth to his smiling one. "So, let's go for it."

JOLENE WAS AWAKENED from a wonderful dream where she'd been reliving her and Aiden's lovemaking. At first she thought the ringing was her phone. Then remembered she'd left it in her purse in the flowered living room.

She felt a loss of warmth as Aiden moved away, picking up his phone from the bedside table.

"Mannion," he answered in a voice she hadn't heard before. Not even when he'd pulled her over for speeding or when he'd dropped by his parents' house for Thanksgiving. It was a cop voice. "Yeah. Give me five, okay? Then call back. Thanks."

His smile didn't match the hardness in his eyes. "It's some leftover business from LA," he said. "It shouldn't take long." He kissed her, but after all they'd shared last night, she could tell that his heart and mind weren't totally in it. "Keep the bed warm. I'll be back in just a few minutes."

"Okay," she said. She considered teasing him by saying to make sure he got back soon or she'd start without him, but every movement as he'd thrown on the clothes that they'd scattered around the room last night radiated a tense, dangerous energy. Whatever had precipitated the call, it was deadly serious.

She decided to take the time to brush her teeth with the toothbrush she'd tossed in her purse at the last minute before leaving for dinner last night. She opted against a shower, because she'd hopefully get sweaty again when he returned. And she liked the musky, manly scent of him, and their lovemaking on her bare skin. Resisting the urge to eavesdrop, she climbed back into bed. And waited.

"THANKS FOR GETTING back to me," Aiden said. "Yeah, I had an interesting Thanksgiving." He knew that news stations around the country had picked up the story of his chase for Eric Palmer, who social media was now calling America's most dangerous rocket science spy.

"I'm calling for a favor." Not knowing who to trust in the department anymore, the message he'd left had only asked for the detective to call. "It's about the ambush."

He didn't have to say which one. It wasn't that often police from a department as well-trained as LAPD ended up getting lured into a death trap. "I had a thought. It's going to sound crazy, but there's something on Bodhi Warfield's phone that you need to see. I'm guessing it ended up in the evidence locker with his clothing after he was taken to the morgue."

Then came the question he'd been expecting. A guy didn't end up with the highest case closure rate in the homicide department without questioning everything.

"I didn't think of it sooner," Aiden said, when asked. "I was diagnosed with a concussion, so maybe I had some memory loss. I also spent several months trying to drink Washington State dry, so my mind was pretty fogged."

The first part *could* be true. The second part definitely was. "You and your partner, Kendall, are going to have to keep this close between you, because I'm warning you that it could be dangerous. So, if you don't want to hear the rest, we'll end this call now."

The curse he got back was short, rude and probably anatomically impossible.

Because he was all amped up, and the fast-moving storm that had blown in from the coast had already passed on toward Seattle, Aiden walked down the steps and began pacing the front lawn. "Okay. Bodhi Warfield was having an affair with the DC's wife. Right. The wife who coincidentally drowned six weeks after the ambush."

That earned another quick question in response.

"I know, I'd already left the department and the state by then. And I can't tell you how the hell I know about it. But I remember hearing it." More truth. "It could've been on the news during my blackout time." It could have. Aiden vaguely recalled the TV on from time to time, though odds were that the channel had been tuned to sports. "There should be texts and calls on that phone proving the relationship. And the fact that she was being physically and mentally abused and was going to leave her husband for Warfield.

"How do I know? He told me."

More rapid-fire questioning.

"Again, I don't remember. Maybe when he was dying." His first lie, that had him cringing and dragging a hand down his face. Any more and not only would he be behaving like a crooked cop, this detective who'd probably interrogated thousands of criminals and witnesses during his career would be bound to pick up on any lies with his well-honed cop sense.

"Like I said, I'm missing a lot of time and details due to the drinking, but I'm sure about the texts." Again the truth. Which he was going to have to stick to if he ended up being a witness.

Yet admitting that he'd gotten his information from a ghost would undoubtedly have the detective bailing on the call from a probably burned-out, possibly still drunk former undercover cop. "When you read the texts, I'm guessing you're going to want to have a talk with the DC. Because I believe we were set up."

Another barrage of questions, peppered by some colorful curses Aiden, in all his years as a Marine, then a cop, had never heard.

"I don't have any solid evidence to prove it. And I'd make a lousy witness, because, like I said, my head got all messed up. Partly from some possible PTSD, and definitely the alcohol. Hell, maybe all this was a hallucination." Hadn't he tried to tell himself that in the beginning? Aiden no longer believed that, but he was smart enough not to share that his dead partner had been providing the information.

"But would it hurt to look?" he pressed. "One more thing." That had just occurred to him as they were talking. "You're going to need the passcode to unlock his phone. It's 082584. Why do I have it? Because we shared in case something happened and one of us needed to use the other's phone in an emergency." Another truth, and Aiden could remember the day Bodhi had told him he'd changed it.

"It's Jess's birthdate," a familiar voice revealed.

Aiden glanced back over his shoulder and saw Bodhi rocking back and forth on the wooden porch swing. "But I'd suggest letting them figure that out for themselves—" he continued his conversation "—because you don't want to get dragged into this by knowing too much. If they're as good as you say they are, they'll make the connection. Since nearly everyone uses a password or phone code personal to them so they can remember it.

"When they match it with the DC's wife's birthday, which his secretary will have, because Jess told me that she was the one who always ordered the roses, it'll be more proof of my relationship with her. Truthfully, I used it because you know I have a lousy memory for dates and I didn't want to forget it. You might also want to mention her fear of water."

Hell. That was the kicker clue. But how to work it into the conversation? Pressing his fingers against his eyes, Aiden punted. "You might want to also ask her friends and family about her fear of water. I don't know. I probably heard it somewhere. We were all invited to that Christmas party after the DC got promoted. Lots of conversations float around at parties. Especially when people are drinking too much spiked eggnog."

"Good off-the-cuff save," Bodhi said approvingly. "That bit of bullshit came so easily off your tongue almost have me believing that you really were Mayberry on Puget Sound's bad boy when you were growing up."

Aiden flipped him the bird, which only made him laugh.

"It's not funny," Aiden said after the detective promised to do some digging and get back to him before ending the call. "Illegal gun sales and drugs equal a lot of bucks. The DC undoubtedly wasn't able to pull the ambush off without help in and out of the department. Tossing adultery into the mix is like throwing a live grenade into a pile of ammunition. If word of this gets back to the DC before they unearth enough to nail him, others could die. Starting with two detectives who happen to be friends. And have families."

Bodhi sobered. "Good point. Now I'm sorry I got you into this. Maybe I just should've kept my mouth shut."

"No. You did the right thing. Dirty cops can spread through the ranks." Aiden thought how Don James had, in a lesser way, started the same downward slide with those damn courtesy cards. "You don't have to apologize. You'd do the same for me."

"In a fucking heartbeat, dude." Bodhi's gesture was his familiar surfer shaka sign, his three middle fingers bent toward his palm, thumb and pinkie extended. "Now that we've set the wheels rolling, I think your lady is waiting for you."

And then he was gone, like morning mist over the water burned off by the sun.

Maybe he *was* crazy, Aiden considered as he walked back into the house. At least one thing he knew for certain. He was still as flat-out crazy for Jolene Wells as he'd once been. But even more, because he was older, more experienced and knew the real thing when he was living it. The challenge, he figured, was to not rush ahead, like he wanted to, but to pace himself and let Jolene get used to the idea to making their relationship permanent. Because no way was he going to screw it up this time around.

He put the case aside for now, replaced by far more pleasant thoughts of tumbling the woman he loved in those rumpled sheets again. Having hoped the night would turn out the way it had, he'd already put in for the day off, putting his new deputy chief in charge. Jennifer Stone was already a good cop. Now it was time for her to practice her leadership skills. And she might as well learn on the job, the same way he had.

Unfortunately, instead of waiting for him in bed,

Jolene was in the living room, her phone to her ear, her expression serious.

"You know I was halfway expecting this," she told whomever was on the other end of the phone. "No, I'm fine. Really. In a way, it's not that terrible. It'll just give me more time to work on my skin care line." She turned when she'd reached the far wall and saw Aiden. Then held up her index finger, promising to be off the call in a minute.

"Seriously," she was saying. "I don't know if I'll make a public statement or not. I need to digest it a bit more first. But big smooches for giving me the heads-up. I have to go—someone's waiting for me."

Just as he was wondering who she was sending smooches to, she said, "Yes." The redhead's blush he loved to watch rose in her cheeks. "And yes." She looked at him while she answered the next question. "It blew the scale up." Despite whatever news she'd received, she smiled. "Gotta go. I'll call you later. Promise."

She ended the phone and let out a breath.

"What happened?" Aiden could tell that despite her brave words and smile, she was shaken.

"That was Shelby. My best friend who's engaged to that chef that gave me the cheesy corn recipe. We met several years ago on a set in Tucson. She's a caterer for movie and TV productions. Apparently the word around town is that I'm being blacklisted."

"For what? And can they do that?"

"I signed a letter addressing sexual harassment to those working in jobs that don't get as much media coverage as the big-name stars. There were over two hundred signatures, and I'm sure I'm not the only person singled out."

"But you're one of them because you have a higher

profile due to your Emmy nomination," he guessed. While he admittedly hadn't been aware of her receiving that until it had been mentioned at the wedding, he figured it was probably a big deal in her business.

"Yes, probably. They're using me to send a warning. And no, it isn't technically legal, but it happens every day, especially in the shadows. That's why I signed that letter."

"So it's happened to you?"

She looked at him as if wondering how naive he could be. "Of course. I'm a woman working in a male-dominated industry. But I've never been forced to do anything sexual to get a job."

"Well. That's a plus," he said drily, the part of his brain still with caveman DNA wanted to go to LA, find any and all of the guys who'd ever laid a hand on her or forced any other sick show of power on her and twist their fucking heads off. A thought belatedly occurred to him. "Damn. You did know I was just kidding about that dick pic I promised not to send you while we were talking in the market, right?"

The concern that had remained in her eyes from her news was replaced by a warmth that he wouldn't mind waking up to every morning for the rest of his life. "Of course I knew you'd never do that," Jolene said. "Though," she suggested, her gaze dropping to below his belt, "it would make a very impressive Snapchat photo."

She walked the few feet toward him and wrapped her arms around his neck. "I'll admit that being blacklisted is upsetting," she admitted. "So, living up to that service part of your civic duty, how about taking me back to bed and making me feel better, Chief Mannion?"

Aiden did not have to be asked twice.

CHAPTER TWENTY-SEVEN

It was more than obvious that the Mannion men—Aiden and Michael—were, as the Facebook page announced, in full courtship mode of both Wells women, providing amusement to seemingly all the residents of Honeymoon Harbor. Seth even informed Aiden that there was betting taking place at the pub as to which Mannion would propose first. Jarle had been put in charge of holding the money.

Two days after the tree lighting, Aiden and his uncle showed up on Lighthouse Lane with three Christmas trees, lights and extra ornaments, because, as Mike explained they figured Gloria wouldn't have enough ornaments for both a tree in the salon and in her apartment, and any Jolene might have had would have been lost in the fire.

"You didn't have to do this," Jolene said as Aiden carried hers into the cottage.

"It's not like my family doesn't have an entire farm of them," he said as he set the trunk in its metal stand.

"I never had a tree in California," she said.

"Not even an artificial one?"

"Nope."

"Any reason why not?" His brow furrowed after he finished tightening the long screws that would keep the tree upright. "Because I can take it back, if you don't like it."

"It's beautiful." And as perfect as any she'd ever seen. Any set director looking for a tree for one of those Christmas movies her mom and Shelby loved so much would've snatched it up on the spot.

Jolene could tell he was puzzled. She wasn't used to sharing personal aspects of her life, which was why, not only was she a serial dater, she tended to stick to guys in the business because all of them—camera operators, gaffers, grips, stunt coordinators—loved to talk about themselves. What shows or films they'd worked on, what stars they'd met, occasionally, most often in the case of the stunt guys, what actresses they'd slept with.

But, she reminded herself, she'd always shared everything with Aiden. The same way he had with her. He knew about how much it hurt to have those false rumors about her mother, and herself, and the difficulties of both loving, but occasionally hating her father. She knew how frustrated he was at feeling that he was always expected to properly represent a respected pioneer family.

Now, they'd finally made love. And not just the night of the tree lighting, but it was as if she couldn't get enough of him, and he'd assured her he felt the same way. They'd shared their lives and now they'd shared their bodies. It seemed wrong to hold anything back.

"It's just that Christmas trees bring back memories of my family's last Christmas together. Before my dad robbed the liquor store." Complicating her feelings about that was his defense that he'd committed the crime to get the money to buy her mother a pair of sparkly CZ earrings for their anniversary. "He got drunk and fell into the tree, knocking it over and shattering all the ornaments."

"As my old surfer partner would say, that's a bummer," Aiden said as he began stringing the lights onto the tree. "I guess the thing to do is to make some new happier memories."

Which they did, as they'd decorated the tall, fat, fragrant fir together, while Bing Crosby crooned about a white Christmas, Elvis sang about a blue, blue one, Perry Como was coming home for the holidays, and John Mellencamp saw Mommy kissing Santa Claus.

Afterward they sat in front of the two-sided gas fireplace Seth had installed, eating decorated cookies Aiden had bought at Ovenly and drinking hot chocolate while Celtic Woman walked in a winter wonderland.

"You even remembered the miniature marshmallows!" Jolene had exclaimed after he'd pulled the package of tiny pastel pillows of sugar from the bag along with the box of cocoa mix.

"I'm a cop," he'd said. "We have good memories and are, by nature, very detailed oriented."

Later, as she'd laid on the soft rug, gazing up at the sparkling lights in the dark, after Aiden had demonstrated exactly how detailed he could be, making every part of her body hum with pleasure, Jolene decided that this was, hands down, the best night of her life.

OVER THE NEXT WEEK, after Aiden would leave the cottage for work, Jolene worked on her skin care line, creating a fluffy coconut almond shea butter body moisturizer with rosemary and lavender oil that felt wonderful going on and made her skin soft and glowing. Gloria tried it out in the spa and all the women with skin dried out from winter heaters had proclaimed it a winner and asked when they could buy it. Another favorite proved to be a hydrating face mask made with yogurt, honey, coconut oil and cocoa. The only problem was it left clients hungry for chocolate, so, along with the cupcakes, Gloria started stocking dark chocolate sables, an intensely flavored delicate cookie from Ovenly that took shortbread to a whole new level.

One of Jolene's goals was to create products that would have a long shelf life without resorting to commercial preservatives that would defeat the organic properties of her line. When using it in the spa, she could make a small batch each morning. But she knew that Gabriel Mannion, who'd called and talked with her for over an hour, after which he'd asked her to send him a projected profit and loss sheet, a business plan and some samples, would want a more commercial product capable of being produced in larger quantities.

She was trying out an avocado mask that would stay safe and fresh for two years, when Aiden returned from work.

"Hey beautiful green-faced alien lady, what have you done with my woman?"

No man had ever called her *his* before, and although even two weeks ago she would have probably told him that he didn't own her, Jolene secretly admitted she liked being his woman. As he was her man. And now she was paraphrasing one of the most sung karaoke songs out there.

"I was trying out a new face mask. And didn't expect you home so soon." *Home* was a slip, but if he noticed, he didn't comment on it.

"I took off early to take you to dinner." He crossed the room, leaned forward, kissed her on her lips and sniffed appreciatively. "I was thinking Italian at Luca's, but now you have me craving Mexican takeout from Taco the Town."

"It's the avocado oil and lime," she said. "It probably reminds you of guacamole."

"That's probably it. It smells great, but I think so far, my all-time favorite is the chocolate."

"That's because it was edible," she said.

He waggled his dark brows in an exaggeratedly rakish way. "That's *definitely* the reason. And I plan on trying that again the next time you make a batch, but in the meantime, how would you like to go on an errand with me?"

"Where are we going?"

"To pick up my dog."

"Oh, yay. Let me go wash my face. How exciting! Are we bringing her back here?"

"Only if you want to. And if your mom wouldn't mind her being in the cottage."

"I love dogs. And Mom has a pet-friendly rental policy." She gave him a huge kiss, rubbing some of the avocado mask onto his face. "I'm sorry. Let me get a wet cloth and I'll wipe it off."

"Or we could both wash off together in the shower," he suggested.

She was so, so tempted. "What about the dog?"

"I told Cam I'd be there within the next hour. Are you up for a quickie?"

"I don't know. We haven't had one yet."

"Well, damn." He scooped her up into his arms and carried her into the bathroom. "We're going to have to take care of that lapse."

Her apartment had burned up, she was being blacklisted and she may or may, at this very moment have reporters from TMZ and other media outlets looking for her. But as Aiden pulled her under the rain shower head, Jolene no longer cared about any of that.

THE DOG WAS, Cam Montgomery told them, a tri-black Aussie, who was black with white markings on her face, chest, legs and underparts with copper points on her face and legs. Her tail had been bobbed, which had her looking a little funny as she wagged her furry butt in a wild welcome at Aiden, who, Jolene learned, had been visiting here at least daily. Fortunately, her leg hadn't been broken, but merely sprained.

"Is that lack of a tail natural?"

"There are some who've been bred to be born without a tail, but most are bobbed by breeders while they're puppies for cosmetic reasons. The AVMA is against bobbing because it's unnecessarily painful and takes away an important way dogs communicate with other dogs. But, as you can see, she manages just fine, anyway."

"She's beautiful." Jolene knelt down and ran her hand through the thick silky fur. "I always wanted a dog, but my lifestyle's never really allowed for one."

"You can share mine," Aiden offered. Avoiding answering, she scratched behind the Aussie's ears, earning more butt wagging and a big swipe of a tongue on her cheek.

"What are you going to name her?" she asked.

"I haven't come up with one yet," he admitted. "It's a big responsibility."

"I vote for Angel." Jolene hugged her tightly, which the sixtysomething-pound dog seemed to like just fine. "Because it's Christmas, and she's such an angel."

"It's not a very manly name," Aiden said.

"She is a female," Cam pointed out.

Aiden laughed. "It's two against one. Though I was planning to have her trained as a police dog and it's not the most fearsome name out there.'

"She's not a fearsome dog," the vet said. "She's easy-going, but she *is* a working dog with a lot of energy, so you're right to give her a job."

"You could do walking patrols with her downtown," Jolene suggested. "Maybe take her to schools. Like those Officer Friendly visits I remember." Though the former chief had brought along a more typical German shepherd.

"You do realize that school visitations are something officers are assigned for punishment?"

"It doesn't have to be that way," Jolene argued. "Chief Swenson came to Roosevelt School when I was a student there. She'd be great with kids, wouldn't you, Angel?"

The dog, hearing the friendly, encouraging tone in Jolene's voice, wagged her furry black butt in full agreement.

"She could also easily be trained as a comfort dog," Cam said. "That could be useful in your line of work."

"I sure could've used Angel to hug the night my apartment burned down," Jolene echoed that idea.

"There you go with the name again," Aiden grumbled, but he didn't sound truly annoyed.

"It's a perfect name," Jolene pressed. "You're not planning to teach her to tear her teeth into jaywalkers, or kids egging cars on Halloween, are you?"

"Of course not."

"Then, not only is it a perfect comfort dog name, it'll also make you seem more accessible. Also, all those negative people who still are waiting for your former bad boy to show up, would cave when they saw you walking or driving around with this beautiful ball of fluff named Angel. You'd be like Officer Friendly, which admittedly might not work as well in the city, but is perfect for Honeymoon Harbor."

"She's got a point," Cam pointed out. "She could be your police ambassador. The same as the dalmatian Flynn Flannery adopted six months ago for the fire station. Sparky has ceremonial duties like riding in parades and greeting station visitors. They also taught him to stop, drop and roll on command. Flynn won over the city council by telling them that kids today like interactive learning and they'll remember Sparky doing that a lot more than reading it in some brochure they hand out. The dog even has his own business card with a paw print signature."

"And I'll bet you wouldn't have thought Sparky was a manly name at first," Jolene continued to press her case. "But it's perfect for a fire station. If you're planning on using her as a comfort dog, Angel is a great fit. Also, as I said, it's a perfect name for a dog who's rescued at Christmas."

Aiden threw up his hands, tossing in the proverbial towel. "I surrender. Angel it is."

CHAPTER TWENTY-EIGHT

FIVE DAYS LATER, after some slow morning lovemaking, as she dressed in a long-sleeved purple T-shirt with black leggings and red-and-purple-striped socks, Jolene looked at herself in the full-length mirror. Wow. If people discovered that the secret to glowing skin was simply a lot of excellent sex, she'd never get her business off the ground.

Aiden, who had to be at the station before she started her work, nevertheless brought her a mug of hot coffee before he took the first shower. Some mornings, when he didn't shower alone, the coffee cooled before she could drink it. This morning, a delicious aroma drew her like a cartoon character out of bed. She slowed only long enough to put a pair of pajamas on (an advantage of working at home), and found him at the stove. Angel was sitting up, watching him with the patient intensity she might watch a herd of sheep she was protecting from coyotes.

"What are you doing?"

"Making breakfast."

"But you always stop at Cops and Coffee."

"I probably still will. But we had some sauce left over from that takeout chicken cacciatore last night, so thought I'd make you an omelet."

"Why?"

"Weren't you listening to the conversation at Thanksgiving? A guy cooking for a woman is supposed to be sexy."

"You don't need to cook to be sexy," she said. "In fact, with your body, if they try another reboot of *Baywatch*, you could win the David Hasselhoff role."

"Now there's a career goal," he said drily as he grated cheese onto the egg in the pan. "If I'd have thought of it, I might've stayed in LA."

She laughed. "I'm glad you didn't," she said, still unsure if she'd be going back, then put that concern out of her mind to watch with fascination as he folded the omelet into thirds and slid it onto a plate he took from the oven's warming drawer. "But that's a pretty impressive move."

"I've been told by a certain gorgeous redhead that I have excellent hand moves," he said, as he took a plastic container out of the microwave and topped the omelet with Luca's spicy Italian sauce.

"Sit. Eat," he said. "From what I've seen, you've haven't eaten anything but dinner since the tree lighting."

"I've been busy." On the outside chance Gabriel Mannion would make it home for Christmas, she wanted to have a good selection of products to show him. "Besides, I'm living on love."

She cut off a piece of the omelet and bit into it. "Okay, if you made me this every day, I might reconsider." She looked up at the clock. "You still have time. Sit down and share. We've only ever had breakfast together on your day off."

"Because we spend so much time in bed before I have to leave," he said, nevertheless pulling up a stool to the bar and sitting beside her. "Being a cop, especially a chief, isn't a nine-to-five job."

"So I've discovered." She took another bite of the omelet that Julia Child might have envied. "This is really delicious."

"Luca did the hard part with the sauce," he said. "I just made the eggs."

"I can scramble an egg," she said. "Some days." Other days, it ended up as sort of a dry egg pancake. "If you'd become a fireman, instead of a cop, they'd definitely make you the firehouse cook."

"Running into burning buildings never really appealed to me," he said.

"You'd rather run into bullets? Like Superman?"

"That doesn't happen that often." He took a drink of coffee. "So," he said with forced casualness, "do you think you could ever marry a cop?"

She froze for a moment and had to tighten her fingers around the fork to keep it from clattering to the plate. Or floor, which was probably what Angel, who'd switched her unwavering gaze to Jolene, brown canine eyes following the fork from plate to mouth was hoping for.

"I've honestly never thought of marriage at all," she said, her own casualness as forced as his. Except that one summer of teen girlish fantasies, which she knew enough not to bring up.

"I never did much either," he said. He polished off his half of the omelet, then took his plate over and put it in the dishwasher. "When I was a Marine, I didn't want to risk leaving a widow at home. Then the jobs I was doing in LA definitely didn't lend themselves to a happy home life. But lately, it's crossed my mind from time to time."

"Fifty percent of marriages don't work."

"Cops deal in facts, and you'd have to prove to me that's an actual statistic and not some number floating around for years," he argued. "But even if it is true, that's a glass half-empty way of looking at it. Maybe because you work in an industry that admittedly doesn't have the best success rate. Conversely, again, even if it is true, that I personally doubt, 50 percent of marriages do make it. Just think of the couples around the Thanksgiving table. Harriet and Jerome, John and Sarah, Ben and Caroline—"

"Who, I heard, had trouble, this past summer."

"A bump. That they overcame because they love one another and Ben was willing to do what he needed to do to fix things. Because he loves Caroline, even after all these years. And what percent are you putting Bri and Seth into?"

"They'll make it. She's loved him forever."

"See. And then there's Donna down at the office and her Hank who made all those animated penguins at the tree lighting. And Seth told me that Otto and Alma Karlsson celebrated their sixtieth anniversary in the town hall this past Valentine's Day. The party was originally planned to take place in the friendship hall of the Swedish Seamen's Lutheran church, but when so many townspeople wanted to join in the celebration, it was moved to the larger venue."

He picked up the stainless steel travel mug he'd usually get filled at Cops and Coffee, then bent down and kissed her. "Why don't you try thinking about it?" he suggested.

Then walked out the door, leaving Jolene feeling as if a hurricane had just blown through her life, disrupting everything.

"WELL, THAT WENT WELL," he muttered as he drove down to the coffee shop. Despite the omelet—which, thank you, Mom, for the lessons—had turned out perfectly, he was in serious need of a sugar boost.

"You're in a mood," Bodhi said. "Trouble in paradise?"

"You don't know?"

"I told you, I'm discreet. When you're in that cottage that looks like Snow White should be living there with a bunch of dwarves—" The glare Aiden shot at him could've melted steel. "Just saying," he said. "It's cute. I just never pictured you living there."

"It beats the crazy cat grandma house," Aiden muttered. "And it's just short term. Until after New Year's."

"When Jolene goes back to LA."

"Yeah. Or maybe no." Aiden swiped his fingers through his hair. "Hell, I don't know what she's going to do."

"Gotta be a problem for a control freak like you."

"I'm not… Okay, maybe I like to know what to expect. Anything wrong with that?"

"I didn't say there was. Exactly. Like you told me a bazillion times, a failure to plan is a plan for failure."

"There's a reason for that other saying I learned in basic training," Aiden said, still annoyed at his situation. "The Marines have landed and the situation is well in hand. That's probably due to planning ahead."

"I may have been a laid-back surfer dude, but when it came to the job, I was dead serious. Which is why I asked to partner with you when you switched from SWAT," Bodhi said.

This time the look Aiden gave him was surprise. "I never knew that."

Bodhi shrugged. "It never came up. But although sometimes running over every single possible outcome could get damn tedious, I figured I had the best chance to stay alive with you."

"Yeah. That turned out well."

"Dude. You never could've planned for that ambush. It was all on me."

"No. It was all on the DC," Aiden said. "No one could've expected one of the top guys in the department to hook up with gangsters to kill a guy who are screwing around—"

"Making love," Bodhi corrected. "There's a big difference."

"You're right." As Aiden had recently discovered. "Sorry. But my point was, murder is never a way to handle a problem. He chose it. Which is why we're going to take him down."

"You hope."

"I know," Aiden said through a clenched jaw. "Because failure is not an option." Not with putting the cop who killed his partner behind bars. Nor with Jolene.

"I DON'T GET the problem," Shelby said. "A guy you love, one you've probably loved since high school, which partly explains you being a commitmentphobe—"

"I am not."

"Of course you are. And you can't change it unless you own it. The guy proposed, Jolene. That's a big deal."

"Why do you think I'm so freaked out?"

"Is it because he's a cop? Like he suggested?"

"No. I mean, sure, that would be hard, but Honeymoon Harbor, while it has problems, isn't that dangerous. His biggest threat may be dying of boredom."

"You said he seems to like the job."

Jolene couldn't help smiling at that. "He does. Just since I've been home, he's rescued a stray dog, gotten a woman out of an abusive situation, put her husband behind bars, hung Christmas lights for an elderly woman, and located a missing gnome."

"Yay for the first three. But I don't get the gnome."

"It's stone and it doesn't matter. The problem is that it's all too perfect. Even if the sex probably registers on Richter scales all over the state."

"Yeah, so you've said. Which is good news because now you don't have to envy me. At least about the sex. I still win on the food."

"He made me an omelet this morning. With cheese. And cacciatore sauce," Jolene wailed.

"The cad."

"I'm serious. It was delicious. And he didn't make it for both of us, though I made him eat half. He made it for me because he was worried I wasn't eating enough. The only person who's ever cooked for me, except your fiancé, is my mother who mostly resorts to her Crock-Pot. And mothers have to cook for their children, so that's a given. And, oh, my God, I just had another thought. What if he wants children?"

"You told me you'd thought about them."

"Not seriously. More in the abstract. My lifestyle doesn't allow for them. Even if I don't get work in LA again, I have my company to establish. And I belatedly realized what a big wedding business we have here. I can always do bridal party makeup. And even include the cities. My Emmy nomination seems to be a big deal up here. *The Seattle Times* covered it."

"Other working women have children," Shelby said. "I'm not going to quit my catering business. I'll cut back when we get started on those three kids, but although I admire them a bunch I could never handle being a SAHM."

"What's that?"

"Stay at Home Mom. I read it on some message boards. But I don't think women say it like 'Sam.' Mostly it seems to be just for writing because it's faster to type."

"Oh, God. You've already drinking the mommy Kool-Aid," Jolene said.

"Or I could be leaning in. I told you, my eggs aren't getting any younger. And I've always pictured myself as a mother. I just never met any man I wanted to have them with until Ètienne."

"I wouldn't know how to be a wife, let alone a mother."

"Do you have any paper bags in the house?"

"I don't know. Why?"

"I suggest you breathe into one before you have a full-blown panic attack," Shelby said mildly. "Then do some of that beachy meditation thing you do."

"That doesn't work anymore. Because I always picture Aiden as the hot beach boy."

"And you're complaining? About your so-called perfect life?"

"I'm not saying it's perfect. That's why I called you. To talk me off the ledge."

Jolene heard a long sigh. "Okay. Here's my advice. Put away work for the day. Go to the market and buy some ice cream and chocolate. Then come home, climb into bed and binge-watch Christmas movies."

"Christmas movies give me cavities."

"See, that's your cynical side coming out again. Yes, they're super sweet and also all about finding true love in the most unexpected places, between the most different people, who face obstacles, then live happily ever after."

"Ha. You notice they never show the happily-ever-after part."

"That's implied. Like an epilogue in those romance novels you down like truffles."

Jolene opened her mouth to argue her beloved novels were nothing like those movies. But the truth was, they were. Just without the fake snow and mittens. "I hate it when you're right," she muttered.

"No, you don't or you wouldn't have called me. You also remember that much of what I'm telling you is what you told me, when I realized I was falling in love with Étienne."

"But the difference is that deep down, you *wanted* to be in love."

"So do you. You're just afraid to admit it. Now I've got to run get ready for Epicure's Christmas party. I wish you were here to do my hair and makeup."

"You couldn't be anything but lovely. Be sure to take lots of selfies."

"I will. Ciao."

Jolene sat there with the phone in her hand for a full minute. Then looked down at Angel, who it was decided would stay home with her until she could begin her training in the new year. "Hey, Angel, girl. Want to go for a ride?" she asked.

The dog's ears flew up and she cocked her head, her eyes revealing hope. "That's right. *Ride.*"

The dog skittered across the floor, grabbed up her stuffed lamb, and ran to the door. After buckling her into her seat belt harness she and Aiden had bought her, Jolene took off, with the lamb squeaking all the way into town.

"Bad day?" Winnie asked as she rung up three pints of ice cream, a huge salted dark chocolate bar, a bag of organic dog cookies made in Olympia and a bottle of Baileys Irish Cream.

"I decided to take a day off," Jolene said. "I'm going back to the cottage, climb into bed with Aiden's new dog and binge-watch Christmas movies."

"Sounds like a plan," Winnie agreed. "Since this place isn't mine, because Mildred still refuses to sell it to me, I may take a sick day and do the same thing myself tomorrow. Though I have cats."

"Cats are wonderful companions," Jolene said. "Self-care is important. Especially during this stressful season."

Winnie looked over at two middle-aged women arguing over who'd scored the last box of blue outdoor Christmas lights. "Blue can be depressing if you don't pair them with white LEDs," she advised. "I saw that on HGTV. But we've got lots of those multicolored ones right next to the blue, that you can program six different ways. They've proven real popular."

As both women abandoned the blue and put boxes of the recommended ones in their carts, Winnie shook her head. "Yep," she said. "I'm definitely taking tomorrow off. But I like the peppermint Baileys this time of year."

She handed Jolene the canvas bags. "If I don't see you at the boat parade, you have yourself a Merry Christmas."

"You, too," Jolene said. She was already feeling better as she left the store.

CHAPTER TWENTY-NINE

SIX HOURS LATER, two of the pints of ice cream were empty and the bottle of Baileys was a third of the way down when the credits began rolling on a story of a mystery writer whose SUV breaks down in the small mountain town of Santa's Village, Washington. The cynical heroine has a reason to hate the holidays until a hunky lodge owner and his young daughter rekindle her belief in love and magic and a years-old Christmas wish comes true.

"That was the best one, wasn't it?" she asked Angel, who'd snuggled up beside her and had seemed to perk up and watch whenever the hero's dog, a huge mutt with PTSD he'd brought home from war, appeared on the screen. The ending, while seasonally sappy, had made Jolene tear up with a joy she hadn't felt for a very long time.

"I hope Winnie does take off tomorrow," she told Angel. "Because Shelby was right, as usual. This was the best medicine."

She was debating whether to move on to the next movie about a heroine magically whisked back to World War II Christmastime when her phone began to chime with "Carol of the Bells," that her mother had insisted she change from her usual "boring" ringtone for the holidays.

Both the area code and the caller were instantly familiar.

"Oliver?" she answered, wondering why her former salon owner would be calling.

"Jolene, love," he said in that British accent she'd never been certain was real or fake. But she'd never asked, and he'd never told. "I hope I didn't catch you at a bad time."

"No," she said. "I'm taking a day off with Baileys, a big furry dog named Angel and binge-watching Christmas movies."

"I approve of the Baileys, dogs are angels on earth, so yours is well-named, but we must get you out of that little hamlet and back down here before your brain turns into cotton candy."

"Dogs are very relaxing," she said. Either them or the Baileys, which had warmed her to her toes in a lovely way.

"First, I wanted to tell you that I'm so sorry what those bastard pricks are doing to you, and of course, you know, if you ever want to come back here, you're always welcome."

"Thank you." Her tongue felt thick, making conversation a bit of a challenge. "Right now I'm working on new products for my line. I think I might have an angel investor."

"Brava, darling," the six-foot-tall salon owner who also performed as Whitney Houston, Tina Turner and did a spot-on impression of Aretha at a local club, said. "I'm sensing an angel theme here. You must have someone watching over you. Which is why I called. I've someone here who'd like to talk with you. She asked for your number, but I didn't feel it was my place to give it out."

"Who is it?"

"Kendall Powers."

Jolene sat up so fast, she startled Angel, who let out a deep, warning woof.

"Hello?" she said as her head was spinning. Kendall Powers was one of the few women powerhouse producers in the movie business. She'd been on Oprah, had been interviewed by Barbara Walters and was a regular on late-night television whenever she was in New York to promote a film. Some producers stayed in the background. Not Kendall, who was larger than life. Just like Oliver's Aretha.

"Jolene," the familiar foghorn voice boomed. "Oliver tells me that you've deserted us."

"Not deserted," Jolene said. Was she speaking too slowly? Too loudly? "I'm just visiting family for the holidays."

"How lovely. And Hallmark commercial quaint. Didn't I meet your mother at the Emmys?"

"You did. You told her she reminded you of Rita Hayworth, which will undoubtedly go down as her favorite compliment ever."

"It was the truth. I'm not known for my compliments, nor my politeness, so I'll cut right to the chase..."

When Aiden arrived back at the cottage, he found Jolene lying on the bed, a wet rag on her forehead and covering her eyes, Angel squeezed against her.

"Is everything okay?" He gazed at the table, taking in the glass, the bottle of Baileys, one empty pint of rocky road and another of Cherry Garcia.

"I don't know... What time is it?"

"About quarter to six."

"Huh. I guess I've lost pretty much all of the day."

"I heard you were giving yourself a day of self-care."

She yanked the cloth off her face. "Please don't tell me it's on Facebook."

"No. Winnie told me. And assured me your secret was safe with her, and wanted me to thank you for the advice, that she intends to take tomorrow, whatever that means. Oh, and she suggested I might get a box of Advil to go with the milk and cereal I stopped to pick up."

"Thank you." She sat up and put her hand to her forehead. "You're right about the drinking. It's a dumb idea. I think Santa's elves are hammering on toys in my head."

"I'll be right back with some pills and a glass of water. You need to rehydrate."

"Or I could just die," she suggested, covering her eyes again.

He was back in a minute, helped her sit up and held the glass while she swallowed the pills. "Drink it all down," he said.

"Thank you. Now, if you'll just excuse me, I think I'd like to lie down again. But if I don't cover my eyes, the ceiling spins."

"I'll wet it again." He went into the adjoining room, rewet the damp rag, wiped her face, and laid it across her eyes and forehead again. Her skin didn't feel clammy, her pulse was fine, and the bottle wasn't all that empty. "Apparently your mother isn't the only lightweight in the family," he said.

"Sometime between the sleigh ride and the Christmas letter from Santa, I forgot I wasn't drinking a milkshake," she said.

"I hope this isn't because of what I brought up this morning."

"No. Yes. Well, a little bit," she said. "You're definitely prime husband material. Like Bill Pullman in

Sleepless in Seattle who Meg Ryan stupidly threw over for Tom Hanks."

"Thank you. I think."

"It's true. You're a catch and any woman with a brain in her head would snatch you up. In a New York minute." She frowned. "Am I slurring?"

"No."

"So I don't sound drunk?"

"Not at all."

"Good. I didn't think I did, but Kendall caught me by surprise, so I was worried. Though she still offered me the job. So, I guess I wasn't during the call."

"A job?"

"A great one. And why haven't you been snatched up? Are all the women in LA and Honeymoon Harbor that blind and stupid?"

"I can only speak for myself. I haven't been snatched up, so to speak, because I couldn't see myself spending the rest of my life with any of them."

She pulled the washcloth off her face again and gave him a direct, though somewhat blurry-appearing, look. Enough that if he'd pulled her over for a traffic violation, he'd definitely do a breathalyzer test on the spot.

"Did you propose to me this morning?"

"No."

"Oh." Her lips turned down. What appeared to be disappointment shadowed her green eyes like mist filtering through the trees outside the window.

"I asked you if you'd ever thought about marrying a cop. Because if I propose—" actually *when*, but he didn't want to scare her off "—and you happen to be inclined to say yes, I wanted you to know what you'd be getting into."

"Oh." She covered her eyes again. "Shelby's right, dammit."

Aiden was hesitant to ask, but they were finally having the conversation he'd wanted to have this morning and was afraid to blow it.

"About what?" He laced her fingers together, encouraged when she didn't yank that hand that was pressing on her forehead away.

"That you're sweet. And perfect. And I'm afraid because I want to let myself love you."

"Is it that hard?"

"No." She took the cloth off again to look at him. "It's that easy." Then she covered her eyes and sighed. "And that's the problem. Also, we get along too well."

"Isn't that a good thing?"

"No. Because it's so easy, I can't trust it. We haven't ever had our black moment. Except for when those guys slipped the Ecstasy in my beer trying to get me to have sex with them. But I told them I was only going to have sex with you. And suddenly, there you were. Like you'd been magically conjured up by my wish.

"So, I have this vague, horrid memory of climbing you like a tree and begging you to take me, which was probably a really bad impression of a porn movie. Not that I've ever seen a porno, but I imagine that's how sexually aggressive actresses behave in them, given that the industry caters to male fantasies."

This time *he* pulled the cloth off her eyes and leaned over her until they were practically nose to nose. "You were nothing like porn. You were a sweet, innocent girl who'd been drugged by some bastard rich college frat boys because I made one of the biggest mistakes of my life by trying to keep you from putting your life on hold to wait for me. If I'd told you the truth then, that I loved you and wanted to marry you when I got out of the Marines, you never would've been at that damn party."

Her eyes widened. And cleared. "You wanted to marry me?"

"Not then because we were too young. But yeah. I always knew you were The One."

"Me, too. You," she admitted softly. "But it's complicated."

"Because of the black moment."

"You're laughing at me."

"Never. Especially now. About this. Though you still haven't told me what the hell it is."

"It's that moment, when all is lost, and the hero, or in a romance, perhaps when the couple, knows they can never be together. In a movie, it's usually at the end of the second act leading into the third. Novels can have a looser structure but it has to happen before the climax."

"You can't tell me that you've faked one climax. At least with me. So maybe we get to skip the black moment."

"You know very well that's not the kind of climax I'm talking about."

"You're talking about fiction."

"True. But fiction mirrors life."

"Not always. I've been to Forks lots of times and have never seen a sparkly vampire."

"That doesn't mean they're not there," she pointed out. "They might be like ghosts. Only visible to those who are supposed to see them."

He wondered what she'd say if he told her how close to home she'd hit with that one.

"What if I don't want a black moment? What if I just want to love you? Forever and ever. Amen."

"You're proposing with a line from a country song?"

"Maybe. But may I point out that you're trying to squeeze our lives into some concept created for screenplays. When I'm talking real life."

"Speaking of real life, I got a job offer today."

"Oh?"

"Yes. From a top Hollywood producer. That Kendall I mentioned. Kendall Powers is a big deal and she and a group of other women are forming a studio. Like D.W. Griffith, Charlie Chaplin, Mary Pickford and Douglas Fairbanks did when they established United Artists in 1919 to allow actors to control their own interests, rather than being dependent upon the big commercial studios. She offered me a job as top makeup artist to a feature-length film that's got Oscar written all over it. She's even got Chris Pine and Jennifer Lawrence on board."

"And you were worried about being blacklisted. I told you that you were too good for that to happen."

"It would mean being away."

"For how long?"

"Six weeks."

"Hell, that's nothing. I was drunk for a lot longer than that. Where is it being filmed?"

"Vancouver, BC. Not Washington."

"Could I come up and visit on an occasional day off?"

"Of course. You could probably even be like Mom and score a part as an extra. You're so ridiculously good-looking, you could probably become a star."

"I think I'll pass. So, problem solved."

"What if I was offered a job in New Zealand?"

"I've always wanted to see those islands."

She lightly slapped his arm. "You're being impossible."

"On the contrary. I think I'm being perfectly logical.

You've worked hard to establish a successful career, so why should you give it up?"

"What if we had children?"

"Are you saying you want to?"

"I don't know." She shook her head, then cringed. Oh, yeah, she was going to be regretting that Baileys in the morning. "Maybe. But how could we, if I had a career?"

"You're talking to a guy whose mom had a career while raising five kids."

"And we've already discussed that she's Wonder Woman."

"Our kid, or kids, if we did have any, would have two grandmothers who'd love a chance to take care of them from time to time. And does this new job offer enough for a nanny?"

"Yes, but..."

He bent down and kissed her, tasting the chocolate ice cream and Baileys. "Problem solved."

"Except you're refusing to give me a dark moment. Which we need. What if we get married, then rush into it and it breaks us up?"

He managed, with effort, not to roll his eyes and reminded himself that she was under the influence of alcohol that had undoubtedly heightened emotions while fogging logic.

"Okay," he said, standing up. "Here's your black moment... Angel and I are going over to my place. Maybe we'll see you at tomorrow's boat parade. Or not. Because this seems to be your hero's journey, so you have to make the next move. Meanwhile, I'm not going anywhere and in a town this size I'll be easy to find when you're ready."

He bent down, framed her face between his palms

and gave her a long, hard, deep kiss intended to not only make her head spin even more, but remind her what she'd be missing if she gave up on him.

Then he whistled for the dog, who immediately jumped off the bed and followed him out of the room.

"Traitor," he heard her mutter. Aiden wasn't sure whether she was talking about the dog, him or both of them.

"Not one word," he said when he saw Bodhi sitting in the passenger seat, singing a Beach Boys song.

"Hell. You didn't screw it up?"

"I don't think so. I'm hoping I set it up. I guess we'll see over the next few days. Have you ever heard of some damn thing called the black moment?"

"Sure, it's a symbolic death when people, or characters, lose everything they've achieved. Wealth, power, love, whatever." He shrugged. "That's when they have to be willing to do anything to win, because, hell, there's nothing left to lose. And then, once they've survived the fire of the black moment and risen from the ashes, they're stronger and more determined than before. That's when they achieve whatever they perceive success to be."

Aiden stared at him before turning onto the Old Fort Road, heading back to his rental house, which he'd decided to take Seth's advice and buy. With all the flowers and cats and antique stuff taken out, and the kitchen opened up, it could make a great starter home for Jolene and him. She did say it reminded her of her beloved *Gilmore Girls* house, which he took as approval. "How the hell do you know all that?"

"You're talking to a philosophy major who had two psychologists for parents. You didn't think we talked about surfing or cop stuff over dinner, did you?"

"Jolene wants a black moment. Said we needed it. I think it's crap."

"You had your own black moment at the coast house," Bodhi pointed out. "The least you can do is give her hers. Then you can both win."

When put that way, it kind of made sense, Aiden decided. "I just hope to hell she hurries up."

CHAPTER THIRTY

FIVE MINUTES LATER, Jolene was lying down again, the wet cloth back on her forehead, rerunning the conversation with Shelby, and the two she'd had with Aiden over and over again in her mind. Maybe she was wrong. Okay, more than maybe. But, then again, she was under the influence of three Christmas channel movies and a third of a bottle of Baileys. So, she wasn't sure her mind could be trusted.

But her heart was telling her something else entirely different. That she had always loved him, that after all these years, they'd been given a second chance, and if she let this opportunity pass, she might never get another. And then she might as well buy Aiden's house, because she'd already have the wallpaper when she became a lonely cat lady. Or worse yet, a gnome lady. Though, at least Mrs. Gunderson had enjoyed a long, happy marriage before her husband's fishing boat went down in a sudden storm off the coast.

That thought had her remembering a story Brianna had told her. About when she'd been working at a hotel in Hawaii and an elderly woman would show up every year with an urn filled with her husband's ashes. She'd stay in the same room they'd stayed together on their honeymoon, and take that urn all over the island to all the places they'd visited together during that honeymoon and decades of anniversary trips. Although it might seem weird, or even a tad creepy to some, Brianna had found it a sweet display of a true and lasting love. Of course, for all her organizational skills, Brianna was, at heart, a romantic who'd married the man she'd loved since second grade.

Jolene had never considered herself a coward. Hadn't she survived years of bullying, that horrible night on the beach, going back to school and getting her degree? And how many girls would set off for Hollywood and sleep in a car, then keep working her way up the ladder to where she could reach the top of her game and be offered a job on a movie with Oscar potential? All that had taken determination, and an unwillingness to surrender. Yet, as she'd already seen, all the success in the world didn't make for true happiness.

Although it took her mother's cancer scare to get her back to Honeymoon Harbor, she was truly happy here. Happy to have reunited with her mother, her friend Brianna, and to be making new friends like, of all people, Ashley.

And she could have Aiden. If she wasn't too afraid to go for him. This wasn't technically a black moment. Because she hadn't really lost Aiden. It just felt as if she had, which was dark and sad and had her feeling wretchedly lonely. But here's where she had to do like all those characters in those movies she'd overdosed on today. She needed to make that leap of faith toward love.

She reached for her phone. "I am not a commitment-phobe," she told Shelby. "I just never met the man I wanted to grow old with. Don't make any plans for next July. And I promise I won't make you wear pink taffeta."

"Go for it!" Shelby said.

Her second call was to her mother at the salon. "Hi,

are you and Mike going to the boat parade tomorrow night?"

"We wouldn't miss it."

"Can I ride with you? I'm planning to agree to marry Aiden and I don't want to be stuck with my car at the dock."

"Of course. And it's about time. How about we have tea at the Mad Hatter tomorrow? Then afterward we'll go over to the Dancing Deer and find you some appropriate seduction clothes."

"Newsflash. The seduction ship has sailed. And I have clothes."

"You have flannel pajamas with snowmen on them."

"They're warm."

"That's not the point. That's Aiden's job to keep you warm. Tomorrow's going to be the biggest night of your life until your wedding night."

"But hey, no pressure," Jolene murmured.

"I want to do this for you. After all, you came home for me."

"A cancer scare is lot higher on the importance scale as after-parade sex."

"If not for that, I may never have blurted out that I wanted Mike as a lover, and could still be waiting for him to make a move. And, for the record, commitment sex is different than just sleeping together. You're agreeing to become a pair, to bond. It should be celebrated."

"You've been talking with Seth's mother, haven't you?"

"Go ahead and laugh, but although Caroline's recently acquired belief system may be thought of as New Age, there's some ancient wisdom in it we'd be wise to follow. I'll make reservations for noon. That'll give us time for tea, and shopping, and then you can get some sexy new lingerie to knock Aiden's socks off."

Jolene was about to assure her mother that Aiden had seemed to like her underwear just fine (not that it stayed on very long once they were in the bedroom), when she realized she did want to knock his socks off. And maybe this time climb him like poison ivy on purpose.

"I'll see you at noon," she agreed.

She hung up, drank another glass of water in an attempt to rehydrate and not be faced with a hangover tomorrow, then pointed the clicker at the TV, and turned to a Christmas movie about a couple set up by their families to be snowed in over the holidays in a mountain cabin.

"THIS SUIT SMELLS like mothballs," Aiden complained as he adjusted the stupid pillow beneath the Santa outfit.

"That's probably because it's been in a trunk since last year," Donna said. "But don't worry, once you get out on the lake, the salt air and smell of the firs will fix it."

"I still think as chief, I should be able to delegate."

"The people will love you," she assured him.

"Yeah, you'll sure turn your girl on wearing that," Bodhi said.

He was just about complain about the beard itching when his cell rang. He pulled it out, exchanged a look with Bodhi and told Donna, "I'm going to start airing it out now."

"Don't go out the front door," she said. "We want you to be a surprise. Go out the back into the alley."

Even better. That way he wouldn't risk stinking up his rig. "What do you have?" he asked the caller, keeping the phone to his ear to prevent any passersby overhearing.

"Enough that the DA is pressing charges this afternoon. On conspiracy, at least two counts of murder, probably more, given some dealers died in that shoot-out, and a host of other stuff that should keep him in solitary confinement for the rest of his life."

"I'm glad to hear that." He gave a thumbs-up to Bodhi. "Are you going to need me to testify?"

"Nah. No offense, Mannion, but with your sketchy memory, I wouldn't want to put you on the stand. We've got some guys on the other side who are willing to flip for a plea deal and they've got the money trail to prove it. You've got to be organized to run a deal as complex as that one was, and they kept records. As for the wife—"

"Jessica," Aiden corrected.

"Yeah, her. My wife had the idea to check out where she'd gone to school and start contacting sorority sisters in case she stayed tight with any of them."

"And?"

"We found three from Alpha Delta Pi. All knew about ongoing abuse from her husband, going back to when they were dating. Two were concerned enough to keep contemporaneous diaries. Just in case they ever needed to testify. They hoped it would be in a divorce case, but wanted to be prepared for the worst. So, two detectives are picking him up any minute, then we'll set the wheels in motion."

"Thanks," Aiden said.

"Thanks back. Dirty cops give us all a bad name. I'm glad to get this one. And I suspect we'll run down more over the next weeks and months. You sure you don't want to come back? It's got to be getting boring up there."

"Hey, when did *you* ever get the chance to locate a missing gnome?"

"I'm not going to ask."

"It's just as well. I'm also getting hitched."

"Huh. Well, good luck with that and we'll keep you updated."

"I heard," Bodhi said when Aiden turned to tell him the details of the call.

"I'm not going to ask how you heard both sides of the conversation."

"Just as well," Bodhi said. "Because I don't have a clue. But hey, dude, just in case this is it, because I'm getting the feeling that now that everything's wrapped up, and you're not only okay with being alive, but crazy in love, and the DC's going to prison, I'll probably be blowing this pop stand soon. So, have yourself an epic time playing Santa and an awesome life. And when you finally get the girl, which you will, don't be surprised if you see me back here for the wedding. Just don't expect me to wear a tux."

And then, just like that, he was gone.

APPARENTLY MOTHER NATURE was feeling benevolent toward this part of the Olympic Peninsula, because with the exception of a lone cloud floating overhead, the night of the parade was as clear and bright as it had been for the tree lighting. While the temperature was briskly cold, everyone was dressed for the weather and enjoying the music from the band yet again, and cups of cocoa being handed out by the high school pep club.

The fishermen, including many retired ones, like Jerome Harper, Sarah Mannion's grandfather, had all gathered at the tree created from crab pots and decorated with red-and-white painted wooden crab pot buoys. With all legally having to bear the name of the crabber, the tree was like a Who's Who of the area's fishing community. When the bugler played a fanfare, Jerome, being the eldest of the group, turned on the multicolored lights.

A moment later, all the boats that had been waiting beyond the harbor sounded their horns, turned on the decorative lights, and began moving toward the harbor. There were big boats, most festooned with green lights along the sides, looking like garlands. Three of the favorites among both parents and kids alike were one featuring inflatables of all the *Toy Story* characters, another with Minions from *Despicable Me* and one from Mannion's restaurant with a pirate dressed like Captain Jack Sparrow (not coincidentally the name of his award-winning beer) dueling with a trio of pirates while the Jolly Roger flew from the mast, the skull part of the skull and crossbones wearing a Santa hat.

Another favorite was from Kira's Fish House where workers had created three large Dungeness crabs with animated snapping claws. The red-and-white Honeymoon Harbor lighthouse drew applause and cheers, as did a boat that featured breaching orcas wearing green-and-blue Seattle Seahawks helmets. Several sailboats had string lights on their sails, other boats had decorated their decks with varying size Christmas trees, and Luca's Kitchen had opted for a gondola, flashing lights strung along the sides, with a gondolier lip-synching to a recording of "Bianco Natale," that was "White Christmas," in both Italian and English. Jolene was too nervous to count, but she supposed there were more than two dozen boats in all.

Then finally, a blue-and-white police car with flashing red, white, and blue lights, like the ones she remembered flashing in her rearview mirror the day she arrived home, appeared and a siren blasted three times before switching to a recording of "Jingle Bell Rock" that had everyone in the crowd not only singing along, but kids and even adults, like Mike and Gloria started dancing.

As the boat pulled up at the dock, Santa got out with a red megaphone shouting, "Ho ho ho, merry Christmas!" with grand enthusiasm for someone who Jolene knew had been dreading playing the role. She was hoping she could help make the experience a little more enjoyable.

Donna Ormsbee, dressed as Mrs. Claus, and two girls from the pep squad wearing red parkas and green elf earmuffs, led Aiden to an oversize red chair where he began handing out candy canes from his bag to the children who'd lined up to meet him and tell him what they wanted for Christmas. He'd stood his ground on no lap sitting, but no one seemed to mind. The more shy children received their candy canes from the perky elf helpers.

Jolene waited until the line had cleared before walking up to him.

"Well, ho ho ho, pretty girl," he said. "Are you here for some candy?"

"No." She climbed up on his lap, suspecting he wouldn't stick to that rule about no sitting. She was right. "I wanted to tell you my Christmas wish."

"Well, then," he said, "that's what Santa's here for."

She leaned closer, only vaguely aware that nearly the entire town had leaned forward, attempting to hear their conversation. "I want you," she said. "Forever and ever, amen."

"Well then," he said. "I think Santa can handle that request right now."

He reached into his bag and handed her a candy cane. Then a red velvet box. "I'd planned to give you this for Christmas. But this finally seems like the right time."

Jolene was certain her heart had literally stopped. Her hands trembled as she lifted the lid and there, sitting on a bed of white satin, was a sparkling heart-shaped diamond ring.

"Dottie and Doris found it for me right after you hit town, and I had it reset in a more modern style in recycled white gold. The stone is rescued from a Victorian age antique and didn't involve any new mining, which I figured you'd prefer. It's said to have belonged to an opera singer who used to perform here back in the town's wealthy heyday. But who knows?" He shrugged. "What really matters is that you've always had my heart. So I wanted to give you this one."

"It's beautiful. And absolutely perfect. And they didn't give away a single hint when I was in shopping today with Mom."

"I swore them to secrecy. Doris, by the way, has been married over sixty years. Dottie would've made that, too if her husband hadn't keeled over playing pickleball."

"What's that?"

"I've no idea," he said. "But all that's important is that I love you, you love me, and I want to spend the rest of my life with you. So, what do you say?"

"I say it's about time." As she slipped the ring on her finger, huge, fluffy flakes of snow began to fall from that single cloud hovering overhead. Then she lifted her lips to his and heard the crowd cheering, before the band, obviously given a heads-up on the event, began playing the old Dean Martin classic, "I've Got My Love to Keep Me Warm."

And for that wonderful, heartfelt moment, kissing the man she loved, the man she'd *always* loved, inside what felt like their own magical snow globe, Jolene discovered that sometimes, if the fates smiled on you, and you got really lucky, life could be even more perfectly romantic than any Christmas movie.

* * * * *

ACKNOWLEDGMENTS

I want to thank, yet again, the most excellent team in publishing. Writing is, by necessity, a solitary business, which is why I'm so fortunate to have you all in my corner!

Huge thanks and smooches to my editor, Susan Swinwood, for never once saying, "You've put a ghost in the story?" Bodhi and I love you for that!

Sean Kapitain, who not only welcomes an author's input, but once again created a stunningly beautiful portrait of my beloved Pacific Northwest. Thank you.

Fantabulous HQN publicist Lisa Wray, who makes magic happen.

Sarah Burningham and Claire McLaughlin, of Little Bird Publicity, who embraced Aiden and Jolene's story with enthusiasm, and proved even more brilliant and wonderful than I could have wished for.

Again, those working so hard behind the scenes at HQN to keep the Honeymoon Harbor train on track, getting my books into the hands of readers.

My assistant, Judie Bouldry, who frees up valuable time for me to write. One of these days we're getting you up here for a ferry ride to lush, green Honeymoon Harbor!

Agents extraordinaire, Denise Marcil and Anne Marie O'Farrell, for their steadfast support, wise advice and friendship. Also for laughing at my jokes.

And, last but not least, to all the readers who've allowed me to live my dream all these past years! Because, in the end, it's always all about you.

JOLENE'S QUICK AND EASY CHEESY CORN-AND-BACON SIDE DISH

This recipe earned rave reviews and an empty casserole dish when I had to whip up something quickly after learning the day before Thanksgiving that my husband had forgotten to tell me that our neighbor had invited us to dinner. Since it proved so successful, I decided to give it to Jolene, who needed something she could make for Thanksgiving with the Mannions.

Ingredients:

1 jalapeño

2 cloves of garlic

2 cans of whole kernel (not creamed) corn, drained. (Chef Ètienne, who rescued Jolene by sharing this recipe, grills his corn, but canned will work just as well.)

1 8oz block of cream cheese. Yes, the entire block and please don't skimp and use nonfat. This is not the time to worry about calories.

A large handful of grated cheddar cheese

A large handful of grated Parmesan cheese.

About 6 pieces (or more, depending on thickness) of bacon, to taste. (If you're like me, you usually eat a piece—just to make sure it's okay—before adding to the dish.)

2 tablespoons of butter

Salt

Freshly ground pepper

For the topping:

½ cup Panko bread crumbs
½ cup finely grated Parmesan
A handful of fresh herbs: I used fresh thyme leaves and chopped sage from my kitchen garden, but these days grocery stores all carry some fresh herbs. (If you can't find any, dry will do, just adjust accordingly. Rule of thumb is 1 teaspoon dried for 1 tablespoon fresh.)

Instructions:

Cook the bacon, chop into pieces, then put aside.

Chop the jalapeño, scraping the seeds out if you don't want the spice, then sauté with two cloves of finely chopped garlic in a saucepan or skillet large enough to fit in two cans of corn and cheese. I recommend adding the jalapeño 2-3 minutes before the garlic, which cooks a lot faster and you don't want it to burn.

When the garlic and pepper start to soften and fill your kitchen with fragrance, stir in the two cans of drained corn, cut up cooked bacon, 2 tablespoons of butter, cream cheese, cheddar and Parmesan. (Be sure to leave out that extra ½ cup of Parm you grated for the topping.)

Season with salt and pepper.

Taste. If you decide it needs more cheese or bacon, toss more in. You've already broken your diet bank and can exercise an extra twenty minutes tomorrow. This is worth the indulgence.

Pour into a baking or casserole dish.

Mix the saved ½ cup of Parmesan, bread crumbs and herbs together, then sprinkle over the corn, bacon and cheese mix.

Bake at 375 degrees for about 15 minutes until the cheese is bubbling and all melted.

And if this isn't already easy enough, you can make it the day before! Just leave off the topping, cover the dish and put it in the fridge. When it's almost time to serve, sprinkle the cheese, crumb and herb topping over it and bake.

Then, prepare for the accolades from diners wowed by their first indulgent, creamy, cheesy, corn-and-bacon spoonful!

Turn the page for a special sneak peek
at the next book in
JoAnn Ross's Honeymoon Harbor series
Summer on Mirror Lake

CHAPTER ONE

New York

THE HEART ATTACK hit like a sledgehammer as Gabriel Michael Mannion carried the casket of his closest friend down the aisle of St. Matthew's Episcopal Cathedral. His heart pounded against his chest, sweat beaded on his forehead and at the back of his neck, and as nausea caused his gut to clench and his head to spin, it took all his steely determination not to pass out.

Which he would not do. Not with Carter Kensington's grieving wife—dressed in a black dress that probably cost more than Gabe's first car, and a pair of five-inch stiletto heels, suggesting that she was feeling a great deal steadier on her feet than he was at the moment—following behind.

And he couldn't forget wives two and three seated in the pews, each with one of Carter's four children. Wife number one, Carter's college sweetheart and the mother of his eldest daughter, had chosen to remain in Santa Barbara. The daughter, Gabe remembered, was taking a gap year in Paris. All on Carter's dime, which he'd bitched nonstop about while tossing back Manhattans at Campbell's in Grand Central Station like he'd time traveled back to 1950s *Mad Men* days. Finally, sufficiently fortified, he'd taken the Metro North home to spend a suburban weekend with his wife, a former swimsuit model, and toddler son in their pricey home nestled into one of the country's wealthiest communities.

Despite having come from "old money," as he'd always point out sometime before Gabe would pour him onto the train, despite a trust fund that would have allowed a normal guy to live a comfortable life, Carter had been an indefatigable force of nature. He'd worked hard, played hard and had, like a comet flaring out, died young. In the bed of one of a string of mistresses, a fact that hadn't made it into his *New York Times* obituary.

Although Carter Kensington had readily acknowledged his many flaws, he'd been a boss, mentor and friend. With the ink from his Columbia business school MBA diploma still wet, Gabe had followed the yellow brick road to Wall Street, when, on his first day of interviews, Carter had taken him under his wing.

"You've got the Midas touch, son," he'd said as he'd handed out a yearly bonus in the high six figures at the end of Gabe's first year. Which was more zeroes than Gabe had ever seen written on a check. Despite his small-town Pacific Northwest roots, he'd proved a natural at trading, and reveled in the take-no-prisoners, roller coaster 24/7 lifestyle.

Though occasionally he had to wonder what good the $1.8 billion Carter had taken home last year from Harborstone Advisors Group had done for him in the end.

Dealing with more pressing issues at the moment, Gabe avoided that question. As he'd been doing for months.

You can do this, he instructed himself. *You will not drop a twenty-thousand-dollar casket.* Although his vision was blurred by vertigo and the sweat dripping into his eyes, his mind created a slow-motion video of the casket bouncing on the stone floor, breaking open, allowing Carter, dressed in favorite James Bond Brioni suit and handmade Brunello Cucinelli shoes, to fall out and roll down the aisle of the Gothic stone church while the choir belted out "Nearer, My God, to Thee."

The church had eight steps. Although they were wide and not all that steep, standing at the top of them was like looking down into the Grand Canyon. Unfortunately, he and Douglas Fairfield, the managing company's sixty-year-old managing partner, were the first tackle to them.

You can do this.

As little black dots swam in front of his eyes like a cloud of gnats, Gabe grasped the brass side rail even tighter and lifted his end to help keep the casket level to prevent Carter sliding downward and upsetting the balance even more. The six pallbearers managed to get him onto the sidewalk and into the waiting white hearse. Then in a group, they moved to the side, allowing Carter's parents, wife and son to make their way to their limo. It was only while he was walking toward the car designated by the funeral home for the pallbearers that Gabe felt himself folding to the ground like a cheap suit.

Then everything went black.

THE NEXT THING he knew, he was in the back of an ambulance, siren wailing, while an EMT stuck an aspirin beneath his tongue, took his vital signs and assured him that he'd be okay.

"Nobody's ever died in my ambulance," she said.

"That's good to hear. So I don't need to go to the hospital." Trading didn't stop just because one billionaire died. It kept ticking along, and every minute Gabe wasn't working was another opportunity missed and money lost, not just for him, but for the firm.

"There's always a first time," the woman said, her musical Jamaican accent at odds with her stern tone. "You don't get to choose a plan B. Once you hit that pavement, you handed the reins over to me."

"You don't understand. I have things I have to do."

"Yeah, I get a lot of guys who tell me that." She strapped an oxygen mask over his face, effectively shutting him up. "But here's the thing. In this case, you'll be glad that I'm the decider."

That said, she went back to monitoring his vital signs, while the guy in front sitting next to the driver was letting the hospital know their ETA.

AN HOUR LATER, on what was turning out to be one of the most fucked-up days of his life, Gabe was lying behind a curtain, listening to what sounded like chaos in the ER. He was thinking that the hum, buzz, chatter and fast-talking reminded him of his summer internship days on the trading floor, when a different doctor from the one who'd examined him on arrival pulled the white curtain back and entered the cubicle.

"Good afternoon, Mr. Mannion," he said. "I'm Dr. David Kaplan and I have good news for you." He came to the side of the gurney and took Gabe's pulse. "Unless you get hit by an ambulance leaving here, you're not going to die anytime soon."

"That's encouraging." That bit of snark from a ginger kid who looked as if he'd just graduated medical school had Gabe feeling a million years old. Which, given that Wall Street years were a lot like dog years, maybe he was. "So, my heart's okay?"

"It's still pumping. It wasn't a heart attack."

"Then what was it?"

"An anxiety attack. Or, another term might be a panic attack."

"No. Way." You didn't survive in his business by being the kind of wuss who panicked.

Doogie Howser gave him a long look that suggested he'd heard that denial before. "The EMT said you're a trader."

"At Harborstone Advisors Group. It's a hedge fund," Gabe tacked on, realizing the name probably wasn't that recognizable to anyone outside the investment world.

He was wrong. The doctor lifted a brow and whistled under his breath as he made a note on the chart attached to the clipboard he was carrying. "Small pond, big fish."

Which was exactly how Carter had described it the morning Gabe had interviewed.

"My brother worked there for a time," the doctor said. "It didn't suit him. He missed the floor, which surprised me, because whenever I see trading floors on the news, they look a lot like what I've always imagined Bedlam to be."

"Says the doctor who chose to work in an Emergency Department," Gabe said drily.

"Believe it or not, I've always found a well-run ED poetry in motion," Kaplan responded. "But we all respond to different stressors. The same way patients view ERs differently than medical staff working in them, Harborstone didn't match up well with Elliott's risk DNA. Also, and this also may sound strange, coming from an ER doctor, he'd lost all sense of any life outside The Street. Which is why I recognize the same signs in you."

That pissed Gabe off. "You don't know me."

"I know that your blood pressure is dangerously high."

"Like you said, we all have our stressors."

"True, and landing in an ER after nearly dropping a casket would cause anyone's blood pressure to spike. The other pallbearers told the ambulance crew that you were already having symptoms of an attack before landing here. They first noticed them midway down the aisle when you got out of step."

"I did not." Gabe was sure of that. He thought.

The doctor's only response was a shrug. "Your cholesterol is also in the high range. I'm guessing from living on takeout."

Gabe couldn't deny that. "Contrary to what people might believe, in my business we don't have time to indulge in three-hour three-martini lunches."

"My business doesn't, either. Which is too bad. Not that I'm in favor of the three-martini lunches, but despite being a hospital, the cafeteria food here is largely made up of carbs, sugars and fats, and Americans all need to take more time to eat.

"The French and the Italians have the right idea. They're not grabbing a bagel and coffee from a food truck, then gulping it down while checking their email. They walk to a café, drink coffee in an actual cup that isn't cardboard and spend time talking with a friend. They're careful about what they eat, they walk more and believe in a slower pace of life with more time off. Which is why they live longer."

"Maybe it just seems longer," Gabe shot back.

Kaplan's half smile was more a smirk, suggesting that this was not the first time he'd heard that suggestion. "Six months after returning to the trading floor, my brother moved his family to Grenoble. He teaches skiing at a small resort at Les Deux Alpes during the winter and spring. Although the glacier there allows year-round skiing, he takes his entire summer off, then gives fall tours of the area until he goes back to skiing. From what I saw while visiting this past Christmas, his family is happier than it's ever been. And it didn't take a doctor to see how much healthier he is."

"I'm happy for your brother. But I don't ski."

"Neither do I, but that wasn't my point. An anxiety attack won't kill you. But it can also be seen as a flashing yellow warning light. When you're anxious, your body reacts in ways that puts extra strain on your heart. That tachycardia you experienced can, in serious cases, interfere with normal heart function and increase the risk of sudden cardiac arrest. Increased blood pressure can lead to coronary disease, weakening the heart muscle, eventually causing heart failure. And it is, of course, a leading cause of strokes."

"Thanks for the PSA." Gabe looked down at his wrist to where his Rolex Submariner should be and found it missing.

"It's in the bag with your other things," the doctor said before he could ask. "Along with your cell phone, which I suspect you could use a break from."

"I need to get back to work."

"And I need to do my job. Which is to prescribe regular exercise, a better diet and a proper amount of quality sleep."

"I get all I need," Gabe said. Okay, so maybe he worked a hundred-plus-hour week, and maybe he was so jazzed when he got back to his apartment, he'd need a couple or three drinks to chill enough to sleep, but that was the life he'd chosen.

"Given that you work at Harborstone, I seriously doubt that," the doctor said, writing something else on

Gabe's chart. "And when was the last time you connected with your family and friends?"

"My family's across the country in Washington State." Although Gabe couldn't remember the last time he'd been in a church before today, he felt a tinge of Catholic guilt that not only had he missed years of holidays, he'd also not shown up for his sister's engagement party.

"Last I heard, planes flew west across the Hudson. When was the last time you hung out with friends outside work?"

"Earlier today."

"But the guest of honor at that party wasn't there. Because he happened to be dead."

"You know what, Doc?"

"What?"

"You've got one helluva smart-ass bedside manner."

"Thank you. It took several years to hone it. Your friend, and I assume he was a close one for you to be a pallbearer, died, according to what one of men at the scene told the EMT, at forty-six. Given that the life expectancy of a male with his birth year is sixty-seven-point-four years, he can been seen as evidence that while working on Wall Street may make you a very wealthy man, the lifestyle can kill you before you have time to enjoy it."

"Carter Kensington's life was excessive," Gabe argued. "Mine isn't."

"Being a workaholic is excessive in its own way," Kaplan said. *The damn guy just wouldn't let up.*

"You do realize that arguing my lifestyle probably isn't good for my blood pressure," Gabe shot back.

"Yet you feel the need to defend it," the doctor said mildly.

"To a guy who probably works the same hours."

"My work's not nine-to-five. But I'm going out tonight with my wife to watch our daughter's ballet recital. She's excited because her tutu has sequins and she gets to wear a sparkly tiara. Which she's going to wear afterward, when we go out for pizza. Because that's her favorite thing. Even if she does insist on pineapple on it. I blame that slight flaw in judgment on her mother.

"You're obviously an intelligent man, Mr. Mannion. Perhaps you ought to consider using some of your brainpower to come up with a way to achieve a better life balance. Before I see one of your friends worrying about dropping *your* casket thirteen years from now."

"Ouch. Mic drop."

Kaplan's lips quirked, giving Gabe the impression that the sadistic son of a bitch was actually enjoying this. "You're free to leave," he said. "But, seriously, you don't have to turn ski instructor. Why don't you try figuring out something that gives you pleasure, and make time for it? While you still have that option. Because I'd rather not see you back in my emergency room anytime soon."

With that he was gone.

CHAPTER TWO

Honeymoon Harbor

"OKAY," CHELSEA PRESCOTT SAID. "We have the summer reading challenge, art lessons with Michael Mannion, the trip out to Blue House farm, so kids can actually see where their food comes from, a tour of Herons Landing B and B from Seth Harper and Brianna Mannion, who'll point out all the construction and tell the story of the Whistler mural, which the reading adventurers will have already learned about beforehand during the trip to the historical museum."

Before the end of workday meeting, she'd written the plans she'd thought of so far on the library conference room wall whiteboard. "What else can we come up with?" she asked her staff, which consisted of one other librarian, Jennifer Miller, who'd moved here from Spokane, two paid assistants, four volunteers and the seventysomething Mrs. Henderson, who, despite having retired, still checked in at least once a week to make sure the library hadn't fallen apart without her.

"This is beginning to sound more like a summer camp than a library," Linda Mayburn, one of the volunteers, said.

"We're in the process of opening minds," Chelsea said patiently. She'd been hearing those objections from Linda since she'd first begun planning the library's summer event in January. She'd continued to bite her tongue, because the truth was that funds were low and she couldn't afford to offend anyone willing to work for free. "While books take readers on adventures to different places and times, we're still talking about our very short Pacific Northwest summers. And although it's hard to believe, there are those kids who don't want to spend those sunny days inside the library."

"Those, especially, are the ones we want to reach," Dorothy Anderson, half owner of the Dancing Deer dress shop and volunteer, said.

"Because reading is fundamental," Doris, her twin, and business partner, said.

"Exactly." Chelsea was tempted to kiss them both. "Those who don't think of a library as a place to find adventure are the ones we want to reach. Because once we get them inside the doors, we can hook them on reading."

"What about the liability issues?" Linda pressed.

"That's covered. Although Quinn Mannion is no longer a practicing attorney, he's still licensed, so he wrote up a permission form for parents to sign. I also talked to the mayor, and he assured me that we're covered under the county insurance."

"People can still sue."

"Any idiot can sue for any reason." Mrs. Henderson jumped in with a huff of the impatience Chelsea herself was trying to hide. "That's what insurance is for."

Although the retired librarian had made her library a safe place for Chelsea during some very difficult childhood years, she'd also run a tight ship. No one had ever argued with her when she was behind the checkout desk. Apparently, Linda wasn't prepared to start now.

She merely crossed her arms and shook her head. But, Chelsea noted, she didn't get up and march out in a huff.

"So," she forged on, "any other ideas?"

"How about a tour of Mannion's microbrewery?" another volunteer asked.

"Great. Let's teach the kids to drink," Linda muttered.

"It could be a special event for the older kids," Susan Long, who taught chemistry at the high school, said. "The same way going out to Blue House farm can teach kids where their food comes from, learning about brewing can show them that by knowing chemistry, you can turn grains, hops, water and yeast into one of the world's oldest beverages. It makes science more relevant to everyday life."

"Also, the first evidence of beer production dates back to Egypt and Mesopotamia in the fifth millennium BC," Jennifer, who'd received a bachelor's degree in art history at WSU before earning her MLS degree, said. "So, there's an opportunity to throw in some ancient history into the mix."

"I like that idea." With the exception of Linda, Chelsea loved her team. "I'll ask Quinn if he'd be willing to do that."

"He's already giving tours to guests staying at his sister's bed and breakfast," Mrs. Henderson pointed out. "I'm sure he'll be willing to do the same for us. I'll volunteer to ask him. He owes me, given that I excused a great many of his library fines over the years. I always knew that boy would grow up to be a lawyer, the way he could come up with all those excuses on why he was returning his books late."

Although Chelsea didn't know Quinn Mannion all that well, she did have trouble envisioning the easygoing, friendly pub owner and microbrewer in his previous life as a high-priced corporate lawyer in Seattle.

"You've got the assignment, Mrs. Henderson. Thank you."

"My pleasure. It gives me an excuse to drop into the pub for those to die for wings he serves."

"There's also the fact that he's not hard to look at," Doris said.

"The man definitely inherited those Mannion black Irish looks," her sister agreed.

"Okay. Any more ideas?" Chelsea brought the meeting back to order when all the women's eyes, even Linda's, had gone a little dreamy.

Chelsea couldn't deny that that Quinn was, indeed, a hottie. But they had work to do. While her library admittedly wasn't the largest on the peninsula, Mrs. Henderson had left her some very big shoes to fill, and not only did she not intend to let the former librarian—and the town—down, she also wanted to make it the best small-town library in the state.

"You're already talking about a lot of activities," Linda pointed out. "And there aren't that many of us."

"I've got that covered," Chelsea said. "Knowing that kids need to demonstrate a sense of responsibility and community service to college admission officers, I gave a talk about summer volunteerism at the high school last month, and we've more applications for volunteer interns than we can possibly use. Jennifer and I will be going through them and choosing three or four this week. They'll be great at helping us herd kids."

Linda folded her arms across her chest, but didn't object to what Chelsea had personally thought was a brilliant idea.

"We've just about got this," she said encouragingly. "Why don't we all think about it a bit longer—"

"Put our thinking caps on," Mrs. Henderson broke in with a decisive nod.

"Yes." How Chelsea loved this woman who, along with giving her a safe harbor when she'd so needed it, had provided a focus that had saved her from aimlessly drifting through life. "That's exactly what we should do. We're all intelligent women, and with the program lasting six weeks, we certainly have more opportunities for engagement." She closed her planner. "Let's ponder the possibilities over the weekend, and meet back here at end of day Monday."

Everyone but Linda seemed receptive to that idea. But again, she didn't say anything. While she appreciated the lack of argument, Chelsea also worried that she might be about to lose a volunteer just when she needed all she could get.

"You're doing a dandy job," Mrs. Henderson, who stayed behind, said. "I was proud of getting funding for our county bookmobile to reach those who couldn't come into town. But this idea will go down in the annals of Salish County as the same type of library milestone."

"Thank you." Her mentor's words meant a lot. "If I mess things up, it could end up an entirely different type of milestone."

"You won't." They walked out of the room, and down the sunshine-yellow hallway lined with library themed posters. "You have mettle, Chelsea Prescott." They'd reached the double glass door and the first poster visitors saw. *Welcome!* it read. *This is YOUR library! A Place to Discover. Read. Learn. Explore. Research. Have Fun. Relax. Connect. Succeed!*

"That was always my mantra," Mrs. Henderson said.

"In the early days, I had it written on an old-fashioned blackboard."

"I know. I remember it well." Chelsea smiled. "Then you upgraded to brightly colored markers on a white board. I hope you don't mind that I had Michael Mannion make the poster."

"You have to keep up with the times. I appreciate you keeping my words."

"I certainly couldn't have thought of a way to improve them." Hadn't the library under this woman's tenure been all those things to her?

"You also have them as a header on the website."

"I loved the photo of the library with the harbor in the back, but I thought putting up a mission statement in its place might draw more people in. I did keep the photo in the right margin where visitors can see it."

"I wasn't complaining, dear," Mrs. Henderson assured her. She knitted her brow. "Perhaps you should add a basic computer class to the learning curriculum. I remember when we first were able to get an internet connection. No one, including me, knew how to use it to our best advantage. It was definitely a self-taught learning experience."

"There are still people who don't know," Chelsea said. "I doubt a week goes by that either Jennifer or I help someone fill out a résumé and search for a job. And then, there's the rush of college applications and some instruction on essay writing. Many of Honeymoon Harbor's students are the first in their family to go to college." She knew firsthand how intimidating that could be. "It can be overwhelming."

"As it was before the computer. But that's the type of thing I had in mind. Also, I've bought some items from local home craftspeople. If more of them had websites, they could reach more potential buyers, but most probably either don't have the skills, or the money to set that up."

"I had a student from the college update ours," Chelsea said. "I'll ask if she'd be willing to teach a couple sessions. One for the older kids and another for the adults."

Mrs. Henderson nodded, her steel-gray head flowing down her back in wild waves. No short, "age-appropriate" hair for her. "That's a very good idea."

"It was yours."

"I know." Another flash of a smile took years from her face. "At my age, I don't have time to bother with bad ones."

That said, she left the library, walking with purpose down the steps. Although she remained hearty, Chelsea always held her breath, waiting for a fall. There was a ramp next to the steps, but the elderly librarian refused to use it.

Chelsea waited until Mrs. Henderson reached the sidewalk, gotten into her Prius and driven off before making one last check of the building. In a back reading alcove, she found the two girls, sitting on the chintz-covered love seat. As they'd been most afternoons for the past week.

"Hello," she said.

Chelsea guessed one child to be about eight years old, but her guarded eyes made her seem older. "Hi."

"Hi!" the younger girl, who looked around five, said with a wide grin. "I'm Hailey and this is my big sister, Hannah. We're reading about dragons."

"What fun. I like dragons."

"Me, too." She bobbed her blond head. "They have fire coming out of their noses." Her brow wrinkled, much as Mrs. Henderson's had. "But they only scorch and eat bad people."

"Then the three of us are safe."

"We are! That's why I don't have nightmares about them."

"I'm glad to hear that."

"Hannah gave me my own dragon." Hailey reached into a Disney Princess book bag and pulled out a fluffy green stuffed one. "It's invisible, but it looks just like this."

"I like it." It was well worn, and missing a leg.

"Me, too. My invisible guardian dragon is always with me, like a guardian angel, and burns away any monsters that try to sneak up on me in the dark."

Chelsea glanced at the older sister, whose return look managed to be expressionless and hard at the same time.

"You're lucky to have such a good big sister."

"I know." The younger girl looked up. "She's always taken care of me. Everywhere we've lived."

That explained why Chelsea didn't recognize them. Apparently, they were new to Honeymoon Harbor.

"Would you like to take that book with you?" she asked. "So you can finish it at home?"

"Yes!"

"We don't have a library card," the older sister said, her tone a challenge.

"That's not a problem," Chelsea said blithely. "I trust you. And when you return it, I'll have other dragon books waiting for you."

"That would be wonderful." Little hands with sparkly nail polish crossed over Hailey's heart. "Wouldn't it, Hannah?"

"Yeah." She didn't seem all that pleased. Or, perhaps,

she was merely guarded. Which was a good thing these days. Even in this small peninsula town.

Getting the message that the library was about to close, Hannah put the book into her own bag and stood up. “Come on, Hailey. We’ve got to go.”

“Okay.” The little hand took hold of the larger one. “Thank you, library lady,” she said.

“You’re welcome,” Chelsea responded. “Can I call your mother for you?”

“She’s working,” Hannah said.

“So there’s no one at home?”

“I have a key.” She pulled it out of her pocket. “We’ll be okay. Like my sister said, I can take care of her.”

“I’m sure you can. But it’s raining.”

A chin went up. “We don’t melt.”

“That’s good to know. Because it would definitely be a disadvantage to living here in the Pacific Northwest,” Chelsea said mildly. “But nevertheless, why don’t I drive you home?”

“We’re not supposed to get into cars with strangers,” Hailey said. “Because of the traffic.”

“Traffickers,” Hannah corrected.

Chelsea was relieved someone had taught the girls, who seemed to be on their own in the afternoons, child safety. “You’ve been in my library a week. Have I acted as if I’m a child trafficker?”

“No.”

“Would it help if I had the chief of police drop over to vouch for me?”

“No!” both sisters said at once.

Hannah placed a hand on Hailey’s head. “That’s okay. I guess they wouldn’t let you be a librarian if you were a criminal.”

“There’s a very extensive background check,” Chelsea assured her, making a note to check with Aiden Mannion about what he might know about these girls' parents. "I was even fingerprinted."

Hannah bit her lip, considering. Then glanced out at the rain that had gone from a mist to a drizzle to a driving rain blowing in over the mountains from a coastal storm. "Okay," she said. "Thank you."

"No problem," Chelsea said, even as she felt something off. While they may not want anything to do with the police, she was definitely going to ask Aiden Mannion about the family. She wasn't sure the law allowed him to share any information, but if it was to keep a child safe, she had to try.

Hannah was quiet on the way to the address she'd given Chelsea, while Hailey continued to chatter away, jumping from dragons to wizards to a book about a giraffe who couldn't dance. "He had crooked knees and skinny legs, and when he tried to join the jungle dance, the other animals teased him."

"Bullied," Hannah murmured.

Hailey continued undeterred. "So, he felt very sad. Because he really was a very bad dancer. He felt sad and alone."

"But then while he was walking home, the giraffe looked up at the moon and was thinking how beautiful it was, when a cricket suddenly appeared and told him how everyone is special in their own way," Chelsea continued, picking up one of her favorite children's stories.

"Yes! And when you're different, you just need a special song." Hailey bobbed her head. "So when the giraffe heard the moon playing just for him—"

"His hooves started shuffling," Chelsea said.

"And he swung his legs around everywhere! And

all the other animals saw him and thought he was the best dancer ever!"

"Like bullies are ever going to do that," Hannah scoffed.

"But they did!"

"The cricket never got any credit for helping him," Hannah pointed out.

Hailey bit her bottom lip as she thought about that. "Maybe the cricket is the giraffe's older sister, who always takes care of him."

Glancing into the rearview mirror, Chelsea watched Hannah's eyes—which, during their short time together had only been expressionless or hard—soften. "Maybe so, sprout," she agreed softly, as she reached over and took her sister's hand in hers.

There was a story there. Chelsea felt it. And not just because she'd been an older sister. But because her once perfect family had crumbled apart when she was about Hannah's age. She knew the need to make things better. Even when it was impossible. Especially for a child not even into her teens.

They'd reached the house, which was a Craftsman bungalow in a neighborhood that had once been mill company housing. Now a house that was renovated and given a modern interior floor plan could bring in several times the original cost. It wasn't always easy growing grass near salt water, but whoever owned this home had apparently thrown in the towel. Where there would have been a lawn, or wildflower garden as many homeowners created instead, there were fir cones and needles scattered over dirt studded with weeds.

Paint that appeared to have once been blue was peeling, and a white shutter was hanging crookedly. While the bungalow could have been darling, with its front porch and low, gabled roof, it was just sad. Chelsea regretted having to drop the girls off here.

"When does your mother come home from work?" she asked, turning toward the backseat.

"Anytime now." Hannah's hand was tightly squeezing Hailey's smaller one. To quiet her sister? Even more concerned, Chelsea decided to definitely stop by the police department on her way home. Maybe Aiden wouldn't be legally allowed to give her much information, but at least he could check to see if there'd been any complaints about or emergency calls from the house.

"Well, that's good to hear," she said in a voice that even to her sounded fake cheery. "I'll just wait here until you go in."

"Great," Hannah said, sounding as insincere as Chelsea just had.

Chelsea watched the two of them walk across the broken pavement of the front walk, across the columned porch and after Hannah had unlocked the door, go inside.

Then she pulled away from the curb and headed to the police station.